In A
Cindy Dorminy

In a Jam
A Red Adept Publishing Book
Red Adept Publishing, LLC
104 Bugenfield Court
Garner, NC 27529
http://RedAdeptPublishing.com/

This is a work of fiction. Names, characters, places, and incidents either are the product of the author's imagination or are used fictitiously, and any resemblance to locales, events, business establishments, or actual persons—living or dead—is entirely coincidental.

To all the small towns throughout the South. Stay sweet.

CHAPTER ONE
Andie

Some might consider waking up in the drunk tank rock bottom. I call it Thursday. Even with my eyelids closed, the light burns my retinas as if somebody is pouring salt in them. The slight turn of my head sends the room into a spin, not to mention the remaining contents of my stomach. Yes, I'm in the drunk tank or, as Officer Tinsley likes to call it, "Andie's home away from home."

"She lives."

"Go away."

"Wake up, Sleeping Beauty." The shuffle of the officer's shoes across the concrete floor scrapes right through what's left of my brain.

I cover my eyes with the heels of my hands. "You walk too loud."

My thick tongue sticks to the roof of my mouth, and every time I try to swallow, a bass drum plays a wicked beat straight into my temples.

Officer Tinsley taps my shoulder. I squint at the burley policeman from South Boston as he hovers over me. He waggles a Dunks coffee cup in front of my face. Nothing better than a large cup of Dunkin' Donuts coffee after an all-nighter. "I got ya something."

On the third attempt, I rise from my scratchy cot of a deathbed and lean back against the concrete block wall, doing my best not to topple over. He sits down beside me, and the slight shift in weight pushes the remaining contents of my stomach into my throat. Tinsley hands me the cup, and I take a tentative sip of coffee. I moan into the paper cup when I taste Dunkin' Donuts's dark roast with a double shot of caramel, exactly the way I like it.

I smile at him even though it makes my head pound. "Yum. You remembered the extra caramel."

He wags his head. "It was Arthur's turn to buy it for you, but he got called away, so you got me to wake you up instead."

I pat his knee. "Thanks, but please stop the room from spinning."

The cot trembles when he chuckles.

"Not funny. God, I'm never drinking again. Ever."

He raises his hands in victory. "Ha! I win. It was under five minutes this time."

"I hate you guys." I lean my head back against the concrete wall and close my eyes. He knows I don't hate any of them. If it weren't for the boys at district C-6, I wouldn't have anyone to spend my holidays with. "What happened?"

Tinsley stands and paces the small room. His jaw clenches. "You were arrested for hitting some fella at the Black Rose pub."

My eyes spring open. "Nuh-uh."

"Ya-huh. But lucky for you, he dropped the charges."

I rub my temples, trying my best to remember the events from last night. "Why would I hit some random dude?"

"Turns out the bouncer said the loser got fresh with you, and that's why you punched him."

Bits and pieces of last night fall into place. I should have known better than to trust a handsome reject from the Vineyard.

"Then why am I still here?"

He groans. "Ya blew a point two and then got mouthy with the sarge. You know how he gets when you do that."

I gulp down the coffee, and the scorching-hot liquid burns my parched throat. "I'm not mouthy anymore. I'll apologize, and we'll be pals again. Case closed."

Sergeant has a soft spot when it comes to me. I think I'm like the daughter he never had.

Tinsley clears his throat and runs a hand through his short-cropped hair. "There's one more thing I need to tell you." He leans against the wall and crosses his legs at his ankles.

I bolt off the cot and pitch forward. If it weren't for Tinsley's cat-like reflexes, my face would be planted on the floor along with my Dunks coffee. A "one more thing" is never something good like "Hey, the loan department decided to let me skip a payment." In my world, it usually means I got fired again or I owe someone money. Or worse, it means someone thinks I have a problem with drinking and I should consider getting help.

He props me against the wall then squeezes his eyes shut. "You need a toothbrush in the worst way."

"Sorry. I even disgust myself."

We sit in silence for a moment. The only sound is the gong crashing through my head every time I swallow.

"I'm not going to rehab. I do not have a problem. I was out celebrating. That's all."

"Celebrating what? Thursday? Andie, a point two? You should be dead. A gal your size can't handle that much booze in the system."

I hold out my hand to make him stop the lecture. "I know. Okay? I can't help it if guys like to buy me drinks. That's hard to pass up. Jeez. Shh. And please whisper."

He takes a deep breath and motions with his head. "Come with me."

Tinsley helps me off the cot, and when I'm able to take three steps without wobbling too much, he leads me down the familiar hallway. My hand finds the wall every third step to keep from pitching to the side. They must have replaced all the light bulbs in this building since the last time I was here because I don't think I remember it being so frickin' bright.

"How's Ginger?"

Tinsley glances over his shoulder. His grin consumes his face. "She's past the first-trimester puking stage. Now she can't keep her hands off me."

"Aw. You are gonna make such a great daddy."

He blushes as he gives me a bashful shrug then points to the last door on the right. I've spent too many mornings in this room, apologizing, and heard too many lectures about how I'm wasting my life away. I don't think I can handle any of that today.

When he opens the door to the sergeant's office, my lungs forget how to work. Instead of the fatherly sergeant in a rumpled police uniform, it's an African-American man about my age, dressed to the nines. Papers spill out of the briefcase he's rifling through. He pulls out a document and places it on the desk in front of him.

Tinsley exchanges handshakes with the man. "Sir, this is Andie Carson, District C-6's favorite gal."

The man is very expressionless. "I'm David Christian."

I shake his hand because I'm not quite sure who he is or what he wants with me. Fear prickles down my spine. Maybe he's a detective and I killed somebody last night. Oh God, it's worse than Tinsley led me to believe. Mr. Christian motions for me to take a seat. It's a good thing because my legs forget they have bones in them. Tinsley sits in the chair beside me, and the screeching sound of metal on concrete spreads through my skull like the noise of the commuter train coming around a corner.

He pats my shoulder and says, "Last night, we were looking through your phone contacts for anyone that would possibly bail you out."

I gasp. "You figured out my password?"

He stares at me like I'm an idiot. "You never changed it from the factory settings."

"Whoops. So who was going to come get me?" I pick at a fingernail, doing my best to act nonchalant.

Tinsley frowns. "No one."

Wow. I thought maybe one of my bar-hopping friends would be there for me, but I guess not. I shrug, pretending it's no big deal while at the same time praying tears don't fall down my cheeks.

"Anyway," Tinsley says, "we did see several voice mails from Mr. Christian that you hadn't retrieved yet."

"Yeah. I thought it was another bill collector. Sorry. You'd think after the third call, they'd get the message that I'm broke."

"Not too broke to go clubbing." Tinsley raises his eyebrows, daring me to argue with him.

Mr. Christian's stoic expression doesn't change.

"So why did you need to speak with me? Did I win the Publisher's Clearing House Sweepstakes? Doubt it since I didn't enter."

Tinsley points to Mr. Christian. "He's an attorney."

Son of a... "It was self-defense. He attacked me, right?" I think Tinsley would have told me if I started the fight.

Mr. Christian crinkles his brow. "I don't know what you're talking about. I'm here about your grandmother, Mary Grace Landry."

The sound of her name sends a warmth through me I haven't felt in forever. I couldn't have been more than five or six years old when I last got to see her. And by the time I was an adult, I was too self-centered to even think about family.

He clears his throat, flips through the folder in front of him, and retrieves a legal-size piece of paper. "She passed away."

A twinge of sadness mixed with a huge heap of guilt rests on my chest. Fifteen years. Fifteen birthdays and Christmases and way too many missed opportunities have passed me by. Tears well up, and I swipe a stray one away before Tinsley or Mr. Christian sees it.

"Oh. I thought she died when I was little. Was she sick?"

"She had a heart attack." His face softens as though he's retrieving a memory. "Nice lady."

"You knew her?"

He nods.

I glance down at my hands, my white knuckles tight around my coffee cup. "I hadn't seen her in forever. She and Mom had a falling out when I was little. Then she told me Granny died, which really ticks me off right now. I didn't know she was still alive."

"That's too bad." Tinsley pats my arm. I almost forgot he was in the room.

"Did you know she liked to play the lottery?" Mr. Christian asks as he reads over the paper in front of him.

A warm grin comes over my face. A flash of one memory washes over me. It's quick, but I see myself as a five-year-old, standing on a stool, helping Granny bake muffins. Her gray hair hanging in a long braid down her back and the red-and-white-checkered apron are about all I can remember of her appearance. That and a nice twinkle in her eyes when she smiled. I do remember she loved to bake, and I loved to eat whatever we made together. The smell of blueberries wafts through the air as if I'm back there with her.

"That's Granny for ya. Did she win two hundred on a scratch-off?"

He swallows hard. "Uh, no. More like two hundred fifty million."

Tinsley whistles. "Holy mother of God."

My jaw drops. I scan the room to see if I can find the hidden cameras. "You're kidding me."

"No, I'm not. She won it a few weeks before she died. Poor old soul passed away before she could spend the first check."

I chuckle as I watch Tinsley. He's going to catch a lot of flies in his mouth if he doesn't close it soon.

"Now I know for sure we're related. That sounds like something that would happen to me. The state got lucky on that one, huh? They don't have to pay her off year after year."

Mr. Christian chuckles. "That's correct, because with your grandmother getting on up in age, she knew she wouldn't be living long enough to see yearly allotments. So she asked for her earnings in one lump sum. She got one hundred fifty million after taxes."

"Holy frickin' cow. Let me guess. She left it to the local church, didn't she?"

"Well, yes and no. It's the church's money if you don't behave."

I blink. I'm sure I heard him wrong. "Could you repeat that, please?"

He chuckles. "You get the entire fortune if you behave. Those were her words."

"Hmmm. Behave?"

Tinsley groans. "Oh dear."

I lean back in my chair and cross my legs then give Tinsley a sneer.

Mr. Christian clears his throat. "Sober up."

Tinsley chuckles until I give him the evil stare-down. "Sorry, but you gotta admit..."

I roll my eyes, pain searing through my sockets from the movement. "Granny hated booze. I remember that much about her. It was, in her words, 'the devil's juice.'"

"She wants you to sober up and settle her debts with her bakery in South Georgia."

I lean forward and read his face. There has to be a catch. The good Lord and Granny wouldn't exactly drop that dough in my lap without some stipulation. But one never knows.

"That's it? Done. Where do I sign?" *Hello, I'm rich!*

Tinsley whispers in my ear, "Point two, Andie. Point two."

Okay, the drinking part will be a challenge, but this time of year is when a cold brewski tastes excellent with everything. I have to keep my eye on the prize, and when it's over, I can party. With that kind of money, I can do anything I want, go anywhere I want. I'll never have to hear I'm fired from another job again. I'll never get another phone message about being late on another payment.

Mr. Christian holds up a finger. "Oh, there's one additional small item."

I lean back and stare at the ceiling. Of course there is one more thing. "Lay it on me, Judge Judy."

Tinsley clears his throat and mouths, "Stop."

"You have to work in the bakery for six weeks, live in the apartment upstairs, and then you can sell it for whatever you can get for it. That is, if you want to sell."

There is no way in hell I'm living in Podunk, South Georgia, for six minutes, let alone six weeks. "That's not one little thing. It's a bunch of big things. I can manage the business from here." My big smile has gotten me out of pickles before. Might as well try it now.

He taps the paper on the desk. "It specifically states you have to live there. Nonnegotiable."

Granny, why are you doing this?

"But if you don't want the money..."

"Of course I want the money, but have you ever been to Georgia?"

He grins. "Born and raised there."

"And that's why you're here now. They eat grits and chew tobacco while they read from their Bibles." I slap my hand over my mouth to keep the bile down. Oh dear, grits and tobacco. I don't need that visual right now.

He raises an eyebrow. "Sounds like you know this place pretty well. Where are you from?"

I cross my arms and stare at him. "Boston."

"Boston? Are you sure about that?" His brown eyes twinkle as though he knows the answer before I say it.

"Yes. Boston... Tennessee."

Tinsley belts out a laugh. "You little devil. You're a closet Southern belle. I have to say, you had me fooled."

"Oh, hush. I moved here a decade ago, so technically, I'm a local now."

He snaps his fingers. "Come to think of it, when you're really lit, you start to draw your words out. I should have known. Can you say 'y'all' for me?" Tinsley's having way too much fun.

I point a finger at Mr. Christian. "You know how small towns work. You can't just go to the store. It's a social event. And the worst part? Everyone knows everything about you. I don't like people in my business."

He slides the document back into the file folder. "So you're saying you don't want the money?"

I stick out my bottom lip and check out a hangnail. One hundred fifty million big ones. Besides never having creditors on my back again, I'd love to go back to school. It seems like ages ago since I even considered a degree. Maybe I could be a teacher or start my own business. Granny's money would allow me to do either of those, or both.

"I didn't say that."

"Because the church has already made their list of things to do with that money when you screw up."

"And I bet the first thing on the list is a bus to drive the blue-hairs to the nearest city for Bible study." It's not the religion part that bothers me, but the church part. It has too many "thou shalt nots" and not enough "love thy neighbor."

He glances over his glasses, and his eyes grow big. "How'd you guess?"

I groan as I rub my throbbing temples. "So, let's back up and discuss the sober clause. That's going to be on the honesty policy, right?"

Tinsley shifts in his seat. "Actually, we've been in contact with the police department down there."

My jaw drops. "You ratted me out? I could probably get my newly appointed lawyer to talk to your superior about messing in my business."

He throws his hands up as if I'm going to take a swing at him. "I only wanted to help. Your attorney gave me the information about your grandmother's shop, but I had no idea about the money. If it makes you feel any better, the dude I spoke to seemed real cool about it all."

I snort. "Great. Could you also tell how big his potbelly is over the phone?"

Mr. Christian belts out a laugh.

Tinsley cackles. "Actually, Diane from intake was in the room when I had him on speakerphone." He taps my nose to get my attention. "And I'm quoting her because I would never in a million years say something like this. She said he sounded like George Clooney with a twang."

Heat rises up my neck. I can resist any comparison except "The George." *Heaven help me.* Crap. I cannot believe I'm going to live the next six weeks in Southern Belle Hell.

"Okay. What do I have to do?"

Mr. Christian sits up straight and pulls out the document again to read the list. "Run the shop for six weeks. Go to church every Sunday morning, Sunday night." He holds my gaze, and I hold my breath. "And Wednesday."

"Fuuudge brownies." Thou shalt not curse during church.

"And—"

"Oh, there's more?" My screechy voice makes my eyes water.

"Try to fit in. Your grandmother's words, not mine." He points to the document as if I forgot it was there.

I slump back in my chair.

If Tinsley guffaws any harder, he's going to get a stitch in his side. "Somehow, the last part will be the hardest of all."

Mr. Christian laughs and puts his glasses back on the top of his head. He slides the document over to me with a pen.

Tinsley dodges me swatting his arm. "It's only for part of the summer. I could do almost anything for that kind of cash."

I sign the document. *Andrea Grace Carson.* "How much do you get?"

Mr. Christian shakes his head. "Nothing. She was a friend of my great aunt. They go way back, even friends during segregation."

I slam the pen down on the paper and slide both back toward him. My head screams out in pain. If I could afford it, I would make an appointment for a deep-tissue massage. After this conversation, I'm going to be one big muscle spasm. Oh, wait. I can afford it now.

After another gulp of my coffee, I stare at the ceiling. "Summer. Ninety-seven degrees in the shade with eighty-eight percent humidity."

"Yep."

"I'll come back to the city with gnats stuck to my skin and Skoal running out of my mouth."

Tinsley's laughter rumbles through the office.

Mr. Christian snaps his briefcase closed. "Behave. You might take a shine to it."

I stand, and after my head stops spinning, I plunk my empty coffee cup in the wastepaper basket. "Well, this was fun. Y'all come back now, ya hear?"

Tinsley gives Mr. Christian a knuckle bump. Time to brush up on my Southernness.

CHAPTER TWO
Andie

Ahh. New car smell. Mr. Christian was so nice to give me an advance on my inheritance so I could make the trek to cow town in style. I'm loving being behind the wheel of my new sporty white convertible. In the past two days, I have driven through big cities, then small towns, then back to big cities. I cried when I reached Atlanta because I knew it was the last of real civilization that I would see for a long time.

Frustration replaces the tears when a traffic snarl post-Atlanta has me at a standstill on Interstate 75. At times like this, I sure could use a cold beer on such a hot day.

For the last leg of my journey, I pop in the new CD I bought before I left and try to read the language guide while I steer with my knees. I should be able to rip right through *How to Speak Southern* in two shakes. It's already coming back to me.

"Hey, y'all," the lady on the tape says. I like to call her Daisy Duke.

"Hey, y'all," I say back to her. I smirk. Not bad.

"Hello, everyone," the tape interprets. *Duh.* I've seen enough episodes of Nashville to figure that one out on my own.

"Hey, y'all," I say as twangy as I can make it. "It's like riding a bike. I can do this."

"I'm fixin' to go to the store," Daisy Duke says.

"Fixin', fixin'..." I glance down at the manual, looking for a clue to what fixin' means, when I swerve and almost hit a semitruck in the next lane. He blares his horn.

"Hey, y'all," I yell at him. "I'm learnin' here."

"I will be leaving for the store soon."

"Huh? Oh yeah."

"I'll have a Coke," Daisy Duke tells me.

"I got this one. Pretty straightforward. I'd like a Coke."

"I would like any cold beverage," Daisy's monotone voice says.

I crinkle my sunburned nose. "That's stupid."

As the hours creep by, I pass homes with yards doubling for automobile graveyards and one church after another taunting me. I fumble with the cooler I've cleverly placed in the floorboard of the passenger seat, underneath a Bible and a *Duck Dynasty* T-shirt I bought at the last gas station. Driving with one hand, I unzip the cooler with the other to reveal a lovely six-pack of my favorite summertime beverage—Sam Adams beer. Got to pay homage to my town, Boston.

I pop the top, but before I can take the first foamy sip, images of me at five, snuggling with my grandmother, filter through my mind. I almost hear her say, "Sober up, Andie." The last thing I need is to get a DUI on the way to fulfill her wishes. *Ugh.* I pull over to the side of the road, pour out the contents, and wedge the open container back into the cooler.

"Granny, are you happy now?"

As soon as I'm back on the road, a big, monster-sized sign welcomes me to Smithville, Georgia, the Colony City. Home of Claire Stevenson, Miss Gum Spirits, and Turpentine. I cringe. *Somebody wants to be known for that?* At least the terms of my agreement don't include beauty pageants, thank God. Although I didn't read the fine print of the legal agreement regarding "fitting in." Even small-town South Georgia doesn't want to witness that.

Right when I cross the city limits, a bug splats on my car window, then another, and another. Then one lands right on my sunglasses. I squeal and flip them into the back seat. It's obvious I've reached downtown because there's a beehive of activity. The drivers of all five cars on the road wave to me. Then everyone on the sidewalk waves to me. I pass by the First Baptist Bank and Trust... I mean Church. The marquee in front of the church reads "Thou shalt not speed." Clever.

Not able to drive one more mile before my bladder bursts, I turn into the first gas station I find. I park under a shade tree so I don't burn my ass on the leather seats when I get back in, a lesson I learned two states ago.

I open the door to the gas station, and a frog croaks, making me jump about three feet into the air.

"Howdy," a man in greasy overalls says to me from behind the counter.

"Hello. Can I use your bathroom?"

"Sure thang, ma'am." He reaches under the counter and pulls out a baseball bat with a leather strap threaded through a hole in the small end. There's a key dangling off the leather strap. He swings the bat in my direction, and I duck. He chuckles then spits tobacco into a McDonald's cup on the counter. I throw up in my mouth.

"Wow. You don't want anyone to leave with the key, do you?" I take the bat from him, doing my best not to touch his grimy hands.

"I've durn near lost a dozen of 'em to kids. Crazy rug rats. It's always on a scavenger hunt list."

I scan the convenience store, but all I see are cans of oil, every tobacco product on the market, and so many bags of chips that I'm getting cholesterol gawking at them. The lottery scratch-off selection is impressive, but I don't see a bathroom.

The man points toward the door. "Bathroom is outside. Hang a left, and the first door on your left. Can't miss it."

I need to pee fast and get the heck out of here while I still have all my teeth. "Thanks. I'll be right back with your bat-key thingy."

Two teenagers enter while I leave for the bathroom. *Ha. I have the bat key. You can't have it!* I stop to stare at this big-ass, jacked-up truck that is parked way too close to my new, shiny baby. I better pee fast before they ding my car door. With one hand, I hold my nose closed, and with the other, I fumble with the bat-key. The typical pungent odor hits me, and I feel as if a muggy funk hovers over me. I tiptoe to the toilet and squat-pee. A loud bang and tires screeching outside cause me to jump and pee on my leg.

"Dang it."

When I finish my business, I drag the bat-key back to the gas station dude. He already has his hand out, waiting for it.

"Thanks. What was that noise?" I might cry if someone ran into my brand-new car.

"Beats me," he says, putting the bat-key back under the counter. "Somebody shootin' something or... someone."

"Comforting." I cannot get away from this Gomer Pyle look-alike fast enough.

"Have a nice day," he says.

"You too," I say over my shoulder as I head out of the store. The big-ass truck is gone, but there is red icky stuff splattered all over my car. I let out a bloodcurdling scream before I can stop myself. I rush back into the gas station.

"Someone's been shot," I yell to Gomer Pyle.

"Huh?"

I rush behind the counter. He's got to have a phone, even if it's only a party line.

"Hey, what do you think you're doing, Missy?" He picks up the bat and cocks it back.

"If you're not going to call the police, then I will."

"Sugar, you don't have to call the po-lice. The fuzz is right there." He points the bat toward the magazine rack.

And holy moly, damn. Standing before me, with his head buried in a *Muscle and Fitness* magazine, is the hottest specimen of a man I have ever seen. In fact, he should be on the cover of that mag. Rock-hard muscles poke out of the sleeves of his police shirt and stress every seam. His dark, super-short military hairdo looks as though it would feel real nice curled around my fingers if he let it grow out a half inch. He peeks over the magazine, and his face lights up. Bam, those soft-green eyes compliment his tan skin, and he has a dimple too. Have mercy. I am in heaven. They sure know how to grow them down here.

"Oh, thank God. I'd never get this kind of service in Boston." I'm impressed with this town's emergency response time. It is very, very satisfactory.

"Can I help you, ma'am?" His words slide off his tongue, slow and sweet, like George Clooney with a twang.

Yes. Yes, he can.

CHAPTER THREE
Gunnar

She snatches the magazine from my hands before I can decide if I want to incorporate reverse lunges into my leg routine. With both hands, she clamps on to my bicep and tugs me toward the door. My cop instincts kick in, and I lean back, one hand hovering near my revolver in case she's a nut job. Already, she's pushing mighty close to that title. She doesn't even come up to my shoulder, but with the clamp she has on my arm, I'm going to lose circulation if I don't investigate whatever's got her dander up.

"That," she says through heaving breaths.

All I see is Johnny Mason pumping gas into his mother's 1960 Thunderbird. I wave to him. He waves back. There's a white convertible parked under a Chinaberry tree. I point at the cool vehicle. "That?"

"Yes." Her head nods so fast she could be mistaken for a life-size bobblehead.

"That?" I ask again, walking out into the parking lot with Charlie on my heels. All I see out of the ordinary is a sweet convertible parked under a Chinaberry tree.

"Yes, that!" She puts her hands on her forehead and leans over. I step back because it appears as though she could blow chunks any second. "Oh God. That's blood on my car! It's new, and I heard a shot, and now there's..."

I like the way she says car. It comes out sounding like "kah." She's definitely not from around here. I take out my notebook and pen and jot down what she says. "Did you see someone get shot?"

She points at the car, then the bathroom, then the store, then back at her car as though she's replaying the whole scene in her head, but nothing is coming out of her mouth. *Yep. Nut job.* Her light-blond hair falls out of a clip, swooshing past her face with every nervous movement. I peer over at Charlie, who is still holding the batkey. He grins, and we both burst out laughing. Charlie has to sit down on the curb to keep from falling over.

The blonde puts her hands on her hips and taps a toe. Her calf muscle flexes with every motion. Uh-oh. I know that stance.

"I do *not* think this is funny."

Charlie crawls over to the car and falls over the hood with tears in his eyes. I clear my throat to tamp down the laughter.

She pushes him away from the car. "Don't do that. You'll contaminate the evidence. Someone could be dying or already dead. Don't you care?"

Charlie's grin is so big, I see the missing teeth on the right side of his mouth. His *she's not from around here* grin causes my laughter to bubble up my throat again.

He hangs his head low. "Sweetheart, don't they have red berry bird crap where you come from?" Charlie asks.

I fist-bump Charlie and laugh again. Inside the woman's car, next to a small insulated cooler is a *How to Speak Southern* book lying in the passenger seat. Cute.

She jumps in her car and shoves the book in her glove compartment then throws her purse over the cooler. This isn't my first rodeo, lady. Her face is as red as the Chinaberry bird shit. Since she doesn't have the faintest alcohol smell on her breath, I'm not going to bust her about that open beer can, although I should.

"I'm so glad you are having fun at my expense."

"Sorry, ma'am. Only small-town humor, I guess."

"What was the bang?"

Charlie chuckles. "Must have been the Jacksons' car acting up again. I need to tell them to let me take a gander at it."

She takes a deep breath and lets it out.

Travis and his wife, Corrine, drive by. I wave. They wave. Three chickens saunter across the road as if they own it. I look back at this cute out-of-towner that has breezed into Smithville. She stares at the chickens and mouths, "What the heck." She has to be Miss Mary Grace's granddaughter. Officer Tinsley's description of her was spot-on. Thank goodness she doesn't favor her granny. But I see glimpses of Mary Grace: her petite frame, pretty blue eyes, that feisty attitude. Yep, they're related, all right.

"Not laughing with you," she replies, cranking her car.

I lean in the open window. Damn, she smells sweet, like vanilla and sunshine. I forgot what I was going to say.

Oh yeah, now I remember. "So, you here to clean up your grand-mother's business?"

Her jaw drops, and she squints her eyes. "You... Tinsley told me about you."

I point my finger at her. "I think you've got it all wrong. He told me about you." I stand with my arms crossed over my chest, legs spread wide apart. I still can't believe I agreed to check in on her, but it's hard for me to say "no." And when a fellow officer of the law asks for a favor, I feel inclined to oblige. Tinsley wants to make sure she has the best chance of inheriting the money. In his words, she needs a fresh start, so I guess I have no choice, especially since she's too cute for words.

Her eyes flick away from mine to scan down my body, taking her time the lower her eyes get. When she's had an eyeful, she works her way back up to my face.

"Ma'am, would you like to file a complaint?" It's nice to know I still have it even though I'm not going there this time.

She bites her lip and gives me a slow-motion head wag. "Not at all." She sticks out a hand, and I shake it. "Sorry. My manners have left the building. I'm Andie. You must be George."

"Huh?"

She gasps, and the Chinaberry red flush creeps up her neck again. "I cannot believe I said that out loud."

She's going to be a pill to deal with while she's here. But at least the scenery will be nice. Those short legs with muscles popping out at every step might be the death of me. Her face doesn't break any mirrors, either.

"It's Officer Wills." I point at Charlie. "That's Charlie."

He spits tobacco on the small patch of grass next to the curb. "Welcome to Smithville."

She waves to Charlie and opens her car door. "Nice to meet you guys. I'll be on my way now."

When she settles into the driver's seat, I close the door behind her. This is going to be fun.

Stop it. You are on a sabbatical from females, remember?

"Follow me, and I'll take you to her shop." I lean in close to her and whisper, "And you might want to get rid of the evidence."

She sneers and reaches over to pick up the cooler then hands it to me. "Can you give me a 'get out of jail free' card since I barely drove over the county line? Plus, my first 'welcome to the neighborhood' gift was a hood full of bird crap. That wasn't very neighborly."

She hasn't been here more than ten minutes, and she's already asking for favors. "Negative."

She shrugs. "Can't blame a girl for trying."

Girls like her peg me for a pushover. Been there, done that, got the scars to prove it.

"Follow me," I say, not giving her another chance to give me any lip. I wave to Charlie when I exit the parking lot in my squad car. He waves to me then to our new guest. From my rearview mirror, I see her give him a cute finger wave. Oh Lord, this is going to be a long, hot summer.

CHAPTER FOUR
Andie

Twangy and muscled Officer George Clooney drives ahead of me through the town. I assume we are on Main Street because it seems to be congested. And by that, I mean three cars are on the road. Wow. And none of them are cabs. Several people wave to the officer as we pass. He gives them a one-finger wave without taking his hand off the wheel. One old lady points at me and whispers to another old lady as we pass. Well, that's a little on the creepy side.

The cop pulls over to the side of the road in front of a shop. The green awning over the front door droops to the left. On the front window, the words "In a Jam" float like steam out of a coffee cup next to a plate of biscuits and, I'm guessing, jam. A rusty bistro table and chairs sit beside the front door, and a wilting plant covers most of the tiny round table. Other than needing a serious window washing, the store isn't in bad shape, at least from the outside.

I step out of the car and observe the other stores on Main Street. Across from Granny's shop is a used car lot. I chuckle at the sign: Hunter's Motors - Bait, Tackle, and Guns. Next to that store is a gym, and from the old-time filling station pump, I assume it was a gas station at one point. The sign says Big Ash Fitness: Tony Ash, Owner-Operator. Maybe I can get a short-term membership while I'm here. For once, I don't have to fake interest in joining to get a few weeks free. A fat guy walks out of the gym with a towel wrapped around his neck and a cigarette hanging out of his mouth. *Classy.* Not that I'm any better when I eat a dozen donuts complemented by a Captain

Morgan and Diet Coke. I guess we all have our vices. Cigarette Man bows his head in a greeting before he saunters toward his parked car.

"Quaint," I mumble to myself as I drag my overstuffed suitcase out from the trunk.

The officer waves to Cigarette Man. "We sure did love Miss Gracie. I would come by every morning for my coffee and her world-famous biscuits and jam." I don't think he means anything by it, but his comment has me clenching my hands around the suitcase handle until my knuckles are white. These people know my own grandmother better than I do. It's embarrassing at best.

He notices I'm struggling with my bag. "Oh, let me get that for you." He takes the luggage out of my struggling hands, and his strong fingers brush across mine. His eyes flick toward mine for a second before he snatches up the suitcase as if it weighs only five pounds. With the other hand, he fishes out a set of keys and unlocks the door of the store.

"World famous, huh?"

Bells on top of the door announce our entry into the store. He hands me the keys, and I stuff them in my shorts pocket. Mr. Christian said the key would be waiting for me, but this is a bit much.

Inside, it seems as though the store hasn't been updated in twenty years. Plastic red-and-white-checkered tablecloths have seen better days. I run my finger across the dust on the Formica countertop that is worn in places. Some of the barstools have two-by-fours for legs. The curtains could use a serious washing. Behind the counter is a stairwell leading to what I assume is Granny's apartment. All in all, the store is run-down but kind of... cute.

"Shouldn't you be patrolling the streets instead of having tea with my grandmother?"

He grins and slides onto a barstool. His uniform pants stretch around his tight butt.

Stop staring. That's rude.

"I know it seems like a bustling city, but the townsfolk behave, for the most part."

Even though I'm not facing him, I know his eyes are on me as I take in my grandmother's place. My heart skitters a bit, and I'm afraid to turn around for fear he's not really ogling at all. I've been in this town only ten minutes, and my Southern roots are already showing. My heart is *skittering*? Ugh.

I don't see any water spots on the ceiling, and the floor feels solid. I walk behind the counter to inspect the kitchen area. The stove is old but clean. On the far side is a pantry with no obvious signs of rodents, thank goodness. Next to the pantry, Granny's red-and-white-checkered apron hangs on a hook. I slide my hand down the fabric, hoping she knows I'm here and that I'll do my best to fulfill her wishes.

I'm here, Granny. Wish you were too.

Officer Wills clears his throat, snapping me back to reality.

The shop is in pretty decent shape. I should be able to sell it for a decent price unless it needs a new roof or if the pipes are older than dirt.

"Cozy, don't ya think?" the officer asks.

I shrug. "Well, it's not Starbucks, but it'll do for now."

He shivers. "Yeah, I ordered coffee at Starbucks one time, and they glared at me like I was insane. I only wanted a cup of coffee. No latte, no mocha cappuccino, Frappuccino, whatever. Just coffee."

I giggle. I don't know where that came from. "I kind of pictured you sitting on your big wraparound porch, with your dog and two point five kids, reading the *Smithville Daily News*, sipping an espresso."

He snickers, and I think I made him blush a bit. "Plain coffee. Miss Gracie made plain coffee." He points at the monster-sized coffee maker perched in the corner of the counter, next to the wall.

That might come in handy if I slip into my old ways and need a massive hangover remedy. I've been semi-dry for two whole days, and I'm already getting the itch. This is going to be a long, hot summer.

"I see the attraction." I pivot to face him. "Wait a second. My grandmother had a coffee shop, and all she served is regular coffee?"

He leans his head to the side then shrugs. "Well, there's black coffee, coffee with two creams, cream and sugar. Actually, lots of options."

"Lots."

He motions with his head to the set of stairs. "Do you want to see your apartment upstairs?"

I cock an eyebrow. "Oh, so you have a key to my apartment too?"

The corner of his mouth twitches, and this time, there's no doubt about the flush across his face. It rests right over that dimple. *Eek.*

"Should I feel safe or scared?"

He points at my pocket. "Uh, it's on the key ring I gave you."

Snap out of it, girl. He's not flirting with you. He's doing his job. "Oh yeah." I pull it out to show him. "Here it is." *Idiot.*

Then he mumbles under his breath, "Except for the extra set I made yesterday."

"I heard that, Mr. Protect and Serve. You were kidding, right?"

"Yes. Of course."

He leads me up the narrow wooden staircase. I'm glad he's carrying my luggage because I don't think I could haul it up the steep stairs. And on top of that, I get a really nice view of his butt. Yep, he fills out those cop pants as well as the cop shirt. I can totally see him as a Chippendales dancer, and he already has the uniform for the job.

"Do you have a first name, or should I keep calling you Mr. Poleece-man Wills, savior of white cars that have been attacked by birds who eat red berries?"

He chuckles, and it rumbles through the small staircase. Nice face, nice butt, nice laugh. Please tell me he's got at least one bad quality.

"Ha ha. It's Gunnar Wills."

"Whew. Way better than 'The George,'" I mutter.

He squints. "What did you say?"

"Nothing." *Girl, stop thinking out loud.*

We get to the top, and I hand him the keys to unlock my apartment.

He drops the luggage, and it almost lands on my foot. "Sorry about that. Tight quarters on this landing."

"I noticed." His chest is at my eye level, and I could so easily reach out and grab that butt of his... to steady myself, of course. I clear my throat in an attempt to clear my mind, which has gone down the dirty trail. "So, Gunnar is a cop... with a gun. Your mama must have known what you would be when you grew up. Lucky for you, she didn't name you Steele Johnson because you don't look like a porn star to me."

He cocks an eyebrow, and I want to stuff the words back in my mouth.

"I mean, you totally could be a porn star. I mean... I think I'll stop now."

Shit. Can I die right here and be done with it?

He chuckles as he fiddles with the stubborn lock.

"I tend to babble when I'm nervous."

"I noticed."

I hold my hand out to him. He gazes at my hand then at my eyes. He licks his lips. Oh dear, that's the international symbol for wanting to kiss someone.

"Pleased to meet you, Officer Wills."

My hand is lost in his large, warm, calloused grip. It's inviting, and like the story of *Goldilocks and the Three Bears*, it feels just right—strong and controlling with a trace amount of grease under the thumbnail. He's definitely not a pencil pusher. That's for sure. And with the guns he has for biceps, my guess is he spends a lot of time across the street at the gym.

Hello, workout partner.

"Call me Gunnar. We're not formal around here."

"Okay, Gunnar."

He throws his head back and laughs. "It's Gunnar."

"Yeah. I said Gunnar."

A smile spreads across his face. "Not Gunnah. Gunnar."

"Gun-errr."

"Better."

Oh, as if he has room to talk.

He glances down at my hand still clenching his. "Don't do anything to make me handcuff your hands together."

My mouth falls open. "That's definitely not original. I've spent enough time around cops to know about their fantasies."

He drops my hand and cocks his right eyebrow. "I meant like drive drunk. I know all about the terms of your grandmother's will."

"Tinsley has a big mouth."

He cringes. "Yeah. Cops are like brothers, no matter where we're from. And I didn't say anything, but the grapevine in this small town is already buzzing about the will. So don't be shocked if people mention it."

I plant my hands on my hips. "Nuh-uh."

"That's affirmative."

Dammit. Every person in this town will be watching me to see if or when I mess up. I'm not going to let them win, no matter how hard the summer might be. This time next year, I won't even remember their names.

"You be a good little girl, and we'll see you in church tomorrow."

He pinches my cheek as if I'm five years old. I swat his hand away. He winks then gallops down the stairs and out the front door. The bells let me know he's gone.

"Thank you," I yell as if he could really hear me.

I survey my home for the summer. A small galley kitchen is to the left of the entrance, and to the right is a tiny but clean bathroom, complete with a shag rug and matching toilet tank cover. It takes no more than two steps, and I am in the middle of my studio apartment. Granny sectioned off the sleeping space with a rustic louvered room divider. The main living space is stuffy and filled to the brim with furniture, but it does have a huge bay window overlooking the street. I imagine sitting on the window seat in the mornings, sipping a cup of tea, and dreaming about how my life will be so much better in only a few short months.

Every surface in the main living area is covered with picture frames of all sorts and sizes. I don't recognize any of the people in the photos until I come across one of my mother. She's holding a baby and appears so pretty. Wait. That baby is me. I pick up the picture and run my hand through the dust covering it. I never realized until now how much I favor my mother. With her short-cropped light-blond hair and freckles sprinkled across her nose, if I didn't know better, I could swear I was staring into a mirror. She seems happy in the picture, but I never remember her that way. We never got along, and as soon as I had the means, I left for the big city and never looked back. I put the photo down, feeling as though I've invaded my grandmother's privacy.

Another photo catches my eye. It's a picture of me in my college graduation cap and gown. I didn't even know she had a picture of that day, much less that she thought it was important enough to proudly display it among her other cherished photos. From the way Mama talked about Granny, I didn't even think she kept in touch with her, let alone cared enough to send her photos of important times in my life. They had a falling out when I was little, and I thought my mother was the best and that Granny had to be the bad guy. It was only later that I figured out my mom suffered from an "I infection." She loved herself more than anyone else. Maybe I had Granny pegged wrong. Maybe Mama had her pegged wrong. And since she lied about Granny being dead, I'll never get a chance to find out.

First things first before I get all sappy. I have to unpack and find something suitable to wear to church tomorrow. I need to make a nice first impression on the townspeople. If they know about the terms of Granny's will, I'll have to work extra hard to walk the straight and narrow.

I stand in the middle of my grandmother's tiny apartment, and the silence is deafening. At times like this, when I'm alone, I'm reminded of how lonely I really am. The only time I hang out with "friends" is when it's happy hour, and I cannot remember the last time I went on a real date. I peek out the bay window to the vacant street below. This small town is too quiet and picturesque to be without some Southern Comfort. Oh boy, this whole staying-sober clause is going to be harder than I thought.

CHAPTER FIVE
Andie

Granny's bed is way more comfortable than I thought it would be. The frame may be something straight out of the fifties, but that memory foam mattress put me in dreamland within seconds of my head hitting the pillow. I fell asleep so fast, I didn't have time to set an alarm. In my typical Andie fashion, I'm late, and to church, of all places. *Dammit.* If it weren't for the church bells ringing, I would still be asleep. Now I only have ten minutes to get dressed. If I had gotten up in time, I could have leisurely strolled to church, but no, I have to drive a measly two blocks in order to get there before it's all over.

I know first impressions are everything, and I'm sucking at it right now, real bad. When I pull the door to the tiny church, it creaks open, and a streak of sunlight hits the pastor's face while he's making the weekly announcements. Our eyes meet, and he pauses for a moment then continues as if no one interrupted him. Several little girls turn around and gawk at the idiot who is late for service.

I slip into a seat in the back row and hope I can fade into the background. I scan the crowd and notice Charlie, the gas station attendant, at the other end of my pew. He waves, and the polite thing to do is wave back, so I do.

I'm trying to fit in, Granny. I promise.

Without realizing it, I do a quick scan of the congregation in hopes that Officer Wills is the churchgoing type. Before I can finish my search, a cell phone chimes, and everyone turns toward one of the old biddies that were pointing in my direction on the sidewalk yesterday. Her thumbs fly across the screen faster than a teenager's can. Her eyebrows furrow when she glances my way, then she focuses again on her phone. Another phone chimes. The other old lady pulls out her phone from her bra. *Gross.* Over her glasses, she reads her phone screen then crinkles her brow before she peeks in my direction. With one index finger, she types a message then returns her phone to its resting place in the nether regions of her bra. They both peer over at me with an "I've got my eye on you" expression that sends a shiver up my spine.

An old pipe organ cranks up a tune, while the pastor leaves the pulpit and starts making his way down the aisle. The two old ladies sit up tall as if they've been paying attention all along. One has the nerve to shush someone.

"Friends, we have a new face among us today. Let's all sing our welcome song. C'mon, everyone. Let's stand and sing."

The entire congregation stands and rotates to face me. This cannot be happening. One of the members, a lady not much older than me, tries to take me by the hand. I stand my ground and am ready to dig my heels in if necessary. I will not be paraded like a calf being sent to the county fair.

"We won't bite," she says. "Come on, honey."

Yeah, I've heard that before.

She pries my white-knuckled hands off the pew in front of me and walks me up and down the aisle. Surely to God they don't do human sacrifices here or drag out snakes. *Please God. Not snakes.* That wouldn't be very Southern of them. Sweat trickles between my boobs. I swear I can hear my heartbeat in my ears as the woman takes me to the front of the church. I'm doing my best to act as if I'm happy to be here, but I'm sucking at it. I wish the frickin' sanctuary floor would open up and swallow me whole.

The congregation sings, "I've got the joy, joy, joy, joy down in my heart."

Someone in the church yells, "Where?"

The booming voice makes me practically jump out of my skin.

"Down in my heart," the rest of the congregation recites back.

"Where?" the person yells again.

"Down in my heart. I've got the joy, joy, joy, joy down in my heart. Down in my heart to stay."

Oh please, God, if you exist, please take me now. Take me out of this hell I've been placed in. When I finally get the nerve to scan the congregation, my eyes fall on Gunnar. He's dressed in a suit, standing on the other side of the aisle, in the second row from the front. And if I thought he was as hot as the third level of hell in a cop uniform, he's beyond scorching in that double-breasted number. Somebody needs to splash some holy water on me to bring my core temperature down a few notches.

He holds a little girl about five years old. Her long dark hair is pulled into a pretty French braid. She snuggles into his neck while he rubs her back. And the chick standing next to him is drop-dead gorgeous. Her perfect brown hair falls to her shoulders with just the right amount of curl framing her pale skin and light-green eyes.

Well, I feel like a doofus for crushing on a guy that's married *and* has a kid. I'm so glad I didn't say anything to embarrass myself yesterday. All those hot-cop notions I was having are neatly tucked away in my brain, and no one has to ever know about them, except God. *Dear God, I promise I didn't know.*

The congregation starts up with the second stanza. "I've got my new friend here, and she's here to stay."

Oh, dear Lord, please let the devil come and take me to hell. It has got to be better than this. This song goes on for five more stanzas until I have the chance to shake everyone's hand. They express how happy they are to see me. This is worse than any drunken state I have ever been in. And a tall shot of whiskey sure sounds good right now.

The pretty lady standing next to Gunnar reaches out to take my hand. She leans in and says, "Nice to meet you. I'm Faith. I'd love to have you over sometime soon. Okay?" She draws out her last word long enough for the congregation to start another verse.

Me? At your house? So I can drool over your husband? Not the best idea. "Sure. That sounds nice."

The little girl grins, and I give her a quick finger wave. *Fitting in, Granny.*

"Mornin'," Gunnar says. His voice rumbles over me and makes me tingle in parts I shouldn't talk about in church. He shifts the little girl to his left arm and holds out his right hand for me to take. *Awkward.*

I smile as I quickly shake his hand, hoping to God that I don't have any tingly feelings for a married man while in church. I yank my hand back and continue my journey down the aisle toward my seat in the back. *Thank God that's over.* Before I can collapse into my pew, the little girl waves me over. I refuse her offer. She does it again and whispers something in Gunnar's ear. He snaps his head around and shrugs. The cheesy grin on her face matches her dad's, even the little dimple on her cheek. She motions again for me to join them, so while the choir director leads us in "When the Roll is Called Up Yonder," I slide in next to them. She hops down from her dad's arms and stands between us, holding both our hands. The lady's eyebrow quirks up, but then her lips curve upward.

The little girl tugs on my arm for me to lean down. She whispers in my ear, "I'm Lily."

"Nice to meet you, Lily."

I realize I have given Gunnar a perfect view down the front of my dress. Even when I cover myself with my hand, his eyes don't dart away. They linger, and with the sluggish speed of the pastor's prayer, they slide up to my face, hesitating on my lips, then locking on to my eyes. There go the tingly girly parts again. No point in calling the roll in heaven because I'm going straight to hell. I'm the biggest chowder head for crushing on a married man.

As soon as the pastor finishes the closing prayer, I'm going straight to Granny's apartment to make a list of items I need in order to get ready for my first day running her shop. Thank goodness Granny left me well stocked with ingredients. If I'm going to fulfill her terms, I need to stay away from married men, especially if they are as hot as a fresh slice of pizza.

CHAPTER SIX
Gunnar

I lean back against my squad car, which I conveniently parked next to Andie's sweet ride. I am walking down a road I shouldn't venture down. She's on a mission, and it is to sell the store and leave by the end of summer. She's not going to stick around, no matter how attracted I am to her, no matter how much I want to keep the town from falling apart. She's the last chance this town has before downtown falls to the big box stores, but she can't know that. She's going to do what she wants to do, and I can't stop her.

But I didn't expect to feel this way. I mean, I knew Miss Gracie's granddaughter would be about my age, but I didn't expect someone like Andie. She's not from around here, so I assumed she would be easy to hate and easy to resist. Tinsley warned me she would steal my heart, but I figured I was immune since I disposed of mine a long time ago.

Even though she seems to have a lot of baggage that she apparently hides with a bottle and a pretty face, I knew she wasn't a bad person after spending a few minutes with her. In fact, she seems really sweet and misunderstood. Her crystal-blue eyes show me an honest and sincere person. More than that, she makes my heart sputter. It has been a long time since I've felt anything. The last time was, well, too long ago, and it didn't end well. So I don't know why I am torturing myself. God only knows.

Lily bounces down the stairs and takes her mother by the hand as they maneuver through the parking lot. Once they are safely to their car, I turn my attention back to that tight little package. Andie can't get away from the steps before she's bombarded by the welcome committee, led by the Jackson sisters, Jennifer and Sarah. She peels her hand away from one person's hand only to get caught by another churchgoer. She does all this with a tentative grin as she slides a strand of hair behind her ear for the tenth time. Finally, Andie is able to pry her hand away from the pastor's and maneuver through a sea of old ladies from church.

Miss Jennifer stumbles over the curb, and before I can take one step toward her to help, Andie grabs her by the arm to steady her.

Miss Jennifer gives Andie a pat on the cheek. "Sooo, you're Andie, Miss Mary Grace's granddaughter." Her sister, Sarah, takes the opportunity to nab Andie's hand again.

Even though I've only known Andie for a day, it's obvious to me that her smile is a painted-on fake.

"Yes, I am." Andie starts to pull her hand away, but I know Sarah's grip is as strong as an anaconda. Andie won't be going anywhere until Sarah finishes devouring her. Jennifer's always been the sweeter of the Jackson sisters. Word on the street is that the two Jackson sisters have taken it upon themselves to make sure Andie doesn't comply with the terms of the will. They've always been the town's gossip gals, but ever since they took a community education class on blogging, they've stepped up their rumor mill to include a blog about all the dirt in Smithville. Sometimes, I wonder if they should be employed at the police department. Other times, I wish their server would go down, especially when it involves one specific out-of-towner.

Miss Sarah confiscates Andie's hand. "We've heard about you."

"Nice things, I hope," Andie says.

Sarah turns to Jennifer then says, "Well, Gracie said you were a souse."

Andie finally has the strength to snatch her hand away. "Excuse me?"

"She means you like the sauce," Jennifer whispers loud enough for all to hear. The woman holds her thumb up to her mouth to pantomime drinking. "That's okay."

Andie scans the parking lot until her eyes land on mine. I wave. She mouths, "Help me."

I motion with my head to keep moving through the shark-infested waters toward me, the ex-king of sharks.

"Well, I'm trying to behave. Isn't that all God can ask of us?"

Two points for Andie. She race-walks my way, or to her car. I'm not sure which.

"If we can be of any help, you let us know," Jennifer yells.

Andie waves to them over her shoulder.

"She means if you need help finding the good stuff, let us know," Sarah says.

Andie rolls her eyes. I eyeball Sarah and Jennifer. They are already in a powwow to devise their next plan of attack. They want Andie's money for the church so badly that they'll take down anyone who stands in their way.

Regardless of what Andie plans to do with the money, she shouldn't be blindsided by selfish old biddies. Although it would really be nice if she didn't sell Miss Gracie's shop... for the town's sake, of course. But if I can show her Smithville isn't such a bad place to live, maybe she won't want to leave. Stranger things have happened.

Even if Tinsley hadn't asked me to keep an eye on her, I would be doing it, anyway. There's something about her that makes me want to go the extra mile for her, as if she needs someone to protect her from the world and from herself.

She stops in front of me, and a scowl replaces that easy grin of hers. She crosses her arms over her chest and stands with a wide stance.

"Are you impersonating an officer, Miss Carson?"

"Trying to but failing. I can honestly say I didn't recognize you without your uniform on." Her eyes get big, and a flush runs across her face. "I mean, without regular clothes on. I mean, you look nice all dressed up."

Her awkwardness is so cute. "You look nice... without regular clothes on too."

Hoo boy, my thoughts head into territory not fit for Sunday school. *Down, boy.*

She surveys her sundress, which shows off nice deltoids. Hmm. I like a girl that doesn't mind slinging a little iron. Her toes peek out of her sandals as she moves up and down on the balls of her feet. There go those sexy calf muscles flexing again. *Have mercy.* And even when she's wearing heels, the top of her head doesn't come up past my chest.

"I can honestly say I didn't recognize you without your groupies singing around you."

She places her hands on her hips. Her mouth tips up on one side as though she's resisting the urge to smile. "Not funny. Actually, it was all okay until they started on the verse about the devil sitting on a tack."

I laugh out loud, covering my face. "At least they didn't break out into a chorus of 'Kumbaya.' That could go on forever." I don't mind it, but it can be a turn-off for someone who isn't used to it.

She peers around. "Shhh, don't give them any ideas."

"They like to make up verses to that one too."

Andie singsongs, "Someone's goin' crazy, Lord. Please take me. Oh Lord, please take me."

I clap. She bows, flashing me a bit of cleavage. She presses her hands over her chest, realizing the view she gave me. Cute and modest, not a bad combination.

"Not bad. Maybe next week, they'll let you sing in the choir."

She puts her hands up, palms toward me. "That is not in the agreement. I have enough to handle with 'the sisters.'"

"Oh, don't let them get under your skin."

She turns around to see the sisters still in the parking lot, scheming. "Who, them?" she asks, giving them a beauty-queen wave.

They scamper away like roaches when the light comes on.

"You do know they'll do whatever they can to get to that money of yours. Don't underestimate their skills." I probably should tell her about their mad blogging skills, but I don't want her to dislike Smithville because of something that might not even happen.

She nods and gives me a slight shrug. "I guess I'd do the same in their situation. But I'm really going to do my best to make everyone proud."

"Hungry?" I ask, ready for a change in subject.

A crinkle forms between her eyes. "Yeah, but what about your little girl?"

"Huh? Oh, Lily. She's at home with her mom."

I catch her quick look-see toward my hands.

"And they're cool with you taking me to lunch?"

I shrug. "I guess so. I don't ask their permission."

Her mouth flies open. "Wow. This town is more progressive than I thought. But it bothers me."

"It's only food. Everyone has to eat."

She mumbles something under her breath then asks, "So, where do you go for food around here? I'm not in the mood for the Tastee Freeze."

I wag my head. It would be funny if there weren't a smidgen of truth to that.

"Let's see. We have two restaurants open on Sunday." I tap my finger to my chin. "BJ's, and then there's Shoney's. Personally, I'd go to BJ's. It's the best food around."

Her eyes get huge, and she scans the parking lot. She whispers, "Did you say... BJ's?

"Affirmative."

"As in..."

I can't bite my grin away. "Why, Miss Andie, I do believe you have a dirty mind."

She swats me on the arm. "You set me up for that." She motions with her head toward my police car. "Do I have to ride in the back seat like a common criminal?"

She is so cute. Although after my conversations with Tinsley, I have a sneaking suspicion she's had more than a few rides in the back seat of a squad car. "No, you can ride in the front seat with me."

Her face lights up. "Can I drive?"

"Negative."

Andie walks over to the passenger's side. I open the door for her. She turns around abruptly, and I don't have a chance to stop. I bump into her and take a quick step back, already missing the contact.

"Can I play with your thingy?"

I stare at her like an idiot. She leans inside my squad car and touches the siren. It makes an obnoxious "whoop" sound, sending her scampering out of the car, bumping into me. This is beginning to be a habit with her. The stragglers from the parking lot all turn to stare at us, giving them fodder for the Jacksons' blog, I'm sure.

"Uh, I was talking about the..."

"Negative, you cannot touch the siren."

She gets in and scoots around on the seat. I shut her door and take a few deep breaths to try to regain my composure, which includes shifting the contents of my slacks while I walk around the car. I should have gone to my sister's house to eat with her family like I usually do. But my niece insisted I take the new girl out to lunch.

This is really not the best idea. Not. At. All.

CHAPTER SEVEN
Gunnar

I can't help but stare as Andie pulls the skin off her fried chicken and plunks it onto her plate. She pats the chicken breast with a napkin to soak up the excess grease. It must be a Yankee thing.

Andie takes a gander over her shoulder for the third time. "Why is everyone staring at us?"

I turn around. They all jerk their heads to look at their plates, not wanting to make eye contact. No surprise why this would be intimidating to someone who hasn't grown up in a small town.

"They don't get out much. You're an outsider."

"Am I that scary?"

"That remains to be seen."

She snarls and dips her fork into my mashed potatoes before I can stop her. To retaliate, I take a sip from her tea glass, causing her jaw to drop.

"And I thought you were a Southern gentleman."

"Southern? Affirmative. Gentleman? Not so much." If she only knew my recent history and how I treated women after Willow left me, she would never consider me a gentleman.

"Pfft." She lifts her tea glass to take a sip but turns it around so she puts her lips where mine were. Her eyes twinkle. She clears her throat, and the flirty behavior is replaced with a more professional demeanor. "So, not many Yankees infiltrate Smithville?"

"Negative. Especially those that really hail from Boston, Tennessee."

She smacks the table, making a roll tumble to the floor. The restaurant turns quiet as all the other patrons abandon their meals to listen to Andie's outburst. "Tinsley's a dead man." Then she gasps, realizing what she just said. "It's a metaphor. I would never tell an officer of the law my evil plans to off my friend."

She takes a swig from her glass. I guess what's good for the goose...

"What's wrong with being from Tennessee?"

"Duh. I worked real hard to get over the dumb-Southern-blond stereotype, and right when I finally ditch the accent completely, I move here. After only two days, bam, it's seepin' back in."

I chuckle. "Like ridin' a bike."

She bobs her head. "You see what I did there? I'm already dropping my Gs. Pretty soon, I'll be ridin' and chewin' and huntin' with all you guys."

"With all y'all."

She points to me with her fork. "I'm not there yet."

"We'll see about that." I wink at her. *Shit. Stop flirting. It never ends well.* I clear my throat. "Like you, most run away from this place when a better opportunity comes around."

She shrugs and scoops another bite of mashed potatoes into her mouth. Through her stuffed face, she mumbles, "Ahh, I see. So why aren't you running from it? Other than the obvious family ties."

I take notice of all the nosy folks surrounding us. What she sees as intrusive, I see as welcoming. I like having people around me I know I can trust, that have my back when times get tough, even if they stick their noses into every detail of everyone's life. They are also there in two shakes if one of us needs anything, like how my best friends were there when I almost imploded after getting dumped by the love of my life.

"I actually like it here." I steal her biscuit. "I know that seems odd to you."

She takes a stab at my hand with her fork. "Hey, you thief. Never a cop around when you need one."

I belt out a laugh. I haven't laughed that loud in years. In fact, I haven't laughed or guffawed or let out a single chuckle for a very long time, but after only two days, this pint-sized Yankee from Tennessee has dragged that out of me. "I lived in the big city for a while."

"Oh yeah?" She takes a long swig from her sweet tea. Yep, she's already taking a shine to sweet tea.

I avoid answering by stuffing my face full of food again. Cassie, the waitress, fills our tea glasses.

"Thanks."

Cassie smiles and walks to the next table.

"Chicago."

Andie drops her fork. "Seriously?"

"Yep. Lived there for two years, working on my master's degree." That lie gets easier to tell the more I tell it. I don't want the people that respect me to know I didn't leave on the best of terms. That is one secret that has been kept from the gossip gals.

She stares while she removes some stuck food off her tooth with her tongue. "You have a master's degree?

I should be used to that reaction by now. I thought I wanted out of this hellhole, and an education was my ticket out. Funny how things end up. Willow and I had plans to run as fast as we could away from here. Funny how feelings change. "Shocking, isn't it?"

"Yeah, so why are you a cop?" She closes her eyes and holds her hands up. "I mean, why did you choose the noble profession of law enforcement?" She peels one eye open to see if I'm offended.

I snicker because at least she has the decency to realize she's being rude. Most people around here blurt it out and don't care how it sounds.

"I get that a lot. I was working on my PhD but decided to settle for a master's instead and left early. Psychology of human behavior."

I'm stretching the truth a little, but she'll get the watered-down version I've fed everyone else in this town. Now that I have a few years' distance from the incident, I'm glad I didn't finish. I would never be happy being in a stuffy office all day. I like being out there with real people, trying to make a difference.

Andie blinks as if she doesn't believe me. "Really?"

"Sounds strange, I know, but I missed it here. I missed the people, the pace. And you might find this interesting, but I use what I learned at Northwestern every day in my chosen profession."

She sits back in her chair and crosses her arms. No telling what I said wrong. That's what I do best with women. She shouldn't be any different.

"You went to Northwestern?"

"I know that's a surprise, but it's true."

She points to herself. "I went to Northwestern."

"No way," I say, but I already knew that. Miss Gracie always talked about Andie. I felt as if I knew her already when she drove into town. And I often wondered if we were only two seconds away from running into each other in Chicago since we were there around the same time. But when I didn't have my head buried in a book, studying, I was deflecting barbs from Willow. Some people marry their high school sweethearts; others thank God every day they didn't.

"Then you must have taken Psych 350 with Professor Roth," she says.

I groan. "And I was grateful to pass. He was a tough bird."

She sits up tall and peers down her nose. Then she puckers her lips and taps her index finger to her mouth, acting like him. "To truly understand someone's psyche," she starts.

"You must first understand your own," I say along with her. We both laugh.

"Small world, huh?" she asks.

"Guess so." I could play the "what if" game forever, and we would still end up right where we are, so it's no use driving myself crazy.

After a pause long enough to gulp down another swig of tea, Andie takes a deep breath. "Okay, I have to know. Are you eating with me to convince me to give the money to church?"

My tea goes down the wrong pipe. I choke out my reply. "Boy, you don't beat around the bush. No. Of course not."

She leans in and whispers, "Then why aren't you eating lunch with your wife?"

"Excuse me?"

"The pretty lady at church. I can't remember her name. And your daughter. Very cute. Why are you here instead of with them?"

She must think I am an idiot because I'm trying to register what she's saying. "Are you talking about Faith?"

She nods. "That's her name. Sorry. I forgot. So many people were introducing themselves today, I couldn't remember them all."

I stare at the ceiling and let out a breath. "I'm not married."

"Oh." She cocks her head to the side. "You sit with your ex-wife at church? Doesn't that give the townspeople fodder?"

"For your information, that's my sister."

She drops her fork. "You were married to your sister?" she screeches, causing a hush to fall over the restaurant.

"Jeez. This isn't West Virginia." I take a deep breath before I choose my next words. "That was my sister and her daughter, my niece. I've never been married. I came pretty darn close one time, but I am not married to a cousin or sister or anyone. Are we clear?" She must really be full of herself if she thinks I would ask her to lunch by myself and leave a wife and kid at home. That is not how I roll.

She bites her bottom lip and flashes those big eyes through those long lashes. "My bad. I guess this *is* a modern town after all."

"I would not—"

I can't finish my rant because Stanley lollygags our way. He's the local doofus. He's a big ole teddy bear but not very bright, and he thinks he's smooth with the ladies, when he couldn't be further from it. Besides, he really only has eyes for his on-again, off-again girl-friend, Jolene.

Stanley licks his thumb and slicks back what's left of his hair. His jeans ride low under his beer belly. If he bends over, we'll all get a plumber's butt showing, I'm certain. He gives Andie a once-over.

I lean over the table near Andie and whisper, "Don't look."

She turns around.

"I said not to look," I hiss at her.

She trains her eyes on her lap and fidgets with her napkin then glances back up. Through gritted teeth, she whispers, "What?"

"Stanley's coming this way." I take a gulp of my tea. "If you make eye contact, he'll start a conversation that will never end."

"Who is Stanley?"

"Nice guy but not the brightest. He lives out near the county dump."

"Great. What does he want?"

"Oh, probably being neighborly. That's all."

Stanley is almost to us. Andie steals a glimpse at him. "Is that a Skoal can in his pocket?"

He stands right next to our table.

"Stan, the man! What's up?" I try to sound as chipper as possible and stick my hand out to take Stanley's, but he ignores me.

He's set his cap on Andie. This is going to be real awkward. I clear my throat. The Friedmans at the table next peer over their tea glasses, waiting to see how this plays out.

"Stan, this is Miss Gracie's granddaughter, Andie. Andie, this is Stanley Culpepper."

He grins like the Cheshire Cat. "I heard of you. You're rich, ain't ya?"

Andie bites her lip but cannot conceal a grin that has started forming at the side of her mouth. If she keeps that up, I'll need to untuck my shirt to hide the evidence of my inappropriate thoughts. That would definitely be awkward.

"No. Not rich yet, that is."

"Miss Gracie was always nice. She'd save her leftover muffins for me. Never went hungry because of her."

Andie grins and glances over at me. I sit back and take in the show. Serves her right for thinking I was married to my sister.

Stanley drags a chair from a neighboring table and sits on it backward, straddling the seat. "She talked a lot about you," he says, licking his lips.

"Really?" Andie visibly squirms in her chair. "That's sweet, I guess."

I casually sip my iced tea and enjoy Andie's reaction to his questioning.

Stanley's grin gets even cheesier. "Yeah, she said you were hot." When her mouth pops open, Stanley points at me. "Sorry, he's the one that said that."

And my iced tea makes an abrupt appearance out of my mouth. I choke and cough. Stanley whacks me on the back a few times then raises my arm over my head like his mama probably did when he was three.

Andie folds and unfolds her napkin. "It's not nice to talk about people behind their back."

Stanley snickers. "I'm pretty sure he meant it as a compliment, and I'd have to agree with him."

Andie bites a fingernail and rocks in her chair. She catches my eye, and I wink at her.

Stanley gets up to leave. "Well, uh, I better go for now. I'll see you around the shop." He takes his Skoal can out of his pocket and deposits a pinch between his teeth and gum.

Andie gulps. I think she threw up in her mouth.

"Save the leftovers for me," he says.

Andie paints on that fake smirk again. "Every last one of them."

As soon as Stanley shuffles off, she pops me on the shoulder.

"Ow! What was that for?" I ask, rubbing my arm. It didn't hurt a bit, but she doesn't have to know that.

"For talking about me, that's what fer," she says, trying to sound hillbilly. *Not working, sweetie.*

"He misunderstood. I said you were going to be hot down here. You know, the temperature." *Liar.*

She crosses her arm and scowls. "Still, the thought of people talking about me..." She shivers. "I like to fly under the radar."

I wave my hand around the room. "No chance of that here. Might as well enjoy yourself."

"Are you the only cop in town?"

"This isn't Mayberry. We have a full force to keep everyone safe around the clock. My shift starts this afternoon."

She rests her elbows on the table, cradles her head in her hands, and groans. Finally, when her anxiety attack has lessened, she meets my gaze and crinkles her eyebrows together, as though she's trying to figure me out.

"What?" I ask.

She shrugs. "What's your story, Officer Welcome Committee? Since I now know that you aren't married, why are you single? You don't seem hideous."

My neck gets hot. I don't like to talk about all my failed relationships, especially one in particular. I drum my fingers on the table.

"I mean, you're young and powerful. And you carry a nice piece."

My jaw drops.

She points to the gun strapped to my belt, which is peeking out from under my blazer. "Your gun."

Okay, I feel like an idiot. Of course she was talking about my gun. I have to get my mind out of the bedroom, pronto.

"Powerful? Hardly." With a cocky grin, I add, "But handsome and modest? That's another story."

"Oh my goodness. I don't know what's worse, Stanley or you. Both of you are very full of yourselves. And you let me think you were married, to your sister. Ugh."

I fight back a chuckle as I take our trays to the trash can. She has no idea how wrong she is. Stanley wouldn't hurt a fly. And my man-whore days are way behind me. It has been years since I had a "one and done," and I don't ever want to relive those days. Ever. I would rather be alone than live that kind of life again. Come to think of it, that's how it's been—alone and lonely. Until now. This is different. I'm not sure different is what I deserve, but different feels good. That's for darn sure. I'm drawn to her, and I am sure I'm going to pay a heavy price for it.

There are so many people wanting a piece of her inheritance, and I sure don't want her to feel that's what I want too. So for now, it's best to be her friend and leave it at that. It sucks because I think with some time, I could really like this girl.

During the short drive back to the church, where she left her car, she sits in the passenger seat, arms crossed, staring out the window, stewing. I am very familiar with that behavior, and I know better than to say anything until I'm spoken to.

"You let me think—"

"Nope. You assumed. I didn't say anything to make you think that."

"You didn't say anything either way," she mumbles under her breath, and I'm not stupid enough to ask what she said. If she wants me to know, she would say it louder.

"And I'm beginning to think you were talking about me behind my back to Stanley. I don't like that. At all."

"I wasn't."

She throws a hand up to stop me. "Don't care."

When I drop her off at the church, she slams the door and stomps toward her car. She's a spitfire when she gets her dander up. As soon as I know she's safely in her car, I drive away, toward the fitness center. In the parking lot, I call Tinsley to brief him on the situation.

"Speak."

"Hey, Tinsley. Gunnar Wills here. I thought I'd call to update you on Miss Carson."

"How's our gal?"

Our gal. I lean back in the seat of car. "She's adjusting. I think with time, we'll grow on her."

"Excellent. I hope so. And you?"

I furrow my brow at the phone as I exit my car to pace through the parking lot. "Not sure I know what you mean."

"Come on. She's adorable. I've had to chase away ten maggots that didn't stack up. She's pretty irresistible."

Oh, he must be into her. *Crap.* "I, uh... I didn't know you and her were..."

He belts out a laugh. "No, no, no. I'm very happily married. She's like a little sister. Pain in the ass, but wouldn't trade her for Red Sox tickets even if they were winning."

I let out a sigh. That shouldn't give me relief. I need to stay professional about this situation, and I certainly don't need to get too close. "That's good, I guess. Not that it matters. She's pretty ticked off with me about a misunderstanding."

"Look, man. I don't know you from Adam, but I feel like I can trust you. We're blue brothers, you know? She's a sweet girl, and I worry about her. All the drinking she does... I mean, she's gotta be wicked lonely to live that way. I think this thing with her grandma may be her way to a better life."

I wave to the Fuller family as they stroll down the sidewalk. Hearing how lonely Andie is saddens me. No one needs to go through life alone, and I hope I can help her see that life doesn't have to suck. "No chance of her being lonely here. By the time she leaves, she'll have her fill of Smithville. That's for sure."

"I wouldn't be so sure."

"All right. I gotta hit the weights before my shift, but I'll keep you posted."

"You do that."

"Oh, Tinsley, maybe you can clear up one thing for me." I scratch my head and assess the area to make sure the Fullers are nowhere around. "Why does Andie call me George?"

I have to hold the phone away from my ear. His laughter rumbles through my eardrum. "She'll have to tell you that one. Bye."

So Tinsley's not her boyfriend. Andie is as lonely as I suspected, and I have no idea why any of this matters to me. I need to do extra sets of weights to work off this pent-up energy before I explode or do something I won't be sorry for. I want her to feel as though she's part of the Smithville family without thinking I want anything in return. And if I can convince her of that, maybe I can convince myself too.

CHAPTER EIGHT
Andie

Like the phrase in my *How to Speak Southern* guide says, I want to wring his neck. I can't believe he let me think he was married to his sister, of all things. And then that stunt about talking to Stanley behind my back before he even had a chance to meet me. That infuriates me. Of all the nerve. If this is Southern hospitality, I don't want any part of it.

I almost trip on the stairs as I bolt up to my apartment in frustration. As I pace back and forth in front of the bay window, I review today's happenings. I didn't completely suck at church, so that's a win for me even though I think I would have been more comfortable running down Main Street in the nude. And lunch with Gunnar started out okay, but things turned pretty sour. I didn't think he would be a part of the church group that wants my money, but it could be why he let me embarrass myself.

None of this matters, anyway. I'm doing what Granny wants and nothing more. But that doesn't stop my heart from skittering when I see Gunnar's police car pull into the fitness center parking lot across the street. He talks on his cell phone before he opens the car door.

His dress shirt stretches tight over his back as he pulls out a gym bag and tosses it over his shoulder then saunters inside. Boy, it's hot in here.

"Yeah, Andie. Nothing more, my butt." I need to get a grip. Six weeks tops, and I'll be gone. Even though my plans include checking out the gym, it would be too much for me to show up when he's there. I would have "crazy stalker out-of-towner" tattooed all over my face. Besides, that would give the locals way too much gossip for one weekend. So I reshuffle my plans and start with number two on my list: buy some things at the Save-Mart to spruce up the shop.

I kick off my sandals, strip out of my sundress, and slip into my comfy tank top, running shorts, and flip-flops. Time to spend some of Granny's money.

IN TWO HOURS, I ACQUIRED a shopping cart full of items and ten stares from the locals, and now I'm heading back to the shop. The cute tablecloths and silk flowers will be perfect on the booths, and the place mats are adorable. It won't take much effort to make this place really shine. Granny had the decency to die with a pantry full of ingredients. All I need to do is figure out how to combine all those items into something edible. No shopping trip will help me in that department. I guess tomorrow will consist of only coffee.

Every thirty seconds, my eyes gaze out the front window just in case I can catch a glimpse of Mr. Muscle and Fitness. When he does exit the gym, my breath fogs up the window. That loose stringer tank top exposes all those ripped muscles I knew were hiding underneath his uniform and—oh God, I think he spotted me.

I stumble backward in hopes he didn't catch me gawking at him, especially since I should still be miffed at him. He drives away, and I can finally suck in a much-needed breath. Before my mind leads me down the dirty path, I grab a bottle of water, my phone, and earbuds then change into running shoes. I'm ready for a nice little afternoon jog, anything to burn off this unnerving tension that has suddenly spread down my body.

I crank up the volume on my cell phone, which only has ten percent battery life left. Steven Tyler's sexy voice sets the pace, and away I go. Considering Smithville isn't a booming city, I figure there aren't many jogging trails, so I keep to the sidewalks. They should lead me safely back to my shop even if I make one or two wrong turns. But if I jog down the street Gunnar lives on, I think I will die of embarrassment.

One swallow of water and two stop signs later, I switch from a walk to a slow jog. The air seems fresher compared to Boston, even if it's very humid. I can breathe out here, and now I know that if I want some peace and quiet, all I have to do is take to the streets because Smithville residents don't seem to be into outdoor fitness activities. Not a single jogger passes me along my jaunt. In Boston, jogging down sidewalks was out of the question. I wouldn't be able to go two steps with the high volume of traffic. I stuck to the jogging trails, especially near the Charles River, and even then, it was usually packed no matter how cold it was.

This is my first glimpse of the landscape of the town. Once I get past the town square, homes start to pop up—cute bungalows with nice-sized front yards. Each house is painted a different color, making it appear almost like a movie set. A flash of memory hits me of the house in which my grandmother lived when we would visit. I know I was little, but I do remember she didn't live far from the middle of town. I'm sure I would recognize her old house if I saw it. It probably hasn't changed a bit in twenty years.

With renewed energy, I pick up the pace and turn down Elliston Street. Thank goodness Spanish moss covers the trees and serves as a canopy across the street. The shade is a welcome relief from the sun beating down on me. Two more gulps of water help me keep pace to the music. A car slows down as it passes me. I wave, but the driver sneers as he proceeds down the street.

With the hem of my tank top, I wipe the sweat from my face. It feels awesome to exercise and rid my body of all the toxins I've been taking in over the last few months. *So this is what sober feels like. Not so bad.* With thoughts of Gunnar to distract me these last two days, I haven't thought much about taking a drink. Maybe if he comes around every now and then, it will be good for me in more ways than one.

I crank up the pace more and turn down another street, blinking the sweat out of my eyes. The sun blares down on me, and it wouldn't surprise me if I got a nasty sunburn today. Next time, I'll have to apply sunscreen.

Every time I reach a stop sign, I see another pretty house in the distance that I want to run by. Because of this, I wind up zigzagging through town so much, I can't remember which way leads back to the center of town. All the streets are named after trees, and I can't remember if I crossed Pine Street before Maple or if Dogwood Lane is perpendicular to Crepe Myrtle Avenue. The street names are as pretty as the homes, but I'm completely turned around now.

I stop at a traffic light to catch my breath. Scanning left and right, I'm not so sure which way to turn to get back to the town square, and I'm too proud to ask for directions from the two little boys throwing a football through a sprinkler. I wave at them, but they only stare back. Steven Tyler's voice stops singing to me. I really need to remember to charge my phone more often.

When the light turns green, I shoot across the street and continue on my journey. My Fitbit buzzes to let me know I'm above my target heart rate. If it weren't for that truck with the rusted tailgate following me, I would slow down to a walk. When I turn right, he turns right. I turn right again, and he's still right on my heels, this time gunning his engine. I turn left, and the truck heads in the other direction, thank goodness, but not before the jerk of a driver wolf whistles. I pick up the pace, my Fitbit screaming for me to slow down. If I can get back to the street with the pretty Spanish moss, I think I can figure out how to get back to my shop. But I don't know how to get back there.

The road I'm on changes from paved to gravel, and the quaint houses change to trailers with chain-link fences surrounding them. A very large dog rushes toward me, showing its teeth. I screech to a halt as the dog runs around me, not doing anything for my maximum heart rate.

A kid from the porch yells, "Buster, get up here now."

After a final "woof," the dog leaves me on the sidewalk, gasping for air. I do an about-face and retrace my steps, but nothing looks familiar. The last drop of water from my bottle drips onto my nose, and my tank top is soaked with sweat. I don't need my Fitbit to warn me about my heart rate because I hear each swooshing beat in my ears, and my head is on fire.

When I get back to the paved part of the road, I stop and lean over, sucking in air. My eyes blur, and the ground spins, not to mention the contents of my stomach do not want to stay down. This is like a sober hangover. I stumble a few steps.

Fear creeps up my spine, and tears well up. Turning right seems like the way I came, but so does going left. I'm not sure anymore, and I can barely see either way now. The houses all appear the same, and my eyes blur so much, I can't read the street sign.

To keep the panic from rising any higher, I lean up against a tree and force myself to slow my breaths. I'm lost in a frickin' one-traffic-light town, and I don't know what to do. I press the heels of my hands to my eyes in hopes of relieving the pressure in my head. But no matter how much I try to slow my breaths, I still pant like a dog inside a hot car.

My eyes close, and the bark of the tree scrapes my back before my butt hits the ground with a thud. I hear a vehicle approach, but I don't have the strength to run away if it's the guy in the rusted-out truck wanting to do more than catcall this time. A car door opens and slams shut, and footsteps crunch through the yard toward me. *Sorry, Granny. Your granddaughter is an idiot.*

"Andie?" That voice. I know that voice. "You okay?"

Gunnar. I close my eyes and say a silent prayer that I didn't get eaten by a large dog or kidnapped by the rusted-truck guy today. "I'm okay. But I'm real hot."

He chuckles. "You don't have to brag about it." He touches my face, and his cool fingers bring me back to life. I open my eyes in time to see his cocky grin turn to concern. "You're burning up."

And if he keeps touching me like that, I'm going to get hotter.

I shrug and try to take in a breath. "At least I'm not sweating anymore."

He groans. "No. That's a bad thing. In this heat and humidity, when you stop sweating, it means you're dangerously close to having heatstroke. Andie, you need to—"

My gut explodes, and I spew every piece of chicken and biscuits I had for lunch all over the grass and down his leg.

"Yep. Heatstroke."

I wipe my mouth with the hem of my tank top then use it to cover my face. "I'm so sorry."

I try to stand, but my knees buckle, and in one quick sweep, Gunnar scoops me up and carries me to his police car. He places me in the passenger seat and cranks the air conditioner on full blast. He takes a water bottle from the console, pours some water into his hands, then lets the cool water trickle down my face.

I jump from surprise and slosh water everywhere. "What are you doing?" If I had anything left in my stomach, it would be all over the floorboard of his police car.

"Cooling you off." He drizzles water down my arms and neck. Then he takes my socks and sneakers off and reclines the seat back, his face hovering dangerously close to mine.

He hands me the water bottle. "Here. Tiny sips. Let's get you to the hospital."

"No! I am fine."

"Hush." He walks around the car and climbs in to the driver's seat. After buckling his seat belt, he guns the engine and races off down the street.

I drift off to sleep but not before Gunnar's strong, soft hand touches my cheek again and slides a strand of hair behind my ear.

CHAPTER NINE
Andie

I cannot possibly have anything left to expel from my stomach. The cold washcloth falls to the floor while I wretch again, dry heaves this time. With each episode, Gunnar holds my hair back to keep it from being sprinkled with hurl. If I didn't have puke breath, I would kiss that man. He doesn't know me from Adam, but here he is, helping me and hardly letting the doctor and nurse in the room do their jobs.

I flop back in the hospital bed, trying not to mess with the blood pressure cuff on one arm and the IV attached to the other. A shiver runs up my spine. "C-C-Cold."

With the back of his hand, Gunnar touches my cheek. His hand is a great combination of strength and gentleness. His eyebrows knit together in a scowl.

"Your core temp is dropping," my doctor says. I think her name is Dr. Ballard.

If I felt better, I would make a wisecrack about that. Her light-brown hair is pulled back into a braid, but by the way the escaped strand coils around her ear, I bet it would be nothing but corkscrew curls if she didn't have it all contained. She checks the IV bag that runs fluid into my vein, while the nurse sticks a thermometer in my mouth and pushes the button for my blood pressure cuff to inflate.

With the thermometer clenched in my mouth, I say to Gunnar, "You don't have to stick around." He's already seen me at my worst, but I have some pride left.

The nurse shushes me.

"I want to. It's no big deal." He flicks his eyes up to the doctor. She has a knowing smile on her face.

"But you should—"

"Shh." He points to the doctor. "You should listen to Mel. I had to pull in a favor to get her to come in on her day off."

"A really big one," the doctor says.

The nurse harrumphs. All three of them have a nonverbal argument, and I have no idea what that's all about.

He grins. "Besides, how are you going to get home? Run?"

The nurse holds up a device to my ear and jots down whatever it displays.

"I thought I'd take a cab. Besides, I'm still mad that you led me to believe you were married."

Dr. Mel gasps. "You didn't."

"I did not."

The nurse snorts as she takes the thermometer out of my mouth. She shows the reading to the doctor.

"One hundred," says the doctor. "Much better. After your fluids finish running and if your temp comes down a little more, I'll discharge you. Don't run in this heat again."

Gunnar sits on the side of the bed at my feet. "See? It won't be much longer."

The nurse taps on the computer keyboard next to my bed. "Not soon enough," she mumbles.

Well, that's rude. I don't know her from Adam, and it's not like I want to be here. It's not my fault it's a hundred degrees and she picked the short straw to be my nurse. I notice the purple streak running down the left side of her jet-black hair. It won't be too hard to pick her out if she ever shows up in my shop. And if she does, I'll give her the same respect she's showing me.

Gunnar's eyes narrow.

"Thanks," I say to him.

"No problem."

I cover my face with my hands. "I can't be sick. I have a business to run tomorrow."

The nurse takes my left hand and places it back down on the bed. "You'll make the IV slow down."

I take a deep breath then focus on Gunnar. "Two days. You've known me for two days. I promise, this is not my usual self. I've had hangovers that feel better than this."

Gunnar chuckles.

The nurse swings around and cocks an eyebrow. "Doctor, do you want me to draw any labs?"

The doctor and Gunnar have another stare-down.

"Yes," she answers the nurse.

Gunnar's jaw clenches.

Shit. They think I've been drinking. Too many times, I've heard officers ask, "Do I need to get the nurse to draw blood?" to see if my alcohol level was over the legal limit. For once, I don't have anything to hide, and they've already assumed the worst. I watch the machine as my heart rate races into the nineties, and I take a few deep breaths to reel in my anger.

The doctor pushes her braid off her shoulder. "Draw electrolytes."

The nurse's mouth drops. "But what about—"

The doctor's face turns red. "Regina, I said electrolytes. Do you have a problem with my orders?"

The nurse turns pale. "No, of course not. I'll get the supplies."

Regina slips out of the room with her tail tucked between her legs. If I had any fluids left in my body, I think my eyes would be spilling out tears. My heart rate monitor beeps faster and faster.

I focus on the floor and take a deep breath. "Doctor, I'm not drunk."

"I know. You have not given me one indication to think otherwise."

"The nurse thought I—"

Gunnar pats my leg again. "And you thought I was married... to my sister."

The doctor belts out a laugh.

I point my pulse-oximeter-covered finger at him. "You, sir, never tried to correct my assumptions."

"Well, you know what they say about assumptions. Besides, don't mind Regina. She's a sourpuss on the best day."

I groan. "Fit in. I'm supposed to fit in."

Gunnar pats my leg. He likes to touch my leg, and I'm not going to complain. "Hey, think of it this way. You met Mel. Maybe you were trying to meet the medical staff that knew your grandmother."

The doctor wags her head. "She was a keeper."

Gunnar chuckles. "You remember the time she slipped on a rug and twisted her knee?"

The doctor clucks her tongue. "Poor thing. She kept hollering, 'Help, I've fallen, and I can't get up.' Even in pain, she was a hoot."

A warmness comes over me, and it has nothing to do with being overheated. But it might have something to do with Gunnar's hand that is still resting on my leg.

The doctor examines Gunnar, and her eyes twinkle. "Unless she's having a seizure, there's no need to hold her legs down like that."

With one quick jerk, he snatches his hand away. The doctor bites her lip in an attempt to keep a smirk off her face. I stifle a giggle as heat rushes to my face, and I'm sure my core temp just shot up again.

"I'm... well... I'll go find a wheelchair." He spins around and crashes into the bedside table before scooting out the door.

My doctor giggles, and in a singsong voice, she says, "Somebody's got a crush on you."

"What? Him? No. We just met."

She shrugs and puts the thermometer in my mouth again. I can't decide if she does it to check my temperature or to shut me up.

"I mean, he's super cute and all, but—"

"Shh."

Dang. Southern women can be so bossy. I wait until the thermometer beeps before I speak again. "Did you grow up here?" If I'm stuck here for a little while longer, I might as well get to know the people that interacted with Granny. Maybe through them, I'll feel closer to her.

"Yep. Except for college and medical school, I've lived here all my life. And some people still see me as the gangly girl they used to pick on in middle school. Never mind I'm the boss on this unit."

I figured there was some Regina-Mel backstory, but I don't want to know anything about it. It's my plan to stay as far away from drama as I possibly can.

"Why would she assume I'd been drinking?"

Mel cocks her head to the side as though I should have figured that out already. "Honey, her daddy is the preacher of the First Baptist Church. Follow the money."

"Oh." Small towns and their drama. "Wouldn't you prefer practicing medicine in a place that doesn't have so much drama? You could make way more money if you lived in Atlanta or Chicago, someplace like that."

She wraps her fingers around my wrist. "I do all right. Besides, the scenery is better here."

Oh. She must be talking about Gunnar. Good to know. I'm glad I didn't make a complete fool of myself.

"So, Doctor…"

"You can call me Mel or Dr. Mel. It doesn't matter to me. I'm not hung up on titles."

"Okay, so are you and Gunnar…"

Her eyes bug out of her eye sockets. "Oh, hell no. Ew. He's my cousin."

Yes!

She wags a finger in front of my face. "There's a lot of stereotypes about the South that are true, but we do not marry our cousins." She motions to the door, where Gunnar stands. His face is as red as mine feels. "When we were little and took baths together, he used to pee in the tub."

Gunnar's mouth drops. "Mel... that was our little secret."

"*Harrumph.* After you read my diary in the seventh grade then told Mitchell Sorrow I had a crush on him, all bets were off."

I gasp and stare at him. "You didn't."

He cringes. "I was trying to get them together. Still am, by the way."

She flings a pen at him. "If you don't keep your nose out of my business, I'm gonna tell Andie that you were in the—"

Gunnar takes a stalking step toward Mel.

In rapid fire, she spits out, "He was in the glee club, chess club, and was a—"

He grabs his cousin and presses a hand over her mouth. A round of giggles bubbles through the hospital room. I've never heard anything like this come from a doctor's mouth before. She pulls back his pinky finger enough to finish her sentence. "Cheerleader."

He flops down into the wheelchair. I pull my knees up to my chest and giggle into my hands. It must be nice to have family to razz. The closest I have to that is Tinsley, and if it weren't for my drinking, I don't think he would have been around at all.

Mel places my arm straight again. She gives me a very satisfied grin. "That'll teach him to mess in my love life, or the lack thereof."

Gunnar's eyes ping-pong from me to her. "Are you two finished?"

Mel shrugs. "Sorry. That was a long time ago. Things change."

He laces his hands behind his head. "Actually, being a male cheer-leader did have its advantages. Why get beat up on the football field when I could have the best view of the female cheerleaders?"

Mel rolls her eyes. "Ugh. And how did that turn out for you?"

Gunnar's mouth forms a tight, straight line. Note to self: he doesn't like to talk about his past. At least we have that in common.

Mel grimaces. "Sorry, cuz. That was low. I grant you one free pass to meddle in my life. But I am shooing you out of here right now while her fluids finish running. She needs to rest."

He heads toward the door. "Watch your back, Doc Ballard. The love doctor is in."

She snarls then glances back at me. In a deadpan voice, she says, "What was it you said about making more money in Atlanta? I think I'll have to check the want ads tonight."

Gunnar chuckles. "She wouldn't leave her loving family." He salutes his cousin, and I watch his retreating frame.

Regina returns with a tray of bloodletting supplies. She removes the blood pressure cuff and wipes down my arm with an alcohol wipe. She wraps a tourniquet around my bicep and sticks the needle in my arm. She may be a cranky girl, but I didn't feel a thing. She draws two tubes of blood and places them on the bedside table. *No frickin' way.* I know a gray-topped tube is the kind that blood-alcohol content is collected in.

I snatch it and hold it up. "I'm no fool, Miss"—I check her name tag—"Regina Price, RN."

Regina's face pales, and her mouth gapes open.

I smirk. "That's right. I know what this color is used to run."

The doctor takes it from my hand. "Regina, what did I tell you? Electrolytes only. We do not need this gray-topped tube." She plunks it into the hazardous disposal container. "I could write you up for that."

The nurse's face loses its color, especially when she sees my shit-eating grin. "I didn't mean any disrespect. Sometimes we draw extra tubes in case the doctor orders more labs later. That way, the patient doesn't have to get stuck again."

She does not deserve an eye roll.

Dr. Mel shakes her head. "When I'm on duty, you draw what I say and only what I say. Do you understand?"

"Yes, ma'am."

Before Regina leaves the room, Mel says, "Oh, and don't forget our strict policy on patient confidentiality."

Regina's spine stiffens. "Of course."

Mel grins. I think the nurse got schooled. Mel is my new best friend. I've never had a best friend before, and I like having people in my corner for a change. Maybe this town won't be so bad after all.

CHAPTER TEN
Gunnar

My phone buzzes with an incoming text while I pace up and down the hallway of the hospital. My nosy sister wants to know how my lunch date went. I text her back, "Not a date." She replies with one single eye roll emoji. People don't get it. I am not interested in Andie like that. She's fun, but I'm not ready to get involved right now, if ever.

I lean against the wall to text her back, when I overhear Regina at the nurses' station. She's speaking to Jolene, another nurse, who is also Willow's stepsister.

"Doc Mel got all pissy when I suggested running a blood-alcohol content on our new town drunk."

Jolene replies with her standard huff. "You know as well as I do she was drunk. Who in their right mind jogs in this heat?"

I storm up to the station and slam my hand down on the counter. "Someone not from around here." My voice booms louder than I mean.

Jolene and Regina jump back.

Jolene bats her fake eyelashes and flips her auburn hair over her shoulder. "Hey, Gunnar. What brings you here?"

As if she doesn't know.

I jerk my thumb in the direction of Andie's room. "Mel's in with—"

Jolene rolls her eyes. "New girl. I know."

"Would it hurt either of you to be kind to our guest? She is Miss Grace's granddaughter, after all."

Jolene stiffens her spine and clicks her pen. "Come on, Gunnar. Two days, and you're already under her spell."

Heat rises up my neck, and if I weren't wearing my uniform, I might do things that I would get arrested for. "No spell, Jo. It's called being nice. You should try it on for size." I need to get out of here before I throw a chair through a window.

I take two steps away from the nurses' station, when Jolene chuckles. "He's so horny, he'll take rejects from Boston."

I jerk around. "What did you say?"

Jolene blows out a breath. "You can't be her knight in shining armor. If you're that hard up, you should call Willow. I bet if you give her another chance—"

"No, thanks. What has Andie done to you?"

She shrugs. "Nothing yet, but if she gets near Stanley, we'll have words."

Regina snorts. "Jo, please. He's a flirt, but he's all yours, and all the women in the county thank you for it."

I point a finger in her face. "Be nice. And if you can't do that, then be silent. Are we clear?"

Her eyes twinkle, but I think Regina is about to crap her pants. "Yes, sir, Officer."

"If I hear one more rumor that you spread about a patient at this hospital"—I point at the room where Mel is—"I'll have a little chat with my cousin."

Now *my* eyes twinkle when her plastic face falls. "Bye, ladies."

"I'll tell Willow you said hello."

I let my middle finger do the talking as I storm down the hall in search of some strong hospital-grade coffee.

AFTER TWENTY MINUTES of grinding my molars to powder, Mel finally strolls into the cafeteria. I'm glad I didn't get a call because I really do want to take Andie home. She has no one else that will help her right now.

"Three texts for me to meet you here is two too many, mister. What's up your craw?"

I crumple my empty paper coffee cup. "Jolene."

She groans. "I hate every time we work the same shift. She and Regina together make me feel like we're back in high school. Regina's not so bad on her own, but together, they have no respect for my credentials."

"They were talking trash about Andie, but I think I put the fear of God in them."

Mel surveys the room then leans over the table toward me. In a hush, she says, "That's not all. Regina tried to slip one past me. She drew a gray-topped tube on Andie."

I motion for her to continue. That means nothing to me.

"I ordered electrolytes. They're drawn into a green-topped tube for the lab to process. A BAC, blood-alcohol content, is drawn in a gray-topped tube. I'm not stupid, and apparently, neither is Andie. She called Regina out on it. I was so proud of her, I could squeeze her."

My mouth drops open. I knew Regina had her suspicions, but I never thought she would stoop to that level. "I bet Jo put her up to it. What did you do?"

"I tossed the tube into the Sharps container. She's not so stupid as to fish it out for risk of getting stuck with a needle. Besides, I know Jo put her up to it. Regina has a little bit of respect for me."

I take a deep breath and stare off into the corner of the cafeteria. It has been a long time since I've gotten my hackles up over a girl, but Jo and Regina's comments hit me the wrong way, and something inside me couldn't stop myself from protecting Andie. She doesn't have anyone in this town, and even if Tinsley didn't ask me to watch her, I would. There's something about Andie that won't let me stay away.

Mel clears her throat, causing me to flick my eyes back in her direction.

"While I appreciate your protective nature, don't you think you're going a little overboard?"

"Not you too. I do not like her. I'm looking out for her because a fellow officer asked me to. And what was I supposed to do? I was driving through town, and I saw her about to pass out. I would have stopped for anyone."

She scoots away from me and puts her hands out. "Okay. But would you hold back Stanley's hair if he was puking his guts out?"

"Stanley hardly has three hairs on his head."

She crosses her arms. "You know what I mean. It's that I haven't seen you this worked up since—"

"Don't you dare say the W word. I've heard her name too many times today." My knee bounces. All this talk about feelings and caring makes me jumpy.

Mel covers my hand with hers. "You can talk to me. I'm not part of the grapevine." She peeks over her shoulder. "I certainly don't discuss personal stuff at work, especially not with Jo or Regina around."

"I'm fine, and I'm not worked up."

She pats my hand. "Can I say something without you chewing my head off?"

I grin. "Considering you've already spilled the beans about my extracurricular activities in high school, I think you're safe."

She stares off into the distance then takes a deep breath. "Would it be so terrible if you were, in some teeny, tiny way, attracted to Andie?"

I rub the back of my neck. If I'm being completely honest with myself, I'll admit there's something brewing. There's something about her that draws me to her. And it's more than my usual Mr. Fix Everyone mentality. I don't know if I'll ever be ready to give myself completely again. Some wounds never heal.

"She doesn't need me in her life."

Mel rolls her eyes. "I know all the shit with Willow."

My jaw clenches.

"And not to mention the way you tried to whore away the pain."

I cringe. One year of lying in a fetal position followed by another year of chasing every tail in three counties is something I don't like to remember. "Thanks for being subtle."

She shrugs. "What can I say? It's a gift. Anyway, you're a great person. All I'm saying is that even though you've only just met her, the way you are around her, it's... sweet." Her mouth tugs up in one corner.

I snort. "Sweet? I don't do sweet."

Her eyebrows dance. "That's my point, cuz." Her phone buzzes. She reads the message then stands. "Andie's fluids have finished running. Should I call her a cab?"

I follow her out of the cafeteria. "Nah, I'll take her home. And while I wait for you to discharge her, I'll see if Mitchell's working today."

She swings around to face me. "Don't you dare."

I wrap my arm around her shoulder and lead her toward the elevator. "You can trust me... maybe."

She shrugs my arm off her shoulder. "Oh, hush. You stay out of my business, and I'll stay out of yours." Barely over a whisper, she adds, "Maybe."

"I heard that."

"Besides, I think Andie likes you."

I don't know if I have it in me to do the whole sweet thing again. When I was nice, I got burned. When I was bad, I almost got killed. Maybe the pendulum is ready to swing back in the other direction.

"You know she only wants the money," I say.

"Pfft. Not so sure about that. But Mitchell... he only likes the chase."

He only chases her because she runs. He's more like a little puppy wanting her to notice him. Andie is different. She's definitely running. Not necessarily away from me, but from the world. I wish I could convince her to keep her grandmother's shop, and not only for my sake. But she has made it clear. Andie is only here for less than two months, no matter what is stirring inside me right now. But six weeks is forty-two long days, and I plan to enjoy every last one of them.

CHAPTER ELEVEN
Andie

Regina checks my blood pressure again and types the values into the computer system. The air is thick with tension. She thinks I was drunk and that was why I was stumbling around town. No matter what I do or say, it's not going to change her preconceived opinion of me. That's her problem, not mine. Now that I know she's got a direct link to the pastor, I'll need to be extra careful of what I say and do around her. But that doesn't mean we have to be besties.

"I think you're going to live to see another day." When she rips the blood pressure cuff off my arm, she actually grins, and if I didn't know better, I would think it was a sincere gesture, a far cry from her judgmental scowl from earlier.

I can't help but think that everyone in this town is going to think the worst of me no matter what I do. I can either be who they think I am or rise above it all. The old Andie would tell them to screw it and get drunk. The new Andie wants to make my grandmother proud. I guess I'll have to kill them with kindness.

"I feel so much better. Thank you." That whole killing with kindness may kill me in the process.

Regina's lips form a thin line. "Only doing my job. From here on out, if you have to run, go early in the morning. I'm talking crazy early, like six o'clock. It's the only time of day it's safe, especially if you aren't used to it."

"I appreciate the tip. I don't know what I was thinking."

In one swift motion, Regina removes the IV from my other arm and wraps a bright-green stretchy bandage around my arm to keep a cotton ball in place. "Keep the bandage on for about an hour, then you should be able remove it without bleeding all over everything."

I let out a giggle, thankful the nausea has passed. "Let's hope I don't do that."

Regina stares, and I'm a bit terrified of what else she thinks of me, especially since her father is the pastor. She swallows hard. "I should not have assumed—"

"It's okay."

She shakes her head. "It was unprofessional and unkind." She takes a deep breath. "Sometimes, living in a small town is a lot like being in high school on a permanent basis."

I shudder, making her laugh.

"Exactly. I let others put thoughts into my head, and I need to grow a pair, especially at work. Jo, the other nurse on duty, likes to stir the pot. She planted the seed about getting your blood-alcohol level, knowing good and well I would be the one to get in trouble if I got caught. Plus, she really likes to get under Gunnar's skin. It's not you. It's her all-access pass to his past."

Too much information. Before she hands me my discharge papers, she scribbles a note on it. "That's my cell phone number. If you want to go for a jog, at a safe time of day, give me a call. We can go to the high school football field and run around the track."

My mouth drops open. I must be hallucinating. She's being nice. I've stepped off the crazy train straight into the Southern Twilight Zone.

Regina giggles. "I'm not pranking you, and I'm not my daddy's little spy. The coaches run the sprinklers. All. Summer. Long. I'm not kidding. Even if we have a water ban. I don't know how they get away with it." She holds up a finger. "Yeah, I do. Football is king in the South. Never mind. Anyway, the coaches are too lazy to watch what's being watered, so the track gets plenty soaked too. It's the only place to run during the summer."

"Really?" I scrunch my eyebrows together. "Are you trying to get me arrested for trespassing?"

She holds her hands out in defense. "Scout's honor. My brother is the head coach. And Jolene hates anything to do with exercise, so no fear of her showing up. She'll probably be pissed if she ever finds out, but that's her problem, not yours."

As much as I didn't like Regina prejudging me, I shouldn't judge her on first impressions, either. She's being nice, and until she's not nice, I should give her the same courtesy. I'm exhausted and not thinking clearly, but it would be very nice to have some female company while I'm here.

"I might take you up on that. And stop by In a Jam tomorrow for a free cup of plain ole coffee."

Regina laughs as she helps me to my feet and holds on to my arm as I steady myself.

Mel knocks on the door before entering my room. "How's it going?"

Regina stiffens her spine. "Vitals are stable. I've gone over her discharge instructions, and she's ready to go when you sign off on her discharge, Doctor."

Mel logs in to the computer system, and with a few clicks, I am officially not their problem anymore. She points her finger at me. "No more running in this heat."

"I promise. Regina offered to share her favorite running spot with me."

Mel gasps as she snaps her head in Regina's direction. "The track at the high school? I'm hurt." Mel faces me. "In all the years I've known her, she's never invited me."

Regina's mouth flies open. "Would you have gone if I had?"

Mel rolls her eyes. "Duh. Of course."

A red flush creeps up Regina's neck. "Okay. How about Tuesday at six a.m.? We'll meet at In a Jam and go to the field together. I wouldn't want the newbie to get lost again."

Regina and Mel knuckle-bump each other then hold out their fists for me. I bump theirs. This is all very strange for me. I've never really had girlfriends before. I've had drinking friends but not hang-out kinds of friends. Being included is an odd but warm feeling. This must be how life is when it doesn't revolve around staying drunk. Or it could be how things are in a small town. Maybe it's both.

MEL WHEELS ME OUT OF the emergency room. Regina waves as I pass by, but all I get from the auburn-haired girl is a resting bitch face.

"Thanks for helping me today, Doctor."

"Just doing my job. And really, you can call me Mel."

"You really knew my grandmother?"

Mel's face lights up. "I'd stop by most mornings to make sure she took her meds and to give her a visual look-see to make sure she was getting around all right. I hated she had to climb those stairs every day and worried all the time about her falling down them."

"Thank you. I really appreciate that." A pang of guilt hits me in the pit of my empty stomach. I should have been the one making sure Granny was safe.

She clears her throat. "Gunnar was there when she had her heart attack, and he called me. I was able to make her comfortable before she passed. She had her DNR orders on her refrigerator, so we didn't initiate CPR. That's 'do not resuscitate.' Those were her wishes, and I had to respect that, but it was really hard. I wanted to try." She swipes a tear away. "She was a good egg."

"Yeah. I wish I had known her like you and Gunnar did." It sounds as though she was close to them and treated them like they were her grandchildren.

"You would have loved her."

"I hope I didn't cause a rift between you and Gunnar."

She waves me off. "Aw, it's all fine. That's what family does."

Family. I wouldn't know. Mom always said this town smothered her dreams of being a singer, but I think she did a pretty decent job on her own. She flitted from one town to the next, taking any singing gig she could get until she landed in Tennessee. That was where, at some nightclub, she hooked up with "the sperm donor," as she always called him. By the time I came along, she had given up singing and gone to work as a bartender. I learned how to make a martini before I was ten and took my first sip of alcohol when I was thirteen. Yeah, my mom was a great role model.

"Do I really have to leave in the wheelchair?"

"Yep. Hospital policy."

Gunnar lounges in a chair in the waiting room, thumbing through a crumpled magazine. His forearms flex with hardly any effort. When he sees us, he jumps up as if his pants are on fire. "I've got my car double-parked just for you."

His bashful grin makes me wish we weren't surrounded by all these hospital personnel. Except my barf breath is a definite turn-off.

As if Mel can read my mind, she slips me a peppermint candy.

"Thanks." I turn back to Gunnar. "Aren't you afraid you'll get a parking ticket?"

"Nah. I've got connections." He takes the handles of the wheelchair, and we continue on our way.

Right as we get to his car, Mel calls, "Hey, Gun." She plants her hands on her hips then brings them up to a clap in front of her face. "Be aggressive. Be, be aggressive." That's an interesting sight—a doctor in blue scrubs, performing a cheer. She even does a high kick. Wow. I'm impressed.

Gunnar growls.

"Family," I say as I wave to Mel.

"Yeah. Can't live with 'em. Can't shoot 'em."

Even though there are better ways to spend a Sunday afternoon than lying in the emergency room, I got to spend more time with Gunnar, and I made two new friends. Plus, they included me in their lives, which is huge for me. Maybe I'm being pranked, and this is all some Southern scheme to keep track of my every move, but I really think I can trust them. I want to trust them. There's only one way to find out. I'm going to dust off my running shoes and take Regina and Mel up on their offer to go jogging. At least if I have another medical emergency, I'll be in the best of care.

CHAPTER TWELVE
Andie

After sleeping like the dead, I feel like a new woman, which I need because today is my first attempt at running the shop. I'm not sure what to expect, but I can make coffee and biscuits. It can't be too hard. Since the IV fluids had me up at five o'clock this morning, peeing like crazy, I put my time to good use. I changed out the tablecloths, placed flower vases on each table, and even figured out that old-fashioned coffeepot and made a great cup of coffee, if I do say so myself. The Piggly Wiggly has a decent assortment of cut flowers, so I purchased some to brighten up the counter and hide what appears to be the remainder of an old bumper sticker. All I can make out is 'ens.' No telling what that said.

I pull my ponytail tighter and commence cleaning off the tables, when an elderly African-American woman shuffles in. She walks all bent over as though every step is agonizing. Surely, I don't have customers this early.

"Good morning. How can I help you today?" I surprise myself by sounding chipper and businesslike. "All I have is coffee to offer you as I haven't figured out my grandmother's recipes yet."

The lady waddles around the counter and puts her purse under it. She picks up an apron that has "It's all fun and games until someone burns their wiener" printed on the front. She crosses the strings in the back and ties it in the front.

"Can I help you?"

"Only a little stiff back. But I's be fine in a while." She opens a drawer and pulls out a rolling pin.

"Excuse me. What are you doing?"

She stares at me as if I've lost my mind then commences pulling out other items from the drawer. "I'm goin' to work. What you doin'?"

I shake the cobwebs out of my head. "I'm sorry. I don't understand."

She moves me out of the way with one strong, bony finger and opens the pantry. She hands me flour, sugar, and baking powder. If she tosses one more item into my arms, I'm going to drop everything on the floor.

"Work. Don't they teach you how to work in Boston?"

Actually, no. I haven't had a steady job in forever, but I don't think she wants to hear about my work or lack of work history.

"You work here?" Having an employee could be a positive thing since I have no idea what I'm doing, but it would have been nice if someone had mentioned it before now.

She snickers. "Girl, you is sharp. Sharp as a tack."

Coffee. I need another cup of coffee. I set all the ingredients on the counter and pour myself a cup then hand one to this lady, whom I'm assuming is my employee. She pours some of the coffee into the saucer and blows on it before she slurps it down.

"Mr. Christian didn't say anything about employees."

She snorts. "Mm, mm, mm. He should be ashamed of hisself. I've been with Mary Grace since the beginning. Let's see... I think it was eighty-two."

If she has known my grandmother since the eighties, then she had to have known my mother too, but I'm too distracted by her scooping out each ingredient into a bowl, combining it all together, and flouring the counter like a boss. She mixes up a gloppy, thick batter, and when she turns the bowl over, it falls out onto the floured surface with a splat.

"Preheat the oven to fo-hunnerd, please."

That, I know how to do.

The woman continues talking as she kneads the dough. "Of course, I ain't been able to do much lately. I got the gout, but Mary Grace, she let me stay on."

"I would appreciate any help you can offer. I'm flying blind here, so thank you."

For ten minutes, I stand in my place as my employee that no one told me about throws a pan of biscuits in the oven, whips up some lumpy gravy, and starts bacon sizzling in a frying pan. The smell takes me back to one of the few memories I have of my grandmother—the smell and the sight of her standing in front of the stove, babbling on about some recipe. But then my mother walked into the room, ruining the moment. It was always about her. If she wasn't the center of attention, she would spoil it for everyone else, especially me.

I snap back to reality. To be polite, I pour some of my coffee into the saucer and blow on it. When I take a sip, I realize this isn't so bad. It's the perfect temperature, and I feel as if I'm drinking my milk from the bowl, which my mother hated. I check my watch to see how much time we have before seven o'clock rolls around when I get to turn the "We're Open" sign around.

"So, what all did you do for Granny?"

The woman shrugs, flips the bacon over in the pan, and peers into the oven to check on the biscuits. "Pretty much everything except clean the crapper. Waited on customers, did some baking, cleaned windows, stuff like that."

"By the way, I'm Andie." I hold my hand out to take hers, but she bats it away, sending a puff of flour into the air. It tickles my nose.

"I know that. I know all 'bout you." She opens the oven door again, and with a dish towel, she scoops out the cookie sheet full of perfect, melt-in-your-mouth biscuits. The aroma wafts over me, making my stomach growl. She drizzles melted butter over the top.

"Who doesn't?"

The lady laughs. "In this town, only the headstones. The name's Mrs. Cavanaugh."

"Nice to meet you, Mrs. Cavanaugh. By the way, how did you know to come in to work today?"

"Is it Monday? Did the sun come up?" She stacks the biscuits on a plate before placing them under a glass cover.

"Yeah."

"Then I work."

I rub my temples. "So the shop hasn't been closed since Granny died?"

"Nope."

I cross my arms over my chest. "And what if I had decided not to move here?"

She cracks a huge smile. "I knew you would come. She knew you would."

I should be miffed at her for assuming I would relocate, but she's right. I am here. My mouth starts to curve upward even though I try to fight it. I glance at the clock on the wall and clap. "It's time." I run over and turn the sign around, announcing to the world that In A Jam is open for all of Smithville to enjoy. *Granny, are you watching?*

I barely make it back to the counter, when the bell over the front door tingles and Gunnar walks in, looking mighty fine in his police uniform. Oh, dear Lord. He is even yummy first thing in the morning. I bet he thinks I slept in my clothes. If it didn't seem rude, I would snatch the dish towel away from Mrs. Cavanaugh to sop up all the drool from the corners of my mouth. *Hubba-hubba.*

"Mornin," Mrs. Cavanaugh says to him. "I got yo breakfast all ready."

"Good morning, Mrs. Cavanaugh." He bows his head. "Andie."

I salute him. "Good morning, Officer."

Mrs. Cavanaugh slides a plate full of bacon and biscuits with gravy toward him.

I pour him a cup of coffee. "Regular coffee, right?"

"Yep. The truck driver stuff." He breathes in the food.

Whatever he doesn't want, I'll certainly take.

"This smells so awesome, as usual." He dives into his plate of food, and I can't stop watching his strong jaw mow through the crisp bacon. His tongue snakes out to catch a crumb at the corner of his mouth, and my knuckles turn white from hanging on to the counter.

Mrs. Cavanaugh clears her throat. *Busted.* "Have you met Miss Andie? Of course you've met."

I bite my lip to hide my smile.

"We've met," he says with a mouth full of food. He glances my way then focuses on his plate. He gulps down some coffee and takes a break from his binge. "Staying out of trouble, I hope?"

I shrug as I wipe the counter. It's not dirty, but it does give me something to do with my hands. It's not what I want to do with my hands, but this won't get me in trouble or start any rumors. Mrs. Cavanaugh scrubs a pan that is already clean.

"So far, so good," I say. "As long as I'm not asked to pray in church, I think I'll do mighty fine." I pull out my water bottle. "And I'm staying hydrated."

Gunnar grins. The bell over the door chimes again, and in walks the two texting ladies from church that I spoke with after the service. I'm not sure, but it seems as though they have on the same gaudy flowery outfits from yesterday. Their wide-brimmed hats are different, but I hope to God no one owns more than one of those loud dresses. I bet some bees mistake them for really huge flowers... really huge. They both have silvery white hair with a blue tint, which sticks out of their hats, and yep, I see that cell phone peeking out from one of their bras. *Ick.* It's way too early for this.

"Mornin', Miss Jackson, other Miss Jackson," Mrs. Cavanaugh says with no expression at all.

They wave to Mrs. Cavanaugh before they give me a sneer as they scoot their wide butts into a booth at the back of the shop.

Mrs. Cavanaugh pours two cups of coffee and shuffles over to them. She sets the cups down on the table. "Now don't you spill that hot coffee on that pretty dress."

The smaller of the two old biddies beams up at Mrs. Cavanaugh. "Why, thank you. I made it myself."

"I can tell," Mrs. Cavanaugh deadpans.

The bigger biddy gropes herself until she retrieves her cell phone from her bra. I'm glad I haven't had breakfast yet because I'm sure it would make an encore performance after seeing that.

Gunnar has his eyes trained on his plate. Smart man. His police radio screeches through the coffee shop. I guess Gunnar understood what was said because he stands, balls up his napkin, and tosses it onto the plate. Mrs. Cavanaugh hands him a to-go cup of coffee.

"Duty calls."

Well, bummer. I know he's got a job, but I was hoping he would stick around for at least a little bit longer, like four or five more hours. I glance at the chalkboard menu and rush over to the cash register. Hopefully, muscle memory from my days of working fast food will kick in and I'll know how to use this antiquated thing.

"Let's see…" It makes a *ka-chunk ka-chunk* sound with every button I push and finally gives me a total. "That'll be two dollars and eighty cents with tax." Dang, there's no way to stay in business with such cheap menu items. I need to think about raising the cost of some things to keep up with inflation.

He stares at me for the longest time then reaches into his pocket and pulls out his wallet. Mrs. Cavanaugh smacks me on the wrist with the dish towel.

"Ow."

The Jacksons snicker, click a photo, then snicker some more. I wish they had a job to go to.

Mrs. Cavanaugh gives me a stern look. "Child, where's yo manners? He don't pay."

"Huh?"

Gunnar hands me a five-dollar bill. "It's okay."

She smacks his hand this time, and he jerks back to escape another hit. I know my eyes are about to bug out of my eye sockets.

He puts the bill in the tip jar and slowly backs away with his hands up, as if he's startled a sleeping tiger. "Better go before she gets the switch out after me." He winks then scoots out the door.

"Mm, mm, mm." Mrs. Cavanaugh shakes her head. "That's the po-lice. You don't make him pay. What's wrong with you?"

I throw my hands in the air. "I'm sorry. I didn't know the rules. It's a dumb rule, by the way." I point at the two old ladies snapping photos of me with their cell phones. "Do they eat for free too?"

She motions for me to come near. I'm not so certain that's the best idea, but as long as she's not holding the dish towel, I might be safe, so I tiptoe closer.

She winks. "Mary Grace always charged them double."

I like my granny more every second I'm here.

The door chimes again, and Gunnar's cousin walks in, wearing a suit so fancy, she probably bought it at Barneys. She is one sharp dresser. With her hair down, her light-brown curls bounce all over her shoulders.

"Hey, y'all." She waves to the Jackson sisters then leans over the counter and gives Mrs. Cavanaugh a kiss on the cheek.

I smile at her. "Hey, Doctor—"

"Nope. I told you. It's Mel."

"Okay, Mel. Would you like some..."

Mrs. Cavanaugh pulls a bowl of cut-up cantaloupe and a cup of vanilla yogurt out of the refrigerator and slides it over to Mel.

"Thanks, Mrs. C. You're the best."

One of the Jackson sisters clears her phlegmy throat. "We hear Andie had to go to the emergency room yesterday after church. Did you have to give her a shot of Narcan for the overdose?"

My mouth drops. Of all the nerve of the old biddy!

Mel wipes her mouth with a napkin and wags a finger at them. "Now you know HIPAA rules prohibit me from discussing confidential patient information, or else I'd be telling Mrs. Cavanaugh about that boil on your ass I had to burn off last month."

Mel is my new best friend.

A twin gasp comes from the Jacksons' table. "Well, the nerve of you. You know that's not true."

"Of course." Mel takes another bite of her cantaloupe.

Mrs. Cavanaugh holds out a fist for Mel to knuckle-bump.

Mel puts on her invisible doctor hat and gives me a once-over. "How are you feeling today?"

I shrug. "I'm okeydokey. I only had to pee about ten times last night, but I'm trying to stay hydrated." I hold up my water bottle.

"Good. If you need anything, you give me a holler." She takes a business card and a pen out of her purse then writes a phone number on the back before sliding the card across the counter to me. "That's my cell number." Mel pulls out a five-dollar bill, which Mrs. Cavanaugh refuses to accept. And exactly like her cousin, Mel stuffs it in the tip jar.

Mrs. Cavanaugh pours four cups of coffee, and I place the lids on them. Then I pull out a drink carrier and place the cups in it for Mel to carry. "Take these for your staff," Mrs. Cavanaugh says.

Mel kisses Mrs. Cavanaugh on the cheek. "What would I do without you?" She points to me. "You show her the ropes, okay?"

Mrs. Cavanaugh snorts.

Mel waves and adds, "Y'all have a nice day. Oh, and we're on for a run tomorrow, right?"

"You bet."

She waves at the Jackson sisters as she scoots out the door.

While I wipe up some drops of coffee on the counter, I shoot Mrs. Cavanaugh a dirty look. "Stop refusing money. This is a business."

Mrs. Cavanaugh snorts. "It ain't gonna hurt you to be nice."

"Nice is one thing, but if you keep this up, I'll have to raise the prices on the paying customers."

The Jacksons perk up and interject themselves into the conversation. "We'll have to take our business elsewhere if you do." I'm not sure which Jackson comments, but the other one nods.

"Don't tempt me." I point a finger at them. "And if you take one more picture of me, I'll dunk your phone in a glass of water. So nip it."

The Jacksons stare a hole through me as both of their mouths open and close like fish out of water. Boom. I think I won that round.

A gurgling noise comes from behind us. "What's that sound?"

"Uh-oh," Mrs. Cavanaugh says.

I scamper around, trying to find the source of the gurgling. "What do you mean, 'uh-oh'?"

With her dish towel, she scoops some crumbs from the counter into her other hand. "Well, the pipes are real old in this building, and if you, uh..."

The sound gets louder. I pace through the kitchen, trying to find the source of the noise. If the pipes are about to burst, that means the value of this building will be diminished. *Crap.* "The pipes? What about the pipes?"

"If you overload them with too much work, well, they tend to leak."

I brave a peek under the sink, and water runs, not trickles, from the pipes. My throat constricts to only let out a tiny "eep" when I really want to scream. This can't be happening.

"Oh God. That's not a little leak. That's a geyser about to blow."

"Yep. It's fixin' to blow, all right."

The Jacksons pull their knees up to their chests to get their feet off the floor. The photographer of the group takes one last photo of me before sealing her phone in a zip baggie.

I glance up from my squatting position. "Fixin'?"

Mrs. Cavanaugh tosses her dish towel on the counter and shoves the crumbs onto the floor. "You're not makin' fun of me, are you? 'Cause if you are, you can run this piss palace all by yo-self. First it was wanting to charge family for food. Now this."

She jerks her apron off and hangs it up then snatches her purse off the hook. The morning started off great, but I now have water gushing out of the pipes all over my inheritance. I pissed off my one employee, the only person who can help me survive the terms of my contract. She's halfway to the door before my brain kicks in. I really need to get some Southern manners in the worst way.

CHAPTER THIRTEEN
Andie

I rush up to Mrs. Cavanaugh and hold her shoulders. "No, no. I'm not making fun. I didn't know what you meant. That's all. Water's everywhere." Water seeps its way toward my shoes. "What do I do?"

She pushes out of my hold. "I'd say you need a plumber."

I slosh through the water, toward the phone hanging on the wall. The two Jackson ladies agree as they sip coffee. One puts a plastic bonnet over her blue hair and hat. The other one positions her phone on the table to take a not-so-inconspicuous photo of me.

I narrow my eyes at her. "I'm watching you."

Her shoulders slump in disappointment as she slides her cell phone back into her bra.

"A plumber. A plumber. Yes." I rush back around the counter and turn toward Mrs. Cavanaugh, who cracks some eggs into a bowl as though this sort of thing happens all the time. "This town has a plumber, right?"

She gives me a dirty stare. I guess that was a stupid question. They have to have lots of plumbers. Everyone needs a plumber from time to time.

"Of course, silly. Jimmy Stokes."

Great. One plumber. That's a shocker.

"Do you know his number?" Water inches closer to my feet. I try my best to slosh it away from me, but it creeps back like the blob in one of those old monster movies. I fling open every cabinet door in search of a mop and bucket. It can't be the first time this has ever happened.

"Five seven eight seven," she says, beating the eggs.

"Five seven eight seven... what? That's not enough numbers."

The two Jackson ladies giggle, earning them a really big Boston-size snarl from me.

"The first three are four two three like everyone else."

Seriously? "Oh." I dial the number as fast as my fingers can use the rotary phone.

"Too bad he ain't there," Mrs. Cavanaugh says.

I slam the receiver down on the cradle. *Ugh!* Tears threaten to spill down my cheeks. I thought I could buy a few muffins from the grocery store, sell them as my own, and close up shop before noon. Easy peasy. And in less than two months, I could lock up the shop for the last time and hand over the keys to the person with the best bid.

Even running a stupid coffee shop is too difficult for me. I can't even do that without making a mess of things. I don't know what I'm doing, and I'm not sure why I even care. It would be best if I called Mr. Christian and told him I can't do it. Granny was mistaken when she thought I should run this place for even one single day.

The click of one of the Jacksons' camera phones pulls me out of my pity party. If they document that I'm not fit to run this shop, I'll lose the money before the week is up. I can't let that happen. For some reason, Granny wanted me here. She didn't want the money to go straight to the church without me at least trying to change. For some reason, she thought I needed this chance, and I owe it to her to try. A little bit of water won't stop me.

I stiffen my spine, wipe the tears off my face, and turn toward Mrs. Cavanaugh. "Why didn't you say so?"

She shrugs. "You didn't ask. And even if you had, you weren't very nice. If you're nice, I'll tell you all sorts of things."

Time to pull out the beauty queen smile I buried years ago. With all my molars showing and the water creeping up over my sneakers,

I say, "I'm so sorry, Mrs. Cavanaugh. Do you know when Mr. Stokes will be back in town?"

"How am I supposed to know?"

I bang my head on the counter. The water is up to my ankles now. Thank God there's a big floor drain so the water shouldn't get too much higher, but I need that water turned off now.

"You knew he was out of town."

I pull out a bucket from the storage bin and slide it under the sink to catch at least some of the water. With my feet, I slosh the water on the floor toward the drain.

"It's a beautiful summer day," Mrs. Cavanaugh says. "He's fishin' if he's alive. Won't be back 'til it rains."

"So I'm supposed to swim until he gets back in town?"

Click. Click. Two more pictures. If one of those women gets a photo of my ass sticking up in the air, I'm going to go all Northern on the Jacksons.

Mrs. Cavanaugh shrugs. She's still so calm; it makes me crazy.

"Attention all In A Jam customers, we are currently having technical difficulties. Please leave while you still can. Mrs. Cavanaugh, what do I do?"

"I suggest you make friends with the other Stokeses."

I sop up some of the water that's not making it down the drain with paper towels. At this rate, I might as well get a canoe and paddle out of this one-traffic-light town. "So the other Stokeses don't like to fish?"

Mrs. Cavanaugh dumps the eggs into a frying pan and sprinkles some salt on top. "Beats me. But they own the hardware store down the street. They could probably help you with your problem."

"Great. That's perfect." I run toward the front door, slipping and almost sliding into the barstools.

Mrs. Cavanaugh stirs the scrambled eggs on the stove top. "You might want to turn off this valve before you leave." She motions with her head toward the sink.

The Jackson sisters giggle. I slop back toward the sink and poke my head underneath it to see the handle she's talking about. I guess everyone in this town has basic plumbing knowledge and is sitting back like flies on a wall, waiting for me to screw up.

Trying to keep my groan to a minimum, I turn the valve, and the water stops. "Pissa!" Through gritted teeth, I mumble, "Why didn't you... never mind. I'll be right back." I point at the Jacksons. "You two better not leave without paying."

I slip one more time trying to stand up. "Would it be too much trouble to ask you to start cleaning up this mess while I go get help?"

Mrs. Cavanaugh pulls out another towel. "Not at all. All you got to do is be nice."

Nice. I used to be nice, but Boston tends to change a girl. Being nice can get a girl taken advantage of in Boston, and we certainly don't waste time saying "hello" to every stranger on the street. That's just not done. One loses a seat on the train by being nice, and guys walk all over nice girls. All the nice guys have bitchy girlfriends, which in turn transforms them into jerks. I need to find a guy that hasn't been tainted yet, and with all the money I'm about to get, I bet lots of guys will be nice to me... until the money runs out.

First, I need the quickest fix for my plumbing problem—I mean, the store's plumbing problem, even though mine is as rusty as those pipes. Next, I'll need to decide how this will affect the property value. With any luck, a buyer will want to demolish the entire building, anyway. Right now, I need to find a nice hardware store.

CHAPTER FOURTEEN
Andie

My ponytail hangs to the side, and my water-soaked jeans drag the concrete. I probably should have asked where the hardware store is, but I can figure this out. For once, I can't bail when the going gets tough. And as much as I would like a shot of whiskey right now to steady my shaking hands, I'm not that desperate... yet. Granny believes in me, so I need to believe in myself. It's a stupid leaky pipe, for crying out loud. It's not like the entire freakin' roof is falling in. It had better not.

To my right is the barbershop with about six half-bald men sitting out front on a bench. That's not an appropriate advertisement for the quality of work the shop does. Across the street is the Big Ash Gym, where I may be able to find a guy to help me, but I need to figure this out all on my own to prove to everyone, especially myself, that I'm not a failure.

Three stores down on my left is a sign in the shape of a hammer, hanging across the sidewalk. I see "Stokes Hardware" printed across it. My first step in that direction in my wet, sloshy shoes almost sends me sailing into the street, so I toe out of them and leave them next to the door of Granny's shop. If anyone wants my ten-year-old, worn-out Keds, they can have them. The bald smoker fitness fanatic across the street tips his head in my direction. Cars pass me as I race-walk on the hot concrete sidewalk. Each driver waves my way as if we're besties. If one of them is Jimmy Stokes, I don't want to know about it.

The Big Mouth Bass over the door of the hardware store about makes me pee in my pants when it starts singing "Take Me to the River." That thing is ridiculous enough in a stinky old bar, but here it is downright creepy.

The cold cement floor is a welcome relief to the soles of my feet. "Plumbing, plumbing," I mumble to myself as I wander down one of the aisles of the cluttered hardware store. By the looks of the place, it hasn't been updated anymore than Granny's store. A lone customer rifles through the paint swatches, holding up various shades of white next to the dingy concrete wall.

"That old sink acting up again?"

I jump about two feet off the ground. When I turn around, I am face-to-face with a guy not much older than me. A cigarette is dangling from his mouth, and his T-shirt is stretched tightly over his big belly. It's apparent that he hasn't spent much time at Big Ash's Fitness.

"Actually, it is. How did you... never mind. Small town."

He sticks out a paint-stained hand for me to take. His blue eyes twinkle, as though he knows a secret about me. "I'm Jake. Jake Stokes. Your grandma has had problems with that old sink for years. I've tried to get her to replace it, but she wouldn't."

I shake his hand. He seems nice enough. Maybe he can fix it for me if I lay on the charm. "But she did keep me afloat with all that plumber's tape she bought."

Sounds simple enough. "Will that do the trick?"

"Until you overuse the pipes again."

I take in his words. "So it's a temporary fix."

"Yep."

Hmm. Maybe it can hold for a few more weeks, and I won't have to spend a quarter of my inheritance on new plumbing. I'm sure Fisherman Stokes isn't cheap. "Will it hold for about, say, six weeks?"

He grins, his lips still holding on to the cigarette. "Until you sell the place?"

A sandy-blond-haired woman with long, lanky legs walks our way, holding a cigarette in one hand and a Mountain Dew can in the other. "Oh my stars. You must be Andie."

She slides one arm around Jake's neck without spilling a drop of her drink. "I'm Liza Jane. Call me Liza. I'm Jake's better half."

"Yeah, I'm Andie. Nice to meet you." No time for chitchat. I've got a business about to float away.

She puts her cigarette in her mouth then holds out her hand, and I take it. People are so polite in this town. She blows smoke away from my face and catches me eyeing the can she's holding. I smell beer. She's a morning drinker like me. The beer calls my name as if it's been searching for me for the past five days since we last connected. It wouldn't hurt too much if I took one tiny sip, if only to take the edge off my craptastic day.

The Big Mouth Bass sings its song again, and in walks the two Jackson sisters. *Ugh.* Tell me they have better things to do with their day than to follow me around.

Liza smirks, and without losing eye contact with me, she says, "Howdy do, Miss Jackson, other Miss Jackson. I'll be right with you."

Keeping my eyes on the Jackson bitches, I grin at Liza. The Jacksons don't seem like the type to do any do-it-yourself projects, so there's only one logical reason they're here—to finish their collage of Andie disaster photos. A paint can moves on its own, and I see Sarah Jackson behind it with her phone. She snaps a photo of me. For spite, I stick my tongue out at her. *Take that.* I have to admit, I'm impressed the AARP member knows how to use a smartphone.

Jake laughs. He crushes the cigarette butt under his boot and lights up another. I guess he doesn't care about the burn mark on the concrete floor. "Bruce told me about your special circumstances."

I hope to God there isn't a pop quiz because I can't keep all these small-town people's names straight, but I'm sure I haven't met a Bruce yet. "Bruce?"

Jake blows smoke in the air. I try to dodge it, but I'm too late. He fans it away from my face while I stifle a cough.

"Gunnar. I call him Bruce. He calls me Bruce. Long story."

Liza Jane fans the smoke away. "One you will hear way too many times before you escape from this one-traffic-light town." She hands her husband her cigarette, and now he's puffing on both at one time. Nothing like getting COPD at twice the speed.

She wraps an arm around my shoulders and steers me away from the lookie-loos behind the paint cans. We stop in the plumbing aisle, and she pulls a roll of plumber's tape from the rack.

"Thanks."

"Now all you got to do is unscrew the pipe under the sink with a wrench." She looks over at her husband. "You'll loan her a wrench, won't you?"

He bobs his head like a well-trained husband.

"Then wrap some of this white sticky tape around where the threads are and re-screw the pipes. Now make sure the water is off first."

"That's it?"

She grins. "Yep. It should do, for the time being. How are you getting along?"

I shrug. "As well as can be expected. The roof didn't cave in at church yesterday, so that's a good start."

She giggles. "If I had been there, it would have fallen in for sure."

Jake chuckles until Liza gives him the stink eye. She glances my way and rolls her eyes. "Don't mind him. I heard you had to go to the ER yesterday."

A wave of nausea flows over me as I remember yesterday's ups and downs. I wonder if Liza is going to be nice like Mel or venomous like the auburn-haired girl at the hospital. "Somebody left heatstroke out of my orientation manual."

She pats my arm. "At least Gunnar was there to save the day."

Yum. Gunnar. My eyes close as my mind flutters back to him eating his breakfast. I could eat him up. "Yeah..." My eyes fly open as I catch her grinning. "I mean yes, he helped me, but so did Mel and Regina."

Jake doubles over in a fit of laughter.

Liza crinkles her nose. "Regina?"

"It was weird at first, but she ended up being real nice, not like that redhead with the resting bitch face."

I shouldn't have said that. This could be her best friend. Or worse, her sister. *Crap.*

"*Harrumph.* You met Jolene. She has the resting bitch face down to a science. But she's had lots of practice."

I peek around the aisle to see the Jackson sisters pretending to read a *How to Install Ceramic Tile* brochure. "And then they're everywhere I go. They should work for the CIA."

Liza belts out a laugh, making the smaller of the Jackson sisters drop the brochure. "They're all right once you get to know them."

I roll the plumber's tape in my hand, remembering why I came in here in the first place. "I really appreciate it. It was really nice meeting you." When I get to the register, I turn around and pat my pockets. I didn't bring any money. *Shit.* I cringe and turn toward Jake, who's leaning against the counter. "I forgot my money."

Sarah Jackson whispers to her sister. Of course they heard I didn't have money.

Liza Jane giggles. "We'll have to get Officer Wills to arrest you. Could be fun." She wiggles her eyebrows, making the Jackson sisters huff in disgust.

My ears burn, but why not have some fun and give the sisters something to stew over. "Maybe this time, he'll let me play with his siren."

Jake laughs so hard, he loses one of his cigarettes. Liza stomps it out with her sneaker. Jennifer Jackson gasps as she tiptoes around the cigarette butt.

"I'll put it on your tab," Liza says.

"Don't stress those pipes," Jake yells.

I wave, and before the door closes, Liza Jane says, "Careful being barefoot on that hot concrete. Bless your heart."

I'm going to need a lot more than a blessing to get me through this summer. I've only been here three days, and I can tell I'm in way over my head. But I can't let the Jackson sisters get my granny's money. If she wanted them to have it, she would have given it to them outright. Granny wanted me to have it, but making me come here must be some damn lesson I'm supposed to learn. *Come on, Granny. Help me out here.* And making me do this without my favorite boys, Jack Daniel and Sam Adams, is pure meanness.

Granny, if you're watching over me, I hope you're getting a big belly laugh out of this because that would make one of us.

I fumble with the plumber's tape as I scoot down the sidewalk, hopping from one shady spot to the next. It's obvious the tape is a temporary fix to a much larger problem, much like my thirty-day Southern intervention is on my sobriety. Once my required stay is over, the patch I've put on my life may burst wide open, creating an even bigger problem.

My phone buzzes in my back pocket. I fish it out as I stand first on one foot then the other to keep from blistering my feet. No telling what Tinsley wants.

"Hey, Tinsley."

"How ya doin'?"

I wave at the car passing by as if I know them. "Fine as frog hair."

His laughter bellows out of the phone. "I'm not going to ask what that means."

"What's up?"

"Checking to see how it's going." That's Tinsley, always thinking of others.

Over my shoulder, the Jackson sisters toddle down the sidewalk toward the country crafts store. Sarah points at my bare feet then does the "I'm watching you" motion, pointing her fingers at her eyes then pointing at me.

"Most people here are nice. Others are freakin' crazy."

"Then you must be fitting right in."

I slide into my sneakers, and my feet thank me for the relief. A gush of water squishes out with my first step. "You're funny."

"Have you met George Clooney with a twang yet?"

A tingly feeling runs up my spine. "Yes. I hardly made it over the county line before I bumped, I mean, met him. I don't know if I should be mad at you or thank you for telling him my situation."

"I thought you'd need someone in your corner."

I belt out a laugh as I lean against the brick wall of In a Jam. "You mean someone to spy on me."

"That's not what I said." He lets out a deep sigh. "I worry about you, and I want you to have a real crack at the money, but you and I both know what you lean on when things get stressful. Don't be tempted. Officer Wills said he'll keep you away from temptation."

"Yeah, but he's an even bigger temptation." I take in a hot, humid breath. "Forget I said that." A cool drink of the alcoholic persuasion sure could take the edge off right now.

Tinsley cackles, and I want to yank him through the phone to smack that Southie grin off his face.

"I have to go. I have a business to run, you know."

"Sure thing. Tell Clooney I said hello."

I disconnect and stomp back into my business, I mean, Granny's business. I've got pipes to fix, customers to tend to, and a contract to comply with. I don't have time for Tinsley's humor right now.

CHAPTER FIFTEEN
Gunnar

Don't go over there. Do not go over there. *Shit.* My treacherous feet force me in that direction, and before I know what's happening, I cross the street from the gym and stand in front of In A Jam. I tried not to think about her all day, but that was an epic fail. Like a drug, I need one more Andie fix before I call it a night. Plus, I really should let her in on the latest word on the street. She's not going to like it, and I'd rather she hear it from me before someone else gets to her.

At the door, I pause. Faint mumbles from the kitchen make my face break out in a huge grin. I press my ear to the glass in the door.

Andie chants, "I'm as nervous as a long-tail cat in a roomful of rocking chairs. What goes under the devil's belly comes back over his back. Well, I'll be a monkey's uncle."

The bell over her door jingles, announcing my arrival.

"We're closed... y'all."

Adorable. I drop my gym bag by the front door and saunter over to the counter. Her *How to Speak Southern* book is splayed next to the sink. Wads of plumber's tape are stuck to the edges of the cabinet door, and one long piece lies on top of the last muffin in the display case. Most of Andie's body is all the way under the sink, so only feet with pink toenails stick out. I had my chance. I could have backed out, and she would have never known it was me. But now those pink toenails aren't going to let me leave anytime soon. *Shit.*

"I heard you were having trouble with those old pipes."

Andie bumps her head as she tries to scoot out of the cabinet. "Ow. Word gets around pretty fast."

"Too fast." When she hears what I have to tell her, she's going to pitch a fit.

She pushes up to a standing position. Her hair is plastered to her sweaty face. So this is what she looks like when she's all hot and worked up. *Don't. Go. There.*

"Let me ask you this. Do people know when I pee too?"

I shrug.

"'Cause if so, why won't someone come forward and give me some toilet paper? I can't seem to find any in Granny's apartment."

I wag my head and chuckle. She peeks under the cabinet and grunts as she tries to unscrew the pipe. Her hand slips, and she bangs her knuckles on the cabinet. A few choice words escape her mouth. "It would be nice if the gossip train would go all the way to the pond where the one and only plumber hangs out." She grimaces from the pain in her hand.

"Don't count on it. Do you want some help?"

She sighs. "Yes. Thank you."

I walk around the counter into the small galley kitchen. No matter which way I move, she seems to move to the same place. She holds her arms up and moves sideways. We are chest to chest as we switch places, and I take my sweet time moving past her, enjoying the view. She smells like freshly baked bread with a hint of vanilla. She keeps her eyes trained on the ceiling. On purpose, I rub against her stomach. When I turn to face the sink, she sucks in a breath.

Before I dive under the sink, I sneak a peek back at her. She leans over the counter, panting. *Sweet.* She bounces twice on the balls of her feet then pushes herself up to sit on the counter. Her feet dangle like a kid's on the side of a swimming pool.

"So tell me... Bruce, how do you know so much about plumbing?"

I'm going to kill him. "What did you call me?" I rotate to get a glimpse of her cheesy mug.

"Bruce." She winks then leans over toward the coffeepot, almost falling off the counter.

I'm grinning so much, I'm sure my dimple has popped out. "You met Jake, didn't you?"

"Yeah, but he didn't explain why you call each other Bruce." She waves a hand in the air. "And to tell you the truth, I don't want to know. Nice guy, though."

"We've been friends since grade school. We had three classmates named Bruce. And in a small town, that's a bit odd. So, to not be left out, we started calling each other Bruce, and it has stuck all these years. Liza's a good egg."

"Yeah, she seems really cool."

I refocus on the pipe I've finally gotten lose. "She's sharp. Don't let that Southern drawl fool you."

"Yeah, and Mel too. She's as sharp as a tack."

I chuckle. "You don't know the half of it."

"I'm meeting her and Regina tomorrow for an early-morning run."

Shit. Regina leads to Jolene, which is a direct line to Willow. I would like to keep my past tucked away, and as far as possible from my present. But in this town, there are eyes everywhere. "Uh, Regina?"

"Uh-huh."

The silence builds like the calm before a storm. No telling what Andie's thinking. "Be careful with Regina."

"I'm not stupid."

"I never—"

She lets out a sarcastic laugh. "Oh, please. I can only imagine what Tinsley told you."

Growl. I climb out of the cabinet, pull my T-shirt down because it had ridden up to my armpits, and hand her the remainder of the tape.

"You're stopping by to 'check on me.'" She uses air quotes, which pisses me off.

I cross my arms over my chest and cock an eyebrow. She has no idea how to handle the Southern rumor mill, and I did promise Tinsley I would check up on her from time to time. "Let's get something straight. You are walking into the snake pit with Regina. If you think you're such a big girl, then knock yourself out. Consider yourself forewarned."

Her mouth drops. *Dammit.* That wasn't nice. I don't know crap about her. Maybe she had her reasons for not visiting her grandmother. I turn my back and take a few breaths to bring my anger down to a simmer. When I peek over my shoulder, Andie averts her eyes.

"Ouch," she says.

I stare at the ceiling and let out a groan. "I shouldn't have blown up at you like that. I only want you to be on your toes when you're around her. All you have to do is be around Regina, and it will make people talk."

"People seem to like a spicy story regardless of the truth." Her expression makes my hostility fizzle away.

I rub the back of my neck. "Regina sometimes can be a pill."

She snorts. "She's better than that redhead."

"True." I blow out a breath. "And just so you know, Tinsley didn't tell me anything that wasn't flattering."

She flashes me another grin, and my anger melts away. "If it weren't for your visits, I'd go crazy."

I bow. "Why, thank you, ma'am. It's a darn tootin' pleasure."

She laughs at my exaggerated accent and hands me a cup of coffee. Taking a break from my mad plumbing job, I slide onto the counter next to her, and my knee bumps into hers. Together we sip coffee in silence. It doesn't feel awkward. It's nice to be with someone without having to talk all the damn time.

I tap her knee with mine, sending a shiver down my body. "Uh, I didn't mean to come off all cranky."

"It's okay. I've been cranky all day. Every time I turned around, the Jacksons were there, documenting my every move."

"Yeah, about that—"

"Then I had the huge, watery mess to clean up. It wasn't my best day." We sit in silence for a moment, and I review in my mind how I'm going to tell her about the latest *Biddy's Blog*.

Andie swipes a bead of sweat from her brow with the back of her hand. "So, what's the story with the nurses? I'm pretty sure it's none of my business, but you know... trying to fit in, and gossip seems to be the trend around here." She gives me a one-shoulder shrug.

I clear my throat. "Jolene is my ex-girlfriend's stepsister, and Regina is her closest friend that never left Smithville."

She grimaces. "From the tension at the hospital, I guess that didn't end well."

"Not at all." I survey the place then focus on our dangling legs. Time to change the subject. "Your grandma would skin us alive if she caught us sitting on her counter."

Andie takes a sip of her coffee then speaks over her cup. "Could be worse."

"Yep. And has been. My sister is five years older than me. The teenagers used to hang out here and, well, you probably don't want to hear about what used to go on in this building."

She puts a hand up. "You're right. I don't need to know." From the flush of her cheeks, I think her mind went down the gutter right along with mine.

I take another sip of my coffee. "Um. This is nice. I think you've mastered the art of making 'plain' coffee."

She bumps me with her shoulder. "Thanks. I'm getting there. Mrs. Cavanaugh has been really helpful. I only burned two batches of muffins. That's way better than I expected of myself. If I could get a handle on Granny's jam, I'd be doing okay. People kept asking for it this morning, but I don't have a clue where to start."

"Better get it right before the county fair in two weeks."

Her hand stops with her cup halfway to her mouth. "The what?"

"The county fair. Your grandmother entered herself. If you read the fine print of your agreement, you'd see you're required to enter. You better get something edible."

She cringes, then her eyes get big. "Can I go buy some at the store and put it in a different jar?"

I roll my eyes. "You've watched too many Andy Griffith episodes, haven't you? For research?"

"No. Okay, maybe a few. But wasn't that pickles and not jam?"

I take one last swig of my coffee and set the cup on the counter before hopping down. "You can do it. Maybe Mrs. Cavanaugh can help. At least you won't have to go to the rattlesnake roundup."

"What?"

I fake a shocked expression. "You've never heard of a rattlesnake roundup? You're missing out."

"Do you put saddles on the reptiles and ride them around?" She pretends to hold reins.

"Silly girl. Snakes are caught and brought to the county extension office to keep the population in check. It's a big deal with food and crafts and stuff."

She pulls her feet under her on the counter as though the thought of snakes creeps her out. "Should I be scared? I mean there can't be too many snakes cruising down Main Street, right?"

I slide off the counter to take one last gander at my handiwork and make sure the pipes are secure. "No, but in the rural areas—"

"This isn't rural?"

I stare at her, making her giggle. I like that sound. A lot. "In the rural areas, like where the farms are, there are too many."

"Ahh. I get it. I think."

One last check of the pipe, and I turn on the valve. I smirk back at her. "No leaks. God, I am the best."

"And modest."

To really see how masterful I am, I turn on the faucet. Water sprays into my face. Andie squeals as I try to get the water turned off. She laughs so hard, she almost slips off the counter. I'm glad she's getting some amusement out of this. I hold the sprayer and aim it at her.

She freezes. "You wouldn't."

I nod. "Oh yes, I would."

With lightning speed, she lunges toward me, trying to pry the sprayer out of my hands. Both of our hands are on the trigger, and we both get a shot of cold water in our faces and down our shirts. If I thought she was sexy to begin with, she's off-the-chart hot as hell when wet. We both let go of the sprayer, and I lean down to turn off the valve again. Drips of water fall off my nose. I shake like a dog, sending a spray of water all over her.

"I cannot believe you did that."

I move close to her, backing her up against the counter. I wipe a wet strand of hair off her face. She bites her bottom lip. *Damn.* She swallows hard and focuses on the floor, while her hands dangle at her sides. I tip her chin up with my finger and lean into her. Her hands find my waist and pull me closer. I bend my neck to be closer to those gorgeous lips. We're only an inch apart. All it would take is for the Earth to tip on its axis a smidgen, and there would be no more space between us. Her eyes find mine, and if she gives me the green light, my mouth is going to find hers, pronto. She clutches my T-shirt and tugs me closer. Right before my lips make contact with hers, the bell chimes above the front door.

Shit.

CHAPTER SIXTEEN
Gunnar

"We're closed," Andie says, not losing eye contact with me. Neither of us moves. The water soaking our shirts feels more like super glue. We're stuck together, and neither of us wants to get out the nail polish remover. After only three days, I want this girl. I know this is not going to end well, but I can't tell my heart that. My stupid, stupid heart is going to get broken again. I promised myself I wouldn't fall for someone who didn't have the same goals as me. I know exactly what Andie's all about. She hasn't made it a secret, and I am already falling for her. She'll be gone soon, and I'll still be here in the same place I was two years ago.

"I know, but I'm here for my leftovers." With hands stuffed in his pockets, Stanley drags himself up to the counter.

Great timing, Stan.

Andie jolts away from me. "Oh. I almost forgot. Yes, we have lots. Pardon the mess. My plumbing is leaky. I mean not mine, but the sink."

Stanley grins for a second before his mouth pulls back into a tight line.

Andie rushes around the store, not making eye contact. From underneath the counter, she pulls out a Tupperware container filled with muffins. "As strange as it may seem, people don't seem to like my baking as well as my grandmother's. It's probably for the best. I won't be in business much longer."

Ouch. Kill me now and get it over with. Stanley waves and stuffs his face with a muffin. He's too lazy to cook, and Jolene works long shifts at the hospital, so it's either go hungry, or eat Andie's leftovers.

She points to the pile in the trash can. "The trash is full of charred globs of crap not fit for the rattlesnakes creeping down Main Street."

I slide onto a barstool next to Stan. "So, whatcha been up to? You seem bummed about something. I mean other than the heartburn that muffin is giving you."

Andie pops me on the shoulder with a dish towel and gives me the death stare.

Between bites, he replies, "I think they're gonna lay me off at the plant."

That's odd. I'm on the town council, and I usually know these things before the public does. "I haven't heard about any layoffs."

Stanley stuffs another muffin in his mouth. Andie pulls out a pitcher of sweet tea and pours glasses for all three of us. Stanley guzzles his down and slides his glass over to Andie for a refill, which she obliges.

"It's only me. Seems like the big company that owns the plant in Boston..." He spits that city's name out as if it is poison and stares at Andie. "They don't want someone without a high school education."

She nibbles on a fingernail.

I crunch down on an ice cube. "I thought you got your GED a while back."

He dives into a third muffin. At least they won't go to waste. It means a lot to me that Andie has a soft spot for Stanley. Just because he doesn't make much money doesn't mean he has to go hungry.

"I tried, but I didn't pass. Not good with tests."

Silence fills the room. Andie drums her fingers on the counter, and tears well up in her eyes.

"But hey, don't worry about that," he says. "Something will turn up. I got connections."

I pat him on his sweaty back. He's such a decent guy. I hate how hard the situation is for him. "I'll let you know if I hear of anything. I'll put in a positive word for you. You're a hard worker."

He swallows the last bit of edible food and stands, dusting off the muffin crumbs onto the floor. He guzzles the rest of his iced tea and burps. *Classy.*

"Thanks, man, but I'm okay. Andie, thanks for the muffins. Not bad."

She gives him a thumbs-up. "See you tomorrow night for more leftovers?"

"Yeah."

"Stanley, I'm really sorry." Her voice quivers.

He waves as the chimes jingle at his departure.

I pick at a hangnail, and Andie rubs the dish towel over the same spot on the counter again and again. A Boston company is laying him off, and even though she has nothing to do with that company and his situation, I can tell she feels guilty by geographic association.

"I feel like a damn Yankee." I detect the slightest Southern accent seeping into her words. She rubs the counter again, and if she doesn't stop, she's going to wear a hole right through it.

I reach out and squeeze her hands. She stares at our joined hands before she braves a glance my way.

"Don't worry about it," I say. "He should have stayed in school. Getting a high school diploma isn't that hard in this town." As if on autopilot, I rub the backs of her hands with my thumbs. She doesn't jerk away. I could easily tug her over the counter, and we could continue that wet T-shirt contest we started before Stanley interrupted us, but the mood is gone. It's just as well.

"I feel so awful for him."

"He'll find work." At least if I can help it.

She pulls her hands away from mine and crosses her arms, focusing on the trash can. "No, I mean, he ate all those muffins. God, he's going to be sick tomorrow."

I chuckle, and I guess now is as good a time as any to leave. She follows me to the front door.

I turn to face her. "Good night, Andie."

She bites her lip and stares at my mouth. Before I can stop myself, I lick my lips. I swear I see her pupils dilate.

"See ya." Andie takes a peek behind her. "And thanks for the... mess."

"Where are my manners?" I take a step back toward the kitchen. "I should help you clean up."

She holds up a hand to stop me. "No big deal. I've dealt with more water than this."

I snap my fingers, remembering what I need to tell her. "One more thing." I pull out my phone and search for the Jacksons' blog. "I think you should see something."

I hand her my phone, and she sucks in all the air in the room. After a moment of near hyperventilating, she reads aloud from the blog. "Miss Andie Carson, granddaughter of the late Mary Grace Carson, has taken Smithville by storm. Not only is she rude to her customers by threatening to destroy their phones, she's disrespectful to the only employee willing to work under harsh conditions that only someone from a big city would approve of."

She blinks away tears and grips my phone so hard, I think she's going to smash it.

"Don't read any more. It's only trash talk."

Andie groans as she collapses into the nearest booth. "Her antics have not included drinking yet, but we're sure since she doesn't have sense enough to wear shoes or even the simplest common sense as to how to shut off a water valve, we are pretty sure her drinking ways will be here soon enough. However, if her inability to pay for something as inexpensive as plumber's tape is any indication, she has probably already spent her way through her inheritance. Tsk. Tsk."

If the Jacksons weren't so old and I wasn't nice, I would have them arrested. This isn't helping one bit in convincing Andie to stay. If I weren't from here, they would scare me off too. I hold my hand out to retrieve my phone, but she rotates so her back is to me.

She reads the rest in silence before relinquishing my phone. Andie clears her throat, throws back her shoulders, and juts her chin in the air. "They 'tsked' me. How rude. But at least they didn't post the picture of my ass in the air while I was cleaning up the place."

Before I can stop myself, I rub little circles on her back with my hand, and her head falls back. "A silver lining in an otherwise rusty situation. You didn't do anything wrong, and you certainly didn't do anything to lose the money coming to you."

"Not yet."

"Don't worry. I'll make sure your attorney knows you're working hard if he doesn't have anything better to do than follow their blog."

Her shoulders slump as she chews on the inside of her cheek. Damn, that woman is growing on me. And this is really, really bad. If it's the last thing I do, I'm going to make sure she gets her money. If it means hovering over her every move, I will, even if it means she won't stick around afterward. She's going to sell the property, leave town, and I'm going to be left with a broken heart and a dried-up Main Street. The town may recover at some point, but I don't think my heart will. Not this time.

CHAPTER SEVENTEEN
Andie

My phone buzzes on the nightstand. That's the third time it has gone off in the last five minutes. The sun hasn't even peeked through the blinds yet. After my first long, exhausting day in the shop, the sexy visitor, and my get-back-at-the-Jacksons plan that had me up way too late, I'm not quite ready to start the day.

My phone buzzes again. "All right." I snatch it off the table before it vibrates onto the floor. "Yeah."

"Up and at 'em."

"Regina?"

"That's right. I'm outside. Time for our jog."

After my waterlogged day yesterday, I completely forgot about our plans. *Gah.* The only thing worse than exercising this early in the morning is having a hangover.

"I think my doctor wouldn't want me to strain myself so soon after my visit to the ER."

"Get up," Mel yells into Regina's phone.

I let out a groan. "Fine. Give me a minute."

"Every minute you stall, the humidity level rises another percentage. Tick tock."

"I'm coming." I fling the covers off me, throw on running shorts and a sports bra, and stumble down the steps with shoes in hand. I lock the shop behind me and shove my shoes on. "Let's do this."

We walk the three blocks to the high school, mostly in silence. Mel's braid swishes around her as she takes long strides. I really should have brought a ponytail holder to get my mop of hair off my neck.

Out of the blue, Regina turns around to face me. "I'm going to get this out in the open right now."

"Oh dear," Mel says.

This isn't encouraging. Regina's brought me out here to turn on me? I'll never find my way back to the shop.

"I'm still friends with Willow. There. I've said it."

She acts as though I'm supposed to know who this person is. "And this means something because..."

Regina blows a strand of hair out of her eyes. "Willow is Gunnar's ex."

So now the hostility at the hospital makes perfect sense. They see me getting in the way of their friend getting back with Gunnar.

"She still lives in Chicago, but we keep in touch."

"You don't owe me anything," I say. "I think you should know by the way I schooled you in the hospital that I can take care of myself."

She groans. "I'm so sorry about that."

"You should be," Mel interjects.

We continue until we get to the high school. It's a typical two-story school in need of repair, but the football stadium lacks nothing. I've seen college stadiums smaller than this one. Even if every resident in the county showed up for the game, it still wouldn't be filled.

"Wow."

"Yep. Football is king in the South." Regina makes a sweeping motion with her arms as if she's a spokesmodel on a game show. With a smile, she walks onto the track that surrounds the field and stretches her legs.

We start out at a slow pace. Regina and I run side by side, our short legs keeping the same pace. Mel runs ahead of us as if she's bouncing off a cloud.

"I would kill to have legs that long," Regina says.

"Tell me about it. I was not blessed with height. That's for sure."

"Don't you hate it that us short girls have to watch every dang thing we eat?"

Mel jogs backward. "Hey now, I have to be careful too."

"Pfft," Regina says. "You gain a pound, and you don't notice. But if I gain a pound..."

I finish her sentence. "You can't zip your pants."

"Exactly."

Mel rolls her eyes. "I'm going to leave you two half-pints so I can get a real workout. See you in a few."

Mel darts off, and before I can take one long, sucking breath, she's halfway down the track.

"Show-off."

Regina giggles then clears her throat. "There's one more thing you might not know about."

Crap. If there is a love child, I think I might puke worse than I did this weekend. I stop jogging and stand beside the goal post. "Lay it on me."

Regina cringes. "There's this blog..."

"I've seen it. Gunnar showed me."

She exhales. "Oh, thank God. I didn't want to be the one to show you the sinister side of Smithville."

I pull a knee to my chest to stretch out my back. "Like I said, I can take care of myself. Let's just say I might have started my own blog."

She throws her head back and cackles. "I love it."

Mel runs past us again if for no other reason than to show off her amazingly long legs.

Regina gets melancholy as she watches Mel run past. "Gunnar is a great guy."

"There's nothing going on between—"

"Not yet, but I'm not blind."

Sweat trickles down my back. I think the humidity level jumped ten degrees in five seconds, especially in my nether regions.

"Here's the backstory. Gunnar was so sweet to Willow when her family lost their home in a tornado, and after that, they were inseparable. She's never gotten over him even though she was the one to break things off. To be the smartest person I know, she can be so stupid sometimes."

"I've made a few boneheaded decisions in my life too." The first time I met Tinsley was one of my lowest moments. He found me passed out next to my car. If he hadn't come by, I could have been robbed or worse. Since then, he has been like my guardian angel, always there when I need someone to help me out of a tangled mess.

"Haven't we all?" She starts down the track at a fast walk.

Mel zips past us again. I don't even think she's worked up a sweat.

"All I'm saying is that Willow can be really sweet. If she wasn't, she and Gunnar would have never been an item. But when she feels threatened, she can turn into a real bitch. She'll say and do things in order to get what she wants. I guess it comes in handy now that she's an attorney."

I think I'm going to hurl. Gunnar's ex is an attorney. Thank God Granny didn't get Willow to control the will.

"I don't want any trouble."

"Of course, but Jolene's already told her about you, so don't be surprised if Willow makes an impromptu visit."

I stop walking and wipe the sweat from my eyes. From the way Gunnar has been flirting with me, either he doesn't have feelings for her anymore, or he doesn't know the grapevine has reached to wherever Willow now lives. Either way, she's not my problem. I have an obligation to fulfill my grandmother's wishes, and while I'm here, I'm going to enjoy myself as much as I can while still being sober. "I've spent the last ten years living on the south side of Boston. I don't scare that easily. And something tells me if he wanted her back, it would have already happened."

Regina shrugs. "Most of Gunnar's friends don't think too highly of her, especially after she dumped him. That was real shitty of her to do that. But there's always two sides to every story."

I chuckle. "Like when someone from out of town shows up in the emergency room dehydrated?"

She knuckle-bumps me. "Nice one."

My instincts tell me I should tread carefully with everyone in this town. Regina could be setting me up to get knocked down by this big, bad Willow person. Or she could start her own rumors about me. I'm taking a huge gamble hanging out with her and an even bigger one showing her I'm not afraid of what anyone can throw my way. My heart wants Regina and Mel and even Gunnar to be real friends. I should stop kidding myself. I especially want it from Gunnar. He's hot and single, and I'm not blind. I see the way he undresses me with his eyes every time he's around me. It has been too long since someone drank me in with their eyes like that. Actually, no one has ever looked at me like that, as if he wants to devour me.

Regina glances down at her watch then yells, "Five, four, three, two, one."

The sprinklers turn on, and we are surrounded by the most awesome spray of water that's meant for the football field but also soaks the track. From the other side of the field, Mel squeals, trying to dodge the spray of water squirting all over her.

Not me. I let the cold water soak me to the bone, and it is exhilarating. I turn around in circles with my arms outstretched. "Woohoo!"

Regina giggles. "Welcome to Smithville."

CHAPTER EIGHTEEN
Andie

My favorite spot in Granny's apartment is the bay window that overlooks Main Street. As the sun sets, I get to watch the townspeople scurry about down the street without being noticed. I wonder if this was Granny's favorite spot too. If we have anything in common, I bet she cursed every time she stumbled on that loose step on the stairs like I do. Doubt it. Not one person in this town has a bad word to say about her. They watched out for her and really cared for her. I've never had that and don't think I'll ever have it anywhere.

It's hard to believe that this time last week I was waking up in the drunk tank with Tinsley standing over me, razzing me like he always does. Seven days ago, I never imagined I would have the opportunity to inherit more money than I can count. But money makes people do crazy things, like move over a thousand miles away to live in a dinky town and make coffee and jam. Crazy things like staying sober.

This week, I've been too dog-tired to even be tempted to relapse, except for that time in the hardware store. And that was a very stressful situation. There have been a few times in which my hands got jittery, and one shot would have calmed them. But I really want to see how long I can go without resorting to the bottle.

Yesterday, after I was nursing sore calves from my run, I learned how to create a blog, and I had a blast giving the Jacksons a taste of their own medicine. I didn't write anything mean, mostly just silly things I notice they do, like stuff their phones in their droopy bras or not cover their mouths when they sneeze, and I wrote about how I caught one of them scratching her butt. My stats show that at least fifty people found my blog, which may have been due to the fact that I left an anonymous comment on the *Biddy's Blog* with a link to mine. And for the last two days, the Jacksons haven't darkened my door, nor have they posted anything else about me. Maybe I nipped that issue in the bud.

My morning jogs with Regina and Mel, my baking lessons with Mrs. Cavanaugh, and even smiling all the time have me falling fast asleep as soon as my body hits my grandmother's lumpy mattress at night.

Nothing keeps me awake except a few fleeting thoughts about the last time Gunnar visited. Had it not been for Stanley's entrance, I would have let Gunnar kiss me and do anything else he had in mind. I know I didn't imagine the desire in his eyes. But thanks to Stanley, I don't have to be disappointed when Gunnar figures out I'm not worth the effort. Plus, I'll be leaving soon, and I don't want to get my emotions all messed up. I would definitely need some liquid courage to get out of that kind of jam.

But Gunnar is an excellent distraction, and if we had met in another time and place, I would have been all over him. He has skeletons in his closet, and from every time the W word is mentioned around me, I have gathered that either the entire town wants them back together, or they are scared to death of her. Not my problem. In fact, I welcome the reminder that he has an old flame out there still pining for him. It makes him easier to resist. At least I try to tell myself that.

I'm pretty sure Gunnar is resisting too because he hasn't shown up since, not even for his free breakfast. And this morning, I didn't even burn the biscuits.

It's just as well. But that doesn't keep my treacherous eyes from scanning the street to see if that fine specimen is patrolling. His police car makes a unique bang when he slams the trunk after retrieving his gym bag. So even though I shouldn't gawk, I do. Every time. And I am never disappointed.

I peruse through a scrapbook I found on the bottom shelf of the bookcase. So much of my life is preserved in the yellowing newspaper clippings. My third-grade spelling-bee-championship picture. A photo of the cast of Godspell, in which I played Andie because that was how that play worked. The character names were our real names. Pretty simple but effective. I'm not sure how Granny knew about all these things, especially since most of them happened way before the Internet. Maybe Granny stalked me, because I'm darn sure Mom didn't share with her.

Granny, I miss you.

I flip the page, and the clipping of my prom-queen photo slips loose and falls to the floor. What a joke that night was. Steven Prescott was ready to make a woman out of me. I wasn't ready, but he was very persuasive. He never gave me a second glance after that night. Like mother, like daughter, except I didn't get pregnant. Somebody must have been watching out for me that night.

No more memory lane tonight. I close the book and let out a deep sigh. I have to figure out this jam recipe for more reasons than the fine print in my agreement. The more I learn about my grandmother, the more I want to make her proud. And I want to be proud of myself too. I scoop up all of Granny's cookbooks, her recipe tin, and the only framed picture of her. Maybe her face will guide me to figure out the mystery. I'm not this stupid. There must be something simple I'm missing.

"Come on, Granny. Help me out. Let's do this."

Careful to miss the wonky third step, I make my way downstairs and into the kitchen. The strawberries I bought from the Piggly Wiggly yesterday are perfect for jam, at least from what I can tell by what I read on the Internet. I am going to figure this out if it kills me in the process.

I place Granny's picture next to the stove for inspiration and begin to prepare the strawberries, being careful to only use the ones that are overly ripe, a tip I picked up from Mrs. Cavanaugh. I mix in sugar, berries, and lemon juice. It should be easy enough. Hopefully this time, it will work, because the last five attempts resulted in big sticky piles of fruity goo. After a quick stir, all I have to do is wait for it to boil. And wait. And wait.

My heavy eyelids flutter shut. I force my eyes open and do a set of jumping jacks. Out of breath, I pull out my cell phone from my back pocket and select my favorite playlist. When Steven Tyler's voice belts out "Janie's Got A Gun," I'm transported back to my scuzzy Boston apartment. With the broom as my dance partner, I boogie through the kitchen, around the counter, and into the front part of the store. It's in everyone's best interest that no one is here because I sound like a dying seagull, but I don't care.

I make up moves I would only do completely drunk, and by the time my playlist starts over again, I'm a sweaty, hot mess. Falling back into a booth to catch my breath, I inhale something sickly sweet and charred. *Crap. My jam.*

"Oh, no, no, no." I run into the kitchen and grab two pot holders to remove the saucepan from the burner. Strawberry goo runs down and splatters onto the stove top. Most of the jam oozes out of the pot like in the movie *The Blob.* What's left in the pan is so hard, it would probably be easier to throw the pan away and buy a new one. I'll never be able to sandblast that crap out of it.

It's probably going to taste disgusting, but I need to know if this recipe is worth trying again. I scrape a spoonful of jam from the stove top and blow on it to cool the gooey glob threatening to spill over on to my sneakers.

"Hot, hot. Oooo." I spit it out. "God, that's nasty." Yep, this pot is going in the trash. I push down the lever with my foot and toss the saucepan.

A knock on the front door makes me jump. If the Jacksons saw any of this, they are going to get an earful. Their blog has focused on other people lately. Maybe the new kid isn't such a disappointment after all.

I tiptoe to the front of the store, hoping to God it's Stanley because I need to talk to him about an idea that is brewing in my head. Regardless of the fact that I don't want to have his babies, he's sweet, and I don't want him to starve or be unemployed.

I peek through the curtains to see Liza Jane standing there. Well, that's odd. I've only seen her in passing since I settled my tab at the hardware store. I didn't think I was on her radar at all.

I unlatch the door and open it for her. "Hey, Liza. What are you doing? Come on in." I wave her inside.

She tosses her cigarette onto the sidewalk and enters. Her nose crinkles.

"I know. A kitchen disaster. Sorry about the smell."

"It's okay. I was on my way to do our monthly moon bathing by the lake and thought you'd want to join me."

"Moon bathing?"

"Yeah, we go to the beach on full-moon nights, get sloppy drunk, and watch the sun come up. Want to come along?"

"Thanks, but I don't think so. It's been a very long week, and I'm trying to figure out this stupid jam recipe. Besides, no booze for me, remember?" But a beer right now sounds very enticing.

She rolls her eyes. "Aw, come on. It's fun. And where we go, no blue hairs around. Plus, Mel said she might join us tonight. She's pretty much a teetotaler with her crazy work schedule."

I scan around at the mess I made then back at Liza. I think I can trust her. She doesn't seem like the kind of person that would be in—how do they say it down here?—in cahoots with the Jackson sisters.

"I really want to, but I should stay here and clean up. Mrs. Cavanaugh would pitch a fit if she saw the mess I made."

Liza puts a hand on my shoulder. "This isn't high school. No one is going to make fun of you if you drink Coke without the Jack."

"I prefer Diet Coke."

"Same thing."

I grin. "What if I wanted a Pepsi?"

She gasps. "I retract my invitation."

We giggle like two schoolgirls, and I take one more glance around at the mess I made. Liza seems nice, and it is really sweet for her to invite me, the strange out-of-towner, to hang out with her local friends. Perhaps I can hang out for a bit and not get tempted to drink. This will be a suitable test of my willpower, and I could use a girls' night out.

I shrug. "I guess I can clean this up in the morning. Okay, I'll go."

Liza gives me a quick hug, almost bringing tears to my eyes. No friend has ever hugged me before or made me feel so welcome. I want to tuck her into my luggage and take her back to Boston with me when I leave.

CHAPTER NINETEEN
Gunnar

No matter how old I get, I still enjoy coming out for our moon-bathing session. And from my house on the other side of the lake, it's an easy stroll to the site of the bonfire. It's stupid, but it's one time when all of my friends get together, forget about work, and chill. The older we get, we spend more time laughing and less time getting wasted. Those who already have kids have a standing babysitting appointment with grandparents so no one misses an event. It's one of the many things I missed while I was away in Chicago. Willow sure didn't, and she would roll her eyes every time I suggested we do something similar at Northwestern. Liza always called her the black Willow spider, and Liza sure had her pegged right.

Someone's already got a fire started, and by the looks of the coolers lined up by the dock, Jake and Liza must already be here. The moon sparkles on the rippling lake water, and with no boats buzzing by, the only sound I hear is Mitchell's boom box blaring Southern rock songs as usual. Mel waves as I get closer to the bonfire. Her schedule keeps her from having much free time, but I'm glad she's here getting to kick back for a change. She has her scrub pants rolled up to her knees, and she runs her feet through the sand. I kick off my flip-flops and carry them in one hand while I tote my cooler in the other. The lake breeze blows through my board shorts and tank top. Before I know it, I'll have to pull out my jacket. It doesn't take long before it gets cold out here next to the water.

"Bruce! You made it," Jake yells, waving me over to the fire.

"Hey, Bruce, Liza, Mitch. Who talked the doc into slumming with us?"

Mel smirks. Mitchell pulls his baseball cap down lower on his face to cover his bashful grin. He takes a swig of his beer as he stokes the fire. The glow on his face makes him appear even more godlike. He's the pretty boy of the group, and even though tons of girls hit on him on a regular basis, he only has eyes for my cousin.

I stop and stare at the newcomer. "Andie? What are you doing here?"

She sits by the fire, nursing a can of Diet Coke. By the way her mouth drops open, I only assume she didn't expect to see me, either. My eyes roam her body. It doesn't matter if she's wearing ratty jeans and a faded T-shirt with something pink stuck to it; she's sex on a stick. I take another long gander down her body, and when I get to her pink toenails wiggling in the sand, I forget how to breathe.

"I got kidnapped." She jerks her thumb toward Liza Jane.

Liza gives me a hug. "Yeah, I figured you weren't going to ask her, so I did."

Mel snickers. My face is on fire, and I haven't even got close to the flames yet. "Thanks, Mom." It's not that I didn't want Andie to hang out with us. I was trying to keep her from any potential temptations, and the lake at night is full of opportunities to slip up.

Liza kisses my cheek. "No problem, honey." She turns to her husband. "His face is titty pink. I love to do that to him."

Andie covers her face to conceal her laughter. I'm glad someone is getting amusement out of my humiliation.

Mel waves the smoke from the bonfire away from her face and takes a sip of her Coke.

Jake throws both of us cans of beers. Andie's eyes scan the group before she sticks the can in the sand next to her while she clenches her can of Diet Coke like her life depends on it. I plop down next to

Andie and pop the top off my beer. I hold my beer can out, and Andie and I toast. "To your first moon bathing."

She clinks my can with hers and beams. "To my virgin bathing."

Jake chuckles. Liza elbows him in the side and clears her throat. "So, Andie, do you want to tell us about your *Lifestyle of the Almost Rich, Sometimes Foolish, but Always Human* blog?"

Andie spits out her drink, and a few droplets hit my foot. I pat her back to help her catch her breath.

"I never thought anyone would read it. It was purely a way to vent about the *Biddy's Blog.*"

My eyebrows shoot up. "What did you do?"

Liza raises her hand. "Let me tell him."

Andie waves a hand in front of Liza. "Be my guest. I have nothing to hide."

She pulls out her phone and reads from the screen. "I'm new to this town, and I'd like to set the record straight about some things. In case there is one person in this town that hasn't heard about the requirements laid out in my grandmother's will, I've included a link. Feel free to read the fine print because I plan on fulfilling everything spelled out there. I want it out in the open what my granny wants me to do."

Andie picks up her Diet Coke and takes another swig. She shoves the can back in the sand, and her lip twitches up in an almost-smile.

Liza continues. "There's a bunch of other stuff about clearing up misunderstandings and how the photos were taken out of context, but my favorite line is this: 'As it says in the Gospel Matthew, first take the plank out of your own eye, and then you will see clearly to remove the speck from your brother's eye.'"

"Boom!" Mitch yells as he high-fives Mel.

Jake leans in to read Liza's phone over her shoulder. "You go, girl. Beat them at their own game."

"What can I say? I was in a mood." Andie's hand gropes for her can, but it lands on my leg instead. She sucks in a breath and snatches it away then picks up her can to drink. I already miss the contact.

"Oh no," she whispers. I look over at her as she holds my beer in her hand instead of her Diet Coke. "I'm sorry." She licks her lips as if she's savoring the taste of my pale ale. Andie holds the can out to me. "You better take this before I chug it down."

I give her a wink as I take it from her. When I take a sip, I realize her lips were in the same place only seconds earlier. A beer has never tasted better.

Griff, the Labrador retriever that lives down the street, gallops up to us and shakes, sending water all over us. Liza squeals. Mitch pulls out a stick from the firewood pile and flings it toward the lake. The dog runs after it.

"Uh-oh, you started the catch game." Liza Jane rolls her eyes. "We won't be able to get rid of Griff now."

Griff comes back, dragging the stick. I take it from his mouth and toss it in the other direction. Jake offers a beer to Andie again, but she refuses. She's actually going to abide by the rules. I'm proud of her.

"Uh... did Bruce here tell you about the time he almost lost his trigger finger?" Jake has told this story a thousand times. As embarrassing as it is, it might loosen Andie up if she knows we've all had our stupid drunk moments.

Mel groans, and Liza rolls her eyes. "Oh, gawd. Here they go." She takes a swig of her beer.

Jake's laughter makes his belly jiggle, and it's a wonder he can even get the stupid story out of his mouth. "We had these thumb cuffs, and I was sloppy drunk."

"Shocker there," I whisper in Andie's ear, making her giggle.

Jake stares at his wife. "Drunk as a skunk, if I remember it right."

"Hey, now," I say. "That was way before I was a cop. Anyway, he put them on my thumbs and pulled them tight."

Griff gallops back to us, and Liza throws the stick again. He takes off after it.

I point at Jake. "Dummy here breaks the key off in the lock."

Andie laughs. "Sounds like something I would do."

Jake chuckles. Liza tries to cover his mouth with her hand, but he wriggles free and adds, "And before we know it, his fingers are starting to turn blue."

"So we go to the hospital," I interject.

Liza Jane mouths the words to the story that she could probably recite verbatim. "But now his thumbs are blue and swollen."

I swallow my beer, thinking back to that stupid night. "And I'm thinking, there goes my career. I'll never play guitar again."

Andie stares at me as if there should be more to the story. Liza Jane plays an air violin with her beer and cigarette.

Mel groans. "You better be glad I was away in med school because I would have cut your thumbs off and been done with it."

I seriously doubt that. "Dusty James comes out with the jaws of life. You know, like they use to rescue people from wrecked cars."

Andie cringes. Her eyes ping-pong back and forth between Jake and me.

"If he touches me with those things, I know I'll lose a thumb for sure."

Jake punches me on the shoulder. "Finally, my boy Mitch here shows up. He's an EMT and happened to have some bolt cutters, and in two shakes, he cuts Gun-man loose."

Mitch stands up and takes a bow. "Thank you very much."

Mel throws her empty Coke can at him, which he catches.

"I thought I was a goner, but I still have both my thumbs." I hold up both hands for Andie to see.

"It's a miracle," Liza Jane says. "Thank you, Jesus." Liza points at Jake and me. "This is what I have to put up with when they get together. I've heard that stupid-ass story about a hundred times."

For the next few hours, we sit around the fire, boring Andie with stories we've told a million times before. She seems like a trouper because she laughs at the stupid stuff we did as teens.

Jake holds up his hand. "How about the time we stole Robbie the Rooster—"

"Enough." She stares a hole through her husband. "Are you trying to run her off before she finishes her sentence here?"

"Huh?" Jake isn't the brightest on a clear day. Get a few beers in him, and he can't take a hint to get off a fire ant bed.

Liza Jane pulls him up and says, "Let's take a walk." She turns back to Andie and says, "Men are so stupid sometimes."

Mitch's beeper goes off, and he groans. I guess he was hoping for some quality time with Mel. "Duty calls." He stands and dusts the sand off his jeans. "See ya."

I mouth to Mel, "Go," and motion with my head for her to follow him.

We have a silent pissing match, but she finally says, "I've got an early shift tomorrow. You can walk me back to my car." Mel holds out her hands for Mitch to help her stand.

If I watch close enough, I would probably be able to see his heart pounding beneath his T-shirt from here. That's the most Mel has given him in years.

Mel leans into him, and he slips an arm around her waist as they walk away.

Andie takes another sip of my beer, and this time, by the way her eyes dart around, I'm pretty sure it was deliberate. The two of us sit next to the fire. She stares off at the water in the distance and digs her toes through the sand as I poke the fire to keep it going.

"Boy, this is awkward," she says.

"Don't worry about it. I'm used to it. I should have warned you about Liza. If I thought she would have dragged you here, I would have—"

"You wouldn't have come?" She drives a stick into the fire, sending sparks flying into the dark sky.

I hold my hands out in defense. "No, that's not what I was going to say."

"Hey, it's okay." She counts on her fingers. "I suck at making jam. You don't need to get involved with someone who's only here for a short time. It's obvious I'm this close to being an alcoholic because one, maybe two sips of your beer, and I'm already craving it again. And oh yeah, there's the little issue about all my money. I'll probably screw that up too."

I whistle. "Boy, howdy. Talk about having self-esteem issues."

"Well, you're the poster child for perfection."

My eyebrows rise.

"Please tell me you've done something wrong in your life."

She has no idea. "I've done plenty wrong."

She snorts. "I'm not talking about being a bad tipper or not tithing a full ten percent."

"Ha. Nice one."

"You know my transgressions."

I clear my throat. "Another time."

She pokes me in the chest with her finger. "I'm going to let you off with a warning, mister, because right now, I've got to pee in the worst way."

Thank God. Saved by a tiny bladder.

CHAPTER TWENTY
Andie

G unnar's grin makes his adorable dimple pop out. If my bladder weren't about to burst, I would jump his bones right here on the beach.

"Either the lake or that rock over there is a pretty private spot."

I survey the premises. Neither is a viable urination option to me. I'm sure I've peed in alleyways when I was wasted, but while sober, I would never even entertain the idea. "No thanks. I'll hold it."

"No one is around. The ones that are won't remember it in the morning."

"That's all right. I'll wait." But I can't focus on anything except the waves coming in and out and in again. I cross my legs. I swear, urine is about to explode out of my nose. If I had driven myself, I would have gone home.

"Suit yourself."

Silence falls over us. He takes another swig of his beer. *Suit yourself, my ass.* He can whip it out anywhere and pee without any shame. I couldn't do that even if I were anatomically able.

Gunnar flicks his eyes my way, and I wonder why in the hell he is not taken. He must eat live chickens or be a devil worshiper or something. He's pretty much the total package. He should have figured out before now that I am not a total package. I'm not even close. I'm a brown cardboard box, crunched up in one corner, with no ribbon or bow, and certainly no delivery confirmation.

"Do you want me to be your lookout?"

"Yes!"

He helps me to my feet, and I'm quite grateful. If I exert too much pressure on my abdomen, I'm going to wet my pants. I follow him toward a huge boulder away from the bonfire. I slap the sand off my pants if for no other reason than to keep me from freaking out about what I'm about to do. If I weren't with a policeman, I'm sure I would get arrested for indecent exposure.

"I cannot believe I'm doing this."

He stops and motions for me to keep going around to the other side of the boulder.

I make a swirly motion with my finger. "Turn around."

He rolls his eyes. "Oh, please. Urinating is a natural act."

"It's not natural for me to pee outside, so if you don't mind, I need my privacy."

He groans but turns around, anyway. "Why don't I... never mind. Would you like me to sing while you go? To drown out the noise?"

I poke my head around again. "That'd be nice. Thanks."

It takes a few minutes because I have a shy bladder, but finally, the sweet release of urine begins. *Ahh.* Gunnar whistles "Whistle While You Work" with his back to me. After I drip dry and zip up, I come around the boulder, still tucking in my T-shirt.

And right at that moment, Liza and Jake walk up. Liza grins. "My, my. Y'all don't waste any time."

I grab her arm. "No, it's not what you think."

She points at Gunnar. "It's about time you figured out how to do it."

Gunnar hangs his head low. I bop him on the arm. He takes me by the hand and tugs me away from Liza. We walk on the beach, near the waterline, away from the crowd, until it becomes quiet. In fact, we've walked so far, I think we're in front of a private residence. I hope we're not trespassing. Fortunately, I'm with the law.

Heat rises up my neck. "People in this town are so quick to judge. Isn't there a Bible verse about that?"

"She's only funnin'."

"I don't like people assuming things about me."

He stops walking and drops my hand. "Assuming you and I are attracted to one another is a terrible thing, right?"

"That's not what I meant." I groan. "People need to stop pushing."

Gunnar throws his hands up in defense. "Maybe I like your company. Is that so terrible? Because if it is, all you have to do is say the word."

My heart sinks. I'm all alone with a handsome guy on a hot summer night, and I'm saying stupid things to chase him away. Something is terribly wrong with me. I blow out a breath so I have time to think of something decent to say.

"I'm not used to people in my business. That's all. I didn't mean to take it out on you." I drag my toe through the sand to form a heart shape. "And for the record, I like your company too."

His eyebrows scrunch together. "Maybe you should blog about it."

I bust out a belly laugh. "I might have to do that."

He sits on the sand near the water's edge and pulls me down next to him. I barely hear the music from where we sit. My knee bumps his as I get comfy in the sand. He rests his arm behind me so he's leaning in to me. His warm breath tickles my ear.

I wink at him. "You like me for my money, don't you?"

"Yep. I'm that shallow."

I laugh and nudge him with my shoulder.

"I'm not impressed with a lot of money. It changes people."

"I don't think I've changed."

"Not yet."

I'm sure since Willow is an attorney, she has lots of money. Maybe from experience, he knows what money can do to people. I scoot my knees up and rest my chin on them. My toes wiggle through the cool, wet sand. "I have had a few daydreams about my life now that I don't have to worry about finances anymore."

He points at me. "That would be nice, I guess. To be able to take care of your family."

If I had a family. I dig my feet deeper into the sand. "I hate to admit this, but it's real pretty out here."

He stares off toward the other people. In the distance, someone starts a volleyball game. "It's my favorite place. I come here to clear my head."

"I can see why. I guess chasing bad guys all day can wear even someone as big and tough as you out."

He pins me in place with a cold stare. "That and when your fiancée dumps you at your wedding rehearsal."

Tears pool in my eyes. He mentioned the ex-girlfriend, and Regina and Mel haven't been shy about their disdain for her, but I never imagined this happening to him. Any girl that leaves this man at the altar is seriously disturbed.

"Oh, Gunnar. I'm sorry. I didn't know." He's probably so jaded now, a girl would have to be near perfect to pass his test. I wouldn't blame him if he never wanted to go down that road again.

He shrugs. "It's okay. I guess I assumed you knew. It's old news, but every now and then, I'll see something that brings back bad memories, and I head here to..."

"To clear your head?"

"Yeah. I bet you think we don't have problems down here, don't you?"

"I was hoping so. What's the attraction, then?"

He rotates so the light of the moon shines on his face, making him even more godlike. "So you're considering staying?"

I goose him in the ribs. "I didn't say that. I was talking about you."

He blows out a breath. "I like it here. I almost drowned in the big city."

My hand finds his, and he squeezes it, making my insides flip-flop. "I bet you'd be okay if you gave it another chance. There's a lot to offer in a big city."

He lies down on the sand, and I collapse beside him. We stare at the stars, still holding hands. There he goes again, stroking the back of my hand with his thumb. If he can make my stomach turn to jelly with a single touch, I'm not sure if I can handle his hands doing anything else.

"I'm content."

"Yeah, I've noticed. I don't know the definition of the word."

He laughs as he threads his fingers through mine. "Always looking for greener grass?"

He focuses again on the stars. I wish I had paid attention in science class because I would love to know what constellation is above us.

"I don't know about that. I guess I've always been too afraid to plant seeds to see if anything could grow."

He lets go of my hand and rolls onto his side to face me then props his head up with his hand. "The grass really will die if you spend more time worrying about it dying than you do making it thrive."

I roll over to face him. "What if I'm a lousy gardener, Mr. Philosopher? What if I put in the effort and it wasn't supposed to grow in the first place?"

He tucks a strand of my hair behind my ear. "It's called faith. You have to trust that you're doing your best and make the most of the results."

I reach out to touch his face. I have to know what that five o'clock shadow feels like. Oh dear, I shouldn't have done that. Now I'll never want to remove my hand from his warm, stubbly chin.

He closes his eyes and takes a deep breath.

"Don't you want more out of life?" I ask.

His eyes flutter open, and I wonder if this is what he looks like when he first wakes up in the morning, because if it is, I could get used to it. "Of course, but I can achieve it without changing my geography. It's not where you are; it's who you're with that matters."

I turn over onto my back and stare at the stars again because his face is way too distracting. "I wish I could be more like you."

He holds up a thumb. "You want to almost lose your thumbs?"

I giggle.

He leans in to me, and I can feel my heart about to beat out of my chest. "No. To enjoy each day, each moment."

He leans closer, putting one arm on either side of me. *Holy mother of God. Please put me out of my misery and kiss me because my ovaries are about to explode.* I'm only talking about a simple kiss. It's not as if we have to get married. But this is the South, so maybe we do. *Okay by me.*

"I do enjoy each day. I'm enjoying right now. A lot."

His eyes flick to my mouth and back to my eyes. I slide my hands up his chest, and he moans. He lowers his face at the same time that damn dog pays us a visit and gives us both sloppy kisses. We bump foreheads in a rush to get away from him.

"Ow," Gunnar yells. "Dammit, Griff. Get your own sexy—"

"If you call me a bitch, you're going to get smacked."

He rubs his nose, and I rub mine, then he helps me to a standing position and laughs. "I would never say that about you."

"I guess Griff can't hold his licker, either." I waggle my eyebrows. "Get it?"

He groans. "That was so bad." He stares at my lips and sighs. "I don't think I'll ever get to kiss you."

I tug him by the collar and plant a fast smooch on his lips. "There. That's better, right?" *Not for me, it isn't.* Holy crap. Those lips are even softer than I imagined.

He grimaces. "Not at all. It's like going to Six Flags and not riding The Scream Machine. I am not happy riding the kiddie mine train."

I throw out my hands. "I'm here, ready to ride whatever ride you're talking about." I know I shouldn't encourage him since I'm leaving soon, but I want this.

He throws his head back with laughter as he pulls me in close, snaking one arm around my waist. The other hand holds the back of my head. *It's about damn time.* His soft lips barely touch mine, when his phone buzzes, causing him to let out a pitiful whimper into my mouth.

"It's a conspiracy."

Gunnar frowns as he reads the text message. "I have to go. Chris Finley is sick, and I've been called in to work."

"If I ever meet this Chris dude..."

He wraps an arm around my shoulders, tucks me in to his side, and plants a chaste kiss on the top of my head. "Don't worry. I'll give him a stern talking-to myself."

He takes my hand, and we walk back to the others. With his other hand, he adjusts his board shorts. Oh my God. I think I'm going to die if I don't get another taste of him soon—one that's longer than a millisecond.

He waves to me as he hustles up to his car and zooms away. When I have the nerve to peek over at Liza, she winks. I guess her mission has been accomplished.

This is way better than getting drunk. Way better.

CHAPTER TWENTY-ONE
Andie

Hovering over the shop's stove, I sneer at my latest disaster, while Mrs. Cavanaugh washes dishes. Every day this week after the morning rush, I tried one recipe after another, and they all resulted in either a "yuck," or a gag, or a quick trip to the bathroom by Mrs. Cavanaugh. Today, I try a new tactic, but Granny's picture perched on the counter beside the stove isn't giving me any guidance. I'm hoping if I stare at it long enough, her wisdom will seep into my brain and saucepan. I'm not getting it.

Mrs. Cavanaugh hasn't been much help in the jam department, but she's invaluable with everything else. She pretty much runs the place. My main job responsibilities include making bank deposits, cleaning tables, and especially making Piggly Wiggly runs with a grocery list of whatever she needs for the day. My first "pig run" took me two hours because, well, it's the South and even a trip to the grocery store is a social event. As long as I get whatever Mrs. Cavanaugh needs, including the exact brand she wants, she's as sweet as sugar.

She doesn't ask for much, and I know Granny paid her a fraction of what she's worth. No matter what happens with the money, I'm going to make sure Mrs. Cavanaugh is well taken care of.

After inspecting Granny's handwritten accounting sheets, it's apparent that she hasn't made a profit in years. She barely made enough to pay for Mrs. Cavanaugh's salary, which is pitiful. *No wonder the place hasn't been updated since the eighties.* But I doubt raising the prices on her baked goods would have made a dent in her bottom line. Fortunately, she owned the building, or she wouldn't have been able to afford a place to live.

I watch over Mrs. Cavanaugh's shoulder as she cracks eggs then dumps the egg whites in one bowl and the yolks in another, all with one hand. She has decided to try yet another pastry recipe on the Jackson sisters. She says they think it's a treat to taste something new, when the truth is she figures no one would miss the Jacksons if they got food poisoning. I love this woman more and more every day.

The Jacksons arrive every day as if they are clocking in to a job, but they don't speak to me. Today, when I tried to compliment Sarah Jackson on her new purse, she peered around me and announced to Mrs. Cavanaugh what her order would be today. With my newfound Southern charm, I made sure they knew to let me know if they needed anything else. Other than the cold shoulder, I have been off their radar as far as their blog is concerned. I haven't seen any new photos of me posted lately, but like an addict, I have to pull it up every night to see if they wrote anything else about me. Thankfully, they have moved on to some other poor schmuck and how the person shouldn't wear leggings since she's sixty. I say if she still has the body to pull it off, then she should go for it. I think the Jacksons are jealous, because to see either of them in a pair of leggings would be quite scary.

Inhaling the aroma of the ingredients takes me back to a time when I visited Granny. She had a knack for pastries, and I would stand on a step stool, begging for one, which of course, she would oblige. I couldn't have been more than three or four years old, but the memory is seared into my brain like the burned jam is on the pot I threw away. Granny pulled out every ingredient she had and asked me to decide what we were going to make. We, or more like I, decided on chocolate princess crown muffins, which was nothing more than chocolate muffins with chocolate chips inside, topped with fluffy chocolate homemade icing and an entire bottle of sprinkles.

Mom was so mad at her for letting me have so much sugar at seven in the morning, but my grandmother shooed her off, saying she needed to let me be a kid. I loved the muffins, and I'm pretty sure Granny did too. We giggled the entire time we cleaned up the cocoa powder from every surface in her kitchen. To this day, when I see chocolate muffins, I get a tingly sensation in my cheeks from all the sugar in the princess chocolate muffins. If only Mom hadn't lied to me, I might have had lots of memories like that one.

I inhale another one of Mrs. Cavanaugh's masterpieces. "No matter what you make, it smells so heavenly."

"That's experience you smell." She takes my hand and places the whisk in it then covers my small hand with her larger, more wrinkled one. "This is how you whip. Better than an electric mixer. It's all in the whisk."

"And the wrist."

She laughs. "That too."

"You've been so nice to me, but why won't you help me with the jam? I only have one more week."

She adds sugar to the egg whites and proceeds to beat them into a fluffy meringue. "You got to win that ribbon on your own. The jackass sisters will notice if I help."

I belt out a laugh. Yep. She's definitely one I want in my corner. "You don't want them near Granny's money, do you?"

She shakes her head so much, I'm afraid it's going to come off. I'm going to miss this lady when I leave. She's the best part of my day.

The chimes over the door ring, and Mel walks in. Only half of her hair remains in her braid, and sweat stains cover her scrubs top.

"Afternoon, Melly," Mrs. Cavanaugh says.

Mel collapses onto a barstool and moans. "It has been a day from Hades today."

Regina barrels through the door. Her scrubs top is so big, she could wear it as a dress. She plops down on the stool next to Mel, lays her head on the counter, and whimpers.

"Bad day?" I'm not sure I want to know, but after a week in this town, the Southern hospitality has already taken over.

Mel wipes her face with her hands. "A compound femur fracture, a motorcycle accident, and Mrs. Betty fell and broke her hip. Bless her heart." She points at Regina. "And she got puked on by a kid."

Mrs. Cavanaugh and I back away.

Regina's head rises off the counter. "Hence the reason for the hospital-issue scrubs so big I could make a sail out of them."

I slide Regina a glass of sweet tea. "Hey, at least I was nice enough to aim with my hurl, right?"

She lets out an exhausted chuckle.

"Anything else?" Mrs. Cavanaugh always knows when there are more words left unsaid.

I pour Mel a glass of tea, and she gulps it down.

"Ah, that hits the spot," Mel says. "I had to see him all day today. He brought in every single case. He gets all doe-eyed when he sees me. It drives me crazy."

"Who?"

"Mitchell," Mrs. Cavanaugh answers as Regina giggles. That gets her rewarded with a nudge in the side by Mel. "He's set his cap for her a long, long time ago."

Mel groans. "And he doesn't take a hint. At. All."

The Mitchell I met at the moon-bathing party was really cute in a reserved, shy kind of way. But I'm new here, so I don't know the whole backstory. I glance over at Regina, and she rolls her eyes. I must ask her for more details later. There I go again, getting all nosy. I'm fitting in too much lately.

Mel stretches her arms over her head. "I try to be friendly because he's an EMT. I have to interact with him. He brings patients in, and I treat them. We have to talk, but he hangs on my every word."

I wiggle my eyebrows at Mrs. Cavanaugh. "Kind of sweet."

"It is sweet," Regina says as she does her best to tuck the XXL scrubs top into her pants.

Mel gives Regina a death stare before she answers me. "Ugh. You don't know the history. I made a promise when I was ten that one day when my mama let me date, I'd go out with him. He hasn't forgotten that."

Mrs. Cavanaugh pulls out some scones and hands one each to Mel and Regina. "You need a man. Get a man, and he'll get the hint."

She snorts. "Yep. That's exactly what I'll do... between clinic, ER shifts, tutoring science at the high school, and every now and then, sleep. A man is not in my schedule."

Regina gives her a sarcastic pout. "Poor Dr. Ballard. At least you got somebody drool-worthy hanging on your every word. I've got squat."

Mel wags a finger in front of Regina's face. "Not so true. What about—"

Regina snatches Mel's scone out of her hand and holds it for ransom. "Patient confidentiality, Doctor."

Mel giggles.

"Sorry if it's none of my business, but what's wrong with Mitchell?" I ask.

Mel crinkles her brow in deep thought. "Nothing, I guess." She motions for me to refill her tea glass. "I wish he wasn't so pushy."

I fill her glass and pour myself one as well. "He asks you out a lot?"

"Well, he never has."

Mrs. Cavanaugh responds in her usual huffy way. "Sounds like he's not pushy enough." Regina knuckle-bumps Mrs. Cavanaugh.

I raise an eyebrow at Mel. "What she said." It wouldn't hurt my feelings at all if one certain policeman would be a bit pushier with me. I would welcome it.

In a separate bowl, Mrs. Cavanaugh gives the chocolate icing one more stir before she lets the gooey heaven drip off the large mixing spoon. She taps it twice on the side of the bowl before she hands it to me. I'm about to drop it in the sink when Mel grabs my arm.

Mrs. Cavanaugh gives me her typical *tsk*. "Child, don't waste that icing." She motions with her head. "Go on. Lick it up. Don't you know nothing?"

She is my kind of lady. "Yes, ma'am." I run my tongue over the back of the spoon, and my eyes roll back in my head. *Yum.*

Mrs. Cavanaugh glances at me. "Going back to your problems we were talking about before we got sidetracked with talk of puke and broken hips, no, I don't want them to have your money. It's yours now."

"Who?" Mel asks. "The Jacksons?"

Mrs. Cavanaugh nods.

Between licks, I ask, "Why not? Because you don't like them, or because you don't want the church to have it?"

"'Cause Mary Grace didn't."

Hmm. I let that sink in while I stir my batch of jam that's simmering on the stove top. I scoop up a spoonful in the ladle and walk it over to her, careful not to drip any on my hands. "Try this."

If I can pass the Cavanaugh test, I may have something. This has to be the one. I've gone over every recipe Granny has. This has to be the one because it had three stars by the title. Mrs. Cavanaugh takes a bite and smacks her lips. Her turned-up nose tells me everything I need to know even before she spits it out into the sink.

"Is it better than the last one?"

She wipes her tongue on a dish towel. "Worse. Girl, I ain't never seen nobody that sucks at cooking like you."

I hold it out for Mel to taste, but she backs away. "No, thanks."

I collapse on a barstool and beat my forehead against the worn Formica countertop. "Ugh. This is so hard." I know I'm whining, but I am entitled. I slide the recipe card over to her. "There's one ingredient that's been erased so much, it's illegible. It has to be important because without that mystery ingredient, it sucks."

She slides the card back to me, and I stare at it, hoping I can conjure up x-ray vision to see what used to be written there. "All the best cooks leave one key ingredient off their recipes."

I squint in hopes the secret ingredient will become visible. "That's the dumbest thing I've ever heard of. What if someone wanted to make that dish?"

"Oh no, you don't never make someone else's dish. And to make sure it never gets stolen, good cooks leave the key ingredient off."

I fling my hands in the air in defeat. "Ooo. Recipe stealing. I can see it now on the next episode of *Cops*. Two grannies duking it out over twice-baked potatoes."

She crosses her arms over her chest. "That ain't funny, girl. Ask Jackie Richards. She made the mistake of loaning her special meatloaf recipe, the one her great granny give her, to Miss Eula Mae. Well, Miss Eula Mae, that snake in the grass, runs that E. coli-infested diner over in Cypress. She started selling the meatloaf as her own family secret."

I feign shock. "The nerve."

"True story. Word got out, because that's what happens in these parts, and she ended up having to shut down that nasty place."

When her back is turned, I run my finger through the chocolate mixture and lick it. Pure T heaven. I used a Southern phrase. Well, Lord have mercy. It's coming back to me.

"I didn't know there was such drama in this slow-as-molasses town." There I go again. I'm becoming a master of all things Southern. With a mouthful of chocolate, I say, "But if others can't figure it out, I sure can't, and I'm not going to enter anything into the contest that's going to make people sick."

"Looks like you ain't gonna get that money."

Maybe if I pitch a fit and throw the spoon across the room, she'll help me figure it out, but somehow I doubt it. "I'm trying. I've done everything in the agreement. I've gone to church." I count on my hand. "I've tried to fit in, and that's even harder. I am doing the best I can. That stupid jam clause was never mentioned when I met with the attorney." I didn't mention my slipup with Gunnar's beer at the moon-bathing party, especially since Gunnar told me to be careful what I say around Regina. Besides, it was one little sip. One sip that led to two, which led to me wanting a third.

Mrs. Cavanaugh snickers. "It was in the fine print." Mel and Regina nod in agreement, as though it's a no-brainer.

"Ugh!" Please God, put me out of my misery. All that's left on this stupid index card of the missing ingredient is a very faint "J" and a "D," so something important is missing. Jam, juice, julienne, deglaze, dust, dice, dredge, drizzle. None of these things make sense with jam.

"What did Granny leave you?" I've been wanting to ask Mrs. Cavanaugh this since the day I met her.

"Not a pot to piss in."

Mel's jaw drops open. Regina plops her head back on the counter, her eyes drifting closed. My eyes bug out of their sockets. "Nothing?"

"Nope."

This makes no sense. Mrs. Cavanaugh had to be her closest friend. I've only known her a few weeks, and I'm already lost without her. "Why not? I bet you were closer to her than most." My hands fly up to my mouth. "Oh my lands. That was rude. I'm sorry."

Regina pops her head up. "I better leave while I'm still awake enough to drive." She turns to Mel and motions to the door with her head.

Mel takes one more swig of her tea, throws some money on the counter, and stands. "Yeah, me too."

I sense they don't want to be involved in this conversation, and I appreciate that.

After they leave, Mrs. Cavanaugh grumbles as she turns her back on me to work on the pastry dough. "She had me in her will for a long time, but I made her take it out when she won that money."

I play with a dish towel. "You didn't want any?"

She turns her head around. "Child, what am I going to do with a whole lot of money? I'm eighty-six years old. We made a compromise. She'd take me out of her will if I let her pay off my house and give me some spending money. It was the only way to get her off my back."

I touch Granny's framed photo, still sitting next to the stove. *Damn you, Mother, for lying to me.* "I bet you think I'm being selfish, trying to take the money and run, huh?"

"No. If I was your age, I'd be doing the same thing. You keep that money. She wanted you to have it."

I bang my head on the counter again as I flop onto the stool. "She should have straight-out given it to the church and left me out of the will. I would have never been the wiser."

She sprinkles the countertop with flour and motions for me to help her roll out the pastry dough. There is something very therapeutic about working with dough. Either I'm going to solve all the world's problems, or I'm going to get arthritis. I'm not sure which will come first.

"Maybe she was watching out for you."

"Pfft. She didn't give a hang about me." Three Southernisms in one conversation. Lord help me.

With the rolling pin in one hand, she rolls out the pastry then dusts it with more flour. She motions for me to cut the dough into triangles like she showed me how to do yesterday. "She talked about you every day."

I drop the knife. "She did not."

"She worried about you being all swallowed up in that big city, especially after your mama died. Worried you were lonely."

This is not happening. If Granny knew about me, she could have reached out, especially after my mother died. I yank out another knife from the drawer and cut swift lines through the dough. "Lonely? I have lots of friends. I was out every night."

Okay, I may have only had a couple of friends, and lately, I was too lazy to go out, but no one really has to know that.

"Don't mean you weren't lonely."

Tears burn my eyes. I pick at the worn edge of the recipe card.

"She knew booze was your best friend."

That's it. I slam my hand onto the counter. "Why is everyone in this dry county so concerned with my drinking? I don't drink any more than anyone else. The only thing different is that I don't conceal it. I am what I am."

There. I've said it. I've said my piece.

She places the cutout dough onto the cookie sheet. "Lonely, that's what you is."

I throw my hands in the air. "Ugh. I'm going upstairs to find another recipe. Maybe there's a *Jam for Dummies* book." I stomp up the stairs, not wanting to hear another word from the wise Mrs. Cavanaugh. She doesn't know me. I'm not lonely at all.

Except I am.

CHAPTER TWENTY-TWO
Andie

If I yawn one more time during this church service, the pastor is going to make me take up the offering. Liza Jane and Jake are probably snoozing the morning away, and I would be too if I were them. Ever since the night at the lake, I haven't seen Gunnar one time. I thought he was into me, especially after that interrupted kiss, but I must have read him wrong.

Boy, that guy acts as though he's so conflicted when it comes to me. One day, he's telling me off about not visiting my grandmother, which, by the way, was not my fault. And the next, he acts as though he wants to jump my bones. We're not in middle school anymore, for crying out loud. I know I'm not going to be here long, but I could do with a casual NSA relationship: no strings attached. But something tells me he's not that kind of person. I'm not, either, but for him, I might make an exception.

Girl, stop it. Get an eyeful, but don't touch. It's temptation at its best. I have to remember: green eyes or green dollar bills.

And to top things off, he's not in church this morning. I'm sure the pastor will forgive him since he had to work all night again. But not having him here makes church super excruciating. Without any eye candy, I'm totally bored. I guess he's sleeping in. Maybe I could go wake him up, or join him. I'm sure it wouldn't take much to figure out where he lives. I really shouldn't be having dirty thoughts in church, but it beats listening to this as-dry-as-toast sermon.

The bratty kid sitting next to me pinches my arm.

"Ow." *Oops.*

Every head in the congregation turns to stare. The kid's mother even has the nerve to shush me. I sneer at the kid, and he feigns shock. If I didn't think I would go to hell for hitting a kid during church, I would do it in a heartbeat. I would love to smack that smarmy smirk off his face.

"Uh. Amen, brother. Amen." That's the best cover-up I can think of.

"That's right," a man says from the other side of the church.

"Amen, Pastor," another says.

Everyone turns back to the preacher, and I can finally let out a sigh of relief. I slump down into the pew, and the little boy laughs. The pastor continues on about the gates of hell, and the kid has the nerve to stick his tongue out at me. And because I'm such a mature person, I stick mine out at him. If he doesn't watch it, I'll push him right through that gate of hell and throw away the key. Right as I'm having a pissing match with the idiot boy, I get caught by the Jacksons. *Click.* Even in church, they have no shame. They must have an unlimited data plan with all those pictures they take. I make a mental note to check out their blog tonight in case I need to make another entry of my own.

I thank the Lord Almighty when the pastor gives the closing prayer. I didn't think he would ever finish that sermon. I smile at the preacher as I leave the sanctuary. On the last step, I twist my ankle and almost kiss the concrete, but I catch myself.

Click. Another photo. I right myself then throw back my shoulders and walk straight toward the blue-haired paparazzi.

"Lovely day, isn't it, Miss Jackson? You too, other Miss Jackson." *Damn.* I surprise myself with that cavity-inducing twang. I smile and pose.

They both stare, unable to move.

"Aw, come on. Is it not fun if I want you to take my picture?" I give them a duck-face pose. I'm sure that will show up online tonight.

My grin becomes beauty pageant large, and I add in a whisper. "No matter what you try or how you try to paint a picture of me breaking the rules, you will not get Granny's money." If it's the last thing I do, I'm going to stick to the plan. I cock my head to the side. "Y'all come back now, ya hear?"

They gasp. "Well, I never." They murmur to themselves and shuffle-walk away from me. Several other church members stand around slack-jawed.

"And you never will, either." I wave as they leave.

Stanley leans against his rust bucket of a car and fills his bottom lip with tobacco. Just the person I need to see.

"Howdy," he says when he sees me. He stands up as tall as he possibly can. "You were getting into that sermon, weren't you?"

I roll my eyes. "When the spirit moves. Actually, I came over to see how you were doing."

Stanley spits, and a tiny bit of it lands on my toe. *Ew.*

"What do you mean?"

"Your job situation. Do you think you'll get laid off?"

"Oh." He peers around and lowers his voice. "Not yet, but I have some time to get my GED, or I'm out."

Here goes nothing. God, I hope he doesn't take this as a come on. "That's what I wanted to talk to you about. When I lived in Boston, I taught adult ed for a while."

His eyebrows shoot up. "Yeah?"

"Yeah." Now I'm the one skimming the crowd and lowering my voice. "I got involved with it when I was on probation one time." I cringe. "You know how that goes."

He chuckles and waggles his eyebrows. "You're my kind of girl."

Oh dear. Through gritted teeth, I continue. "I feel bad about your situation, so if you would like me to help you prep for your exam, I will. You can study while you eat my leftover muffins."

A wiry grin moves across his face. *Oh dear.* He does think it's a come-on. "You'll help me?"

"It's real studying, okay. Not..."

"Making out?"

"Exactly. Don't want to get involved with anyone here. You understand, don't you?"

He pouts, but he throws a grin in there too, so I know he's not too disappointed. "Okay. I might do that."

I sigh. "Great. I'll see you tomorrow night." Lord, I hope Gunnar doesn't think I'm leading Stanley on, or worse, that I am into him.

Stanley salutes, and I scamper away, but not before he yells to the Jackson sisters, "She loves me."

Great. That's all I need.

CHAPTER TWENTY-THREE
Gunnar

To protect and serve. That's my job. Okay, maybe I go out of my way to protect one little out-of-towner, but no one has to know that. She doesn't have a clue how many times I check in on her, follow her to the bank, and make sure she's locked up tight. She's used to living in the big city, but that doesn't stop me from being overprotective. And if I get caught, I can hide my excuse behind my badge.

Tonight is no different. After a half-assed workout, I saunter down Main Street. In case anyone's watching, I check to make sure each storefront is locked up tight. When I get to In A Jam, I stop in my tracks. The front door is ajar, but the lights are off in the shop.

My gym bag slides to the sidewalk as I creep into the dark coffee shop. My heart races as adrenaline pulses through my veins. I hate this part of my job. We rarely have a break-in, but it does happen. I feel for my gun in my ankle holster to make sure it's ready in case I need it. In all the years I've carried one off duty, I've never had to draw it, and I'm hoping tonight isn't going to be any different.

The light from the street lamp casts shadows around the store. Anyone could be hiding behind the counter, or worse, in the stairwell leading up to Andie. I hear a stumbling noise on the steps, then another, and a string of curse words.

Slurring her words, Andie says, "Don't make me use my weapon."

"Put the gun down, Andie. It's me. Gunnar."

She staggers down the rest of the steps. My eyes adjust to the darkness enough to see her silhouette. I walk toward her until I am at the bottom of the steps, terrified that I might have to draw my gun and shoot her if she raises her weapon at me. I blink twice when she comes into full view, only wearing a tank top and panties. *Shit.*

"I was only bluffin'. Don't have a gun." She holds her hands out so I can see she doesn't have anything in them.

"You left your front door open."

"Oh. Oops. I went out for an... errand, and I guess I forgot." She snaps her finger. "Did you know this is a dry county? I figured out where Mason County started." She jerks her thumb over her shoulder. "It's that way about five miles in case you needed to know." She giggles. "Then when I got back, I found Granny's stash. Who knew?"

I let out a huge sigh. She flops down on the last step, and even with the filtered light from the streetlight outside, I have a clear view down her tank top.

She leans to the side. "What are you doing here? You scared the crap out of me."

I cross my arms over my chest. "You're drunk, aren't you?"

Andie leans forward, and I reach out to keep her from face-planting onto the floor. I shouldn't have made contact with her. This is not going to end well.

"You're trying to change the subject."

I hold out a hand for her to take. After two attempts, she latches on, and I help her stand. There she goes with the leaning thing again. I take her by the shoulders and aim her in the direction of the stairs. "Let's get you back upstairs."

She's putting me in a difficult position. If I keep this from her attorney, I could lose my reputation in the community. But if I let him know, she'll lose her money, and I'll lose a chance with her.

Her left foot goes up, then her right foot goes up on the same step. Then she sighs and rests her head on my shoulder. I prop her up, and together, we attempt another step. With each step, she leans more and more on me, and before I know it, she's dead weight on my arm.

"Damn, girl. You're heavy when you're drunk."

That was the wrong thing to say. Andie swings around so fast, I almost lose my balance. With her on the step above me, I can almost see her squinty eyes.

"Are you saying I'm fat?"

Oh boy. Even when she's drunk, she's as cute as all get-out, and I can't help but laugh. "No, sugar, you're not fat. Never mind."

She points a crooked finger and sways. I catch her before she sends us both tumbling down the steps. "'Cause if you think I'm fat, I can show you someone who's fat. Peggy Shiflitt down at the Piggly Wiggly. Now she's fat." She wags her head, confirming her assessment of poor Peggy. "Peggy, Piggy." She laughs at her own joke and snorts. "And for that matter, here's proof that I'm not fat." She crosses her arms and grabs the hem of her tank top then pulls it up over her belly button.

I quickly stop her. I've daydreamed about her doing this for me, but not on the steps and definitely not inebriated.

"Hey now. I believe you. This isn't necessary."

"Pffft." Okay, that confirms the as-drunk-as-a-skunk assumption I had. I need to get her up to her room fast and make her brush her teeth. She misses a step and tumbles into her living room, crashing into the couch. At least we made it.

This is a bad idea, but I sit on the couch next to her, anyway. "You're not supposed to do this, or you'll lose all the money."

Andie stares off, and when she looks me in the eye, I can see how glassy her eyes are. "Oops." She laughs, which turns into a whimper, then a full-blown crying jag. She slumps down, rests her head on my shoulder, and pats my thigh. That feels too perfect.

"What's the matter?"

After a beat of silence, she asks, "Do you think I'm lonely?"

Well, yes, I do, but she doesn't want to hear that right now. "I don't know. I don't know you very well."

She rubs her cheek on my shoulder, back and forth as though she's trying to find the right spot. Her bottom lip sticks out. "Mrs. Cavanaugh thinks I'm lonely and that's why I drink."

Mrs. Cavanaugh is wise. "Is it?"

She bolts up and stumbles to the bathroom. With a toothbrush in her mouth, she mumbles, "I got lots of friends in Boston. Already made some here too."

She spits in the sink, grabs a crumpled piece of paper off the kitchen table, and tumbles back into the living room. When she sits next to me, she melts into my side, and before I can stop myself, I put my arm around her and lean back on the couch. She snuggles in with me. It feels right, as if we've done this a thousand times before.

"You can still be lonely."

She rests her head back, and all I want to do is kiss her neck. It's there for the taking. Apparently, she can't see what she does to me.

"Is that answer listed in the city manual?" she asks.

Andie makes me laugh, and I kiss her silky, fruity-smelling hair. I shouldn't have done that. She should push me away because I want to do it again and again. "But it's true."

She shrugs and flips her hair off her shoulder, exposing more of her delectable neck. *Crap.* "Maybe she's right, but until she started harassing me, I didn't care. Can you arrest her for harassment?"

"No, sweetie, I can't. But why do you care now?"

"Because when all my 'acquaintances'..." She makes air quotes with her fingers and leans more into me then places a hand on my upper thigh. *Jesus.* "They'll find out about the money; they will all want to be best buddies with me." She turns abruptly, and her resting hand moves way too close to my groin. "When I needed a job, were they around? Nope. When I needed a loan, were they around? Nope."

"And you don't want to share with them."

Andie runs her hand down the side of my face. I clear my throat.

"I don't want to waste it on them."

As much as I don't want to, I take her hand away from my face and hold both of them. That seems to be the best place to have them so they don't get any closer to my fun zone. She's drunk, and I'm not going there again with any girl. "You could do something worthwhile with it."

She groans and focuses on the floor. Then she wipes a tear from her face and licks her lips. "I don't even like the taste of alcohol anymore." All of a sudden, she doesn't sound drunk. She sounds completely with it. She sniffles and holds up the wadded piece of paper with a pink gingham-checked border. "See what I found in one of Granny's photo albums?" She smooths out the wrinkles and hands it to me. "A note from me to Granny." She pokes at the page. "By the date on it, I would have been in middle school." She shoves it toward me. "Go on. Read it."

I clear my throat. "Granny, I don't know why you hate my mother so much, but leave us alone. She doesn't want to hear from you again, and neither do I." I peek over at Andie, who works her teeth over her bottom lip. "Ouch."

"Yeah. But there's one little fly in the ointment. That's the stationery Granny sent me one year for my birthday, but this note is typed, and the scribbled signature is not mine."

"No way."

She snatches it away from me and wads it into a ball. "Thinking back, that's about the time Mom told me Granny was dead. She lied to us both."

My heart breaks for Andie. She missed out on a chance to have a real relationship with her grandmother. I don't even know what I'm supposed to say. I'm angry with a person I've never met. I'm sad for Miss Mary Grace because she wanted to know her granddaughter in the worst way. And this selfish act, for whatever reason, ruined it for everyone.

"I'm sorry."

Andie snorts. "Not your fault." She stares off into the corner of the room and, for the longest time, stays silent. Then she takes a deep breath and turns back to me. "I am so lonely."

She curls into me, and her bare leg brushes mine. I can't hold back anymore. I cup her face in my hands and raise it until she's peering into my eyes. I wipe a tear off her cheek.

Leaning in, I whisper, "You don't have to be. I'm right here." At first, my lips barely touch hers. It's not nearly enough. My hands roam down her arms and rest on her waist. I slide a hand under her tank top to feel her burning-hot skin. She lets out a sigh and runs her hands up my chest. When she kisses me, it's just another light, feathery peck. I can't take it anymore, so I run my hands higher and pull her closer to me. My lips press against hers, and she moves with me. Suddenly, a skimpy tank top and panties are way too much clothing for me. My lips leave a trail down her neck, and I curse the days I've lost thinking about this moment. But it's not supposed to be this way. She's not supposed to be drunk.

Then I get a vision of her waving goodbye, leaving town with her convertible loaded down. Even though it's the last thing I want to do, I push her away from me. Both of us breathe as if we've been running a marathon, and her lips are so perfectly swollen. Her hair is a gorgeous mess.

"We shouldn't do this." I stand up to put some distance between us. "Uh, we shouldn't do this." I pace the living room, trying to find the words, trying to keep myself from diving back in and pressing her into the couch with me on top of her.

She plays with a loose string on her tank top. "I'm sorry."

It's not a great idea to touch her again, but I hold out a hand to help her stand. "I'm not sorry in the least. It's not the right time. That's all."

She bows her head and wipes another stray tear away. "You don't want me like that, do you? You're so perfect, and I'm a hot mess. I bet you've never even gotten a parking ticket."

Her words make me freeze. She has no idea how imperfect I am. I turn around and hold her face in my hands again then give her one last kiss on the lips. Dammit, I shouldn't have done that. "You are not a hot mess. And if your blood-alcohol level wasn't so high, I would show you how not sorry I am."

She chews on her lip. I wish I were doing that.

"I won't tell anyone about your little slipup, especially your attorney. We all mess up sometimes."

Some more than others.

I kiss her cheek. I have to touch her and kiss her. Leaving is harder than I thought it would be. "I'll lock your door on my way out."

She blows out a breath.

"See you soon, sugar?"

She clears her throat and paints on that fake, beauty-pageant smile. "Of course."

I wave and jog down the stairs. If I don't leave now, I'll still be here in the morning, and that tank top will be ripped to shreds.

CHAPTER TWENTY-FOUR
Andie

Every time I close my eyes, I see Gunnar's beautiful face, feel his breath on my neck, and taste his lips. In my dreams, he kisses me everywhere, and I let him. But when my dreams turn to me breaking his heart, I bolt up in bed, causing my head to pound. This isn't my plan. He's not supposed to be so yummy.

Damn it to hell. If I hadn't been drunk last night, he might have carried me up the stairs, and my dreams would have become a reality. He thinks I was too drunk, or so he said. I wasn't so sloppy drunk that I don't remember every detail this morning. But a few more shots, and I would have been there.

Tired of tossing and turning and getting turned on with thoughts of his lips on mine, I throw the covers off, do a quick spit bath, and head downstairs to study that damn recipe card. Mrs. Cavanaugh won't darken the door for another couple of hours, so I'm going to attempt another batch. Something tells me this recipe is the one I'm supposed to use. There's something about that missing ingredient.

The open Jack Daniel's bottle I left on the counter last night taunts me as if to say, "Come to Mama," but I'm not going to do it. Last night was it, and it's not because of the money, and it's not because Gunnar saw me wasted. The more time I spend in this town and in Granny's home, the more I know she was trying to protect me from myself. Yes, this is a test, but one I plan to pass with flying colors.

I should have never gone in search of clues about my mother because all I found was the bottle of Tennessee's finest whiskey. I bet

Granny never intended for me to find that tucked neatly away in a box labeled "country crafts." Or maybe she did, and it was a test of willpower, one that I failed miserably. But finding that letter sent me spiraling out of control, especially when my mother made Granny think I didn't care. Needless to say, I reacted to unsettling news in my normal fashion—drinking enough booze to suppress the hurt.

"Here goes nothing." I drag out all my ingredients and place them on the counter by the stove. My shiny saucepan I bought at the department store welcomes me like a new friend, and it begs me not to ruin it. While the strawberries simmer on the stove, my eyes wander back to the whiskey bottle. The amber liquid sloshes around when I tap it with my wooden spoon.

Only a few people in the city have even cared enough to text me after I didn't show up at my old haunt. But even they don't keep in contact anymore. Out of sight, out of mind. Like I told Gunnar, they don't care. They would care enough to help me wash my money down their throats with the finest liquor it can buy, but when the cash ran out, they would be on to the next person. Tinsley is the only person who keeps in touch, but I think it is part of the agreement he made with Gunnar more than his concern for me.

It has been so long since I've had someone I could talk to. I never understood why my mother was so angry with Granny, and she always took it out on me. "You're exactly like her. One day, you will be grown up and make mistakes, and I'm going to be there to throw it in your face." Those were the last words she said to me as I packed my bags and moved out after I graduated college. I never heard from her again until I got the call two years later that she had ended her life. I was bound and determined not to make the same mistakes she did, whatever they were.

I pick up the bottle and take a quick scan around to see if anyone is snooping in the windows. It would be so easy to toss it back where I found it and forget about my messed-up life. No one cares about me, anyway. This town with these nice people only like me for one reason and one reason only—money. Once I'm out of their lives, they won't remember me.

Maybe I should let the church have all the money and run away. I could take the advance Mr. Christian gave me and start over somewhere new. My faux friends would never be able to find me. Or I could drain this bottle dry in hopes that I wouldn't see another day.

The bottle calls my name, begging me to wrap my lips around it. It tells me it is the only one that understands and the only thing that can give me relief. I raise the bottle, and right before it touches my mouth, my eyes land on Granny's picture. This is not what she would want for me. I jostle the bottle over and over, and some of the contents spills on my hands.

"No! No. You are not going to win."

The bottle slides out of my hand and lands in the saucepan, the rest of its contents spilling into my latest jam attempt. "Shit." I scoop it out with my wooden spoon, grab it with a dish towel, and toss it in the trash. In case the Jackson sisters saunter in, I bury it deep under other trash. I cross my arms over my chest and stare at the bubbling strawberry and Jack Daniel's concoction. *Hmm. I wonder.*

Before I know what I'm doing, I dip the wooden spoon in the saucepan and scoop out a glob. I blow on it so I don't burn the roof of my mouth and count to ten. It's still steaming hot, so I take a tentative bite. With an open mouth, I breathe in and out, trying to cool the burning, congealing glop in my mouth.

I cock my head to the side and lift one eyebrow. "Not bad."

My phone buzzes, notifying me of an incoming text. Tinsley's message reads, "Hope you're doing well. Have you found your twang?"

I giggle as I reply. "Yep. I'll call you later."

The bell chimes over the door, and I place my phone on the counter.

"Morning," Mrs. Cavanaugh says. She goes through her daily routine of hanging up her purse, sliding on her apron, and dragging items out to start on breakfast.

"Morning, Mrs. Cavanaugh." I get out a clean spoon and scoop another spoonful of my latest jam for her to taste. When I wave it under her nose, she tries to swat my hand away.

"Oh, come on. Please try it. I think I'm getting the hang of this."

She backs away from me. "I'm in no mood for food poisoning."

Maybe if I whine, she'll try it. "Please? Pretty please with sugar on top?"

She lets out her typical huff, knowing she's not going to win, and opens her mouth. I grin, hoping my positive attitude will help her be open-minded about this batch. She takes a bite and smacks her lips. That's more than I've gotten out of her in the past.

"Well? What do you think?"

She wags her head back and forth as though she's trying to find the right words. "Not bad."

Hallelujah. I give Mrs. Cavanaugh a big hug and plant a kiss her on the cheek. "Woo-hoo! Oh yeah, oh yeah." I strut around the kitchen like the chickens that roam Main Street.

Mrs. Cavanaugh giggles. "It tastes pretty much like Mary Grace's. What did you do this time?" She cracks eggs into a bowl without even glancing my way. I'm still mesmerized at how she can do that. Her arthritic hands don't seem agile enough, but they are.

"Uh... I followed the recipe." I shrug. "The only other thing I did was not burn it to hell."

She dumps flour into the bowl and pours milk into the well she's created. While she mixes the muffin batter, she says, "I guess you figured out the secret ingredient."

I shrug and try my best to conceal my surprise at what exactly that ingredient was. "I didn't do anything different, except..."

Mrs. Cavanaugh stops her work and stares at me. "What?"

"Nothing. I need to write down my steps so I can replicate what I did." I turn my back to her and focus on the recipe card. I peer at the tiny writing on that one line with the missing ingredient. Since it's in faint pencil, I can barely make it out, but I'm sure of it now. It says, "1CJD." One cup of Jack Daniel's. I gasp.

Mrs. Cavanaugh studies me. "Something wrong?"

"Not at all." I do a happy dance in the middle of the store, boogying with a broom. *Granny, you little souse. Mama did say we were a lot alike.* If I can submit this to the county fair, I can check one more item off my "get out of hell free" card. I'll be kissing this small town goodbye faster than a hot knife slices through butter. *So long, hillbillies.*

The bells above the door chime, and my happy dance is interrupted by Gunnar, the one sexy fly in the ointment. *Dang it.*

CHAPTER TWENTY-FIVE
Andie

His eyes rake over my body, and I grip the broom tighter, pretending to actually sweep. Damn, he's more handsome with sober eyes. I hope he doesn't lecture me about my slipup because I've already given myself a massive tongue-lashing for the both of us. I slide the broom back into the closet if for no other reason than to have something to do besides gawk at him.

"Mornin'," Mrs. Cavanaugh says to him, throwing some bacon in the skillet. "Where you been hiding?"

A flush creeps up his neck. He glances my way, and I busy myself with cleaning the sink. *Scrub, scrub, scrub.* Don't give him one single peek. But I can feel his eyes on me.

Mrs. Cavanaugh pulls out a cup and pours him some coffee.

"Morning, Mrs. Cavanaugh. I've been working some late nights, so trying to sleep in."

He sips his coffee, and his eyes peer over the cup at me. I forget how to breathe and can't keep from staring back. We do this 'look away, glance back, focus on anything but each other' dance several times.

Mrs. Cavanaugh clears her throat. When I snap my head toward her, I see her eyes twinkling. *Busted. Gah!*

She takes off her apron and picks up her purse. "I seem to have forgotten my rheumatiz medicine. Do you mind if I go down to the druggist to get some more?"

It's not actually a question. It's more like a statement wrapped up in a polite Southern request. I'm starting to get the hang of these phrases, and I don't think I need my translator anymore.

"Oh, why don't you let me do that for you? You shouldn't walk if you don't feel well." *Please, pretty please with sugar on top, please let me leave.* This coffee shop is heating up with pheromones.

She waves me off as she's already at the door. She has never mentioned being on medication before, so I'm pretty sure she's trying not to be a third wheel. "Nah. Fresh air will do me some good. It's hot in here."

Ain't that the truth.

The bells chime, and she's gone, leaving me and Gunnar and a whole lot of silence between us. He sits on his usual stool at the bar. I put a few pieces of bacon onto a plate and slide it toward him. He crunches down on a piece and nods his thanks.

I point in the direction Mrs. Cavanaugh went. "I wish she hadn't done that."

He winks as he takes another sip of coffee. "Now you have to talk to me, huh?"

Planting my hands on the counter, I lean over. "And you, sir, have to look me in the eye." I'm still not sure if he meant it when he said he wouldn't tell Mr. Christian. There's nothing to prevent him from changing his mind.

He grins, and I melt when that dimple shows up again. "I'm sorry if I offended you last night."

I take a step back. "You didn't offend me. I was the one that was, how do you say it? Three sheets to the wind and rambling on and on." I tug on the neckline of my T-shirt to hopefully create a breeze to cool me off.

He motions for me to sit next to him.

I slide onto the barstool and fiddle with the dish towel in my hand. After another awkward moment of silence, I have the nerve to speak. He deserves to know my excuse for the slipup, no matter how lame it was.

"It's like this. My mother didn't get along with her mother, so I knew Granny hardly at all. In fact, Mom told me Granny died a long time ago."

He agrees without interrupting me.

"This seems to be a pattern. I hadn't spoken to my mother for a few years when she died. I'm not proud of that, but I guess I wound up feeling like the only person I could depend on was myself. Then last night, I found that letter to my grandmother. My mother forged my name on it, making it look like I didn't care about my own grandmother. Who does that? Lovely family, huh?" My fake grin shows up.

He sets his coffee cup down and puts a hand over one of mine. "You're not used to people caring about you, really caring."

I close my eyes and focus on his hand stroking mine. "Yep. And now with all this money, I really don't think I can trust people, especially in this town."

He rotates me on the barstool until I'm facing him and rests his hands on my knees. "Why is that? Liza and Jake can't stop talking about how sweet you are. You even befriended Mel and Regina. Mel's a pushover, but Regina's a hard egg to crack. These people are your friends." He glances down at his hands on my thighs before his gaze rakes up my body and lands on my face. "And there's me."

I blow out a breath because everything he said is completely true. But there are others out there that aren't so friendly. I point at the front window, which looks out on Main Street. "Every day, the blue-haired duo comes in this store, hoping to catch me doing something wrong."

He laughs, and his hands slide up my thighs. *Stay focused, Andie.*

"By the way, did you read their latest blog entry? I can't believe they said they were going to issue hard hats to the church members for fear that when I walk in to the sanctuary next time, the roof might cave in."

"Don't waste your time. I'm sorry I even told you about that stupid blog. But most around here are decent folk. Simple, maybe, but not out to get you."

I lean toward him as though I'm trying to examine his thoughts. "Are you one of the decent ones?" If he's not, he sure has me fooled. He had a perfect opportunity to rat on me, and he didn't.

He chuckles as he bows his head. "I'm out to drain your account dry."

I love his sense of humor. I glance down because it hurts too much to focus on him for very long, especially since he's drawing circles on my thighs with his thumbs. *Have mercy.*

"I enjoy your company, Andie, but I think we went a bit too far last night. I'm, uh... glad we stopped."

My shoulders slump as I lean back. "You are?"

He stares at the ceiling as though he's trying to find the right words. And there's that dimple again. "Well... it was the right thing to do. You were drunk. I should turn you in."

No! It was one little slip.

"But I won't."

A huge gulp of air I didn't know I was holding escapes my mouth. I hop off my stool and walk in a straight line, and one at a time, I touch my right index finger to my nose, then my left. "I'm not drunk now." I wink at him. "Want to give me a sobriety test?"

He tugs me toward him by a belt loop until I crash into that solid body of his. "How about a Breathalyzer test?" He leans down, and those soft lips are on the sensitive spot behind my ear.

If it weren't for his strong arms wrapped around my waist, I would be a puddle in the middle of the floor. He nips at my bottom lip, and his tongue leaves a sweet, bacon-scented trail down my neck. I moan into his face.

"You pass," he whispers into my neck.

"I need a retest." My mouth finds his.

He groans, grabbing my butt with one hand and holding my head in place with the other. My hands roam through his hair, down his thick neck, and latch on to his wide shoulders. I could do this all day long.

The bell over the door chimes, and Liza Jane enters. "Hey, y'all," she says, zapping us back to reality.

We jolt away from each other. Gunnar wipes his mouth and adjusts his uniform pants. I smooth my hair down then race-walk around to the other side of the counter and drum my fingers.

Liza's wide grin says it all. "Have mercy, it's hot in here. I guess I interrupted something."

Gunnar clears his throat. "I better go do some public service work." He salutes us both and practically runs out of the store.

Liza watches him go then turns back to me, never losing her smirk. "Our coffeepot is on the fritz. I need two large cups to go, please."

My hands tremble as I drag out two paper cups and pour coffee in them. "Sure thing. These are on the house. You've been so nice to me. It's my way of thanking you for not treating me like an outsider."

"Thanks, hon. But I'd rather pay for the coffee and get the scoop for free."

I melt over the counter, almost spilling the coffee. She pats me on the back, enjoying my reaction, as she continues to giggle.

"Tell me. I promise I won't tell a soul, not even Jake."

I bang my head on the counter. "Why does he have to be so cute and sweet and..."

Her eyebrows rise. "And what?"

"Ugh. He's such an excellent kisser."

She cackles and pats me on the back again. I prop my elbows on the counter and rest my head in my hands.

"What's wrong with that?"

Here comes whiny Andie again. "Because I'm leaving soon, and I don't want any hard feelings."

"Sugar, it's not his feelings that are hard."

I gasp, but it's true. Every time he's near me, he has to adjust his package.

"Gunnar is one of the sweetest guys God has ever made. Have fun and see where it takes you."

I shrug. I would love to spend more time with him—more quality, lip-locking time with him for sure.

Liza taps me on the hand, and I peek over at her. "He's not after your money. Surely to goodness, you know that by now."

"I know." I pour myself a cup of coffee, and we sip in silence. "I'm afraid he's out for me." I put my cup down and play with a spoon. "I'm not sure I can give him that. I don't let people near me often, and I sure as hell don't need to let in someone that lives a thousand miles away."

She shrugs, and I think she gets it. Her usually perky face has a slightly tipped-down mouth, almost a frown. She has been so sweet to me without wanting anything. When I leave, I'll be leaving more than this town and Gunnar. I'll be leaving others that really seem to like me—the crazy, sometimes drunk me. I still feel Gunnar's hands all over me, ready to devour me, and I'm ready to let him do that.

I groan. "God, he's such an excellent kisser."

Liza Jane laughs loud and pops me on the shoulder. I lose my grip on my coffee cup and spill it all over the counter, making her laugh even louder.

"Ain't love grand?"

She did not say that. I'm not in love. But the more I think about it, there's nothing keeping me and Gunnar from having something casual while I'm here. He's not attached, and if it means getting more kisses from him, I am more than willing to consider it. No strings attached is not usually my thing, but if it involves him, I would definitely give it a shot.

CHAPTER TWENTY-SIX
Gunnar

Anytime I have girl troubles, I go to one place—straight to Jake. Not that he's an expert or anything, but I trust his advice. He and Liza know me better than anyone else. I don't even have to say much for him to pick up on the fact that I'm all messed up.

He sits at his desk in the cramped office located in the back of the hardware store. Dented filing cabinets line one wall, and a mini-fridge rests in the corner within easy reach of his desk. He enters purchase orders into a spreadsheet, while I perch on the edge of his desk, clicking his stapler.

He snatches it out of my hand and stares. "Out with it."

I focus on my hands, remembering what they were touching only a few minutes ago. "God, she's an excellent kisser."

Jake leans back in his chair and belts out a laugh. "Man, you got it bad."

"It doesn't matter. She's made it clear she'll be leaving soon. Why do I do this to myself?"

He abandons his accounting work and puts his feet up on his desk. "Because you haven't been laid in two years. Not since that redneck from Ocilla sent a bullet whizzing right past your left ear."

My jaw clenches. "Don't remind me."

"Or because it's been three years since Willow dumped you at the altar?"

The mere mention of her name makes bile rise up my throat. Willow and I grew up together and went off to college together. She was my first, and I thought she was the one. She left me for a bigwig real estate investor, and I took a downward spiral, landing in every honky-tonk in the South, trying to sex her face out of my mind. All that did was give me a huge case of regret and a stare-down with a shotgun from a redneck's boyfriend.

"Rehearsal. She left me at the rehearsal, not on the wedding day."

He holds his hands out. "Oh, my bad. Like that's any better. You didn't listen to me when I told you she was using you as her ticket out of this town. She knew her daddy didn't trust her to go off to college unless you were right there beside her, keeping watch over her. You were in looove." He draws out the word and makes kissy-face noises.

I roll my eyes. "No one likes a 'told you so.' But I know. You told me so. I get it."

"Or could it be that this sassy out-of-towner tight little package blazes into town and brings something in you back to life?" Jake drops his feet to the floor and leans over the desk to make sure I'm listening. "You think she's too good for you, don't you?"

I shake my head. "Nope." Suddenly a hangnail is way more interesting than this conversation. I should have ridden around in my squad car, talking to myself.

Jake pokes me in the side. "Let me tell you something, brother. No one is too good for you."

The door is flung open, and Liza walks in, holding two coffee cups. She kisses me on the cheek. "Sugar, I'm so sorry about that."

"Don't worry about it. Please don't tell anyone else."

Jake takes one of the coffee cups from Liza, and she sits in his lap. He stares at her. "What did you do this time?"

She bites her lip to hide her smile, but it overcomes her face. "I didn't mean to, but I walked in when he and Andie were in the middle of a huge lip-lock."

I groan. "Stop, Liza. It wasn't that bad... was it?"

She waggles her eyebrows at her husband. "Lord have mercy, I have never seen him all over somebody like that. I swear, if I was two minutes later, there would have been clothes flying everywhere. The health department would have shut down In A Jam in two shakes." She fans herself.

Jake chuckles, his big belly jiggling her. I shoot him the bird.

"You know I love you. I'm happy for you."

"Whatever." I check my watch. Time to cruise the streets in search of criminals.

"He was telling me Andie is too good for him," Jake says.

My mouth drops open. "I did not say that."

"You better not." Liza tosses her empty coffee cup in the trash then picks up a cigarette and lights it. "She's not. You are perfect for each other." She ruffles Jake's hair. "Like us."

He runs a hand under her T-shirt, making me cover my eyes. "Guys, please. I'm right here."

"I love to make him squirm," she says to Jake before looking back up at me. "I could tell you stories about your sister and my—"

"Stop. She's going to be leaving soon. I'll be here. End of story."

Liza holds out her hands as she takes in my crappy excuse. "Okay. Sure. Then why the hound-dog face?"

I stand and bang my head against the wall. With the whine of a teenager, I reply, "Because she's such an excellent kisser."

Jake laughs, and Liza jumps off his lap. She squeezes me around the waist. "See, you guys are perfect for each other. Those were her exact words about you." She waves and slips away to straighten up the plumbing aisle.

Hmm. Maybe Andie feels it too. Maybe she'll want to give us a chance, and she'll want to stay here. Maybe she'll love it here and want to help revitalize downtown. *Yeah. When pigs fly.*

In my crazy dream-like planning state, I forgot where I was.

Jake smirks. "Hey, Bruce," he says when I turn to leave.

I put my hands on my hips. "What?"

He makes kissy-face noises again. I flip him off and hear his cackles as I exit the hardware store. Andie feels it too. *Sweet.* Now I need to ever so slightly convince her to stay. And not for the town, but for me.

CHAPTER TWENTY-SEVEN
Andie

My fingers glide over the dozen Mason jars lined up like jam soldiers on my counter. They may be globs of sugar and fruit to other people, but to me, they are like my children. I'm proud of them and can't wait to present them at the county fair this weekend. It was Mrs. Cavanaugh's idea to use some leftover ribbon from an old set of curtains to dress up the jars, making them appear as though they are wearing gingham skirts tied with a rough cord. The hot glue only seared three of my fingers in the process, so I will count that as a win. I may not win the blue ribbon, but I consider myself a winner already. For the first time in my life, I'm proud of something I've accomplished.

The bell rings, and I jump five feet off the ground. It's Stanley. He's not who I was hoping for, but I pretend I'm not disappointed. My lips are still swollen from my make-out session with Gunnar, and I'm eager for more of that action, but Stanley is here for his muffins.

"Hey, Stan." I slide the Tupperware container toward him. "I think I'm getting better."

He chows down on a muffin, and his eyes roll back in his head. *Nice.* "Not bad, Andie. Not bad at all." With a mouthful of food, he says, "I've been thinking about what you said."

My eyes spring open. "To get you ready for the GED?"

A blush creeps up his neck. "If the offer still stands, I think I'd like to do it."

I bounce up and down. "You won't be sorry, and I won't tell a soul. It will be our little secret." I was hoping he would mention it, and in anticipation of his change of heart, I picked up some work-books and supplies at the office supply store. I hold up a finger. "Wait right here."

I zoom upstairs to get the supplies, and by the time I get back, he has devoured all of my muffins. I really must be getting better at bak-ing than I thought. After I fix us both glasses of sweet tea, I spread out all my school supplies. His hand glides over the workbook, and when he touches the word GED, his fingers retract, almost as if it's an involuntary response.

"I, uh..."

"You can do this. I'll help you."

He backs away from the counter. "It's too much."

I sling my hip out and put my hand on it. "Stanley Culpepper, how would you eat an elephant?"

"Uh, I wouldn't. I like venison."

I pat his shoulder. "You eat an elephant one bite at a time." I wave my hand over all the materials. "You tackle this one problem at a time. Let's start with addition."

"If you say so." Poor guy. By the way he stares at the workbook, I get the sense that he has no confidence in his abilities to pass.

I pull my phone out of my pocket, find a Southern rock station, and crank it to an ear-bleeding level. He bops his head to Lynryd Sknyrd, and seeing him relax makes me happy, so happy that I even sing along to "Sweet Home Alabama."

After thirty minutes of reminding Stanley that whatever he does on the left side of the equation, he has to do to the right, I think it clicks. He relates it to dipping, which makes me shudder, but what-ever works for him works for me.

"See, Andie, if I put my Skoal on the right side of my gum, the next time, I have to put it on my left. It helps with the buzz."

I almost throw up in my mouth. "I believe you. Next step: if Mark purchased X T-shirts at six dollars apiece and Y sweaters at twenty dollars apiece, which expression represents the total value of the purchases? The key word here is..."

He cringes. "And?"

I high-five him. "Yes. The key word is 'and.' So which one of the choices is correct?"

He studies the question and the four choices I've written on the dry-erase board. "Hmm. I think I start with putting my plus sign here for the 'and.'" I encourage him to continue. "So that eliminates A and C because they have a minus sign."

My smile gets bigger. In one lesson, he has already learned how to beat the system by eliminating the obvious wrong choices, which is a positive sign that he's a better problem-solver than he thinks. "X goes with six, and Y goes with twenty, so it has to be B."

I do a whip and nae-nae only for him. "Woo-hoo. Watch me whip. Now watch me nae-nae." I freeze, hoping he didn't think anything more of that than an expression of excitement for his correct answer.

Stanley covers his eyes with his hands. "I think I'm blind."

"I'm not that bad of a dancer. Anyway, you are way smarter than you've let yourself believe."

He lets out a yawn, which makes me yawn. "We better call it a night. I got the big county fair this weekend."

I snap my finger. "Do you want to sample my jam? You know, give me an honest opinion? I think I've got Granny's recipe nailed."

"Yeah. I've got room."

I pull out the lone Mason jar that I kept back for myself and attempt to pry it open. I tug and tug, but it's not going to open.

Stanley holds out his hand for me to give him the jar. "It is bull strong and pig tight, isn't it?"

"Uh, if you say so."

With ease, he turns the lid, and the loud popping sound tells me I sealed it properly. *Yay for me.* I pull out one lone biscuit left from this morning and place it on a plate. I spoon out some of my jam onto the biscuit and scoot the plate in front of Stanley.

"Be honest. That's the only way I can learn."

He takes a bite and swallows but doesn't say anything.

"Oh no. What did I do? I thought this time it was better."

"It's dang good, Andie."

I flop onto the stool next to him. "Oh, thank the Lord. So you like it?"

He shoves the rest of the biscuit into his mouth. "Tastes pretty much like Mary Grace's."

I clutch my chest. "Aww. Thanks, Stanley. That means so much." If it passes the Cavanaugh and the Stanley test, I must be on to something.

"It's got a kick like hers did. What did you use?"

"Nope. It's Granny's secret recipe. Not going to tell."

He slides off the stool, dusts crumbs onto the floor like he always does, and finishes off his iced tea. "Thanks, Andie. See you at the fair?"

"Wish me luck."

He stops before exiting and clears his throat. Without turning to face me, he says, "I appreciate you."

Aww.

He leaves, and I pull down the shade and lock the door. In the dead quiet store, I collect all the study supplies and nae-nae all the way up the stairs. "Woo-hoo. I'm going to win."

Even if I don't, I tried my best. I never thought I would even care about impressing a bunch of hillbillies, but it is important to me that they know I cared about my grandmother and her traditions. It doesn't change my mind

CHAPTER TWENTY-EIGHT
Andie

So this is a county fair. The town square, which is usually a vacant plot of dried grass, has been converted into a miniature fairground, and it's an easy walk from my shop. All I have to do is follow my nose, and in no time, I'm in the middle of a small-town festival. I never knew these kinds of things actually existed, but here I am, surrounded by inflatable bouncy houses, a dunking booth, and an honest-to-God food stand that offers fried pickles and funnel cakes. I've always thought "funnel cake" was an odd name for a pastry. It's not in the shape of a cone at all. I might have to try one later.

At least I'm not overdressed for the occasion. My simple yellow sundress and low-heeled strappy sandals don't make me stick out like a sore thumb. My wicker basket filled with jars of jam swings from my elbow. I'm a woman on a mission to fit in. *Granny, you'd be proud of me.*

I walk up to an elderly man sitting under a green canopy. Next to him is a sign that reads Contestant Registration. I guess I'm in the right place.

The elderly man smiles. "Let me guess. Jam contestant." He must be psychic.

"That's right. This is for my grandmother."

He slides a clipboard over to me, and I register my strawberry jam, leaving out the part about it being spiked.

"The jam contest will be at five o'clock at booth number three." He points in the direction of the line of booths with banners advertising various items and events like food, country crafts, 4-H, and

Girl Scouts. "It's behind the petting zoo and before the Tilt-A-Whirl ride."

I glance down at my watch, noticing it's only midafternoon. "Thank you, sir."

In no hurry to get to booth number three, I take in the sights and smells of the fair. Children rush past me toward one of the bouncy houses. To my left, men try to impress their ladies by ringing a bell with a sledgehammer. And my nose is overwhelmed by the smell of fried everything. The first day I got here, this smell would have made me throw up, but now I want to try everything, including the fried pickles. But first, I have to try one of those funnel cakes. They are only a dollar fifty. *What a bargain!*

Gunnar's niece runs up to me. Her dark hair falls past her shoulders in two long braids. In one hand, she holds an ice cream cone, and with the other, she tugs on the hem of my sundress.

I grin down at her. "Well, hello there."

She smiles, and a dimple pops out. "You're Miss Andie, aren't you?"

I bend down so I can see into her pretty blue eyes. "You know my name. You're Lily, correct?"

She nods as she takes a lick from her cone and holds it out for me to have a turn. In my old life, I would never have shared food, especially with a kid who probably has more germs than the CDC can categorize. But here, it would seem rude not to, so I take a lick and taste homemade peach.

"Yummy. Thank you for sharing your ice cream with me. That is so sweet of you."

She offers me another lick, which I oblige.

"Where's your mother?"

She shrugs and takes another lick. "She's working the dunking booth. Uncle G is supposed to be watching me."

"Where is your Uncle G?"

She takes another lick. "Don't know."

I hold out my hand for her to take. "Why don't we find him together?" *Yes, let's find that hot uncle of yours.*

"Uncle G talks about you all the time."

A warm sensation flows from my chest down to my toes.

"He uses the word captivating a lot. Not sure what that means, but it doesn't sound fun to be captured."

I bite my lip and watch this adorable child chasing her melting ice cream with her tongue. I comb the crowd for Gunnar. He can't be far. He's a policeman. He has to be searching for her. I'm about to give up and find Lily's mother, when I see a flustered Gunnar in the distance. He runs his hands through his hair as he darts around, hunting for Lily. Even with armpit sweat stains and disheveled hair, he's still as sexy as sin.

I point at him. "I think we found him."

Lily drops my hand and runs his way. His terrified expression turns to complete relief upon seeing her. He scoops her up and swings her around. She holds her ice cream out for him to lick. Now all three of us have swapped spit. She points at me, and when my eyes meet his, he goes from relief to a full-on smile.

I walk to him, and he drinks me in from head to toe. That look is yummier than the ice cream.

Without losing eye contact with me, he asks Lily, "Where did you run off to?"

"I wanted to see the bunnies."

He grins at me then turns his attention back to his niece and tickles her stomach. "Your mama would have skinned me alive if I lost you again. You wouldn't want that, would you?"

She pouts, and my heart melts for her. "No, but I found your captivating friend."

I cover my mouth to keep from laughing.

Gunnar's face turns as red as a sunburn. "I see that."

"Lily shared her ice cream with me. It was delicious." Maybe after she's safely returned to her mother, Gunnar and I can share other things, in private.

Lily holds her cone out for me again. I refuse this time.

"She likes to scare the 'you know what' out of me. Her mother's over there." He motions with his head to the dunking booth.

Some large guy sits on the bench above the cold water, waiting to be submerged. On such a hot day, that wouldn't be a terrible thing.

"My guess is you're not in the mood to be in the doghouse with her."

He sucks in a breath through his teeth. "Exactly, and she might sic her fireman husband on me." He points at the guy manning the Ferris wheel. The man is built like a tank.

I cringe. "I'm glad it all worked out."

"Uncle G, let's go see the bunnies."

He tickles her again before his eyes rake over me one more time. "We must see bunnies. Good luck today."

Well, crud. I've been bested by bunnies. "Thanks." My grip on the basket tightens. I really am proud of what I've done, and I'm shocked that my grandmother gave me such an interesting, ironic secret.

With my shoulders back, I put on a happy face and practically skip toward the taste-testing booth.

The other nurse that works with Regina stomps toward me, her red hair whipping around her face. She's no bigger than me, so when she stops in front of me, we are eye to eye. Her resting bitch face doesn't do anything for her.

Out of the corner of my eye, Gunnar race-walks toward me, flailing his arms.

The redhead pokes me on the arm, almost impaling me with an acrylic nail. "Excuse me. Are you Andie?"

"Yes." Of course she knows who I am, but something in her tone tells me this is not going to end well.

She rears back and slaps me so hard across the face, I fall to the ground, landing on my knees and dropping my basket full of jam jars.

"Ow!"

Gunnar grabs her arm before she hits me again. "Jolene, what are you doing?"

She tries to wriggle free, but he has a viselike grip on her arm as he holds out his other hand to help me up. Lily picks up the jam jars and puts them back in my basket. I examine the jars to make sure they are still intact. Jolene should be glad they survived because I was ready to go all Southie on her. The woman jerks away from Gunnar and moves toward me, but he blocks her path.

She points at me over his shoulder. "That's for messing with my man."

Ugh. Girl drama. I'm not messing with her man. But I would like to be messing with the man holding her back from me.

I rub my cheek. *Damn!* I think I'm going to have a bruise from her slap. I'm grateful she didn't punch me. She may be petite, but she packs a mean punch. A small crowd has formed around us, and some people have their phones out to take pictures. That's peachy. I'll be the topic of someone else's blog by tonight.

Jolene takes a deep breath, jerks away from Gunnar's grasp, and holds her hands out in surrender. I hope that means she's done using violence.

"Have you been spending time with Stan?"

I'm sure Jolene has a sweet side, but right now, I'm not seeing the attraction. It's either that, or Stanley is used to her craziness.

"Yes, but you need to have a little more faith in your boyfriend."

Jolene rears back to take another swing at me. I cover my face, but there's no contact. When I peek through my fingers, I catch Gunnar wrestling with her.

Jolene backs away from us. When she gets to the Tilt-A-Whirl, she yells, "You Yankee bitch better leave my man alone."

"Bring it," I yell back.

Gunnar touches my cheek, and I grimace.

"Thanks for protecting me, but I had it all under control. In my wildest dreams, I never imagined I'd be in a Southern catfight."

Gunnar scans the crowd. "It's over, folks. Nothing to worry about."

The crowd filters away as though it's just another day at the fair.

Gunnar raises an eyebrow. "You know she's Willow's—"

"I know, and I don't care. People need to mind their own business."

"You and Stan?"

I rub my face. "It's not what you think."

He wags his head and cracks a grin. "I'm not sure what to think."

"I promise it doesn't involve any physical contact."

His eyes burn into me, and I can't peel my gaze away from his. He leans close to my ear and whispers, "I'd like some physical contact later." His breath tickles my neck, and a shiver runs down my spine.

"I'll see if I can make it happen." Oh, it's on. If it weren't for a little girl and a jam contest, I would drag him back to my shop right now. We could give the Jacksons something really juicy to write about.

His eyes sparkle, and a wide grin spreads across his face.

Lily tugs on his arm. "Come on, Uncle G. The bunnies."

My eyes dance. "The bunnies."

Gunnar waves as the four-year-old girl takes control of him and leads him away from me.

Sigh.

CHAPTER TWENTY-NINE
Gunnar

B unnies, bunnies everywhere. Lily almost had me talked into buying her one when Liza Jane saved the day. She's decked out in a prairie miniskirt, cowboy hat, and boots. On any other person, it would look ridiculous, but Liza pulls it off. She knows her best friend, my sister, well enough to know that I would be in the dog-house permanently if Lily came home with any critter that would ul-timately be one more thing for Faith to take care of.

Lily walks between Liza and me, holding our hands as we walk through the middle of the town square. Liza saved the day by re-membering the hand sanitizer. The germs from the bunnies, goats, and every other living creature don't need to stay on her hands, espe-cially now that she's making a beeline to the cotton candy machine. Nowhere in the rules did Faith mention a maximum amount of sugar, so cotton candy it is.

Liza waves me off when I pull out my wallet for the tenth time this afternoon. "I'll get this one."

My eyes roam the crowd, hoping to catch a glimpse of a certain someone in a yellow sundress. She could be anywhere by now. I don't see any jars of jam on the ground, so at least Jolene's not bothering her anymore. Hopefully, she's occupied with Stan and has forgotten all about Andie. The band starts playing a country line dance song, which is not my thing. Liza and Lily run back to me. Lily is pulling sticky pieces of pink cotton candy off the cone and shoving it in her face. She's going to be a gooey mess in five minutes flat. I'm glad I don't have to bathe her tonight.

Liza points at the band. "That's my jam." She leans down to Lily and whispers something in her ear, making my niece snicker. Liza kisses Lily on the cheek and rushes onto the dance floor, holding her cowboy hat on her head with one hand while she whistles with two fingers of the other. *Crazy girl.*

I watch Liza as she dances. She waves me over to join her, but I refuse. I would rather keep scanning the crowd to see if I can find Andie.

And for the second time in one afternoon, Lily has scooted out of my eyesight. My sister is never going to let me watch her ever again. Finally, I spot Lily hugging Andie's legs next to the ring-toss game. *Thank God.* Andie's arm cradles Lily's head as she strokes her hair. She leans down to talk to Lily, and her face displays a shocked but happy expression. She searches the crowd, and when she finds me, her smile widens.

They meet me halfway.

"Tell your Uncle G that I would love to," Andie says to my niece.

I can read a whole lot into that open statement, but we are in public, and there are little ears ready to pick up on every word said. "Lily, what did you say to her?"

"That you wanted to dance with her."

It's either an intense, five-second sunburn or embarrassment that creeps up my neck. Andie throws her hands up in surrender. Lily runs off again before I can catch her, but Liza snags her then waves at us and mouths, "Go for it." I stare at my boots before daring to look at Andie.

"Smithville should be called the matchmaker capital of the world," Andie says.

"I guess so. Why don't we get hitched so we can get some peace?"

Her eyes get big.

"I'm kidding." Or maybe I'm not.

She laughs. "Of course."

I turn in a circle. "I don't see broken jars anywhere. Is it safe to say the jars safely made it to the contest booth?"

Andie rolls her eyes. "Yes, Officer. Every single one of them."

I hold out a hand, and when her fingers intertwine with mine, I forget what song the band is playing. I slide one arm around her waist and hold on to her hand with my other hand while I lead her in this two-step song. I think I can make my clumsy feet move to this beat.

"I don't know how to do this." Her soft voice trembles.

I lean into her and whisper, "I've got you. Easier than making jam."

She giggles in my ear, and now I'm worried she's going to have to hold me up. Her free hand holds firmly to my shoulder as we step, step, step-step over and over around the dance floor. After a few rounds, she gets the hang of it and relaxes in my arms. I imagine how I would really like to hold her. If we weren't surrounded by ninety-five percent of the townsfolk, we might get arrested for a public display of affection. If anyone is gawking or blogging about us dancing, I really don't care.

The song ends, and I swing her out and back into me. Her chest smashes into mine, and her eyes are heavy lidded. I lean down to kiss her right as the band starts up with an old Southern rock song.

Her face lights up as she jumps up and down. "I know this one." She dances around me and sings the lyrics to the Allman Brothers song, "Ramblin' Man."

I put my fingers in my ears as she boogies around me, singing.

"I love this song!" she yells over the music.

"I can tell, but we have laws against this kind of indecency."

She gasps and swats at my arm. I pull her close again, and she doesn't resist. I swing her around, and every time her face is close to mine, her grin gets bigger. When the song is over—and I'm not complaining that those Allman Brothers know how to write super-long songs—I spin her around. Her sundress fans out to show her muscular thighs.

Have mercy.

Those words could be Andie's anthem. I don't think I will understand when she leaves.

Over the loudspeaker, Fred Calhoun makes the announcement that the jam contest will start in five minutes. Andie bounces in my arms, making her breasts brush up against my forearm. She really shouldn't do that unless she wants my lips permanently attached to hers.

"It's time! Do you think I'll win?"

She's gone from hating this place and despising everything Southern to actually wanting to win this silly jam contest. I think we're rubbing off on her.

"You have as much chance as anyone." For her sake, I hope so, even though it will be highly unlikely given the fact that Mrs. Cavanaugh teases her so much about how bad her attempts have been.

She darts toward the jam booth then stops and turns around, waving for me to come with her. I freeze. My focus is on the splash of platinum-blond hair I thought I saw slicing in and out of the crowd. I must be hallucinating. I hope to God I am.

"Aren't you coming?"

I snap out of my confusion. "I can't miss this."

Watching her weave through the crowd to get to the front reminds me of Lily on Christmas morning. She actually is eager to know how well she did. I hope even an honorable mention is enough to keep the Jackson sisters off her tail for a bit. They stand in the front row, cell phones in hand, ready to capture the moment as it happens. They would like nothing more than for Andie to fail. If her jam is terrible, it might give Andie another reason to leave after her required time here is up.

Even if Andie doesn't win the blue ribbon, I want her to do well because she wants to do well. She nibbles on a fingernail, waiting on the judges to announce their decision. One by one, the judges taste each entry, bobbing their heads up and down as they write notes. Andie fidgets as she waits. I stand behind her and put my hands on her hips. She slides her fingers through mine and squeezes.

As sappy as it sounds, I whisper in her ear, "You're the sweetest thing I'll ever taste."

She squeezes my hands tighter and rotates her face enough to give me a quick peck on the cheek. I don't think she cares if the Jackson sisters catch it on film. I know I don't care. Maybe it will give them something to blog about. Their eyes and phones are focused on the judges, anyway.

While the judges are in a huddle, making their decision, my eyes roam the crowd in hopes the platinum-blond hair was only in my imagination. Willow can't be here. She hates this town and most everyone in it, even her family. There's no reason for her to come back, especially after all this time, unless Jo dropped some hints to pique her interest.

The judges agree with one another. Fred Calhoun holds up the blue ribbon and takes the microphone. "This year's blue ribbon goes to..."

Andie crosses her fingers and closes her eyes.

"Andie Carson for her Saving Grace Strawberry Jam."

CHAPTER THIRTY
Andie

He said my name! My jaw is on the ground next to the discarded funnel cake and cigarette butts. Everyone around me claps and whistles for me.

Gunnar squeezes my shoulders and says over the crowd, "Go get your ribbon." He gives me a slight shove to make my feet move.

When I get up to the booth, I turn around and notice all the people cheering. Liza and Jake are right in front, woo-hooing for me. Gunnar's sister and niece stand next to him. Lily jumps up and down and waves my way. Even the Jackson sisters clap, and to my surprise, they high-five each other. Of course, they pull out their phones to take pictures of me. I'm sure those photos have me with a huge, face-covering grin. *Granny, I did it!*

When Mr. Calhoun hands me my blue ribbon, my hands tremble so much, it slips out of my hand and floats to the ground. Lily picks it up and hands it to me.

Mr. Calhoun pats me on the back. "Nice job, Miss Carson. Your grandmother would be proud."

A tear escapes my eye, and I bat it away before anyone can see it. "Thank you so much." I hold up the blue ribbon for all to see, and Jake whistles again. I take a bow. Never in my wildest dreams did I ever think I would win something like this, much less be ecstatic about it.

"Now, folks, if you'd like to taste test Andie's jam, please stick around. She'll have more in her shop to buy. Isn't that right?"

I shrug. "I guess so." All it takes is for one person to hate it for my excitement to dwindle.

The Jackson sisters almost knock me over, getting in line to try my jam. Oh, this isn't going to end well.

"I wouldn't eat too much. You know, lots of carbs on a hot day... you know." *Crap.* Surely they can't get drunk off jam. I didn't use that much, and the simmering had to burn off some of the alcohol. I should have tried it out on myself to check the alcohol-tolerance level.

The Jackson sisters don't listen, and neither do all the other blue hairs in the county. Dang, there are a lot of old people in this town. I try to make eye contact with Gunnar, but he's in a powwow with his sister, Faith, and Liza Jane. Liza's arms flail around, and Faith nibbles on a fingernail as she scans the crowd. They have been all grins and giggles up until now. I wonder what has them all in a tizzy.

Gunnar rakes a hand over his face. When our eyes meet, the stress leaves his body. He walks toward me, smiling. I hold out the ribbon as if he didn't see me win it, and he busts out a huge grin. "I'm impressed."

"So am I." I check out all the old folks gobbling up my jam. "I wish they wouldn't eat so much."

He takes my hand. "Relax and enjoy the day. I think you made some friends today."

I cringe while I watch the Jackson sisters eat a jar of jam all by themselves. "Oh, I don't know about that."

"When do I get to try some?"

"Uh... maybe later."

Sarah Jackson runs up to me.

Oh dear, here it comes.

Her sister is right on her tail.

"Andie, I need to talk to you about this jam."

I hold my hands out. "Hey, I did my best, and I'm sorry if it's not like Granny's."

She grabs me by the arm, and dang if she doesn't have a tight grip. "You made it precisely like Mary Grace. She'd be so proud. We must have more. We miss her jam so much."

Hmm. I think I'm getting the picture now. Maybe they were the source of Granny's covert booze in an otherwise dry county.

"Yes, we miss her jam... and her, of course."

"Thank you. I miss her too." That's so odd considering I didn't know her very well. But I feel her presence around me, and I know we would have gotten along really well had Mama not told me she'd passed away years ago. Maybe that's why she kept me away from Smithville and told me all those mean things about her very own mother.

"Do you have some more at the shop?"

When I say no, they pout like two five-year-olds.

"We wanted to sell some at the church bake sale next Sunday."

If I can get in cahoots with the Jacksons, I might be able to fulfill the "fitting in" requirement of Granny's will. It might be harder than making jam, so if I have to play nice with the Jacksons, I'll do it.

"Would you be willing to make it a charitable donation since it's a worthy cause?"

Time to lay on the charm and pull out whatever Southern accent I can. "Anything for the church. Stop by and get all you want on Monday."

The Jackson sisters beam at each other. "That would be perfect," one of the sisters says. I can't ever keep them straight.

The other one waves. "See you on Monday."

"You mean Sunday. At church, right?"

She waves me off. "Yes, of course. You can sit with us if you want."

I turn to Gunnar. His jaw is on the ground. "You certainly made a favorable impression on them. I never thought that would happen."

I shrug. "What can I say? I'm an acquired taste."

He points to the Jackson sisters, who are fighting over a jar of jam with another blue hair. "I think the holy trinity might have to change their opinion of you after today."

"After a keg, I mean a jar or two, they may be sick."

He cocks his head sideways as the band cranks up again.

I'm shocked that I know another Southern rock song. "Oh my God. It's 'Champagne Jam.' So perfect."

"You know this song? From the Atlanta Rhythm Section?"

"Shocker, huh?" One thing my mother bored into my head was Southern rock music.

Gunnar slides his arm around my shoulder. "You're full of surprises."

Before I can stop myself, I slip my arm around his waist. I fit right at his side as if I were made for him.

He canvases the crowd, and his spine stiffens. Then he jerks his head toward the photo booth. "Want to preserve the moment? Get it? *Preserve* the moment."

I roll my eyes. His jam humor is so corny but totally adorable. He escorts me to the booth and shoves some dollar bills into the machine before he scans the crowd again.

Behind the curtain, he places me on his lap, and his hands slide up and down my thighs. I can't help but lace my fingers through his. "Are we going to take pictures or make out?"

He kisses my neck. "Can't we do both?"

I gasp as he kisses my neck. The camera's flash goes off. I take his face in my hands, turn it toward the camera, and make a duck face. Then I cross my eyes and hold up my blue ribbon. *Flash*. Next Gunnar and I stare at each other with our foreheads touching, and my heart races. *Flash*. He holds my face and kisses me on the lips. *Flash*. The kiss deepens, and I forget where we are until a kid pulls back the curtain to interrupt our kissing booth.

"Sorry." I grab Gunnar's hand and scoot out of the way so the kid can use the booth for its intended purpose. We wait outside the booth for our pictures to be developed, staring at each other as though we're both hatching a plan to finish what we started. When the pictures drop from the slot, we both grab for the strip of photos, but I'm faster.

"Hey now, it was my dollar," he says.

With a pouty face, I hand over the photos.

He groans. "Oh, all right."

He takes out his key chain with a Leatherman tool dangling from it. Then he cuts the strip of photos in half, handing me two photos and keeping two for him. I get the neck-kiss and duck-face photos. He gets the forehead-stare and kiss photos.

"Satisfied?" he asks.

I grab him around the neck and give him a big hug. He slides his arms around me and holds me tight.

"Very satisfied."

He has no idea how satisfied I am, and before I lose my nerve, I ask, "Go out with me?"

He makes a face as though he's mulling over his answer before he kisses me on the cheek. "I'd like that."

Whew.

A super-tall, model-perfect blond girl glowers at us from across the field. Her arms are crossed, and she looks at me as if I stole her blue ribbon. Maybe she needs to try some of my jam. I let Gunnar go, and when he turns around to see her, his entire body stiffens. The perky blonde cocks her head to the side, sending a nonverbal message our way that I'm clearly not understanding.

"You okay?" I ask Gunnar.

He closes his eyes and nods. When he opens his eyes again, he glares at the blonde. Then when his eyes meet mine, his expression softens. Oh, that must be Willow, and I feel as if I've been caught with my hand in the cookie jar. Too bad. I'm still taking the cookie.

He takes my hand. "Hungry?"

"Sure."

I'm not the smartest person in the world, but something tells me I'm not going to like Willow being back in town. Even though I'm not sure what I mean to Gunnar, I don't want to lose him, and I can't believe I'm admitting that to myself. He may have never been mine to lose. The lyrics to the next song ring true. "That old flame may not be stronger, but it's been burning longer than any spark I might have started in your eyes."

CHAPTER THIRTY-ONE
Gunnar

*S*on of a bitch. She's back in town. I haven't seen hide nor hair of her in three damn years, and she shows up right when I've finally let myself move on. I worked through all the stages of grief: shock, denial, depression, anger, chase-every-skirt-in-the-county phase, and finally acceptance. I'm over her. My molars will be ground into powder before the night is over.

Seeing her now makes me question what I ever saw in her. Her white-blond hair is even more shocking than before, and it matches her cold personality. As usual, she has to make sure she's noticed by everyone. The way she carries herself, so in control as if she's on the prowl, makes me want to hurl. No matter which direction Andie and I walk through the town square, Willow appears, watching our every move. She has got stalking down to a science.

I found someone that makes me happy. Andie doesn't try to change me even though I would like to change one part of her. I want her to stay. But I can't make her stay any more than I could make Willow.

Andie and I eat corn dogs while we walk through the fairground, and I hope we don't run into Willow. Liza Jane and Faith are spitting mad she showed up, so I don't think Willow has the nerve to cross their paths tonight. Liza texted Mel and put her on high alert, so with all those women against Willow, I don't think she will confront me tonight. She'll want me to come to her. It's a power play, one that I'm not going to comply with. Except she knows everything about me. I thought my secrets left when she did. This is not the best time to air dirty laundry.

"You okay?" Andie asks, bumping me with her hip. She chases the mustard dripping off her corn dog with her tongue. *Damn.* She has no idea how sexy that is.

"Yeah, sure. Long day." *And going to get longer.*

"Great. I wanted to make sure you didn't miss this." She holds out her blue ribbon, and her eyebrows bounce up and down. "Huh? What do you think? Not bad for a Yankee." She is so adorable.

"You're very proud, aren't you?"

"Heck yeah. I worked my tail off trying to figure it out."

I stare into her eyes. "I'm proud of you too."

She stands on her tiptoes, her hands grabbing my bicep for balance. "Can you keep a secret?" she whispers.

"Sure."

She peers around then places her mouth so close to my ear, I can feel her lips moving against my earlobe. "That jam has booze in it."

My head snaps around, and we are nose to nose. She holds out her hands in defense.

"I followed Granny's recipe to a T. I promise. And I only had a smidgen for a taste test. Aren't you proud of me?

A chuckle bursts up my throat. No wonder all the old folks loved Miss Mary Grace's jam. Andie's eyelashes tickle my nose when she flutters them.

"Yes, I am, and I guess that special ingredient will be our little secret." I take in the dancing grannies. "They seem to like it."

Mayor Duncan and Tom Harding wave to me as they greet each person that walks past them. The portly and balding mayor may technically be the head of the town, but Tom Harding really runs the place. He's younger, and with his easy grin and orange-red hair, people want to please him.

I take Andie by the hand. "There are some people I want you to meet."

Both men smile as we approach.

"Hey Gunnar," Mayor says.

"Mayor. I wanted you to meet Andie Carson, Miss Mary Grace's granddaughter."

"Pleasure to meet you."

The tall ginger grins down at her. "I'm Tom Harding."

Andie cuts her eyes toward me. "Nice to meet you. You should stop by the shop sometime."

Tom points at her blue ribbon. "Congratulations."

She almost bounces. "Thanks. This has been the best day."

"I'm sure your grandmother would have been very proud."

She swallows. "I hope so."

The mayor pats my shoulder. "You two kids have fun."

As they walk away, they are surrounded by townspeople asking them if the rumors about a developer wanting to buy up all the shops on Main Street are true. I don't want to think about that right now. Tonight is all about Andie.

She dances around me in a circle. At every turn, she makes sure I get a full view of her blue ribbon. I snatch it away and run toward the Ferris wheel, where Jake is the operator. That should scare the bejesus out of me, but I trust him.

Andie grabs for her ribbon. "Hey, you stealer. Where's a cop when you need one?"

Jake fist-bumps me as he holds the bucket open for Andie to step in. While she is securing her blue ribbon so it doesn't fall out, I slip Jake a wad of cash and wink at him. Sometimes, no words are necessary.

I jump into the bucket, and it swings forward and backward, making Andie latch onto my arm as if her life depends on it. As soon as Jake moves the lever, we start our way up to the top. Andie lets out a screech.

On our way down on the other side, she squeals, "It took my breath away." When we start back up, she says, "Did I ever tell you I'm afraid of heights?" Her grip on my arm is so tight, I may never be able to use my gun again.

"It's a little late for that information. We're perfectly safe."

I lean over to see how high we are. Below us, lights strung up from booth to booth twinkle in the night. Couples still sway back and forth on the dance floor to country music, and children continue to stuff themselves with every fried food imaginable. I sure hope I don't drop my corn dog on somebody's head. I take one fast scan of the crowd in hopes that Willow isn't staring up at us. I want this to be a special moment for Andie and me, one that will help her decide to stay.

"Yeah, perfectly safe," Andie says nervously. "It's a fair ride that was assembled yesterday by a bunch of Joe Dirts."

I laugh and put my arm around her neck, pulling her close. She fits next to my side as if she's made for that spot. Her hand rests on my thigh on the way up, and on the way down, she squeezes. Then the ride stops, hanging us in midair.

She grabs on to my arm. "What's happening? Are we stuck?"

I point at the ground. "Jake's letting people off."

"Oh." That satisfies her, and little by little, we get closer to the ground. When all other riders are off and it's our turn, Andie starts to stand up. I grab her arm, making her sit back down. Jake turns the crank and sends us back up to the top.

She gasps. "This is bad."

I wink. "Wait. Trust me."

"What did you do?"

She crosses her arms, then a small boom, boom, boom sounds across the field. Fireworks light up the dark sky. They are right above our heads. Reds, blues, and greens explode everywhere, and we're so high up, it feels as if we are part of the show. Later, I'll have to thank Liza for the suggestion because this is pretty awesome.

"Oh, Gunnar. This is so pretty." She sinks into me, and I play with her hair as she continues to point each one out. "Did you see that one? So pretty." Her face glows with the colors of the fireworks, but her eyes light up her face. She turns to back to me. "Can you keep another secret?"

I nod.

She looks at all the townspeople on the ground staring up at the fireworks then back at me. "I kind of like it here. Like... a lot."

That's music to my ears. I kiss her nose. "Maybe you can buy the Ferris wheel."

She giggles.

I turn away from her beautiful face and try to focus on the fireworks, because if I gaze too long into her eyes, I might say things I don't want to take back.

She takes my face in her hands, forcing me to look at her. "I like the scenery."

She blushes, and my heart melts. I know I'm falling for her. She kisses me on the lips softly then again with more passion. I wrap my arms around her waist and deepen the kiss. When I pull her onto my lap, the bucket swings, making her squeak.

"I've got you, sugar. I won't let go. I promise."

There goes my mouth, saying things I don't regret. My hands slide under the straps of her sundress. I kiss her shoulders and neck. She lays her head back, allowing me more room to kiss her neck.

"Oh, Gunnar."

"You taste so sweet. Now about that date you asked for."

"Name the day."

We're nose to nose, and I stare into her eyes. I want her to know I'm dead serious. "I want lots of dates. Lots of days." My hand roams down her dress, and right when I roam under it to feel her creamy thigh, Jake starts our decent. I growl, making Andie giggle. "To be continued?" I ask, hoping I know the answer.

Her head nods up and down, making her look like a human version of a bobblehead. *What a ride.*

If I had my way, we would continue as soon as our feet hit the ground, but as I expected, Willow is waiting for me, leaning up against the photo booth, with her arms crossed over her chest. I don't want her to ruin my life again, so after walking Andie back to her home with my shadow not very far away, I make up a lame excuse about having to check in at work. I have to clarify to Willow that it's over between us and that she has no right to stalk me like a predator. She won't approach me with so many of my friends around. That's not her style because she knows they would be all over her. So I'll have to do what she expects me to do—go to the lake. If I want her gone, I need to do this sooner rather than later.

Before I leave Andie, I give her a spine-tingling "I need you more than air" kiss, leaving us both out of breath as my shadow throws daggers with her eyes.

CHAPTER THIRTY-TWO
Gunnar

The lake at night clears my head like nothing else. The water lapping at my feet, the sun setting, and a Boston lager sliding down my throat are precisely what I need. Willow's back in town. Coincidence? Hardly. Everything she does is calculated, right down to the last "I can't marry you." Thinking about that night almost makes my beer rise back up in my throat. She crushed me. She changed me into a person that didn't even resemble me at all: a cold, take-what-I-want prick. Thank God I came to my senses and left those days behind me.

Many times, I wondered what I would do when I saw her again. Her parents still live in Smithville, so I knew she would have to come visit eventually. Every time they see me around town, I sense the bile churning up my throat again. They still blame me for them wasting fifteen grand on a no-show wedding.

My phone buzzes in my pocket. If it's Willow, I may throw my phone in the lake. But it's only Tinsley. "Hey, man."

"How's our girl doing?"

Our girl? She's mine. All mine. "She won a blue ribbon for her jam."

Tinsley's booming laughter bellows out of my phone. He yells at someone. "Hey, Andie won a blue ribbon." I hear a few "woo-hoos" come through the phone. "That's awesome. So is she, uh, staying out of trouble?"

I close my eyes and think back to the night of her relapse, which was the same night of one fantastic kiss. "She's great. I'm real proud of her."

202

"That's what I want to hear. So, you keeping your hands off of her?" His chuckle tells me he's kidding with me.

"Nope."

"Ha. She's a delightful girl."

I drag a stick through the sand. "Yes, she is. She's even said she likes it here."

"Wow. Didn't see that one coming."

"Yeah. I don't want to read too much into it, but I kind of hope she sticks around, you know, for the long haul. She's starting to grow on me, if you know what I mean."

A silent moment passes before he responds. "I wish I could help you out there, but I can't get a good read off of her the few times I've talked to her. But hey, if she doesn't, I've got a buddy at the Boston University Police Department. It's kind of like a small town within a big city. You up for that?"

I shake my head, knowing good and well he can't see me. "Thanks, but I like it here."

"Man, I gotta go. Tell Andie I said hello and to behave."

"Will do."

I stuff my phone in my back pocket and take in the silence for a few minutes before I smell that signature over-the-top lavender perfume.

Willow sits down beside me in the sand. "Hey, Gunnar."

"Hey, Wills. I'd like to say 'Nice to see you,' but my mama taught me not to lie."

She chuckles under her breath. "I guess I deserved that."

"And then some." I take a swig from my beer bottle. "You're on private property. *My* property." Even though I knew she would be here, I have to get one dig in for old times' sake. If she wants to reminisce, she should go on the public side of the lake.

"Ouch."

We sit in silence, listening to a boat putter pass in the distance.

"You have something on your mind? Spit it out, then please leave."

She hugs her knees to her chest and shivers. "It's cold out here by the water."

Maybe she should wear something besides a skimpy top. And for God's sake, she could put on a bra. This isn't her first time at the lake at night, for crying out loud.

I groan and shrug out of my jacket, knowing I'm playing right into her plan. I place it around her shoulders, and her fingers graze mine when she latches on to the collar. I snatch my hand away before I feel something. She snuggles into my jacket and inhales my aroma. I think I'll have to burn it to get out her scent and the memory of her in it.

"What brings you back to Smithville?"

"Family business, and I miss you."

I snort and almost choke on my beer. "I doubt that. You've got Brad or Tad, or what was the last one's name? Tristan? Seriously, why didn't you throw a Fabio in the mix while you're at it?"

She throws her hands out to stop me. "Okay, I can see one of us still lives in the past."

"Don't you get all high and mighty."

Willow holds out her hands. "Okay, I get it. You're still mad. I treated you like shit. You happy?"

I take another swig of my beer. "Actually, I am, but it has nothing to do with you."

That shuts her up, at least for the time being. She flings her hair off her shoulder and swats a lightning bug away from her face. Willow and bugs go together about as well as orange juice and toothpaste.

"We used to sit out here all the time, you and me."

"Yep." I don't want to go down memory lane with this vile person. But in order to completely move on with my night, I need to face my demon head on. Get her out of my head forever.

"Remember the time we stole a bottle of Jack Daniel's from my daddy's liquor cabinet?"

"I think that rock over there is where I hurled my guts out."

She giggles. "Not your finest hour." She nudges me with her knee. "Come on. Let's take a walk."

"No, thanks."

She reaches out for my hand, but I stuff it in my pocket.

"I know I hurt you, but I've had a lot of time to think, and I want to make it up to you."

"That's not necessary. I'm fine." And I am. It has taken me a lot of anguish to get to this place, but with a little help from a lot of friends and one sweet out-of-towner, I am one hundred percent fine.

"I'm not."

I snort. "That's your problem, not mine. I'm sure Jo filled you in about Andie."

"Yes."

"And this trip home conveniently happened to coincide with all this. How lucky for you." I'm sure my sarcasm doesn't go unnoticed.

She turns to face me. Pain etches across her face. "Gunnar, I still love you. I want to try again."

I stand up to leave. "I don't."

"Don't what? Don't want to try, or you don't love me anymore?"

I shrug. "Maybe both."

She folds her arms over her chest. "Tell me more about... Andie." She spits out Andie's name as if it's poison.

Through clenched teeth, I say, "Whatever you don't already know is none of your business."

She laughs. "Oh, please. Smithville's grapevine is faster than the Internet. I'll find out sooner or later. It might as well come from the source. And the blog..." She sucks in air through her teeth. "I trust that more than CNN."

I focus on the water rushing past my ankles. "She's inherited her grandmother's coffee shop and lottery winnings. You remember Miss Mary Grace. Andie's only here for the summer, so leave her alone."

Willow gives me a humorless grin.

"But she's starting to like it here, so I have a feeling she might change her mind. Who knows? She might be the newest member of the Smithville community." It may or may not be the truth, but either way, it's another way to get under her skin.

Willow's smile fades. She pulls me close and slides her hands up my chest. A shiver runs up my spine. She wraps her arms around my neck and pulls me down so we are eye to eye. "She should leave."

She places her lips on mine. First, it's a soft, gentle kiss, then it turns into something with more urgency. Old feelings bubble up, and she wraps her arms around my neck, pulling me closer and moaning into my mouth.

The last time I kissed her was the day I showed her the house I built for us, the one I still live in even though I can't bring myself to enter the master bedroom. While she was still living in Chicago, finishing up at Northwestern, I was working like a dog to surprise her. Boy, was I ever surprised. She said it didn't fit into her "plan." Right after that, she dumped me.

Within an instant, the image of the spunky, petite blonde dancing around me and bragging about her blue ribbon floods my mind, and I don't care anymore about how Willow used to make me feel. It's not worth it.

I push away from Willow. "I can't do this."

She stops me from moving away. "Yes, you can. You want this." She takes a step toward me, but I hold my hands out in front of me.

"No. And the answer is 'no' to both questions, by the way."

She cocks her head to the side in confusion.

"I don't want to try again, and I don't love you anymore."

She crosses her arms over her chest again and raises an eyebrow. "We'll see about that. Does your little Andie know what really happened at Northwestern?"

My breaths are so fast, I may hyperventilate. Through a clenched jaw, I reply, "Leave that in the past."

Willow tsks me. "Oh, Gunnar, dear. I'm sure everyone would love to know you got kicked out of your PhD program for cheating."

Every muscle in my body is going to cramp up from the stress I'm putting on them. "You didn't used to be vindictive. That's low even for you."

She tsks me again, which pisses me off. "And to think everyone here really thinks you came back because you missed this place. How long could you keep up this charade?"

Forever. A cop that cheats at that level can't be trusted, especially in a small town.

She kisses me on the cheek before I can recoil. "I've kept your secrets all this time, but I don't have to. Let that sink in a bit." She slithers away.

Before she's out of earshot, I yell, "Why now? After three years, why now?"

"Maybe it's time for me to fix your little cheating problem."

I shake my head even though I know she can't see me. "I don't need fixing."

"Wouldn't you love to have that guilt off your shoulders?"

I squeeze my eyes shut and wait for her sports car to rev up and speed away. Only then can I breathe. It's only then that I realize she's still wearing my jacket. Now I'm sure I don't want it back.

CHAPTER THIRTY-THREE
Gunnar

No matter where I go today, Willow's there. She was at the gym, and now she's sitting in the park while I patrol on foot. She doesn't talk to me, and I certainly don't strike up a conversation with her. At least she can't attend the town council meeting. In the two years I've been on the council, I've never wanted to be at the meeting more than I do today. Anything to get out of her view. But soon, we need to have a talk about her threat to expose my secret. I'm not sure how far she'll go to get her way. With her, anything is possible.

Mayor Duncan and City Manager Tom Harding are in a pow-wow when I enter the room. Most of the other council members guzzle down the weak coffee that's needed to stay awake during these meetings.

When Mr. Harding sees me, he waves me over. "Gunnar, you are precisely the man we need to talk to."

This is bad. If Willow already leaked my secret, I may be out of a job. This town has zero tolerance for dishonesty. The council wants trustworthy personnel, and if they find out I wasn't completely truthful on my job application, they could fire me on the spot. And if that happens, I may not be able to show my face in this town again. A bead of sweat trickles down my back, and I do my best to control my breathing.

I exchange pleasantries with the two men before I ask, "You wanted to see me?"

They escort me to the corner of the room. The mayor cranes his neck to see over his shoulder before he speaks.

"Fred Wilkins is closing his shoe-repair shop next week."

Damn. I was afraid of that. Another small family business is shutting its doors. At least he's not asking about my shady past. "That's a shame. He does fine work. Why? "

"Not enough people want shoes fixed anymore. And Stokes Hardware is losing business to the big chain store over in Buxley."

I squeeze my eyes shut. Jake puts on a happy face, but I know it's been hard ever since Mason's Home Improvement opened up in the next county.

"That leaves only two businesses on that side of Main Street. Big Ash Fitness is on shaky ground, and with Mary Grace passing, I don't know how stable In A Jam is."

I cock my head to the side. "It's as stable as it ever was."

The mayor raises his eyebrows. "Son, there's no chain coffee shop in town yet, so her business is vital to the community."

"All are vital, wouldn't you say?" I turn to the city manager, and he shrugs.

The mayor puts his hands on my shoulders, and it forces me to look him in the eye. "Gunnar, we need Andie to stay in this town to keep the promise to the community. We said we would do everything in our power to keep it primarily small businesses and not fall prey to the lure of big chain stores. Now I know you've gotten cozy with her."

My spine stiffens. "I'm sure I don't—"

He holds up a hand to stop me. "I'm not blind, and I don't care about what you do in your private life. All I'm saying is that maybe you can use your charm to keep her from selling. If I thought someone in town could afford to buy it, we wouldn't be having this conversation."

"You want me to get... *cozy* with her for the sake of the town?" I can't believe I'm able to spit out the words from my clenched jaw.

The mayor and city manager nod as though it's the greatest idea they've ever come up with. I'm not stupid. They want me to sleep with her to convince her to stay. I guess my man-whore reputation still hangs over me like the off-kilter awning over In A Jam's front door.

"If she wants to stay and run the shop, I'd be the first in line to welcome her. But if she decides to sell, I can't stop her. It's not my place."

The mayor crosses his arms.

"The rumor about the developer. It's true, isn't it?"

He cringes. "They've already approached Big Ash. Not sure about Stokes. If they get to Andie without her understanding the bigger picture, she could be easily persuaded."

The rest of the town council begins to filter into the room and take their seats for the meeting. "We'll talk about this later. Think about it. Okay?"

I nod because it's the easiest way to end this conversation, but there is no easy way out of this situation. I want the town to survive and even thrive again like it did when I was a kid, but I don't know how bad I want it. This community welcomed me back without question. Maybe I owe it to them. Maybe I owe it to myself.

THE THREAT OF THUNDERSTORMS keeps me away from my typical brooding place, so getting drunk while watching the Atlanta Braves on television in my living room will have to do. After that town council meeting and running into Willow at every turn, I need to be left alone to stew. I know I'm an idiot, but I've avoided Andie ever since the fair. I didn't even go to the gym after work this week because I didn't want to see her. I kiss her like crazy then run away like some stupid middle school kid. I have to get this Willow situation settled before I go further down the road with Andie.

I can't believe she's still in town, and worse, my brain still can't get over what the mayor and city manager want me to do. As much as I want both things—to sleep with her and to save the town—I can't do one for the sake of the other. I have some scruples left. And if she ever found out, she would never think I really had feelings for her.

Every time Dansby Swanson gets a hit, I down another beer, and he's on fire tonight. If he connects this time, I may not remember the rest of the game. Another rumble of thunder booms in the distance. Good thing the Braves are playing in Los Angeles tonight. Otherwise, they might have a big rain delay. The crack of Swanson's bat sends the ball over the third baseman's head, and I pop open another beer.

A *tap, tap, tap* on my door jolts me out of my one-man tailgate party. "Who is it?" I yell, not moving from my supine position on the couch. Faith wouldn't walk over from her house with a storm brewing, and her house is next door. If she needs something, she usually texts me.

"It's me," Willow says from the other side of the front door.

I'm going to need another six-pack.

"Go away."

Thunder rumbles in the distance, so with a huge groan, I peel my body off the couch and force my feet to move toward the front door. When I open the door, instead of seeing her typical sassy grin, she has fear all over her face. She hates storms.

"Can I come in?"

Thunder claps a little closer this time. Willow covers her ears. Ever since her house was flattened by a tornado when we were in eighth grade, she has been terrified of even the smallest storm.

I open the door wider and motion for her to enter. When I shut the door behind us, I lean against it, trying my best to figure out why she's here.

She inspects the living room, the pictures on the wall, and the tongue-and-groove paneling. "It's real pretty."

"Thanks."

She points to the empty beer bottles on the coffee table. "Am I interrupting something?"

I collapse onto the couch. "Watching the Braves. Chilling. Pondering the meaning of life, and oh yeah, wondering why the hell you decided to come back after all this time to torture me."

Unfazed by my snark, she picks up the only unopened bottle on the table. "Can I?"

"Sure. I think I've had enough, anyway."

She holds the bottle out to me so I can open it for her. She never had the best grip strength. My fingers graze hers as she transfers the bottle from my hand to hers. With one quick rotation, I loosen the cap then slam it back down on the table.

After one swig, she sighs and relaxes on the other end of the couch, too close for me, especially after five beers. "This tastes great. I forgot how a cold beer can taste going down."

"You can take the girl out of the country..."

A smile forms on her lips. "Shut up."

"Did you come here because you wanted a beer, or what?"

She picks up the bottle cap and fiddles with it. "I need to tell you something."

I stare at the television in hopes she'll get the hint I'm not interested. Watching Swanson run the bases is far more interesting than her, anyway. "You could have saved yourself a trip and sent me a text. I know you have the number."

Thunder booms again, making Willow jump. "God, I hate that."

"Say what you need to say so you can get back on the road before all hell breaks loose out there."

She swallows. "I talked to Professor Gibson."

Bile rises up my throat. He ruined everything for me. "So? The damage is done."

"He said he would reconsider letting you finish the PhD program."

The Braves take the field, and I stare at the television while Jaime Garcia warms up on the pitching mound. "Can't even if I wanted to. I have a job, and people depend on me."

She scoots closer, and I feel trapped with no more room to move on the sofa. I move to the recliner and pop the footrest up.

"He said he would expunge your record of the plagiarism."

"Why?"

"Because..."

I pop the footrest down and bolt out of the recliner. "What are you up to?"

"Nothing." Her high-pitched voice screeches through the room. She places her bottle on the end table, stands, and takes my hands in hers. The lamplight flickers on and off. "I better go. We'll finish this some other time."

I grab her arm to show her to the door.

Her eyes graze over my chest and up to my eyes. "I miss you, Gunnar. I'd do anything to have you back. It could be like old times."

A flash of lightning and a sudden boom of thunder send Willow into my arms.

"Hate storms."

"I know."

Her breaths are hot and fast on my neck, sending me scampering down memory lane, back to the days when we were inseparable, when I would do anything for her, even build a house.

She kisses my neck, and my willpower, fueled by too many beers, starts to falter. She kisses my cheek and the tip of my mouth. I force a moan back down my throat. My hands find her hips, and she flings her arms around my neck. Her lips crash into mine, almost knocking me over. I pry her mouth off of mine.

"Show me our bedroom," she whispers.

I flinch. Our bedroom. I built this house for us after I was kicked out of school. When I surprised her by showing her "our" bedroom upstairs, she broke up with me. I found out later that she had been seeing another student, a professor's son.

No matter how horny I am or how I wish I could turn back time, I'm not going there. Not. Going. There. I don't want her anymore. I push her an arm's distance away from me. Through flashes of light, I see shock running across her face.

"That guy... the one you were seeing when you broke off our engagement. Phillip. You're still with Phillip, aren't you?"

"Gunnar, let me explain."

"And that's Professor Gibson's son."

The lights pop back on, making her blink. She crosses her arms over her chest. "Yes."

"And it's only a fluke that you show up now and he will clear my name. What are you up to?"

She turns her back to me and clears her throat. "He said he would clear your name, get you a job on the Northwestern police force while you finish your PhD. I think that's very nice of him."

I snort out a hateful laugh. "So generous of him."

She snaps around. "We can be together again. And I know how much you wanted that PhD. You were so close. It wouldn't take you any time to finish."

I pinch the bridge of my nose. She knows more than anyone what I wanted to do with my life, and she thinks when I came home, I was settling for a consolation prize. At times, it does feel that way.

"What about him?"

Her lip trembles.

"Jeez, Willow. I'm not going down that road again."

"He needs your help."

There it is. She finally had the guts to say it. "My help? I don't see how."

Willow stiffens her spine and cocks an eyebrow. "You don't want your name cleared? All you'd have to do is alter the evidence against Phillip. He can't have a DUI on his record."

I stumble backward, and even though I've had five beers, I am completely sober now. "A 'you scratch my back, and I'll scratch yours' kind of deal?"

Her face lights up with a huge grin as if we are on the same page. "Exactly. No one would ever know. And we could be together again... eventually."

"Ha. Eventually. No, thanks."

I walk away from her, but she grabs my arm. "I already told Phillip you'd do it. And his father will fix things on his end."

Hail beats down on the rooftop, almost sounding like a million shotguns going off at once. "I will not owe anyone anything. I don't care who knows my past. You are the most selfish, conniving person I have ever known." I point at the door. "You need to leave right now."

She gasps and shakes her head so fast, I think something is going to come loose. "I can't drive in that mess." She points to the window, which has hail bouncing on it, threatening to break the glass.

Crap. I take a deep breath. Even I wouldn't want to be driving out in this storm. I know she would have a panic attack to beat all others if she was out there. Through gritted teeth, I say, "Fine. You can sleep in my room." I point down the hall to the main-level bedroom I use. "I'll take the couch."

"But—"

"And I swear, if you try anything... come tiptoeing in here wearing nothing but your underwear, anything, I will kick you out, no matter if there is an EF-3 tornado barreling down on us."

Her eyes are as big as saucers.

"Are we clear?"

She nods and backs toward the bedroom.

"And Willow? We're done. We've been done for years."

She closes the bedroom door behind her, and I feel like a large chapter in my life is finally closed too.

CHAPTER THIRTY-FOUR
Andie

Gunnar hasn't stopped by to visit for over a week. I thought he would stop by the night of the fair, but he said he had to take care of some things, and I didn't want to pry. And then I hoped he would drop in last night to make sure I wasn't scared during the storm, but he didn't. It's better this way... for him and for me. I think. Maybe. *Ugh*. I'll stick to my original plans of doing my time and getting the heck out of this small town.

But as I scan my sweet little coffee shop, it's not so easy anymore to up and leave. I love everything about this store, from the creaky steps leading to my apartment upstairs, to the cranky cash register. It has grown on me, and I am having second thoughts about leaving.

To torture myself, I read the *Biddy's Blog* this morning. If the thought of Willow wearing Gunnar's coat wasn't enough, her staying over at his house was. I know what he's been up to, and I don't play that game. If he caves in at the first sight of his ex, then he's not over her, and I'm not getting in the middle of all that drama. I can hardly blame him. She's gorgeous with her model-perfect body, and she's successful—everything I'm not.

I've kept it from Liza and Mel that I've been talking with a developer who is interested in buying the building. I think I can get a fair price for the building, but I don't want them to tell Gunnar about it. It's not his business.

Liza and Faith plop down on a barstool after Faith gives her customary squeeze-hug to Mrs. Cavanaugh.

Liza gulps down the coffee and sighs. "This is not bad."

"I'm getting better, huh?"

"Mrs. Cavanaugh made it, didn't she?"

I gasp. "No. Maybe."

Mrs. Cavanaugh chuckles.

"Where's Lily?" I ask.

Faith's face lights up. "Kevin's off today, so I've been shooed out of the house. He wants Lily all to himself."

Liza stirs her cup of coffee and nibbles on a biscuit I made that turned out perfect. "It's hard to believe my brother was afraid to hold her when she was first born."

I lean toward her. "Wait." I point at Liza then at Faith. "You're married to Liza's brother?"

"I better be. I mean, we've been having sex since—"

Liza covers her ears with her hands. "Gawd, don't talk like that about my brother. Ew."

With a confused expression on my face, I ask Liza, "So, if you are Kevin's sister, and he's married to Gunnar's sister, what does that make you and Gunnar?"

"Cousins," Mrs. Cavanaugh replies.

Faith high-fives Liza. "Probably so."

That is so cliché but funny. I love that they're such a tight group. Some are related, and some aren't, but they are all family.

While they giggle over some crazy story about some guy that got sloppy drunk and peed off the Ferris wheel at the county fair, I check my phone for messages.

Liza chews on the coffee stirrer. "Not to change the subject or anything, but have you seen the town's hottest cop lately?"

I give her the stink eye and glance over at Mrs. Cavanaugh, who busies herself with some bread dough. She probably knew on day one, but we haven't talked about it.

"No. Should I?"

Mrs. Cavanaugh sighs. "Child, you should jump his bones the first chance you get. He's mighty fine."

Liza Jane spits out her coffee. Faith cringes.

Mrs. Cavanaugh eyeballs us as if we're two of the dumbest people on the planet. "Well, he is, and you know it. All this sexual tension in the air every time he walks in the door even stirs my old girly parts."

Liza Jane rests her head on the counter, and her whole body trembles. I try to stifle a grin, but that's too funny.

Faith gasps. "Mrs. C., that's my brother you're talking about."

The bell chimes, and there's a chill in the air. Mrs. Cavanaugh stops smiling and growls. *Whoa.* I turn to see Willow and Jolene standing behind Liza Jane. Willow crosses her arms and clears her throat. Happy Liza turns to see who it is, and she instantly changes to bitchy and ice cold.

Liza snarls. "What do you want?"

Faith chews on her bottom lip. Okay, I can safely say there is some history here, and I'm not sure I want to know about it.

Willow's high heels click on the tile floor as she approaches the counter. "Nice to see you too, Sliza."

Liza's gaze lands first on Willow then on Mrs. Cavanaugh. "Well, well, well. If it isn't the black Willow spider."

Jolene stays silently behind Willow, as if she's her shadow.

Willow rolls her crystal-blue eyes and drops her designer purse on the counter but not before she snatches ten napkins out of the dispenser and places them down as a barrier. I don't mind when a customer uses them, but using them to protect her precious bag is not cool.

Willow holds out a jeweled hand in front of Faith's face toward me. "I'm Willow, and I think you may have already met my sister, Jolene."

"Stepsister," Faith says to clarify.

I take her hand and am not sure if she intends on scratching me with those claws of hers or what. "I'm Andie. Nice to finally meet you."

Not really, but I pull out my best manners and try not to squeeze her hand too much.

"I heard about you." She gives me the quickest smirk. If I had blinked, I would have missed it.

I wipe the counter down for lack of anything better to do. "And I've heard lots about you."

Liza snickers, making Willow glare at her.

"Can I get you anything?" Nice change of conversation. Point one for me. She wants to reel me in and fight over Gunnar, but I'm not going to bite. She can have him.

"Hmm." She taps her bottom lip with her manicured nail.

I curl my fingers into the dish towel to hide my chipped nail polish. It has been forever since I've cared about splurging on something like that.

"I'd like an iced caramel macchiato, please. Grande because I don't need too many calories."

Liza Jane snorts. "Yeah, Andie. Hop to it. Iced car-mel blah blah whatever else she said. And make it a grrrrande."

"I'm sorry. All I have is coffee. Regular coffee." I slide the bowl of individual creamers toward her. "But we have three varieties of creamer." I hold up a finger. "And we have tea if you'd rather have that."

"Chai tea?"

Faith smacks her hand on the counter, making Jolene jump. "This isn't Starbucks, Willow. Regular coffee or regular tea."

Willow lets out an exasperated sigh.

"Sweet tea?" I ask.

"Fine. Give me a glass of... sweet tea." Those two words sounded like venom coming out of her mouth.

"Cheer up, Willow. Maybe if you drink enough sweet tea, it will turn you sweet." Liza doesn't hold back.

"No chance in that," Mrs. Cavanaugh says.

Willow's mouth drops. I kind of feel sorry for her. Not really.

I pour Willow a glass of tea and hand it to her.

She takes a dainty sip and cringes. "That sure is sweeter than I remember."

Faith pats Willow's arm. "I will hand it to you. You're back one week, and you're already getting your accent back."

Liza laughs. "How... convenient."

Willow turns on her stool and stares at Liza Jane, who is not intimidated in the least. "What's your problem?"

Liza smiles, and if I didn't know better, I would think it was genuine. "Bless your heart. You really are dumb as a box of rocks. You know exactly what my problem is. The nerve of you coming back after all this time."

Jolene stands. "Maybe we should go. This was a bad idea."

Willow's face turns red. "This is my home too, remember?" Her chest rises and falls with her rapid breaths.

And I thought the Jolene catfight was tense. I walk around the counter to stand between the two with my back to Liza.

"Willow, I think you should leave. Don't worry about paying for your tea as I'm sure it wasn't to your satisfaction."

She grabs her designer purse so hard, her knuckles turn white.

Faith snorts. "You told everyone you knew that Atlanta was your home, and when you moved to Chicago, you ditched that accent faster than you ditched my brother."

She gulps down her iced tea and slams the plastic cup onto the counter. "That's none of your business."

Faith gently places her paper coffee cup onto the counter, licks her lips, and with the most syrupy voice I have ever heard, she replies,

"When you ditched him the day before the wedding, it became my business. Now do what you need to do in town and get the hell out."

Willow blinks. "You don't scare me."

Liza pushes me out of the way, but I push back. This is my store, and I have to be the adult in the establishment. I hope Mrs. Cavanaugh can help me out because I'm not sure what to do. I am like a fly on the wall, and at any minute, I'm going to get squashed.

Over my shoulder, Liza yells to Willow, "That's because you don't learn fast. You should be scared of me."

"Stop!"

All the women in the store freeze and stare my way.

The door chimes, and Mel walks in. Even in her rumpled, slept-in scrubs, she still oozes class.

Willow's eyebrow rises far into her hairline. "Melanie?" She rests her bag back on to the napkin-lined counter.

Mel's stare scares the crap out of me. "It is Doctor, thank you very much."

Oh my. Mel never wants to be called that.

Mel slides onto the stool next to Liza.

"Hey, Mel," I say. "I was about to call 911 when you showed up. Lots of hostility in the air." I give everyone in the room a death stare, daring anyone to start more crap. While I love the way they cannot stand Willow, I have a business to run. They need to take their cat-fight somewhere else.

Mrs. Cavanaugh wipes the counter, the dish towel sliding dangerously close to Willow's Louis Vuitton purse.

I let out an exasperated sigh. "Would you like something to drink, Mel?"

Mel gives Mrs. Cavanaugh a kiss. "Thank you. Tea would hit the spot."

Liza points at the door.

Oh dear. Round two.

"You need to leave now, and if you dare mess with Gunnar, I promise you, it won't be pretty."

Mel snorts. "Ditto."

Faith smirks at her. "What they said."

Willow turns her attention to me and shows off an evil grin. "You have no idea why I'm here. Maybe you should ask him." She picks up her purse and swings her hips as she walks toward the door with Jolene at her heels. "Nice to meet you, Andie. If you see Gunnar, tell him I'll give him his jacket back tonight. He's such the gentleman."

The bells chime so loud, I think they are going to fall onto the floor. Her cryptic "you should ask him" rings in my ears. I would ask him if he would ever show his face again. For once, the *Biddy's Blog* was right about something. He has been with her. Blood rushes to my head, and my ears burn with anger.

Mel slams her empty tea glass down on the counter. "Shit."

"Wow." I motion to the women in my shop. "Remind me not to get on your bad side."

Liza pulls out her phone and texts something. She slams the phone down. "That bitch gets my dander up. I hate her."

Faith stares at the door. "No more than me."

"No need getting all riled up." Mrs. Cavanaugh refills Liza's coffee cup. "She'll leave soon enough when she realizes she done pissed up the wrong tree."

"I don't understand, and I don't think I want to," I say as I collect all the empty glasses.

Liza points at the door. "That skank had the best guy in the world wrapped around her little finger, and she cheated on him. Over and over, and he wouldn't believe me."

Mel snorts. "Wouldn't believe me, either. I even caught her multiple times in college, but he thought I was trying to start trouble."

Faith shudders. "She's evil."

Liza agrees. "I threatened to tell him if she didn't, and finally the night before the wedding, she broke it off. I'm glad she did, but she humiliated him in front of everyone."

My heart breaks for Gunnar. He is the total package, and to be treated that way makes my stomach turn. Hearing this makes me think this is why he's been staying away. Her reappearance has probably made him have second thoughts about getting involved with anyone else, especially me.

Faith growls. "Pissed me off that she said she couldn't marry a cop. It was not fittin' for her image. What a—ugh, I don't want to insult all the female dogs in this town."

Mel paces the floor. "All she had to say was she had a change of heart and didn't want to get married. But she blasted him about being so small town. That was the one thing she harped on about him that he wouldn't bend about. It ended up being his saving grace."

"It was terrible," Mrs. Cavanaugh said. "He would come here, and Mary Grace and I fed him, let him go on and on about how much he loved Willow. All the time, we wanted to jostle him and say that her dumping him was the best thing that could have happened to him. She would never deserve him. Not in a million years."

Liza stands and heads for the door. "Come on, Mel, Faith."

The three rush out of the shop faster than girls shopping on Black Friday.

Mrs. Cavanaugh wags her head. "That Willow girl is full of spite."

There has been way too much girl drama today. I thought I left all that mess behind in Boston. I'm not about to fight someone over a stupid guy, but Gunnar isn't some ordinary guy. I've never felt like this before. I've never longed for someone to touch me. His kisses take me to another place. And if he would ever show his face again, I'll remind him of what he's missing. After I chastise him for ignoring me for an entire week.

CHAPTER THIRTY-FIVE
Gunnar

Liza slams the door of the hardware store so hard, the back two legs of the chair I'm balancing on almost slide out from under me. She stomps up to me and Jake, throws her hand on a hip, and huffs. Mel's right on her heels. *Uh-oh.*

"Uh-oh," Jake says under his breath.

Liza blows her bangs out of her eyes. "Tell me you aren't getting back with that... that... ugh! I can't even say her horrible name."

I hold my hands out in defense. "Whoa. Slow down."

"Is it true what the Jacksons are saying? You've seen Willow since she's been back, haven't you?"

I fumble with my holster, mostly for fear she may jerk my gun away and shoot me with it when she hears what I have to say. "Yes, I've seen Wills."

Liza groans. "That pet name disgusts me. She's pretty willing and able, all right."

I clench my jaw. I know Willow hurt me, and when I saw her again, all those feelings, both good and bad, bubbled back up to the surface, but I did care for her at one point, so she can't be all bad. "Be nice."

Mel rolls her eyes.

Liza gets in my face, and Jake has to pull her away. "Be nice? Are you kidding me? She needs to be nice. Her coming around the coffee shop, sizing up Andie. God, it was pathetic. She practically pissed on Andie's leg to mark her territory."

Jake chuckles, and I pop him on the arm.

225

"Is Andie okay?" If Willow pulls any shit with Andie, I might blow my stack. And she better not have said anything about North-western. I can't believe I'm even entertaining the idea of taking Willow's offer to have my record cleared. The thought of being near her on a regular basis again nauseates me. But to be able to finish what I started is enticing.

"No. Andie can hold her own. She wasn't intimidated by your ex in the least."

Of course she can, but Willow is a snake and knows how to cozy up to someone right before she bites the person's head off.

The door slams closed again. *Shit.* Faith stomps my way. I can hardly deal with Liza and Mel. When Faith's in the mix, I might as well crawl into a fetal position and cry uncle.

"What the hell is your problem, Gunnar James?"

I throw my hands up in disgust. "Calm down, Faith Marie." If she can start pulling out the middle names, so can I. "She came by last night."

Faith huffs. "I'm not calming down. That girl is—"

"Enough." I close my eyes and do my best to calm my breathing.

Faith takes me by the hand and guides me back into the chair. She sits on Jake's desk in front of me and holds my hands in hers. Before she speaks again, she takes a deep, calming breath. "I know how you're wired. She was your first true love."

I close my eyes. It is completely embarrassing talking about my love life with my sister, sister-in-law, cousin, and best friend. It's obvious they have nothing better to do.

"You believe in forever love, and she's... not wired like that."

"You don't think I know that?" I hate it that my voice cracks. *Shit.*

"I don't know why she's back. All I know is she needs to get out of Dodge fast before you spiral down that rabbit hole again. Do you really want another year of depression followed by three more years of self-harm with every ho-bag in the South?"

She makes me sound like I was a man-whore, which if I'm being completely honest with myself, I kind of was. I would rather not think of those years. But Willow cut me so deep, I wanted to die, and when that wasn't going to happen, I wanted to forget. If I had the smell of every girl in a hundred-mile radius of me, maybe I couldn't smell her.

"No."

Jake clears his throat. "Why is she back?"

"She said she could get me a job as a Northwestern policeman. She thought that would make me happy, and we could try again. She says she misses me." There's no need to tell them all the details.

Liza sits on the edge of my chair and wraps her arm around me. "Oh, boo hoo hoo. Cry me a river. She doesn't get it, does she?"

I shake my head. I love my job, but that's not what keeps me here. I love this town. My family is here. My soul is here. But Willow knows everything.

"What did you tell her?" Faith's eyes plead with me to say I told her no.

"I told her no."

They let out a collective sigh.

"Y'all need a hobby. I'm not that stupid. Give me some credit, okay?" Although the thought of never having that dark cloud over me anymore is a little tempting.

Jake takes another puff of his cigarette. "Bruce, with Willow, there is always an ulterior motive. You know that."

"Yep." Her motives are worse than they think, but I can't tell them that. I can't let them know Willow has some leverage over me. She may think she does, but she doesn't really want me. She doesn't want anyone else to want me. I'm still pissed at myself for letting Willow in my house this week. She wormed her way back into my town, my life, and into my bed. Thank God she left me alone on the couch and didn't try anything. Before I woke up this morning, she was gone. She thinks I've been waiting for her to want me again. But the truth is, I've been waiting for the right person to want me, and I think I've found her. If only I can accomplish with Andie what I never could with Willow—give her a reason to stay. That starts by not avoiding her.

I lean over and kiss my sister on the cheek. I whisper to her, "Thanks, sis, but I've got this. We'll talk later."

She kisses me back. I kiss Liza, and she squeezes my shoulders. Mel hugs me, then I lean in to fake-kiss Jake, and he pushes me away.

"If this powwow is over, I need to go to work. We've got to have some sort of law in this town."

They salute me, Jake's being the middle-finger salute. I love my family. I won't put anyone ahead of them ever again. All I have to do is avoid Willow, make sure Andie knows how I feel about her, and convince her to stay. I'm not sure which one is the hardest. The middle one will be the most fun, so I'll start there.

CHAPTER THIRTY-SIX
Andie

Stanley stuffs a third muffin in his mouth while he wags his head to the beat of the rock song blaring from my cell phone. He says he concentrates better if Lynyrd Skynyrd plays at twenty decibels. I'm getting used to the music and caught myself humming "give me back my bullets" a time or two over the last week. I write a sentence on the whiteboard and turn it toward him.

Since Willow's "mark her territory" visit yesterday, I've had a lot of time to think. First off, if she's what Gunnar is attracted to, then that knocks him down a peg or two on the hot-o-meter. And secondly, I'm not jealous of her at all. In my worst drunken state, I was a nicer person than she is completely sober. I would never cheat on someone then decide years later that I have a right to come back to claim the prize. That's not how life works. If he wants her, I hope they are eternally miserable together.

Liza assures me there's nothing going on between Gunnar and Willow, but until I hear it from him, I have to assume there is the slightest possibility that Willow's words and *Biddy's Blog* have at least an ounce of truth to them.

Handing Stanley the marker, I say, "Circle the nouns."

He studies the board, and with a big grin on his face, he circles "squirrel" and "tree."

"Excellent. Now which word is the verb?"

He draws a circle around the word "ran" and slams the marker down on the counter. He sits back, proud of himself.

"Woo-hoo." I scurry around the counter and give him a big hug. I jerk him off the stool, and we boogie to "Sweet Home Alabama," his favorite tune. "Say, 'Pissa!'"

"Pissa! Whatever that means." He swings me around, his gut jiggling from all the dancing and too many muffins.

"You are going to pass. I know it. Just keep Jolene away from me, okay?" I rub the cheek she slapped at the county fair a week ago. I can still feel the sting.

"She thinks I'm working double shifts." He dances around me, when the door chimes go off. I forgot to lock the door again.

Gunnar raises an eyebrow as he drops his gym bag off his shoulder and onto the floor. "Stan, I didn't you know you had it in you."

Stanley blushes. I throw a dish towel at Gunnar. He can't come in here a week later, smelling like his ex, and think I will want to play.

With a stutter, Stanley says, "We, uh, we were, uh..."

I pat Stanley's back. "Go ahead. Tell him. You should be very proud of yourself."

Gunnar's eyes widen when he looks my way. Then he looks at Stanley and back at me. Our eyes meet, and I'm putty.

Don't care. He's not worth it. If he's that wishy-washy, she can have him.

Stanley shifts his weight from one leg to the other. "She's uh..."

I walk over to Gunnar and pick up the dish towel I threw at him. "I'm helping him get ready for the GED."

Gunnar cocks his head to the side. "Seriously?"

I plant my hands on my hips and huff at him. "Yeah, seriously. I'm a nice person when I want to be. Plus, I'm an open book."

Stanley chuckles. "From what I hear, she's a nice person in a lot of nice ways when she wants to be."

My mouth drops open. Gunnar laughs. They high-five over my head.

Stanley gives me a one-armed, brotherly hug. "I'm kidding."

I poke his Pillsbury-Dough-Boy belly. "You better be, or else you'll lose your tutor and my delicious muffins."

Stanley gulps down the last of his iced tea and walks toward the door. "I gotta go before Jolene gets suspicious."

Gunnar waves. "See ya, Stan."

Stanley turns and grins. "Maybe she'll make you stay after for detention. It could be fun being punished by her."

Gunnar belly laughs, and I reward him with a poke in his not-at-all-dough-boy stomach.

"Stan, I mean it," I yell as he rushes out. I pop Gunnar on the arm. "Not funny."

Gunnar walks over to the door, locks it, and pulls down the shade. He shrugs. "Could be fun, though."

When he turns to me again, he's a different person and stares into my soul. He's no longer the playful, joking Gunnar. The guy striding my way appears more like an animal stalking his prey.

"Hey, stranger." Maybe my tone will resonate with him that I've noticed he's been avoiding me.

He walks so close that his minty breath tickles my neck.

To keep myself under control, I turn around and busy myself with all the supplies lying out on the counter. All the whiteboard markers must be organized this minute, or I'll lose myself in those eyes.

"How have you been?" he asks.

Stop being so damn sexy. Actors work their entire life to sound Southern, but there's no denying a fake. And Gunnar is far from fake. I shrug. *Stay focused. Act nonchalant. Act like him being so close doesn't send tingles all over your body.*

"Oh, okay, thanks. Mrs. Cavanaugh makes your breakfast every morning, but when you don't show, she feeds it to the stray dog. Griff thanks you."

His hands rake down my arms, leaving goose pimples in their wake. "We need to talk. I am so sorry for not..." He lets out a breath.

"I had stuff to resolve, and it's been taking longer than I thought it would."

"No need." With my back still to him, I have the courage to say, "I met Willow."

His hands grip my arms tighter.

"She's so... interesting."

"Yes, she is."

"I see why you... never mind. None of my business." I scrub the same spot on the counter for the tenth time. "Have you two had a chance to catch up?" I wiggle out of his arms and toss the supplies into a box under the counter. I pour myself a glass of tea and guzzle it, waiting for his reply.

He won't stop taking me in, and he won't leave more than one inch of distance between us. I face the sink and wash my glass. Again, his hands are on me. They rest on my shoulders.

"We've had a chance to clear the air."

I let out a deep chuckle. "I bet you have. I'm real happy for you, Gunnar." *Not really.*

"Andie, please look at me."

I hang my head low as I dry my glass. "She wants you, Gunnar. I want you to be happy. You deserve to be happy. Will Willow really make you happy?" My breath hitches. Gah. I hate it when I sound so girly.

"I haven't been happy in so long, I don't remember what it feels like, but yes, she does want me."

My heart falls into my shoes. He said what I knew he was going to say, but I was hoping he wouldn't. I can't blame him. She's gorgeous and tall, and by the way she dresses, she must be very successful. And she's the ghost that's been haunting him. I was the placeholder until she came back.

I should be happy. This makes selling the property and leaving this town all the easier. Without Gunnar in the mix, I don't have anything to hold me here. This is the best outcome. This is what I need. I should be happy about this.

He squeezes my shoulders, and after a deep breath, he says, "She wants me, but I want you."

I let out a snort. "So that's why you haven't stopped by all week? Because you... want me. Makes perfect sense."

He swings me around so I have to face him. His eyes are stormy, and his breath comes out fast, tickling my nose. "I didn't want her to mess with you, but I guess it happened, anyway. Again, I'm sorry I didn't stop by, but I was trying to keep her away from you."

"I'm a big girl from the south side of Boston. Trust me. I can take care of myself." *All but my heart.*

His eyes undress me. I can't breathe. My heart beats way past a marathon pace. He leans in to me, resting his forehead against mine.

I close my eyes and soak in the contact. "Why do you want to be with me?"

He chuckles and kisses my nose. "Because."

"Did she stay at your house?"

He growls.

"It was actually a relief for the blog to be about someone other than me."

"Yes, she stayed over the other night, but if you knew her history, you would understand. Nothing happened. I made it very clear I didn't want her." He blows out a breath. "I still don't want her."

I bow my head, trying to figure out what I believe and what's completely a line. He takes his index finger and tips my chin up so he can see my eyes. He has no reason to lie to me. If he wants Willow, there's nothing to stop him from getting his first love back. But he's not running to her. He's here, with me, and that's enough for me.

I tilt my head up to get a better view of the desire in his eyes. His lips touch mine, and I had forgotten how supple they are. He slides his hands through my hair, removing my ponytail holder. My hands roam under his shirt, and he groans.

He whispers in my ear, "When I say I want you, I mean, well, you know."

Oh. My. God. I can't make my mouth say anything. I nod. He holds up a finger for me to stay still. He rushes over to pick up his gym bag. "There are some things in here we might need."

I put a hand on my hip. "Officer, I do not do bondage. So if your handcuffs are in there, you can forget about it."

He slings the bag over his shoulder, takes me by the hand, and leads me upstairs. "You have a dirty mind, Miss Carson. What's in here is more of the latex variety. Trust me. I think you'll want it."

CHAPTER THIRTY-SEVEN
Gunnar

When I kick the door closed behind us, it slams a little louder than I mean for it to. A picture frame on the wall tilts to the side. I guess I'm more eager than I want to admit. Andie's arms are clenched tightly around her middle, and she trains her eyes on the floor.

"Sugar, look at me."

She glances up, and I know I've made the right decision. She holds my heart now, and it feels right. It's been so long since I've wanted to be with a woman, wanted to hold her, make love to her. I've had boatloads of sex since Willow left me, but none of it could thaw my heart. Andie walks into my life, and I'm alive again.

"I know we've only known each other a few weeks, so we don't have to do anything you don't want to do. Okay?"

She leaps into my arms. Her legs wrap around my waist, and she kisses me hard on the lips. "I want you, Gunnar."

I pull away from her. "You said my name with an R at the end. Gunnar, not Gaannah."

She smirks. "I guess you're wearing off on me."

I kiss up and down her neck. "Stop teasing me."

I walk us to her bed and plant her feet on the floor. She clutches the hem of my T-shirt and slides it over my head then flings it across the room. She gasps when she sees my bare chest. Score one point for me. All those hours in the gym pay off with that one delicate expression. Now it's my turn. My fingers brush across her bare skin on purpose as I take my sweet time removing her T-shirt. God, she's beautiful—petite and fit. And her breaths make her breasts move up and down, driving me crazy. I want to rip off that bra so fast, but I need some bit of control, or we won't even get to use any of those condoms I brought.

She holds on to my arm with one hand while she struggles to re-move one sneaker at a time. I toe my shoes off and peel out of my socks. We stand there, staring at each other. She is only wearing sexy faded cutoff jeans and a bra, and I'm wearing nothing but gym shorts with a very large bulge in the front that has not gone unnoticed. She licks her lips, taking her deadly sweet time unhooking her bra. When she throws it at my face, I almost pass out at the beauty standing be-fore me. I toss the bra to the side and wrap my arms around her body. Skin to skin with Andie is where I want to be for the rest of my life.

She pushes me backward onto the bed. The mattress squeaks and bounces with my weight before the bed frame cracks, sending me crashing down, along with the bed, onto the floor. My feet fly in the air as I hang on with all my strength to the side of the mattress, with only my pride hurt.

Andie gasps with laughter and flops beside me, tears rolling down her cheeks. "How am I ever going to explain this?" She kicks her leg in the air as another round of giggles bursts through her mouth. She claps her hands. "Be aggressive. Be, be aggressive."

I pull her to me, our feet still higher than our heads. "That's ex-actly what I plan to do."

Her eyes flick up to mine. Doubt falls on her face.

"You, Andie, are the most beautiful person I have ever known."

She grabs my face and kisses me so hard, I think I'm going to be bruised, but I don't care. My hands roam, and so do hers. In a single flick, I unbutton her jeans and help her shimmy out of them. *Have mercy.* Pink lace. I'm going to be a dead man by morning. She fid-dles with my shorts, and I bat her hand away. If she does that, I'll be a goner in five seconds flat.

"Not yet, darlin.'"

I stand to drag the mattress onto the floor with Andie still on it. She lets out a squeal. I crawl back to her and leave a trail of kisses down her neck, on each ripe breast, and down her stomach. Her sexy moans make me melt into her. I'm glad I brought an entire pack of condoms because one foil package will never be enough to satisfy either one of us. Not tonight. Not ever.

I DRAW FIGURE EIGHTS on Andie's bare stomach as she plays footsie with me. I don't care how late it is or that I have to work in the morning. All I care about is that I'm here in Andie's bed, or rather on her mattress, making love to her over and over. I'm floating, and I never want to land. I think I've found my happy place.

Her stomach growls. "Sorry." She plants another kiss on my shoulder. "I've worked up an appetite."

"Me too." I stand up, and her eyes get big as she stares at my package. If she stares long enough, it will be an even larger package.

"You're so... perfect."

Heat flushes my face. "Far from perfect, sugar." And if she ever hears my Northwestern secret, she'll agree. "How about I steal some food from the shop downstairs? Do you think the owner would mind?"

Andie giggles. "I'll make sure she doesn't even know it."

I sling on my boxer-briefs and shorts and back out of the room. "Be right back."

In record time, I haul butt downstairs, grab some day-old bagels and a carton of milk, and take the stairs two at a time to get back up to her. I slip on the throw rug, almost losing one bagel. She giggles the whole time. I hand her the bagels as I snuggle back onto the mattress with her. She nestles into the crook of my neck and tears off a bite of bagel, feeding me like a bird. I open the carton of milk, and we both drink straight from it.

"Your phone buzzed while you were down there."

"It can wait." God, it had better not be Willow calling me. Talk about ruining the moment. "I need to be honest with you."

She stuffs a piece of bagel in her mouth. "This can't be fun."

"After Willow left me, I was... I didn't take it well. I did things I'm not proud of."

She swallows, digesting my words. "Had to numb the pain?"

"Yeah." I offer her the carton of milk. "When Willow left me, I did some really stupid stuff. One hookup after another, hoping it would make me numb. And it did, but I'm done being numb. I was done way before you showed up, but you... you sealed the deal."

She cranes her neck to meet my gaze and bats those eyes. "Aww, shucks." We sit in silence for a moment before she adds, "Can I be honest with you?"

"Of course."

Andie clears her throat. "Not to bring down the mood, but when you left to get the food, I thought you were..."

"Leaving?"

"Yeah. That's the standard operating procedure."

I roll over on top of her so we're nose to nose again. "I'm not going anywhere. I want you to know that I've never felt this way about anyone before."

I tickle her and take a bite out of her bagel.

She squeezes her eyes shut. "Anyone?"

"Anyone. You make me happy."

She flings her arms around my neck and crushes the milk carton between us. Cold milk oozes all over us. She squeals.

"God, that's cold," I say, laughing.

"These sheets need to be washed, anyway. How about a shower?" She wiggles her eyebrows up and down.

Uh, you don't have to ask me twice.

"Try not to break my grandmother's bathtub, okay?"

I pick her up and carry her to the bathroom, where we spend the next thirty minutes getting dirtier before we get clean. I can't say this out loud because Andie would think I'm acting like a girl, but I'm already picking out a wedding date, china patterns, and the names of our first three children, all with the knowledge that she still may leave me.

LYING ON A CLEAN SHEET that we flung over the mattress, I kiss every inch of her body. I can never get enough. I hope she feels the same. By the glow of complete satisfaction and the way she can't stop her fingers from roaming through my hair, I think she does.

"There's something else in my past I want you to know about. Only one other person knows this."

"Willow?"

"Yeah." It's time to be completely honest with Andie. Of all people, she would understand.

My phone buzzes again. Terrible timing. I groan.

"You better get that. Somebody really wants to talk to you."

Son of a...

With one arm still around Andie's waist, I fish out my phone from the gym bag on the floor. It's five o'clock in the morning already. *Crap.* I answer the call and listen to my dispatcher.

"Yeah. Oh. Sorry. Battery died."

She covers her mouth to stifle her giggles.

"Yeah, okay. Bye."

I hang up the phone and groan. I find my shorts and sling them on fast before my body can react to seeing Andie stretching out on the mattress, the sheet sliding down to expose part of her right breast. *Nice.*

"Train wreck," I say.

"I am not an expert by any means, but it wasn't that bad, was it?"

I roll my eyes and fall on to her.

She giggles. "Be careful. You might break the... Oh, wait! You already did that."

I prop myself up on my elbows and examine the disheveled, beautiful mess below me. "A train wreck off Highway 92."

She yawns, and even with her mouth wide open, she's gorgeous. "That's terrible, I guess."

I nibble on her ear. "No injuries except for Mr. Clairmont's tractor." Thank God it wasn't anything more serious. I wasn't on call, so I didn't expect to get called away.

Her laughter bubbles out louder. "Give my condolences to Mr. Clairmont."

"Will do." I give her an Eskimo kiss and force myself off of her. "I better go while I can."

She yawns and props herself up with an elbow. "Bye, Gunnarrrrr."

I lean down and kiss her one more time. "Bye, sugar."

There's no way I'm going to focus on work today. I hope no one notices the goofy grin on my face, but I really don't care. Before noon, the whole town will know I am off the market permanently. Even Willow will leave me alone. But to have my record clean would make me hold my head up high again, and that would be nice. I have to decide if the price is worth losing whatever Andie and I have started.

CHAPTER THIRTY-EIGHT
Andie

My thigh muscles scream with every step I take down the stairs. I hurt so badly, I'm surprised I'm not bruised. *Totally worth it.* I haven't had sex in forever, and I've never had it with that much passion. They sure do things differently down here in the South.

"Morning, Mrs. Cavanaugh," I say, hobbling into the store.

She scans me up and down and grins. "Busy night?"

"You could say that." I pull the notebook closer to me and train my eyes on my list of orders for the day. "Twelve orders for jam?" I throw on my apron. "Better get started."

Without stopping her biscuit-making, she motions with her head toward the stove. "Lucky for you, I picked up your secret ingredient last night after bingo."

I pull out the whiskey jar and bite my lip. "How did you know?"

"Mary Grace thought she was sneaky, but why else would she have all that booze around? She was a teetotaler."

Realizing she could have put me out of my misery by revealing this weeks ago should make me angry, but it doesn't. I had to figure it out on my own. I hide the bottle under the counter and give Mrs. Cavanaugh a big kiss on the cheek.

"What was that for?"

"For being so sweet to me. I can never thank you enough for what you've done for me and what you meant to Granny."

She focuses on the counter and sighs. "She was my best friend, and you're so much like her."

I give her shoulders a squeeze. "Thank you, Mrs. Cavanaugh."

She slams down the wooden spoon and huffs. "When are you going to call me by my first name?"

I blink. "I thought I was being polite. My Southern book says it's proper manners to call someone by their last name until they tell you to do otherwise."

"I'm telling you now."

"There's one problem with that."

"Hmm. What's that?" She rolls out the biscuit dough, and I hand her the dough cutter.

"I don't know your name."

She turns to me and chuckles. I wipe some flour off her plump cheek.

"Etta. My name's Etta."

I stand up tall. "Okay, then. Thank you, Etta."

She points the dough cutter my way. "It's Miss Etta."

I hold up my hands in defense. "Yes, ma'am. Miss Etta." I kiss her cheek again. "Thank you," I whisper.

She hums a hymn as she goes about her business. I scan around the shop and notice it's emptier than usual. "I haven't seen the Jackson sisters in a few days."

"Jennifer is in the hospital."

"Oh dear. What happened?"

Mrs. Cavanaugh lines the pan with the cutout dough. "She got real confused and passed out."

My jaw drops. "When did this happen?"

"Yesterday."

I slam the dish towel down on the counter. "Why didn't you tell me? As much as they drive me crazy, I kind of like their special kind of crazy."

She shrugs, putting the baking pan in the oven. "I thought you knew. Everybody knows."

I throw my hands in the air in disgust. "Well, I'll be. I guess I should have gone to the Piggly Wiggly last night."

"Guess so."

Gunnar walks in, and my knees buckle. I can't stop the vision in my head of him completely naked on top of me only a few hours earlier. He winks, and I'm so glad I didn't go to the Piggly Wiggly.

"Morning, Mrs. Cavanaugh, Andie."

"Look what the cat dragged in." Mrs. Cavanaugh slides a plate of bacon and eggs over to him.

I pour him a cup of coffee, spilling half of it on the counter.

"Thanks," he says, his eyes darting around.

Mrs. Cavanaugh chuckles. "You two seem rode hard and put up wet."

Gunnar spits his coffee all over the counter. I open the refrigerator to cool off the flush on my face.

"I was young once. Enjoy it while you can."

Gunnar grins. "I plan to."

I try to peek at him over the refrigerator door without him seeing, but he does anyway and winks again. I close the refrigerator and steady myself by leaning on the counter.

"Andie, would you like to go out with me tonight?"

My hand slides across the counter, and I drop all the paper coffee cups on the ground. Mrs. Cavanaugh kicks them out of her way.

"Like on a date?"

He shrugs. "Yeah. A date."

I'm not sure what to say about that. A date means he's ready to go public about how he feels about me. I'm used to guys who never call me back, so this whole dating thing is an odd concept.

Mrs. Cavanaugh points a wooden spoon at me. "Child, if you don't, I will."

I peek over at Gunnar's twinkling eyes. "I better if I know what's good for me."

He guzzles the rest of his coffee and walks around the counter to give me a kiss on the cheek, turning me into a puddle.

"See you later, sugar." His fine ass walks out of the store.

Mrs. Cavanaugh catches me licking my lips. I stiffen my back and turn toward the stove. I must focus on my jam, or else I'll run down the sidewalk and jump Gunnar's bones. That would give the Jackson sisters a lot to talk about, but I don't think it's against any of the rules. I'm about to bust a gut to tell Liza and Mel what happened. They've been my biggest supporters. I'm sure one glimpse at me, and they'll figure it out all on their own.

While I contemplate the different ways I can violate Gunnar's body tonight, the bells over the door chime again, and a FedEx delivery person walks in carrying a cardboard tube. "Delivery for Andrea Carson."

I wipe my hands on a dish towel and take the signature pad he holds out. "Morning. Would you like some coffee? On the house?"

"Sure. Thanks."

I pour him a cup to go, and after he leaves, I investigate the package. My eyes light up when I see it's from Bilkins Properties. David Bilkins, the developer that is interested in buying my shop and others along Main Street, emailed me to tell me the blueprints were on the way.

I fling off my apron, turn off the stove, and give Miss Etta another kiss on the cheek. "I'll be right back."

With all the effort I can muster, I hustle up the stairs. Each step reminds me of my wonderful night with Gunnar. In my hands is something that might break his heart.

I pop open the tube and roll out the blueprints of what David has planned for Main Street if I sell. A Starbucks, a Pier One store, and the cherry on top is the supersized Buy For Less store. It takes up the entire block, and now I can see how they can afford to offer me such a pretty penny for my property. The stats he enclosed have his projections for the next five years. Even after he buys me out and with the cost of construction, he still plans to turn a profit within three years. *Wow.* He must know what he's doing. The blueprints are a thing of beauty.

But in order for this to work, Liza and Jake and Big Ash Fitness would have to sell too. The Stokeses seem pretty settled in, but it will be hard for them to pass up this kind of cash.

I sit at the table, staring at the blueprints. This should be easy for me. This is what I want. I think. I get Granny's inheritance plus more from the developer than the store is worth. I could go anywhere and do anything. Sitting still makes me jittery, so I pace back and forth. Every step I take, I sense Gunnar, feel him, smell him.

I'm going to be like Scarlett O'Hara, and I'll think about all this tomorrow. I roll up the blueprints and stuff them back into the tube. I toss the tube into the coat closet, and step by painful step, I go back down to the shop to help Mrs. Cavanaugh prepare for the day. And I've got a date to prepare for. But first, I need to pay a visit to Miss Jackson. It's the proper thing to do. Land sakes, I'm as busy as a three-balled bunny rabbit.

CHAPTER THIRTY-NINE
Andie

The last time I was in this hospital, Gunnar was holding my hair back while I puked my guts out. I tiptoe down the hallway, peace lily in hand, wondering what the heck I'm doing here. Miss Jennifer is my nemesis. She wants my money for the church. I shouldn't care if she's not feeling well, but somewhere along the way, I started caring.

Ever since I figured out the secret ingredient in Granny's jam, the sisters have been nothing but friendly toward me. And today is my way of offering the olive branch.

"Andie?"

I swing around, and my plant whacks Mel in the stomach. "Oh, I'm so sorry."

"What are you doing here?"

"I've come to see Miss Jackson."

She steps back. "Really?"

"Yeah. Shocker, huh?"

"I think it's really sweet that you're here." She wraps an arm around my shoulders and guides me down the hallway. "So... any progress with Gunnar?"

My face flames with heat. "You could say that."

She lets out a muffled squeal and squeezes my shoulder. Mel enters the hospital room ahead of me, giving her hands a dousing of hand sanitizer foam at the door. She checks the pump next to Miss Jackson's bed that delivers something from a bag into a tube in her arm.

246

She taps Miss Jackson on the arm. "Miss Jackson, you have a visitor."

Miss Jackson opens her eyes, and when she sees me, she laughs. "I never thought you would come visit. I'm glad I wore my best nightgown." Her pale face and sunken eyes don't resemble the perky pest that invades my life on a regular basis.

I give her a half hug and place her plant on the bedside table. "I didn't know what kind of flowers you liked, so I went with a plant."

She pats my hand. "Look at you, being all neighborly."

Mel gives her a kiss on the cheek. "I'll check in on you later. No Zumba class today."

"Buzzkill."

Miss Jackson is the hippest old person ever. She texts, has a Facebook account, and uses words like "buzzkill."

I sit next to her on the hospital bed and stare at the pump. "How are you doing?"

"Better. I got real disoriented and passed out. Turns out, I have a UTI. I guess I haven't been keeping my hoo-ha clean enough."

I bust out with laughter before I can stop myself. "I'm sorry, but the image... oh boy."

Miss Jackson laughs. "It's seen better days."

Please make her stop.

"When my Harvey was alive..."

I gasp. For some reason, I thought they were spinsters.

She nods. "Yep. Married, then he went off to war. He died, and I never got over it. Never remarried."

Tears prickle my eyes. To have that kind of love must be the most awesome feeling. "I'm so sorry."

"I'm not. He was everything to me." She blinks a few times then fidgets with her blanket. "Thank you."

"I would have come earlier had I known. You and your sister are my only steady customers." I take in the room. "Where is your sister?"

She fidgets with her blanket. "Sarah never learned to drive."

"You mean she can figure out the inner workings of a smartphone but can't manage to drive two miles on a flat road?"

She giggles. "Too proud to let anyone know. I always drive us around."

I take her hand in mine. "Would she throw something at my head if I picked her up to bring her here?"

Her bottom lip trembles. "You'd do that?"

"Well... yeah."

A tear trickles down her cheek. She grabs me and smothers me in a bear hug. "Thank you so much. And I'm so sorry about the blog. We only wanted the church to have the money. We didn't realize how much hurt it could cause you. I'm so sorry."

"It's all water under the bridge now." When I manage to pry myself from her viselike grip, I stand up and smooth out her blanket. "I'll be right back." Before I leave the room, I walk back to her. "I almost forgot. You need to ask Dr. Mel first to make sure you can have this."

I pull out a jar of jam from my bag. She almost pulls the IV out of her arm, snatching the jar from my hand.

AFTER I PRIED SARAH'S bony hands off my shoulders from hugging me to near death, I drove her to the hospital. She insisted we ride with the top down, and she put on a scarf to hold her gray-blue hair in place. She even let out a "woo-hoo" a time or two along the way.

She sprints into her sister's room, and it's as if they haven't seen each other in years. They finish each other's sentences, and in rapid fire, Sarah catches Jennifer up on what's been going on in town. Sarah grabs my arm, and they surround me in a hug. *Awkward.*

"Oh, okay." I'm not used to group love, but I can get used to it.

A snicker at the doorway interrupts our love-in. Mel gives me a wink.

I tear away from the sisters and walk toward the door. "I'll let you two get reconnected, but I'll be back in a bit."

"Hungry?" Mel asks me.

She leads me to the cafeteria, where we get hospital food and sit in the "doctors only" dining area, which is almost empty.

She plays with the mystery meat on her plate. "So, you and Gunnar..."

I try to tamp down my grin, but I fail miserably.

"I knew it." She does a seated happy dance. Several doctors glare at her as if they are ready to commit her to the psych ward. "I'm sorry. I'm very, very happy for both of you."

"Still not on Team Willow, I see. Not that I'm complaining."

She sticks her finger in her mouth as though she's going to induce vomiting. "She used to make fun of me because I was all knees and elbows growing up."

"And look at you now."

Mel's face flushes. "I did all right. I need to tell you something, and it's only a rumor, so take it with a grain of salt, okay?"

I put my fork down and take a deep breath. "There's usually a grain of truth to most rumors, so out with it."

Mel stares at the ceiling before she clears her throat. "I don't like the rumor mill, so I hope to God it's all lies, but I heard something bad happened when Willow and Gunnar were at Northwestern, and he has a chance to fix it, but that would mean he would go back with her."

I lean back in my chair. "Huh. He said there was something he wanted to tell me, but he got called in to work. If he was going to leave with her, why would he want to... he made it sound like he was done with her. His exact words were 'I'm not going anywhere.'" I rub my temples so hard, I'm going to crush my brain.

"Like I say, it doesn't make sense, and it's so out of character for him. I'm a jerk for mentioning it. Besides, I never could figure out what he saw in her. But you... you make sense."

Now, I'm the one with the flushed face. "Don't go picking out my china patterns. We're having fun. That's all."

She rolls her eyes. "If you say so."

But in my mind, I've already decided on a Noritake Cardinal china pattern, like my grandmother's. But a more urgent task is that I need to get ready for my date with George Clooney with a twang, and he needs to tell me what kind of game he's playing with my heart.

CHAPTER FORTY
Gunnar

It's been so long since I've been on a date, I don't remember how to act. What do people do on dates these days? My sister, the high school literature teacher, keeps up on what's hot and what's not. When she told me about rage parties, I figured I would stick with bowling. It's safe, and everyone loves to bowl, I think.

"You're taking her bowling?" Faith stares at me as if I grew horns.

I haul Lily around on my shoulders through her backyard, which backs up to mine. "What's wrong with that?"

"Uh, everything. You need something romantic."

"Uncle G, what's mantic?"

Faith shoots me a warning glance.

I am not going there. "I better let your mother handle that conversation."

I put Lily down on the ground, and she spins in circles. "Is it like Burt's Bees?"

Before she has a chance to face-plant onto the grass, I grab her. "What did you say?"

"Burt's Bees. Jeffy Taylor says his brother said he was too young to know about Burt's Bees. Why? Mama puts that on her lips all the time."

I nudge Lily toward Faith. "She's all yours."

Faith takes her daughter by the hand and guides her to the house. "Why don't you play in your room for a while?"

"Can I watch TV?"

Faith contemplates that for a bit then nods. Lily wins that round. Faith turns to me, and we both crack up.

"Burt's Bees? Oh dear." She clears her throat. "Okay, mister, you are not taking Andie bowling on your first date. You are going to do dinner and a movie."

I groan. "Sis, there's no place around here to eat a nice meal, and the theatre closed down years ago. I'd have to take her to Moultrie, and she'd hate that more than here. At least we have a traffic light."

She holds up a finger. "I've got it all figured out. Trust your big sister for once."

I BARELY GET ONE RAP on the door, when I hear her barreling down the stairs to meet me. Maybe she's looking forward to this date as much as I am.

Out of breath, she locks up the shop and smiles. Andie is so adorable, I could devour her. *Damn.* Her tight capri pants don't leave much to the imagination. *Yum.*

"Where to?" she asks.

"Dinner and a movie. My sister insisted, but I think you'll like it."

I help her into my truck, and we drive out to the lake. We both slip out of our shoes, and I hand her a blanket and cooler, while I grab a huge picnic basket and my gym bag.

"If I didn't know better, I'd think you're moving in."

"Sometimes, I wish I could."

We find a quiet spot away from the joggers that frequent this area at sunset. She spreads out the blanket and pulls out the cold items from the cooler.

"Compliments of Faith." I show her a container of chicken. "Baked chicken. I know you don't like fried. Potato salad, her specialty, Boston baked beans, and even an apple pie."

She clutches her chest. "This is... nice."

"Nice? All I get is 'nice'? Are you all right? You've been kind of quiet."

"I'm hungry."

Something's up, but I know better than to push a woman. When she's ready to talk, she'll blast me with more words than I'll ever be ready for. I motion with my head. "There's a gallon of sweet tea in the cooler."

"I've actually grown to love sweet tea."

"That's step one in the 'fitting in' process, and I'm glad you can check that one off your list."

We sit crossed-legged, eating our picnic dinner. I make every excuse in the book to touch her. I graze her knee with mine. I feed her potato salad; her moans are about to kill me. She feeds me a piece of pie, and the way she licks her lips makes me want to devour her and forgo the pie.

She flops back onto the blanket. "Best meal ever."

I hover over her and swipe a stray hair away from her face. "Pleased you liked it."

"The other night, you mentioned there was something you needed to tell me. I'm all ears."

Well, damn. Either I can lie to her and say it's no big deal, or I can be completely truthful with her. I know all her secrets. She should know mine.

I sit up and pick at a blade of grass. "It's not pretty. You always think I'm so perfect. Well, sugar, you're about to find out everything you think of me is what I want you to think. I made a terrible mistake in college and got kicked out."

Her mouth drops open.

"Yep. I did something. It doesn't really matter what I did, but it was bad enough to lose my chance of getting a PhD. You see, I told you I left because I missed this place, and I did miss my hometown, but I came back because I had nowhere else to go."

She can't even maintain eye contact. The hem of her blouse is more interesting. "And where does Willow fit in?"

I pinch the bridge of my nose. "She says she can fix everything and get my PhD."

She snaps her head to attention. "Your PhD. At Northwestern? With her?"

"Yeah."

She finally finds her voice, and she's not shy about using it. "And you want that?"

"I don't know."

She starts slamming dishes back into the basket. "What part do you not know about? Because you are confusing the hell out of me. First you tell me a whopping lie about why you left Northwestern. Then Willow comes prancing back into town, and you start panting like a dog. Was last night with me because you were bored?"

I clench my jaw. "Not at all." She makes it sound so much worse than it is.

"Oh, really? And what does she get out of this? You get your PhD, but people like Willow don't do anything without getting something in return. What does she want?"

My silence answers her question.

She groans. "That's what I thought. She wants you back, and you are still in love with her, so it's a win-win... for you."

"No, that's not true. She wants—"

Andie throws her head back and lets out a dry laugh. "We all know what she wants."

I crawl over to her and take her hands in mine. She won't let me hold them at first, but finally she gives in. "I don't love her. She only wants me long enough to fix her latest plaything's DUI record. I don't want to be with her. I'm sorry I'm not the man you thought I was."

"Gunnar, so what? You're imperfect. You're flawed. Well, big whoop. Everyone is. But I don't like lies. I'm the most messed-up person on the planet, but I own my mistakes, and I try to do better. That's all I can do. That's all anyone can do. And if people don't like you because of your flaws, then screw them."

I'm an idiot for even entertaining the thought of being near Willow again. I'm miserable thinking about it. What I have in front of me is the most beautiful mess I've ever seen. For me to even think about losing Andie makes me want to beat myself up.

I slide a hand down her cheek. "I'm so sorry I hurt you, but if the truth comes out, which is what Willow is threatening to do, it will ruin my career in law enforcement."

Barely above a whisper, she asks, "She's blackmailing you?"

"Yes."

Andie throws her hands around my neck and squeezes me so tight, I can hardly breathe. "Oh, Gunnar."

I kiss her neck and pull back from her, realizing she is absolutely correct. "You know what? Screw them." I chuckle. "I need to be more like you."

"I don't know about that, but since I've been here, I've been able to face my demons head-on, and you know what? It feels really fantastic." She grins, and I know I made one more giant leap toward a forever with Andie. And I like it. I hope I haven't messed things up so badly that she will leave me.

She bites her lip. "Where's the movie?"

I breathe a sigh of relief because I think her anger has subsided. I give her a quick peck on the lips. "I'm glad you asked."

I pull out my laptop and start up *My Cousin Vinny*.

"I love this movie."

I'm not surprised. Nothing about her surprises me anymore. We snuggle together on the blanket, with the laptop resting on my stomach. I wrap my arm around her and play with her hair. We only get to the part where Vinny gets awakened by the train before we abandon the movie to make our own entertainment. I thought making love to Andie was wonderful on a broken bed, but having her on the beach at night gives a whole new meaning to seeing stars.

She wraps us in a blanket, and we kiss well into the night. Neither of us cares to move. I never want this night to end. Best dinner and a movie ever. For once, I'm so happy I listened to my sister.

AROUND MIDNIGHT, THOUGH neither of us want to, we pack up the supplies and leave our beach spot because we both have to work early in the morning. When we get to her place, I walk with my arm around her, guiding her toward her shop.

"It's quiet this time of night," she says.

"Yeah. So many of the stores are abandoned. Main Street used to be bustling even in the middle of the night." The mayor's words invade my brain.

"I bet it was fun back in the day."

I remember hanging out on Main Street as a kid. There were so many stores, every store one can think of. My mother would let me and Faith roam around while she did her errands. We had plenty to keep us occupied, and everyone knew us, so we felt safe. All the storekeepers watched over the local kids.

I let out a big sigh. "I wish it was still that way."

She squeezes me tighter. "You okay?"

I shrug. "When I came back after my Northwestern fiasco, I vowed to make this place better than when I was a kid. I haven't done that. This city, this street could be so much more, but people keep leaving instead of coming here."

She cranes her neck so we can see eye to eye. "You're such a wonderful man. You want so much for this town. I don't want any hard feelings when it comes to my money."

I cup her face in my hands. "Sugar, that's your money. You can stuff your mattress with it for all I care."

She buries her face in my chest. "What if I sell?"

Shit. I don't want to have this conversation right now. "It's not my place to tell you what to do. But I was hoping at least some of Smithville had rubbed off on you."

Andie grins and pulls me down for a kiss. "Some parts are unforgettable."

She nudges me toward her door and unlocks it then pulls me inside with her. We kiss our way up the stairs and finish our dinner plans there. I love second helpings of dessert.

CHAPTER FORTY-ONE
Andie

Gunnar is so cute, rocking back and forth, hands in his pockets, while he stands outside the church. When our eyes meet, his dimples pop out. He takes my breath away every time I see him.

"Hey," I squeak out.

"Mornin."

Gah. That drawl is going to make me melt faster than this hot sun. He takes my hand, and together, we walk into the church. He escorts me past the Jackson sisters, who can probably smell that we had sex less than five hours ago. And by the way Sarah gives me a thumbs-up, I'm even more certain. With a hand on the small of my back, he leads me into the pew with Faith and Lily.

Lily grabs my hand. "Sit by me."

"Okay."

Gunnar sits on the other side of me and wraps an arm around my shoulders, resting his hand on the back of the pew. I guess he's not afraid to show affection, so I rest my hand on his leg. I swear I hear photos being snapped behind me. *Calm down, Miss Sarah and Jennifer. We're buds now, right?*

"Tell me they didn't take a picture," I whisper to Gunnar.

He chuckles. "I think so. Don't worry about it." He runs his hand through my hair. *Snap. Snap.*

When the preacher enters, we all stand for the opening hymn. Gunnar pulls me close. His baritone voice rumbles down into my chest while he sings "Leaning on the Everlasting Arms."

As we pass the peace, the pastor approaches me. "Would you like to take up offering today?"

My throat closes up, not allowing any air to get in or out. "Uh, I don't know."

Lily pushes her way into the aisle. "Can I help?"

The pastor laughs and pats her cheek.

I give her little body a squeeze. "I would love your help. Come on." I take Lily's hand, and she leads me up to the altar. She picks up two baskets and hands me one. I take a peek over my shoulder at Gunnar, and he beams with pride. Lily begins on one side of the aisle, and I follow her lead. We walk down the aisle, stopping at each row for people to pass the basket back and forth. The Jackson sisters snap another photo then wave. For that picture, I hold out the basket and pose. Maybe they should put that phone down long enough to add some cash to the basket.

On the back pew sit Jolene, Stanley, and Willow. Jo slides her hand through the bend in Stanley's arm, I guess to remind me of her territory. He gives me a cheesy grin as he drops a few dollars in the plate. Willow juts her chin high and doesn't even acknowledge that I'm in front of her. We are in the house of God, so I'm not about to start a catfight in front of the pastor and the Jacksons. If she came here to start something, she will be disappointed.

After Lily and I finish the collection, we march back up to the front and place our baskets on the altar. I hold out my hand, and Lily high-fives me, making the entire congregation laugh. I nestle back into my pew by Gunnar, and he gives my shoulder a squeeze. He glances over his shoulder and groans. I assume he realized who was sitting in the back pew.

He leans over to whisper in my ear. "Next week, you might be ready to baptize some sinner."

I cover my mouth to keep from laughing out loud. The term *hell freezing over* comes to mind. "As long as I don't have to preach."

"You could talk about the splinter in your eye and the log in theirs," he whispers.

His breath tickles my neck, and I stifle a giggle, thinking about my blog post. "I'll just stick with love one another."

"I like that L word."

Holy crap. He's flirting with me in the middle of church, in front of God and the Jackson sisters. If he's not careful, I'm going to slide my hand up his thigh to see if I can feel the love.

FAITH WAS SO KIND TO invite me over for Sunday lunch. If I thought Gunnar was a walking muscle, he is nothing compared to her husband, Kevin. He worked all night as a fireman then dragged himself out of bed and to the table. His dark hair is still tousled. Lily favors him, and it's obvious by the way he talks to his daughter, he adores his little girl. With Lily, it is "Daddy this" and "Daddy that." And he goes along with it. That completely explains his pink toenails. Most men would hide them in shoes, but he wears flip-flops. I think my ovaries did a summersault.

Gunnar chuckles. "Bubble-gum pink is your color."

Kevin hikes up a leg and wiggles his toes. "If Lily likes it, then I like it."

Gunnar throws his head back in laughter. "I think your daughter shredded your man card."

Faith puts the lasagna dish in the middle of the table. "Actually, I burned it a long time ago." She leans over the table and kisses her husband.

Gunnar covers Lily's eyes, making her giggle.

Kevin drags Faith onto his lap. "You wait 'til you have a young'n of your own. You'll do anything she wants, and you'll love every stinkin' minute of it."

Gunnar's neck turns a splotchy pink, far pinker than Kevin's toes.

Faith stares at her husband. "Can I tell them?" she asks him.

He throws his hands in the air. "Sure."

"Tell us what?" Gunnar asks.

Lily pipes up. "Mama's going to have a baby."

I gasp and jump up to give Faith a hug. "That's so exciting."

Gunnar grins like a proud papa. "Another baby?"

"It's like this," Kevin starts. "When a man loves a woman, they—"

Gunnar covers his ears. "I don't want to know what my sister has been doing."

Kevin yawns and stretches his hands over his head. "It's not like you've been celibate, right?"

I freeze. Gunnar takes my hand under the table and gives it a squeeze.

Lily jumps up and down. "We're going to celebrate? Yay."

Faith tickles her daughter. "Sit. Let's eat before we have more Burt's Bees talk."

"What?" Kevin and I both ask.

Faith rolls her eyes. "Nothing. Let's eat."

We dive in to the most amazing lasagna I have ever eaten. Turns out, Faith uses beef and pork in her recipe. Right as I stuff my face completely full of food, Lily asks, "How was your date last night?"

I draw in a breath, and the food goes down the wrong way.

Kevin jumps up. "I've got this." He grabs me around the middle and performs the Heimlich maneuver on me, sending a huge hunk of pork like a projectile right onto Gunnar's face.

"I'm so sorry," I gasp.

Gunnar wipes his face. "The date wasn't that bad, was it?"

"Of course not," I say, coughing and waving him off. "It was one of my all-time top-ten dates."

Faith cocks an eyebrow. "Top ten, huh? Must have been the rotisserie chicken."

Gunnar spews iced tea all over my dress.

"Oh... Burt's Bees," Faith says.

I can't make eye contact with Gunnar without losing it. He wipes tears of laughter from his eyes. When we dare to look at each other, he cracks a grin that I can't resist. I know I've made an error in my best-ten-dates calculations.

"Okay, I admit it. It was the best date ever."

Gunnar drops his fork.

Lily picks up his fork and hands it to him. With a deadpan expression, she says, "Yep. Burt's Bees."

I have no idea what that is, but Gunnar and Faith collapse onto the table, crying with laughter. Kevin shrugs then takes another bite of lasagna as though it's a normal day at their house. It would be so nice to have a lively family like this. When I was growing up, all my mother did was throw a TV dinner in the microwave and say, "Eat up." Seeing Faith regard her husband with a twinkle in her eyes as she subconsciously rubs her belly wakes something up inside of me. I want that. I never thought I did, but I do now. I sneak a peek at Gunnar, who gives me a faint longing expression.

Surely he doesn't want that with me of all people. I'm a walking mess. If he knew what was best for him, he would run away from me as fast as he could. I am terrible, and he'll figure that out soon enough. This newfound sobriety is on shaky ground at best, until a rough patch comes my way to test how shaky it really is. I already messed up really bad that night when Gunnar thought someone had broken into the shop. I can't afford for anything like that to happen again.

"Uncle G, can Miss Andie help me pick out my bedroom in your house? You promised when I turned five, I could have my own room in case Mama was driving me crazy."

He drops his second fork.

Faith grins. "Oh, he did, did he? Actually, I think that's a great idea. Andie, have you seen what Gunnar's done to his place? There's a shortcut from our property to his through our backyard."

He stares at his sister, his eyes bugging out of their sockets.

"No, he hasn't shown me his house." This is becoming a pattern with him.

Gunnar stuffs his mouth with a roll.

Faith points out the back window. "You can almost see it from here. I can't believe he did it himself."

"Hey," Gunnar mumbles, a piece of his roll falling out of his mouth.

Kevin points his fork at his wife. "Wait a second. I think I remember putting in a whole bunch of hours on my days off."

She kisses him on the cheek. "Yes, but I've come to expect that from you." She side-eyes Gunnar. "Him? Not so much."

Lily giggles.

"Oh, you think that's funny, don't you?" Gunnar tickles her.

She squeals and runs around the table to hide behind me. I block her from Gunnar's wiggling fingers.

"Silly girls don't get to pick out their bedroom at their favorite uncle's house."

She peeks out from around me. I give Lily a squeeze, and she takes me by the hand and drags me to the back door.

I point at the dirty dishes. "I should help your mother clean up."

Faith waves it off. "Nonsense. Go check out the Ponderosa."

Gunnar stands and sneers. "Stop calling it that."

Faith gives him a smirk. "Wait 'til you see it. All that's missing is the map with the fire burning through it."

Gunnar and I walk down a brick walkway, with Lily holding our hands. When we turn a corner, I'm faced with a huge log cabin. I gasp. His house does resemble the Ponderosa. When I was a kid, we didn't have cable television, so if I wanted to watch anything, it was the channel that showed old westerns from the sixties. In *Bonanza*, the Cartwrights lived in a huge log cabin called the Ponderosa, and if I didn't know better, I would think we were on the set of that old television show. And Michael Landon was hot back in the day, so I certainly didn't mind watching the show.

"Oh my, Faith wasn't kidding."

"Not you too."

Lily and I run up to the broad front porch and climb the steps. Gunnar lollygags behind us. She pulls me down into the porch swing, and the warm breeze rushes past us. From his front porch is a perfect view of the lake. I bet sunsets are crazy beautiful from this view.

"Any chance you've got one of the Cartwrights tucked away in there?"

Gunnar leans against the porch railing, watching us swing back and forth, my hair flying in my face.

"Don't tell me you're a Little Joe fan."

I stumble out of the swing, and Gunnar catches me. "Who isn't? I bet Lily even knows who Little Joe is."

Lilly nods. "Uh-huh, and he's hot."

I gasp, but I can't argue with her.

Lily takes my hand and leads me inside. I almost cry. The front room is enormous, with real log chinking and a vaulted ceiling. A stone fireplace accents one large wall. Above the mantel is a huge flat-screen television. The open floor plan allows me to see all the way into the immense kitchen that includes a wraparound granite bar. The massive dining room table has to be one of a kind. Photos of Gunnar in various stages of his life line the hallway. Lily's face adorns the end tables. I'm drawn to the kitchen. It is Old West meets modern Southern, and it's perfect. I run my hand across the cool granite countertop, taking it all in. To the left is a hallway that leads to more rooms. To the right is an enormous staircase.

"Gunnar, this is a masterpiece."

He walks up behind me, rubbing my shoulders. "I did okay."

I lean into him. "Okay? I've never seen anything this beautiful. It fits the landscape too."

"There's a great view of the lake from the upstairs balcony."

"It's perfect."

He pulls out a water bottle and hands it to Lily. "Not everyone thought so."

My heart breaks for him. He poured his heart and soul into this home for Willow, and she turned her nose up at it.

He walks over to help Lily open up the bottle. She runs up the stairs. At the top, she turns to us. "Well, come on."

Gunnar's expression is distant. I touch his cheek. "You okay?"

He wags his head. "I don't go upstairs much. You go on up. I'll be down here."

I pull him down to sit on a barstool and stand between his legs. He rests his hands on my hips.

"You don't go upstairs in your own home? Do you sleep on the couch?"

He chuckles. "Sometimes." He motions down the hallway. "There's a guest bedroom on this level that I use."

"Are you going to tell me why, or do I have to beat it out of you?" I rear back, and he grabs my fist.

He kisses every knuckle.

I stand and take his hand. "Come on, big boy. You can do this." I tug him toward the steps.

He follows me. We find Lily in the first bedroom on the front side of the house. It has a window seat, built-in bookshelves, and a huge walk-in closet. It's a little girl's dream.

"Wow, Lily. Is this the one?" I ask.

She bobs her head and wraps her arms around Gunnar's leg.

"It's all yours, baby. You can stay here anytime your mother approves."

"Can I get a big bed with a canopy?"

He picks her up and hugs her tight. "Anything you want."

"Yay!"

I high-five her. "Yay!"

She wiggles out of his arms and barrels down the steps.

Gunnar cringes. "Careful. Please don't break your neck. Your mother would have my hide."

"God love her."

"She has no idea how much she's saved me."

I think I get it now. I take his hand, and we walk down to the end of the hallway. He stiffens when we get to the last door on the left. I open the door to find a master bedroom that takes up the entire back part of the second level. It's bigger than any apartment I have ever lived in. The California king bed seems more like a twin in this enormous room. I turn in circles, taking in the room. The huge picture window on one end gives a clear view of the field and the lake in the distance. I open a door and about wet my pants to find a massive second-level porch that runs the entire length of the house.

Gunnar leans against the French door. "I built this for Willow. It was a surprise. On weekends and nights, I would work from sunup to sundown, and Kevin did a lot during the week when he was off work. It wasn't complete, but I couldn't wait to show it to her. So the night before our wedding, I drove her down here. I made her wear a blindfold, which she hated. I walked her up the steps, and in that very spot where you are now, I removed her blindfold to show her what I had done for us."

"I'm guessing she was underwhelmed."

He snorts.

If I ever get Willow alone, I'm going to give her a piece of my mind. The nerve of her to break him like that.

"Is that why you've never brought me here?"

"Yeah. Stupid, I know."

I take his hand and pull him out onto the balcony. From up here, we both see Lily running back to her house. Her daddy picks her up and swings her around.

"It's not stupid. Not at all. This was a labor of love, and it wasn't enough. I'm so sorry." I pause for a moment. "Just to be clear, when Willow stayed at your house, did you..."

He pulls me close. "She hates storms for a very legitimate reason, and in good conscience, I couldn't let her drive during the storm. As much as she hurt me, I couldn't do that to even her. But I am not lying to you when I say nothing happened."

I swallow hard and fight off all the doubt I have swirling around in my mind because I want to believe him. "You promise?"

He cups my face. "I promise. And I am not going to Northwestern."

I wrap my arms around him, and he pulls me close. If I wasn't sure before, I am completely convinced now. I'm falling hard for Gunnar, and I like how it feels.

"Tell me something." I point toward the lake. "Is this the same lake where we did our moon bathing?"

"Affirmative."

"You let me pee behind a rock when a real bathroom was on the other side of the shore?"

A pink blush creeps up his neck. "I'm sorry. I wasn't ready to let you in. I am now." He kisses me on the lips and runs his hands through my hair. When we come up for air, he whispers, "Stay with me tonight. Here, in this room."

"I'm not Willow."

"I know. Thank you for not being her."

I lick my lips. "I'll stay, but you have to do two things for me."

His eyes grow big with anticipation.

"One: make sure that front door is locked."

He grins. "Done. What's the second?"

"Can we fire up that Jacuzzi tub?"

He tickles my neck with kisses. "Absolutely."

CHAPTER FORTY-TWO
Gunnar

Not more than thirty seconds after Andie leaves my house this morning, there's a knock on my front door. I rush downstairs, my heart skipping a beat. Andie must not be ready to leave. I'll be late for work if it means more time with that beautiful girl.

I fling the door open. "Did you forget—"

Instead of Andie standing there, it's Willow. She's wearing her standard-issue short shorts and wedge heels. She threads a strand of her long hair through her fingers. This cannot be happening. I peer over her head to make sure Andie's gone. *Whew.*

"Don't worry. She left before I knocked." Her snarky smile makes me doubt her words.

Every muscle in my body stiffens. I want to scream. "What do you want?"

She slides her claws down my chest as she pushes past me. What once made my body come alive now sends shivers down my spine.

"To talk."

She roams through the living room and toward the kitchen as if she owns the place. I know that look, and she's evaluating every piece of furniture in my house. In the kitchen, she pilfers through my cabinets until she finds two coffee cups.

"Can I make you some coffee?"

"Nope. I need to get ready for work so..." I point toward the front door.

She opens the refrigerator and pulls out a bottle of water, takes a sip, then licks her lips.

I roll my eyes.

"Have you thought any more about my plan?"

I point at the door, hoping she'll get the hint. "I don't need to think about it."

Her hips sway back and forth as she walks toward her prey—me. "Perfect. I'll have the movers here by the end of the week. We can sell this place and start over."

I chuckle as I swat her hand away from my face. "We?"

She blinks, realizing her slip. "I meant you, of course." She bats away fake tears. "I miss you so much."

"Sure you do. That's why you were screwing around on me and why you've been shacking up with Miles ever since you've been back, right? Does Phillip know?"

She winks, and I think I'm going to hurl. "Aww. Are you checking up on me?"

I turn my back to her. "Don't flatter yourself. It's a small town, remember? I don't care who you "do." I am over you. I thought you were smart enough to get the hint the other day."

She shakes her head, her platinum-blond hair swishing around her shoulders. "I don't believe that." She twirls in a circle, her arms open wide. "Look at this place. You built this for me. You want me back."

What I should be doing is showing her the door, but I need to get this off my chest so I can move on. "All these years, I wondered what it would feel like to have you here, wanting what I want."

Her eyes grow big with anticipation. I walk toward her and put my hands on her shoulders. She sighs. Of course she would think it was a gesture of affection. I only want her complete attention.

A loud gasp comes from the living room. I swing around to see Andie standing there, a single eyebrow raised.

Dammit.

"Andie." I rush to her. "It's not what you think. Let me finish."

She walks around me, past a grinning Willow. She runs up the stairs and to the master bedroom, with me right on her heels. She rushes around the bedroom and finds her phone on the nightstand.

"Please, Andie. Let me explain."

She snatches up her phone. She shows it to me and walks out of the room. I grab her arm and turn her around toward me. She stares at the floor, her chest rising and falling.

"Don't leave. Not like this."

"Gunnar—"

"She's here to cause trouble. I don't want her here."

She smiles, but it doesn't reach her eyes. "I know, but why is she here? She's always around because you let her. I can't deal with it."

My heart sinks. I cup her face and swipe a tear from her eye. "Can we talk later?" *Please, please, please.*

She groans. I place my lips on hers for a soft, loving kiss. She holds on to my T-shirt before she gives me a slight push away. She walks down the steps, her chin jutted out, making sure she doesn't make eye contact with Willow. With all the grace of a true Southerner, she walks through the living room, toward the front door.

"Toodles," Willow says.

Andie walks up to Willow and cranes her neck to make eye contact with her. "I may not be from around here, but I know better than to get in a pissing match with a hellcat." She points at me. "Gunnar's a great guy. Near perfect. He deserves someone perfect for him. It may not be me, but I'm damned sure it's not you. Oh, and that Jacuzzi tub... fantastic."

She opens the door to leave, when Willow throws her last barb. "You know, he got kicked out of Northwestern for cheating."

Andie freezes. The glint in Willow's eyes turns my blood boiling hot.

"That's right. This perfect man got caught plagiarizing on his thesis."

"Willow, stop!" I yell.

Willow slides her hand up my arm, causing a shiver to run up my spine. I snatch it out of her grasp.

"Did you know he's moving back with me?"

"No, I'm not."

Andie walks out the door, and when I hear it click, I stare down at Willow.

"What?"

"You need to go. Now."

She rolls her eyes. "She's going to leave you. She's going back to Boston, and you'll be stuck here in this big ole stupid house all by yourself, unless you take me up on my offer."

I don't know who she thinks she is, but she's crossed a line that can never be uncrossed. I take her by the arm and lead her to the front door. I open the door and plant her on the front porch.

"There are two things you need to know. The first is you don't want what I want. You never have and still don't. And secondly, even if you did, I. Don't. Want. You."

Her mouth drops open.

"That's right. I'd rather be alone in this 'stupid' house than be with you."

With that, I slam the door. I stomp upstairs to get ready for work. After all this time, when I've decided to move on, she comes back into my life and pulls this shit. I have finally moved on and found someone who truly cares for me, who doesn't try to change me, and I think I'm in love with her. Now I have to deal with this shit.

Willow doesn't care for me. She doesn't want me. She only wants to make sure no one else can have me. It's not going to work.

CHAPTER FORTY-THREE
Andie

I t took only two blocks on the drive of shame before the tears began streaming down my face. I'm so stupid. It's not that I don't think Gunnar's feelings are real, because I know they are. I see it in his eyes, feel it in my heart, but I'll never be able to compete with her. Willow is so perfect. She's got perfect hair that doesn't frizz in this Southern humidity like mine does, and her face is flawless. She doesn't even have one freckle. I'm not sure if that's even legal in the South. I've only been here for a short while, and I can already find constellations in all the freckles popping out on my chest and shoulders. And I don't even want to start on those long, sexy legs of hers. Who knows how many times they've been wrapped around Gunnar? The thought sends chills down my spine.

Mrs. Cavanaugh is already rolling out dough when I walk in. Without even missing a beat, she asks, "Rough night?"

I slump onto the barstool in front of her and wipe a stray tear away. "The night was wonderful. The morning is another story."

She stops what she's doing and pours cups of coffee for both of us before motioning for me to follow her to the nearest table. We both pour coffee into our saucers and slurp from them.

"Child, what's wrong?"

I play with the spoon as it gives me a distorted reflection of myself in the metal. "Miss Etta, I like him. A lot."

When I have the courage to face her again, she cackles. "Glad to see you're finally admitting it."

I cry into my hands. She pats my arm and waits for me to catch my breath.

"It's Willow," I finally say.

Miss Etta tsks. "She's a viper. He's not stupid... anymore. Don't you worry about a thing. She'll be gone soon enough to toy with her next prey."

"And I'll be gone soon too."

"That's up to you."

I think about the blueprints I have in my apartment upstairs. That's the easiest thing to do. I can sell my property, run away, and forget all about this place. I can do that. I think I can.

"It's probably for the best. I get what's best for me, and Willow gets what she wants."

"What about Gunnar? Does he get what he wants?"

I shrug. "If I leave town, I leave him. He's made it very clear this town is what he wants. He wants this town to thrive, and he wants to be a part of it."

"Nice of you to speak for him. I think, given the choice, he might surprise you at what he'd choose."

I shake my head. "If he wouldn't move to Chicago for Willow, he won't move to Boston for me. And he doesn't care enough about me to be fully honest with me. I don't know if I trust him."

She slurps her coffee then smacks her lips. "Again, nice of you to speak for him. You aren't Willow. I've known both of them since they were in diapers. As long as he was doing what she wanted, everything was fine. When he wanted something different, she'd pout. I think he knew things were going south with her and needed her to say it. He didn't build that house for her. He might think so, but he built that house to test her. And she failed."

The door chimes, and in walk the two developers. "Hello, Ms. Carson."

"Morning. I didn't expect to see you today." *Crap*. I don't need this today.

Mrs. Cavanaugh stands and grumbles under her breath. "We got lots of jam and scones orders today. I'll get right on it."

"I'll be there to help in a second."

The developers take their place at my table and pull out documents. "We did some comps to find out what your store is worth, and you'll see here our offer is way above what it's worth."

The offer is very appealing. I could sell, leave this place and everyone in this town behind, take my inheritance, and never have to step foot in this city again. I peek over their shoulders as Mrs. Cavanaugh cuts out biscuits in record time. She hums a gospel hymn that I actually recognize. "Leaning on the Everlasting Arms" has become my earworm this summer. I've really become attached to Mrs. Cavanaugh, and to Gunnar.

"In thirty days, we could have this building leveled and start working our way down the street. In six months, we could break ground for the new Save A-Lot."

In a soft voice, Mrs. Cavanaugh sings the words to a gospel tune. "No, never alone, no, never alone. He promised never to leave me, never to leave me alone."

A car creeps down the road, the driver waving at the pedestrians as they go. Stan knocks on the window and waves as he heads to work at the mill. The Jackson sisters walk in and take their usual seats. I wave to them. Even though they are cantankerous, I've grown fond of them. As usual, they take a picture of me with the two men.

Then Willow walks in.

She smirks as she sashays up to the counter. Mrs. Cavanaugh takes her order, but I wouldn't put it past her to spit in Willow's coffee. While she waits on her coffee and scone, she wanders close to our table. Her acting skills are terrible because even though she appears as though she's checking out the plants in the window, I know she's listening to every word we're saying.

"So, do we have a deal?"

I stare at the two men, at Mrs. Cavanaugh, at the Jackson sisters, and then at Willow. She cocks an eyebrow. Mrs. Cavanaugh clears her throat and hands Willow her cup. Willow takes a sip of her coffee, scrunches her nose up, then walks to the door and freezes. She turns around and, with a smarmy sneer, she asks me the most off-the-wall question.

"Have you met the mayor?"

"Yep. I've checked that off my 'how to fit in' list. Why?"

She taps her cup with her finger. "Just wondering, because he would do pretty much anything to keep this town from sinking. I bet he'd even go so far as to suggest that someone do a little time in the sack to encourage a person to see things his way."

I cackle at her insane comment. "I have a business to run, but thank you for your input."

"Okay, but one day, I'll say 'I told you so.'" Her syrupy, singsong voice makes me want to claw her eyes out.

And with that, Willow prances out of the shop.

I don't care about anything that comes out of her mouth. I watch her get in her car and drive away, then I look back at the two men. "I don't know anymore. If you had asked me a month ago to sign the papers, I would have done it lickety-split."

The man furrows his brow. "Lickety-split?"

I chuckle. "I would have signed in a heartbeat. But now, this place, these people..." I point at Mrs. Cavanaugh and the Jackson sisters. "They're like family. I need more time. I don't know if I want to sell anymore."

The man's jaw drops. "You're staying here?"

I shrug. "I don't know about that. All I know is this store is important to them... and to me. So either you can give me more time to think about it, or I'll have to say no right now. What will it be?" Even if things go south with Gunnar, I don't know if I can bail on this town and these people.

Both of the Jackson sisters' jaws have hit the table. Miss Jennifer winks and gives me a thumbs-up.

CHAPTER FORTY-FOUR
Gunnar

Time to face the music. I didn't want to believe Willow because, well, she's Willow, but curiosity got the best of me. She texted me that she saw developers at In A Jam, going over plans, and that Andie was very interested in what they were saying. I know she's trying to get under my skin, but even if there is a grain of truth to her observation, I have to know for sure. So I drop the dumbbells I'm lifting and run across the street to see for myself.

Through the store window, I see Andie talking to two men, mulling over paperwork, exactly like Willow said. *Dammit.* Andie's going to sell. She's not the person I thought she was. I'm so stupid.

The two men almost knock me down as they fling the door open to leave. I watch them as they stomp down the sidewalk, one of them flailing his hands in the air.

With eyes trained on the floor, I sulk into the coffee shop and sit down on a barstool.

Andie comes out from the back and freezes when she sees me. She gives me a half-smile then pours me a glass of sweet tea.

"Hey," she says, her voice soft and tentative.

I motion with my head but find the newspaper someone left on the counter more interesting. I immerse myself into the front-page article, not giving a hoot about what the school board voted on for next year.

"I'm glad you stopped by. Things got a little... crowded this morning."

I focus on the article.

She clears her throat. "Are you okay?"

When I don't answer, she uses a finger to pull the newspaper away from my face so I have to make eye contact with her.

"I'm fine."

"I was hoping you'd stop by this morning, and when you didn't—"

"I'm busy. That's all. Keeping things safe in this dried-up, podunk town."

She takes a step back. "Huh?"

My eyes bore holes into hers. "Nothing."

She turns to Mrs. Cavanaugh but still speaks to me. "Are you sure you're okay? You don't normally have this tone."

I fold up the newspaper and slide it away from me. With a chuckle, I say, "So you know me a few weeks, and you think you really know me. Right?"

She folds her arms across her chest. "Did I do something wrong this morning? I'm sorry I came back to get my phone. I wish I hadn't because I don't want to get in the middle of things."

She thinks this is about Willow. I stand, chug down the last of my iced tea, pull out a few dollars, and slam them onto the counter. "Add that to your coffers."

"What?"

I turn to leave. "As if you don't know."

The Jacksons stop mid-bite to listen. I don't give a damn if it shows up in their next blog or not.

Andie runs around the counter and grabs my arm. "Really, I don't."

I snatch my arm from her grip. Her eyes pool with tears. *Too bad.* She's brought this on herself.

She snaps her head around toward Mrs. Cavanaugh. "What did I do?"

"I ain't gettin' involved." But that sneer tells me I've overstepped my bounds.

"Smart woman. Good day, Mrs. Cavanaugh."

When I stomp back to the fitness center, I brave a glimpse at Andie standing in the doorway of her shop, wiping tears off her face. *Way to go, idiot.* I let Willow drive a wedge between Andie and me. The cop in me should have gotten her side of the story, but the man who has been hurt before overtook my brain.

IF SHE LEFT HER DOOR open on purpose, I'm going to be pissed. I peek into the dark coffee shop. It appears to be fine. The cash register door is open, showing the drawer is empty, a clear indicator Andie went to the bank earlier tonight. No tables are overturned; nothing is out of the ordinary. If I don't investigate and something really did happen, I would never forgive myself, so I tiptoe toward the steps.

"Andie, are you up there?"

The door to Andie's apartment opens, and she gasps. "Gunnar, what are you doing here?"

I jerk my thumb toward the front door. "You left your door open... again."

She descends the steps and flips on a light. "You're kidding."

I put my hands on my hips. I'm not buying her naive act. I've had too many years with Willow to know bullshit when I see it.

"Did you do that on purpose?"

She cringes. "Guilty."

I groan and head toward the front door.

She grabs my arm. "Wait. Don't leave. As long as you're here, we need to talk."

She takes my hand, and I yank it away.

"You're already here. Come on."

"Make it quick."

Andie leads me upstairs, like a calf to the slaughter. She plops me down on the couch and kneels on the floor by my feet.

"What?"

"What?" she mimics.

"What?"

Andie grins.

I stare at her with no expression. The faster I can get out of here, the better.

"What is wrong? Please tell me what I did wrong. I thought a lot about it, and I don't care what Willow said. The fact that you cheated is really none of my business, anyway."

"So you met with the developers today, right?" I motion with my head to the corner of the room, where the rolls of blueprints rest in the corner.

"Oh. That."

My jaw drops. "Yeah... that."

She sits next to me on the couch. I move as far away from her as I can.

"I never kept that a secret from you. You always knew that was a possibility. I have fulfilled every part of my grandmother's will. I can sell if I want to. But let me explain."

I stand. Sitting next to her fogs my brain. I walk into her kitchenette. She has the photos from the county fair on the refrigerator, secured with a Georgia peach magnet. That seems like ages ago, but I have relived that night a thousand times in my mind.

"I know. I only thought that..."

She stands next to me and touches my arm. "Thought what? That since we—"

She backs away and bumps into the counter. I turn to sneer at her. She stumbles out of the kitchen and into the living room. Her eyes are wide, and her mouth drops. "No. Please, no."

"No, what?"

She covers her face with her hands. "Please tell me you didn't... we didn't... you weren't trying to... what Willow said." She collapses onto the couch and buries her head against her knees. "Oh God, no."

I walk toward her. Even though I'm angry, if something is going on I don't know about, I want to know if there's anything I can do.

She stares up at me, her eyes pooling with tears. "Did you use me?"

I freeze. "Are you kidding me? For all I know, you used me. You know, get in good with the cop so he wouldn't rat you out."

I've hit a nerve because she bolts off the couch and stomps toward me. She pokes me in the chest. "I don't need your protection."

And I don't need this. I walk away from her but yell over my shoulder, "You don't need anyone, do you, little rich girl? You don't need anything or anyone, and you sure as hell don't need me."

I take two steps down the stairs, and she's right behind me. "You're mad that I won't give all that money away to your... your Podunk town. Isn't that right?"

I stand at the bottom of the steps. "That's not it."

"Sure it is. You used me to get the money, but it didn't work. I know about the mayor."

I turn to face her. She's on a step above me, so we are almost nose to nose, and I guess by my expression, she senses there was some truth to the rumor.

"I don't give a damn about your money." She takes one step up on the stairs, and so do I. "What I do care about is this town was great at one time, and little by little, it's changing because big corporations come in and take over. There's hardly any small businesses anymore.

It's unethical to make lots of money by making everyone around you poor."

She stumbles on the top step and splats down on her butt. I hover over her and get real close to her ear so she won't miss anything I have to say. Her eyes are huge, and her chest rises and falls with every heavy breath.

"When you sell, this entire downtown will fold. There won't be anyone left."

"I didn't know—"

"Just stop it." I straighten up so she now has to crane her neck to see me. "But remember this. You had a chance at a family. This entire town welcomed you like you'd lived here your entire life. You snubbed it. You snubbed us all." I lean back down and whisper, "But you'll have all that money and maybe a bottle of booze too. Maybe all that will keep that cold heart of yours warm at night."

I stiffen my back and walk down the steps. "Good night, Miss Carson."

Before I storm out of her store, I hear her sobs from the stairwell. I don't really care, but that doesn't keep me from feeling like a total jackass.

CHAPTER FORTY-FIVE
Andie

My pillowcase is soaked with all the tears I shed last night. I never thought I could create that many tears. My eyes are almost swollen shut from the puffiness. If it weren't for Mrs. Cavanaugh downstairs tending to customers, I would have had to close shop today. I sit on the floor with my back resting against the couch, flipping through my grandmother's scrapbooks and hoping some sort of solace will fall out of the worn pages. Three empty tissue boxes rest beside me, and snot rags litter the floor. A picture of me when I was little falls out, and I pick it up off the floor. On the back, in faint blue pen, someone wrote, "Andie, age six." I vaguely remember that day. It might have been the last time Mom brought me down here to see my granny. I guess I'll never know what happened between them.

But I feel so close to my grandmother here. It's almost as if she's still alive. The scent of brown sugar always seemed to float all around her. I close my eyes and see her putzing around her kitchen, me right on her heels. I wish Mom had let me spend more time with her. All I have left of her are a few sparse belongings and this shop.

A knock on the apartment door jolts me back to reality. Maybe it's Gunnar. Maybe he had a fitful night too and wants to talk, really talk this time.

"Andie, can I come in?" Liza Jane asks, and my hopes fade.

"I don't feel very well." My voice cracks. "Maybe later."

"Honey, please let me in."

I let out a big sigh and unlock the door. Liza puts down a cooler and holds out her arms. I fall into them, which starts another wave of tears.

"Come on, honey. We need to have some girl talk." Liza lets me cry until I can't produce any more tears. She holds a beer out to me, but I wave it off.

I sip from my water bottle, trying to replenish the fluids I've lost. "I had him figured for a really nice guy."

She touches my arm. "He is."

"It's always been about the money. Even our..."

"No. That's not true. I don't believe that for one second. I don't care what it seems like. It's not his way. He really cares about you."

I wipe my nose on the hem of my T-shirt. "He didn't give me a chance to explain. I was having second thoughts about selling, but maybe I should. The developers weren't happy with me putting them off but said they'd call me in a few days." More tears pour out. "He was downright mean last night."

Liza hands me a fresh box of tissues and hugs me for the umpteenth time, never judging me, always treating me like the sister and friend I need. "Do you care about him?"

"I don't want to."

Liza giggles. "You didn't answer my question."

I sit upright and wipe my nose again.

"Well... do you?"

I nod. "I love him, but it doesn't matter anymore."

"What did he say when you told him?"

I squeeze my eyes shut, and more tears escape.

"Oh, Lord have mercy. You haven't told him? Sweetheart, I don't know how you do it in Boston, but down here, the boys are so dense, you have to knock them upside the head to make sure they know how you feel."

I almost grin at that.

She bumps me on the shoulder with hers. "That's probably why he hasn't told you how he feels about you."

"You don't know that, and right now, I'm so mad at him, I don't care."

"Oh, honey, I know. I know Gunnar better than he knows himself. He is In. Love. With. You."

I wipe another tear away. "He accused me of single-handedly letting the town fall apart if I sell. I didn't know how bad it had gotten." *Sniff, sniff.*

She nods. "Yeah, we're barely keeping our heads above water, but that's not your fault. Trust me. He loves you. He's just being an ass right now."

I blow out a raspberry. "How can he love me when even I don't love me?"

Liza lights up a cigarette and puffs away from me. "None of us are worthy of the people that love us. Hell, as much as I tease Jake, he's a saint for putting up with my shit. I'd be lost without him. Tell me this. When you wake up in Gunnar's arms, do you feel like running, or do you feel like staying?"

Every time I've slept with Gunnar, I've prayed the night would never end. I fit in the crook of his arm as if I were tailor-made for that very place. I love waking up to find him with a content expression on his face. I'll never find that with anyone else, no matter where I go.

I know the answer but can't make my mouth say the words. I chance a glance up at Liza Jane, and she cocks an eyebrow.

"That's what I thought." She chucks her cigarette butt inside her beer can then gathers all the tissues and bottles up and tosses them in the trash can. "Don't make a rash decision based on this one misunderstanding. I'm sure that's all it is. Do you want me to beat some sense into him?"

I shake my head, causing my snot-filled sinuses to explode with pain. "Oh no. Please don't."

She pouts. "I won't, but if he comes to me, I won't hold back."

We sit in silence. She sips on a beer, and I blow my nose for the twentieth time. Finally, I have the nerve to ask. "What about Willow?"

She mimics sticking a finger down her throat. "Don't make me lose my breakfast."

I bite my lip to keep from laughing. "You are terrible."

Liza giggles. "I tell it like I see it."

"But if he's not interested, he sure has a funny way of showing it. He seems to jump every time she snaps her fingers."

Liza rolls her eyes. "She knows how to play him, but trust me, he's not interested. She's only here to stir up trouble, and when she realizes it's not working, she'll start sniffing around somebody else, hopefully back in Chicago so we don't smell her stench down here."

I stand and give Liza a big hug. I love her like the sister I never had. "And you see me as one huge mess, don't you?"

"Girl, I see you as flawed, like the rest of us. But what I really see is someone who is madly in love with one of my best friends, and that makes me really happy. You deserve each other, so please, don't do anything in haste."

I kiss her cheek. "I promise. Thank you so much."

"That's what sisters do. Talk to him, okay? Don't let this fester."

"I'll think about it." I wrap my arms around her neck and cry some more. "Thank you. I needed to hear that. I don't have any family, and for you to say that to me..."

"Girl, what are you talking about? You have a huge family here. We all love you. Even the Jacksons."

We both get a giggle out of that.

She points at me. "Now, missy, you take a long, hot bubble bath, put an ice pack on those puffy eyes, and get down there to help Mrs. C. because it's packed."

My eyes widen. "Really?"

"Yep. People love your jam."

I bet they do, and I love them.

My phone buzzes. It's Tinsley. "I need to take this."

"Sure thing. I'll show myself out." Liza picks up her empty cooler and scoots down the stairs.

I take one more sniffle before I answer the phone. "Hey, Tinsley."

"Hey, how's it going?"

"Okay."

"Hmm." He's not usually so lost for words.

I collect my used tissues and toss them into a trash can in the kitchen. "It's been a bad day. That's all."

"Bad as in..."

"No, not that kind of bad. I'm completely sober, unfortunately. It's... I don't know what to do."

"About what? The money? 'Cause I got a kid that's gonna need college in about ten years. Just saying."

I chuckle. "I'll keep that in mind. I don't want to leave, but..." My voice quivers. "Things didn't work out like I thought they would."

"With a certain George Clooney with a twang."

I roll my eyes, and if he wasn't dead-on correct, I would come back with a snarky remark. The pictures of Gunnar and me on my refrigerator catch my eye. "Maybe."

"I'm sorry about that, kiddo. You're a great person. Don't let anyone tell you different. You hear me?"

"I hear ya." I pluck the pictures off the refrigerator and toss them into a drawer.

"Here goes nothing. I'm no romantic, but sometimes people are afraid to show how they really feel. And us guys are the worst about feelings and stuff like that. So don't give up on him. I think he's a fine guy."

"Tins, you've never even met him."

"No, but I got spidey senses, and my superpowers say he's one of the good ones. You deserve to be happy."

The bells over the door downstairs ring, reminding me I need to tend to customers. "I need to go, but thanks for the pep talk. I'll see you soon."

As I descend the stairs, I do a quick evaluation of my life. I have a business and friends and a place to call home, but I may need to give it all up because Gunnar had them before I did.

CHAPTER FORTY-SIX
Gunnar

Here I am again, sitting in the hardware store, waiting on some divine intervention from my best friend. I hate having these feelings. It's so much easier being closed off to everyone. It's even easier to be the "one and done" guy because there's never any emotional attachment. This thing I feel for Andie is physical, emotional, with even some spiritual feelings all rolled into one messy ball.

Jake mixes a can of paint, while I sit on the counter, flipping through the color-swatch cards. He takes the can out of the mixer, opens the lid, dabs his finger into the paint, swipes some paint onto the lid, then hammers the lid closed with a mallet.

"I can't believe she accused me of sleeping with her so she wouldn't sell."

Jake raises a shoulder and cringes. "You did tell me what the mayor said."

"But that never entered my mind when we were, uh, when I... I'm not the kind of person who does stuff like that anymore. She's too..."

Jake whistles. "Man, you got it bad."

"I do not. Okay, maybe I care about her a little bit. Man, I was a jerk to her. Something snapped, and it was like I was a ventriloquist dummy and somebody was pulling my strings."

The fish over the door starts singing, and Stanley walks in, holding a Styrofoam cup.

"Hey, Stan."

"What's up?" He spits tobacco juice into the cup.

Jake lights up a cigarette. "Talking about Andie."

Stanley snickers and spits again. "You like her, don't you?"

I throw my hands in the air. Nothing goes unnoticed in this town. "All right, I care about her. A lot. You happy?"

Stanley and Jake wait for me to continue.

"I knew better than to get involved with her. I knew she wasn't going to stay, but..."

Jake puffs smoke in the air. "Were you listening to the little head?"

Stanley chuckles.

I whack him in the chest, almost knocking over his spit cup. "It was like I had known her all my life."

Stanley removes the Skoal can out of his back pocket. He turns around to show us his backside. He points to his pants.

"You see how these jeans are worn where my can's been?"

I glance over at Jake. He shrugs. He doesn't seem to have a clue where this is going, either.

"Uh, Stan, are you saying you need some new jeans?"

Stan shows me the can then slides it back into his jeans pocket. "See how nice it fits right in that pocket? Like it belongs there?" He pats the pocket. "Like the pocket has stretched to hold it jusssst right."

Jake and I stare at each other. He shrugs.

"Yeah? Go on," I say.

Stanley takes the can out of his pocket again and shows it to me. "Without the can, the pocket droops and feels all empty."

I try not to grin, but it's not easy. "Okay."

Stanley pops open the can and puts a fresh plug of tobacco in his bottom lip. "She's your Skoal."

Jake's jaw drops open.

"She fills my... pants?"

Jake turns around and chuckles; his whole body trembles.

"No, silly," Stan says. "She fills your heart. Your heart is like the droopy pocket. Without her, it's missing something. She fills in the missing pieces of your heart."

Wow. Stanley rocks back and forth on his heels then bows. Jake high-fives Stan.

"Uh, Stan. I don't really know what to say to that. When did you get all philosophical?"

He grins a toothless grin. "When I met my Skoal. Jolene means the world to me."

I pat Stan on the back. "I don't care if you ever get your GED. You are one of the wisest people I've ever met. Thanks, man."

When I didn't think his smile could get any bigger, it does.

The bass song starts up again, and Liza walks in. Her eyebrows are raised, and her hands are on her hips.

"Hey, Liza," Stanley says.

Jake points to Stanley. "Liza, who is Stan's Skoal?"

She rolls her eyes at her husband. "Duh. Jolene."

Stan hugs her. She paces the room. *Uh-oh.* I don't like it when she gets like this.

"Gunnar, that girl is a mess. You have to make things right."

Sometimes, I want to hide and not let anyone know anything that's going on in my life. "Liza, some things aren't meant to be. She's great, and it's been fun, but she doesn't want the same things I do. She doesn't care if downtown folds when she sells."

"Bullshit," all three of them say.

Liza gets right in my face. "You are a jerk for making her feel guilty about selling. It does not fall on her shoulders whether the town sinks or swims, so you owe her an apology. Gunnar, talk to her."

"No. She's angry, and I can't blame her. Besides, we've already said everything that needs to be said. "

She smirks, and I lean back, waiting for her comeback. "Everything but three sweet, simple words."

I chuckle. "Okay, Yente."

Her face turns beet red. She hates it when I call her matchmaker.

"I appreciate what you're doing, but I need to be alone for a while. I might even go to Chicago to clear my head."

Steam practically shoots out of Liza's ears. "Mister, if you do that, you will be disowned. That chick is so full of herself, I bet she screams out her own name during sex."

Stanley backs out of the room. "On that note, I'm out of here. Remember. Pocket. Skoal. Think about it."

I don't have any plans of going to Chicago, especially when it would mean being with Willow, but I love getting a rise out of Liza. She deserves it. I love her like a sister, but sometimes, she needs to butt out. And the best way to stop the freight train of her mouth is to freak her out.

"Relax. I'm not going anywhere with Willow."

She points her finger. "You better not, or I'll knock you into the middle of next week, looking both ways for Sunday."

Jake leans over to me and whispers, "Don't try her. She's as ornery as an old mule when she hasn't gotten any."

She pops Jake on the shoulder. "I heard that."

"Listen, I need to tell you something before word gets around."

Liza backs up into the paint mixer. "Willow's not pregnant, is she?"

"No! But it does involve her."

I pick up the color palette wheel for no other reason than to have something to do with my hands. I never knew there were so many different shades of white. "I need to tell you all something, and I should have confided in y'all a long time ago. Now that it might get out, I don't want any of you blindsided. I did something really dishonest in graduate school." My eyes stay trained on the paint swatches. "I wasn't doing very well in school. I was so far behind in my research project, I was ready to quit—give it up and come back home. Willow talked me into staying, and I wanted her to be proud of me." I chuckle. "We both wanted out of Smithville so bad, and I didn't want to let her down. So one night, we were at a bar, and there was this guy. We were chatting him up, and he told me he knew a guy that could hand deliver me my research project, for a price. And before you say it, it was not Willow's idea. She tried to talk me out of doing it. Apparently, I suck at cheating because the one time I try to pass off someone else's work as my own, I get busted."

"Oh, Gunnar," Liza says, squeezing my arm.

Thinking back to that day brings back all the humiliation. "Willow knew someone high up, and she talked them into granting me a master's degree since I had the courses to qualify. That's the only thing that kept me from going off the deep end."

Liza wraps her arms around my waist and gives me a big hug.

"I thought she did it because she loved me, so I moved back here and waited for her to finish school. Turns out, she did it because she was embarrassed. That came out when she broke up with me."

No one in the room moves. The only sound being made is the hum of the air conditioner. I turn to face my friends. "So, when I go on and on about trying to save this town, it's because this town, you two included, saved me."

I blow out a breath. Those words needed to be said years ago, but I was too embarrassed. Now I don't care who knows.

Liza hugs me again.

"I could lose my job for lying about my school record."

Jake waves me off. "Explain it to the chief. You did get the degree. You only left out the little details surrounding it."

Liza waves her arm through the air in front of everyone in the room. "We love you exactly the way you are. But there is someone that loves you even more. Don't let her go."

CHAPTER FORTY-SEVEN
Andie

After a serious cold compress session and a pound of concealer, my puffy eyes are finally presentable for church. I've come this far; I'm not about to let my heart mess all this up for me. He'll probably be there, and everyone will stare at the physical and emotional distance that's between us. He has to know that I have to be at church, so the nice thing to do would be to let me have my time. He can have the church the rest of his life. God, I hope he doesn't show. But I want him to.

I slip in right as the organ cranks up for the first hymn and slide into the back pew, next to my favorite brat who throws spitballs at my face. I give him a warning glance before he settles in next to his mother. Sweet Lily scans the crowd, and when our eyes meet, she grins real big and waves. She whispers something to her mother. Faith looks over at me with her mouth turned down. She mouths "no" to Lily. Lily turns to me one more time and frowns before she slinks down into the pew. I sure could use a Lily hug right now, but it is right of Faith to not get Lily caught in the middle of all this.

Gunnar walks past me and sits next to Lily. She climbs onto his lap and whispers into his ear. He shakes his head and stares straight ahead. Please don't let me cry in front of all these people. I'm so glad I don't see Willow because the few bites of breakfast I did manage to eat might make an appearance all over the sanctuary's carpet.

Someone taps me on the shoulder. I jerk my head up to see Liza standing there. She never goes to church. My mouth drops, and so does the pastor's. She motions with her head for me to scoot over. She slides into the pew next to me and holds my hand. I rest my head on her shoulder and whisper, "Thank you."

During our passing of the peace, the pastor says, "Andie, this is your last required attendance. I would love it if you would take up the offering."

I take a gander around the room, and as soon as my eyes land on Gunnar, he snaps his head in the other direction. "I'm not feeling well. I don't want to give anyone a virus."

He hands me a bottle of hand sanitizer. "Nonsense. One last time."

"I'll help," Lily says, running up to me. Bless her heart. I'm going to miss that darling angel so much.

"Lily, that is so sweet of you to volunteer. Thank you." The pastor gives her shoulders a squeeze.

Faith gives me the faintest of smiles and a single nod. Gunnar bows his head to read the church bulletin. He is the definition of handsome, especially when that dark lock of hair falls over his eyes. I want to brush it away like I've done plenty of times, but I can't. He hates me, and he hurt me.

During the offering, Lily insists I take up the collection on the side of the congregation where Gunnar sits. I train my eyes on the offering plate and try to pretend I'm happy while I walk down the aisle and stop at each pew. When the plate is being passed back to me, Faith takes it and hands it to Gunnar. Without looking in my direction, he shoves it my way but misses my hands. The offering plate clangs to the floor. Dollar bills and coins fly everywhere. A red-hot flush runs up my neck. Making a fool of myself in front of the entire congregation is what I've always been afraid of happening, and to do it at Gunnar's feet right after he broke my heart is more than I can take. I wipe a tear away as I kneel down in the aisle.

"I'm so sorry." I don't know if I'm apologizing to the congregation for disrupting the service or to Gunnar for the miscommunication. Or maybe it's to myself for falling in love with this man and this community. With shaky hands, I grab the money off the floor. Lily runs up to help me. My breaths are rapid. On my knees, I lean over to grab some money by Faith's foot, when Gunnar's hand stops mine. He picks up the money and hands it to me. His touch lingers for a millisecond longer than necessary. I miss his touch. This may be the last time I ever get to feel his hand on me, so I savor the moment, even though we're in the middle of church.

As though he suddenly realizes what he's done, he snatches his hand away, and the moment is gone.

"Thank you," I whisper. I doubt he heard me, but it was mainly for me, anyway. My "thank you" was for more than helping me collect the money I dropped. It goes beyond not reporting my slipup when he could have. It even goes beyond the intimate times we spent together. It's for welcoming me into his family and never treating me like an outsider. I felt more at home here than I have anywhere in my life. But I don't anymore.

When we finish taking up the offering, Lily and I march back up to the front and place our plates at the altar. Lily gives me a high five, and the congregation giggles.

"Let's give a round of applause to Andie. No one is an official member of this congregation until they've dropped an offering plate." The congregation stands and claps for me. All except Gunnar, who stays in his pew, focusing on the floor in front of him.

I shrug as I walk back to sit next to Liza. She hugs me. Even the brat next to me gives me a thumbs-up. Regina gives me a faint finger wave, and Sarah Jackson dabs at her eyes with a tissue, which makes me want to give each of them a big, crushing hug. After today, I will have fulfilled all the stipulations in Granny's will. I should be happy. It's only money. I don't need it, and I surely don't want it anymore.

TEARS AREN'T USUALLY an ingredient in Granny's jam recipe, but they are today. It's never too early to get started on Monday's orders, and after I scooted out of church like a scalded dog, I had to do something, or I would go crazy. I measure out the whiskey and pour it into the boiling pot of fresh strawberries from the Jackson's garden. The golden liquid calls to me. On a day like today, I could use a little bit of liquid companionship. It would be so easy to drown my sorrows. I've done everything I needed to do to inherit the money, and the developers want an answer by tomorrow, so I need to make up my mind. Today's church service was the last on the checklist. I'm free. I can do anything I want. I can drink until I pass out. It would be nice to sink back into my old ways. It would be so easy.

I hold up the bottle, and the familiar smell wafts over me. Screw you, Gunnar. You don't deserve me. This town doesn't deserve me. I'm done. I bring the bottle up to my lips, but before I take a sip, my hand freezes.

No.

This isn't what I want. Even without Gunnar or this town, I don't want to be that person anymore. I've gone over a month without even the desire to get drunk. I'm not going to start now. I'll have to get through my sadness in other ways, like finding friends to lean on, or hey, maybe I'll even read Granny's Bible. It may give me some strength like it did for her all those years.

With this being my last batch of jam I'll ever make with Granny's secret ingredient, I pour the remainder of the whiskey down the sink and toss the bottle into the trash. I can actually breathe again. I feel ten feet tall right now. I can do this. I know I can.

After sterilizing the Mason jars, I line them up on the counter and, one by one, spoon the scalding-hot jam into each jar like a pro. I don gloves, screw on the lids, and let the jars cool on the counter. They are my babies. I label each one and decorate the lids with ribbon and a gift tag.

"Granny, I hope you're proud of me. I've tried super hard. I really have. Thank you for making me come here."

A peace comes over me like I can't explain. I know she's watching over me, and in that moment, I feel her loving arms around me, telling me she's proud of me. And this time, happy tears flow down my face.

A knock sounds on the door, making me jump. Maybe it's Gunnar. I wipe the tears from my face and rush toward the door. When I fling open the door, as Mrs. Cavanaugh would say, I could have been knocked over with a feather. It's not Gunnar.

It's Regina and Willow.

CHAPTER FORTY-EIGHT
Andie

Crap. I barely trust Regina, and the encounters I've had with Willow have not been pretty. Regina gives me a tentative smile. Her normal tan face is paler than mine.

"Hi. Uh, I'm not open."

"We know." Regina points at Willow. "She needs to talk to you."

"I don't think that's a wise idea."

I start to close the door, when Regina stops me. "She's not here to cause trouble." She sneers at Willow. "Are you?"

Willow's eyes dart around. "I'm not going to cause a stink. I promise."

"No."

Both of their mouths drop open. As I start to close the door, Regina throws her body in the way. She holds her hands out as if she's the referee and Willow and I are on opposing sides, about to have a throw-down.

"Willow, give me a minute."

Willow's face turns a splotchy red, and she blows out a breath. It's not as though she has any choice in the matter.

Regina whispers in my ear. "You'll be doing me a favor if you hear her out. Everyone is on her ass to tell you the truth, even Stanley."

I blink like an idiot. "Stanley?"

Regina nods. "He's your number-one fan, so please..." She glances over her shoulder to where Willow stands, nibbling on a fake fingernail.

I roll my eyes and open the door wider for them to come in.

Willow tiptoes in and sinks into the first booth she comes to. Regina pats my arm and points at the counter. "I'll be over here, minding my own business unless she goes into full bitch mode."

Regina motions for me to approach Willow, who acts as though she could throw up at any minute. From the little I know about her, she's usually in control. I bet this is new territory for her.

I slide into the booth so I'm sitting directly across from her. "Would you like something to drink?"

Willow shakes her head. "Not unless you got some whiskey. I sure could use a shot right now."

Regina giggles, and I bet she's thinking back to our first encounter at the hospital.

"Sorry, I don't have any." I glance over at my jam jars, and for a fleeting second, I consider sharing with her what my secret ingredient is. "You want to talk?"

She focuses on her shaking hands. "I wanted to..." Willow's pained expression makes it seem as though she's about to cry.

"You got this." Regina gives her a thumbs-up. Then she smiles at me. "She's not used to apologizing. Go easy on her."

Willow swallows. "I am here to say I shouldn't have gotten in the way. I should have stayed away, but somewhere deep down, I never let go completely of Gunnar. I always hoped we'd get back together one day."

"Oh."

"But that was me being selfish. I wanted Gunnar to be a certain way, act a certain way, be around certain people. When he could be himself around you... I realized I had lost him."

"It doesn't matter."

She chuckles. "Oh, but it does. I tried so hard to convince him to take me back, to move back to Chicago with me, but he wouldn't have it. And as recently as yesterday, he told me he wasn't leaving Smithville and that I was free to let his little transgression out for the world to see, and that was after I let it slip about seeing the developers here. He didn't care anymore. I realized then and there that we'd never be able to fix our relationship. We're too different."

I sneak a peek at Regina, who quickly focuses on her phone.

"That's sweet, but this has nothing to do with me."

Her big blue eyes bore into mine. "Oh, but it does. It's my fault, you know. I planted seeds of doubt in his mind about you. I reminded him every chance I could that you were only a temporary attraction." She lets out a dark, unamused chuckle. "I even told him about the developers at your shop, even though I could see it in your eyes the way you soaked in every person in there that day that there's no way you're going to sell."

"I haven't decided."

"I guess what I'm trying to say is I'm used to getting my way so I used the only thing I could think of that would put a wedge between you two. He loves this town, and I knew how he would react if I manipulated the facts to suit my needs."

I lean back into the booth, doing my best to analyze the conversation. This is not the Willow everyone talks about. She doesn't just throw out the white flag and surrender. "I don't know if I believe you."

She bats her eyelashes, causing a tear to trickle down. "It's the truth. That and the fact that if I didn't talk to you, Jolene was going to kick my butt." A goofy grin slides across her face. "Apparently, Stanley has cut her off in the bedroom department until I make nice with you."

I throw my head back and let out a huge cackle. "Now *that*, I can believe."

Willow pulls out her phone from her purse and slides her fingers across the screen. She turns it around for me to see. "And if you need more proof, read this."

My eyes get big as I read the Jacksons' blog interview with Gunnar. "Oh my stars. He confessed to the entire town?"

"Yep. And that one line at the bottom makes it very clear that even if you are not in his life anymore, he's done with me. Needless to say, the Jacksons had no problem putting me in my place."

"I don't know what else to say."

Regina slides in next to me. "You don't have to say anything. Willow finally realizes she can't control every situation. Right?"

Willow rolls her eyes, and a tear trickles down her cheek. "I really did love him, you know."

"I'm sure you still do."

Willow grins. "Yeah. But I need to let go of the fantasy. We're different people wanting different things. I didn't want to admit it."

After a beat of silence, Willow clears her throat. "I'm sorry."

Regina claps her hands. "Hallelujah! See, that wasn't so hard."

Willow blushes. "Don't get used to hearing those words out of me." She holds out a hand for me to shake. "Truce?"

I'm not so naïve as to think that she's a changed woman, but I want to turn over a new leaf and be the better person. It's on her to keep the truce, not me.

I take her hand, and she chews on her lip. "He's a great guy. Be sweet to him."

"No. As much as I'd like for things to be different, we're not together."

"Don't give up."

I tighten my ponytail. "It has nothing to do with giving up. We said some really bad things to each other, and he doesn't trust me. It was fun, but it wasn't meant to be." I suck at lying.

Willow slides out of the booth and smooths back her hair. "I hope for both of your sakes, things work out because he's one of my favorite people, and I want him to be happy. You make him happy."

She motions for Regina to follow her out the door.

"Thank you," I say.

I think that conversation was more for her sake than mine because I still feel as crappy as before. But for her to accept responsibility is huge, if not for my sake, for hers. I'm still shocked we didn't bring out the claws and fight over Gunnar. Maybe in the South, they do things more civilized. Besides, neither one of us "gets the guy." If the church scene is any indication, he's over me, and I need to get over him.

CHAPTER FORTY-NINE
Gunnar

L ast night, I checked her front door after I left the gym. Part of me was happy that she finally remembered to lock it, but the other part was disappointed because it would have given me an opportunity to talk to her. I probably should have called her, but I really didn't feel like getting hung up on, so I left a note on her car windshield using a page out of my citation book. I'm an idiot. I know that, but I can't make my feet go over there and talk to her.

Hell, this morning, I'm sitting in my patrol car across the street, watching her wait on tables, chitchat with the customers, and even give the Jackson sisters gentle hugs as she serves them their morning coffee. She scoots around her shop as if nothing ever happened. Her days here are coming to a close, and that must be what's making her happy. She's going to leave, and I'll have to deal with whatever happens to this town.

Yes, she'll be walking out of all of our lives, but she'll be taking my heart with her, and I don't want it back. This is worse than when Willow left me. In all honesty, I built my house as a test to see if she loved me enough to stay here, to change her party-girl ways. And she ran away as fast as she could. She left me in a fetal position for a year, but when I finally got my head out of my depressed state, I realized I'd wanted her to run. There was something niggling at the back of my brain, telling me she wasn't the one.

I had to do my own whoring around to figure out that wasn't what I wanted, either. I even had to endure two years of celibacy to realize what I want. And what I want is right across the street, her ponytail swishing around her face. What I want is going to leave this city forever, and I'll never be the same.

A knock on my window scares the crap out of me. I squint to see Willow standing next to my car, arms crossed over her chest. Through the closed window, I hear her say, "Gunnar, we need to talk."

I do not need this today, but she's not going to leave me alone until she says her piece. Well, I have a few things to say to her today. When I get out of my car, I slam the door behind me.

"What do you want?" My jaw is clenched so tight, I'm not sure if she could interpret what I just said.

"What is your problem?"

I storm over to her and get right in her face. "You are my problem."

She points to In A Jam. "You are making a big mistake."

I squeeze my eyes shut and count to ten. I have never hit a girl, and I don't want to start now. "It's my mistake to make. You've caused enough damage. Please go." And with that, I turn my back on her, rest my arms on the hood of my police car, and rub my temples.

"I know. That's what I mean."

"Please leave." I sneak another peek at Andie, who has now taken up dancing with a broom. God, what a woman.

"Not until you go over there and apologize to her. I did. And let me tell you, I almost chewed a hole in my cheek from biting it so much. I do not admit I'm wrong, and you know that."

I swing around to make sure there isn't a smart-ass smirk on her face. She's dead serious. "What did you do?"

Willow bites on her bottom lip and stares over at Andie's shop. "Well, it was under duress, but I meant every word I said. I told her I fed you half-truths because I know you well enough to know which buttons to push."

I let out a breath as I stare at my shoes. "Doesn't matter. I saw the plans she had in her apartment. She's going to sell."

Willow stomps her foot. "You saw physical evidence of what you wanted to see to substantiate what I wanted you to believe."

Her big words make me chuckle. "Did you spout lawyer speak?"

"Maybe, but what I saw, in the shop with the developers, is a girl who was hearing the words from those two men, but... it's almost like she had a thought bubble over her head because as she took in every single person in the shop that day, I swear I felt her thinking, 'I can't leave them.' Gunnar, things aren't always what they seem."

I turn back around to watch Andie as she has a conversation with Mrs. Cavanaugh.

Willow steps up to stand beside me. "Gun, I have nothing to gain from this conversation. I know we're done and have been for a very long time. But as a friend, someone who has known you almost your entire life, I beg you to apologize to her."

I agree. She's right. I have to at least try. "I'll stop by tonight after my shift."

Andie pulls out something from underneath the counter and, after she says a few words to Mrs. Cavanaugh, walks to the front of the store. With a tape dispenser in one hand and a sign in the other, she proceeds to tape the sign to the front window. She slides her hand over the sign then nibbles on a fingernail. She pats the sign and walks away, back into the store.

Willow squints to read the sign. "I can't read it."

"I have to go."

I yank the car door open, and before I can get my seat belt on, I have the engine cranked. I pull my patrol car into the street and roll down Main Street to get a better glimpse at what she put in the window. I think a kick to the nuts wouldn't hurt this much. My heart drops into my stomach, and I bite my lip to keep a tear from escaping when I read the sign again.

For Sale by Owner.

CHAPTER FIFTY
Andie

The blueprints rolled up in the corner of my living room call out my name. They taunt me to take a peek at them. The business card posted on my refrigerator is like a beacon in the night. Every time I get near the kitchen, it catches my eye. I don't need the card for me to know the developer's number. They've called me ten times this week. They want an answer today, and with each call, they get a little more impatient with me. I don't know what to do, and I'm sure not going to make a hasty decision. It's not like I need the money. I'm in the driver's seat in this deal, so they can wait, or they can move along. Putting the sign in the window was my way of telling a certain someone I'm on my way out of here, no matter if I sell to the developers or not.

Speaking of driver's seats, Gunnar had the nerve to give me a parking ticket last night. I saw it first thing this morning, waving in the breeze. I tore it up into tiny pieces and threw it in the trash. He can arrest me for not paying the fine if he wants to. I've been in jail for far worse things.

Mrs. Cavanaugh has her apron on and is already working on the morning pastries. I don't think I can take this place away from her. She runs this shop as though it's hers, and I would have been lost without her. I've bent her ear so much, and she listens and only offers advice when asked for it. I love her and know Granny felt the same.

"Morning," she says without stopping.

From behind, I wrap my arms around her shoulders and hug her as if my life depends on it. She pats me, leaving flour palm prints on my arm.

"You've been so wonderful to me. Thank you."

"Being neighborly. That's all."

I kiss her on the cheek. "It's more than that. I know you loved Granny like a sister, and you wanted me to succeed. I'll never be able to repay you for your kindness."

She pats my cheek, and a flash of a memory comes to me from a day when I was little. Granny showed the same expression of love to me.

A tear slides down her cheek. It's the first time I've seen any sadness in her eyes. "Mary Grace was my best friend. Even through all the civil rights mess, she never left my side. She was my maid of honor in my wedding." She giggles. "That was a sight."

Thinking about how close they were warms my heart. I bet they ruffled a few feathers. If things were different, maybe Liza, Mel, and even Regina could have been my best friends for life too. "Tell me what to do."

"I can't do that, child. Besides, from the looks of that For Sale sign in the window, I thought you had decided."

I chuckle. "That was all for show. I had all but decided to stay, and then everything with Gunnar..."

She kisses my cheek. "Stay or leave. Sell or keep it. You've always got a home here."

I hug her, and the tears flow again. "Thank you. Can I call you Granny?"

She wraps her arms around me and holds me tighter than I thought she could with those frail arms. "Of course you can, child."

She wipes my tears, and something clicks in my mind. "If I could ask, what is your maiden name?"

Her eyes twinkle. "It took you long enough to ask. Maiden name is Christian."

I throw my hands in the air. "Of course. My attorney is your great nephew, isn't he?"

She giggles.

I place my hands on my hips and give her my smirkiest expression "You are a sly fox."

"If you had asked, I would have told you."

I give her another hug. "That's your answer to everything, isn't it?"

"Yep. I keep my nose out of people's business unless they ask." I grab her purse and pull out her wallet.

"Child, what are you doing?"

She has a ten-dollar bill and two one-dollar bills. I snatch one of the dollar bills out and wave it in front of her face.

"This shop is for sale for one dollar." I survey the empty coffee shop. "Any takers? Going once. Going twice... Sold to the lovely lady with the silly apron." I tuck the dollar bill inside my bra and rush over to the window to snatch the For Sale sign. I write SOLD across it, tape it back onto the window, and blow her a kiss.

And like a little schoolgirl, she grabs the kiss out of the air and places her hand to her heart. "And if you ever want to come back home, I'd hire you in a heartbeat."

MY BAGS ARE PACKED, and I've made three tearful attempts to say goodbye to Mrs. Cavanaugh, my new granny. I promised her I would stay in touch, and I will. She's promised to not work so hard and to hire some extra staff so she can enjoy her life but still be in charge of the shop. I can't imagine anyone else more deserving of it, and I know she'll keep my grandmother's memory alive and do her best to preserve Main Street.

My phone rings. Of course, it's Tinsley. "Hey, buddy. Miss me?"

His deep, rumbling laugh rushes through my phone. "So, you really are moving back here?"

"Yep. It's the right thing to do."

"Can't wait to see you but hope I never have to take you down to the station again."

I giggle. "Nope. I don't even know who that girl is anymore."

He's silent for so long, I think we've lost our phone connection. "Uh, have you said goodbye to Clooney?"

I promised myself I wouldn't cry any more tears over him, but dang it, I'm on the verge of another crying jag. "Let's talk about something else."

He lets out a deep sigh. "Be careful."

"Always."

"Andie, I'm proud of you."

My phone pings, notifying me of a message. "Thank you. I'll see you soon. Gotta go."

I hang up and read the message from Mel. "Check the blog."

Oh dear. No telling what the Jacksons have to say about me leaving. When I pull up the blog, I can't get past the first sentence before tears stream down my cheeks.

"Our little out-of-towner, who crashed into our city a little over a month ago, is leaving today. After the last few weeks, we realized we were wrong about her. We thought she was an insensitive, selfish drunk. She's none of those things, and we wish her the best in whatever life has in store for her. Andie Carson will always be one of us, a true Southerner with a heart of gold. She's leaving with more than the well-deserved inheritance. Andie's taking a piece of us with her. Godspeed, Miss Carson. You passed the test."

Bless their hearts.

Now it's on to part two of the hard part: saying goodbye to Liza and Jake. I peek into their hardware store, hoping Gunnar's not inside. I haven't seen him or Willow since Sunday, thank the Lord. It's helped me focus on making the right decisions for me without starting the pain in my chest all over again.

Liza walks from the back room and freezes when she sees me. She walks toward me with arms open wide and wraps me in a loving sisterly hug. "I'm going to miss you so much."

I tear up, hearing her confession. "Me too, Liza. You've been so sweet to me. You didn't have to. From the very beginning when I had my first leaky pipe, you were more than kind."

Liza laughs.

"You included me like I had always lived here. You didn't make fun of me. Well..." I glance over at Jake. "Maybe *you* did a little bit, but that's okay."

He chuckles.

"And when things went south with Gunnar, no pun intended, you were still my friend. I'll never forget that."

She hugs me again then pulls away fast. She grabs a pen and piece of paper and hands it to me. "Now, you write down your address. I'm coming to visit you, and we're going to have one hell of a time in Boston." She wiggles her eyebrows at her husband. "I might not come back."

I write down my address, not knowing how long I'll be there. I don't know what my plans are for the future. I don't have to stay in Boston, but it's familiar. With all the money waiting for me as soon as I meet with Mr. Christian, I will have enough to do whatever I want, go wherever I want to go. I hand the paper back to her. "Here. You have my number, and I would love to keep in touch."

Jake gives me a hug. "Please keep in touch with her. I don't want to live with a mopey wife."

Liza nudges him in the stomach. "Is there any way I can talk you into staying?"

"It would be too awkward. This is Gunnar's home. I don't belong. But thank you for making me feel at home while I was here. It means the world to me."

I kiss her on the cheek. "Tell Stanley I said goodbye and good luck. If I have to see him in person, it might kill me. I'm already on the verge of a big ole Southern crying jag. He's ready for the exam. I know it."

"Will do. Stop by the hospital to say bye to Mel if you get a chance."

"Of course."

With one more wave and before I burst into another round of tears, I leave the hardware store and rush to my car. With my head held high, I drive down Main Street for the very last time as I head toward the interstate. When I get to the Leaving Smithville sign, a police car sits on the side of the road. I keep my eyes focused on the road, but I know Gunnar sits in the driver's seat of that patrol car. In his nonverbal way, he's saying, "Godspeed."

Farewell, Gunnar. I'll never forget you.

CHAPTER FIFTY-ONE
Gunnar

It's been three days since Andie left, and I haven't left the house since. Faith insists I eat dinner with her and Kevin tonight. I'm not sure if I bathed until Faith imposed the forced meal on me. She says I'm starting to get skinny from lack of food and from a broken heart, and I need a home-cooked meal. I don't have an appetite, but maybe Lily can make me feel alive again. When I open the door to her house, I see Liza, Jake, and Mrs. Cavanaugh sitting at the table. *Shit*. I back out of the house, but I bump into Stanley and Mel.

"Where do you think you're going?" Stanley takes me by the arm and forces me into Faith's house.

"What's going on here?"

Kevin walks up and takes my other arm. They place me on the couch, and the rest sit around me. Lily sits on my lap.

Faith clears her throat. "Sorry to lie to you, but it was the only way we could get you here."

Liza touches my arm, but I jerk it away from her. "We love you and know you're hurting real bad."

I shrug. "It doesn't matter. It's over. I'm over her, and life goes on."

"Bull," Lily says.

My eyes nearly pop out. "Lily, where did you learn a word like that?"

She points to Faith. "My mama."

Kevin takes his daughter by the hand. "I think it's time I take her for a bike ride." He pats my back on the way out the door.

Faith turns back to me. "I've put a lot of thought into this, so please hear me out. You love this town. It's where you were born, where you grew up." She waves an arm around the room in front of my family and friends. "It's where we all grew up, and we all feel the same way. We all want the town to thrive. But the thing is, this town will be here long after we're pushing up daisies in Woodlawn Cemetery. Love won't be."

"She had an agenda. She doesn't care about any of us."

Mel pulls out her phone. "I guess this is what 'not caring' looks like."

I gape at the picture of Andie sitting next to Miss Jackson in the hospital.

Mel smirks. "She brought the other Miss Jackson to see her sister, and the three of them played Would You Rather."

God love this woman.

I close my eyes, and all I see is Andie's beautiful face. She's in my mind when I go to sleep and when I wake up, and she's in every dream I have in between. Faith hands me a plane ticket and a scrap of paper.

"What's this?"

Mrs. Cavanaugh points to what is in my hand. "It appears to be a plane ticket, but I'm not the sharpest tool in the shed."

I chuckle. "Yes, ma'am, it is. I guess my question should be, what is it for?"

Liza squeezes my shoulder. "We all collected money and bought this ticket to Boston for you."

No, this can't be happening. They can't butt in like this.

"We also got you an interview for a position at the Boston University Police Department."

Mrs. Cavanaugh holds up a finger. "Compliments of my great-nephew. He called a certain person who had connections."

Before she can continue, I add, "Tinsley."

"Yep."

I belt out a laugh. "Of course it's him."

"My nephew went to law school there. He said it's—"

"Kind of like a small town within a big city. Yeah, I'm pretty sure Tinsley said the exact same words." I let out another chuckle. I take in each person in the room. "But she doesn't want me. She sold the shop. It's over. She doesn't want me, and she doesn't want this town."

Mrs. Cavanaugh shoos Liza out of the way and sits down beside me. "Son, she sold that shop to me for one dollar."

My eyes bug out of my head. "She didn't sell to the developers?"

Mrs. Cavanaugh shakes her head. "Nope. She cares about this town too."

"How did I miss that?"

"You were Mr. Mopey Pants, that's how. You holed up in your house for three long days. A lot has happened. Didn't you even read the blog?" Leave it to Mel to be blunt.

"I opened and closed the page about ten times before I decided it would only make me feel worse."

Jake hands me a bottle of water. "She had decided not to sell a while ago, but the black Willow spider fed you enough information to turn you against Andie. She tried to tell you, but you're a bit on the thick-skulled side." He thumps me on the side of the head as if he's checking a melon for ripeness.

Faith kneels at my feet. "She left because this was your home, and she didn't want any ill feelings between you two."

Andie didn't really sell. She had decided to stay before I pushed her away. I am the biggest bonehead. First I chewed her out for something she didn't do, then I clammed up and wouldn't apologize when I had the chance. And the weak attempt to apologize with a stupid note didn't change anything. This all could have been avoided if I wasn't so busy being a moron.

Faith pats my knee. "Now, you've had two women leave you for the big city. One you let go. One you're about to let go. What are you going to do?"

The age-old phrase "home is where your heart is" rings true. No matter where Andie is, that's where home is.

"I'm going to Boston."

"Yes," everyone in the room says.

Stanley holds out his Skoal can, making me laugh.

"Yes, I love her. She's my Skoal."

I stand and give each person a big hug, lingering a bit longer with Faith. "Thank you so much, sis," I whisper in her ear.

"I love you, baby brother. I want you to be happy. We'll visit all the time. I promise."

I nod and hug her again. I let out a big sigh. "I've got to pack."

MY INTERVIEW WENT WELL, and I was shocked they offered me the job on the spot. I think I will fit right in with the group. Being a university cop is a lot like being a small-town police officer. It's important to slow down, get to know the community, and try to keep the students from getting too crazy. It's not Smithville, but I'll do anything to be with Andie. I was hesitant to take the offer until I had a chance to smooth things over with her. After today, I'll have my answer, and so will they.

Thanks to Tinsley, I have Andie's address. Boy, I am a huge fish out of water. They're going to eat a simple Southern boy alive up here. At least my favorite beer is Sam Adams, so I've got that going for me. After three wrong turns, one missed subway, and walking right past her apartment building twice, I'm finally standing in front a brick building located a stone's throw from the Boston Athletic Club.

Now it's time to grovel. I hope after all this, she takes me back. If a thousand apologies don't work or the fact that I'm moving here for her, maybe the engagement ring in my suit pocket will do the trick. I took a big chance on uprooting my entire life without talking to her first, but I wanted to show her how much she means to me.

My heart races as I go over my apology in my mind. What if she doesn't care? She could hate me by now. If she doesn't feel the same way about me, I might jump off the dock into the Boston Harbor. Things could go south real fast, but it's a chance I have to take.

When I notice her walking toward me, my heart skips a beat. There's my girl. She doesn't see me yet, so I can enjoy the view without any distractions. And it's the most gorgeous view I have ever seen. Her skin-tight jeans leave nothing to the imagination, and her hundred-watt smile could melt an iceberg on a cold winter's day.

And then she sees me.

CHAPTER FIFTY-TWO
Andie

This must be a mirage. I blink to see if he's still there. He is. He's got on that sinful double-breasted suit he only wears to church, and he is every bit the six-foot-two yumminess that I remember. A few girls stumble as they stare at him.

Move along, girls. He's mine. Or at least he used to be mine.

I try to calm my nerves as I clutch the legal documents in my hands. Only moments earlier, I signed over most of my lottery winnings to twenty different small businesses in Smithville. The police and fire department, the hospital, and of course, the church got hefty donations too. That still leaves me with plenty to live on for the rest of my life and enough to put Lily and her baby brother or sister through any college they want to go to. I don't need that money, and neither do the developers.

Gunnar cracks a grin and saunters toward me. I want to wrap my arms and legs around him, but I don't know why he's here yet. There's no way he could know about my legal decisions. There's no way he could have gotten on a plane that fast. The ink isn't even dry yet.

Only two inches separate us, but it's two too many.

"Hey," I croak out.

"Hey."

This isn't starting off very well. "What are you doing here?"

He sighs. "A couple of reasons. The first is to apologize to you. I am so sorry for the things I said. I didn't let you explain. I took what Willow said she overheard and thought the worst of you. I hope you can forgive me because I am so sorry. I will never do that to you again."

I swipe a tear away. I nod in hopes that he knows I accept his apology. I forgave him the moment I saw him waiting on me, pacing in front of my apartment. "You said you had a couple of reasons."

He takes a step closer and slides his hands down my arms. "Stanley passed his test."

I drop my documents on the sidewalk. "He passed?"

"Yep. He won't get fired because of you."

I cup my hands over my mouth to keep from screaming hallelujah. "Oh my stars. That's fantastic."

I bounce up and down, and before I can stop myself, I leap into Gunnar's arms. He holds me so tight, I can hardly breathe, and I never want him to let me go.

"He wanted you to know."

"That's awesome."

Gunnar leans back, and my feet dangle off the ground. My whole body is pressed up against his, and it feels so wonderful. He puts me down, and I take a step back.

"I appreciate you telling me all this, but you could have done it with a phone call."

"I could have, if you were taking my calls."

I cringe. "Guilty. I needed time to think some things through."

He takes my hands in his. "Besides, I already had a phone interview. Today's was in person."

I cock my head to the side. "What are you talking about?"

He pulls out his wallet and shows me a Boston University Police Department business card. "I want to be where you are, sugar. If you're in Boston, I'm in Boston. You're my life. I love you."

I bite my lip to keep it from quivering.

He strokes my face with his hand. "Say something, please."

I take a deep breath. "You came here for me?"

He waggles his eyebrows then pulls out a black velvet box, and I suck in all the air in the city. When he kneels down on one knee on the sidewalk in front of hordes of people going about their business and opens that box to show me an engagement ring, I almost pass out.

"Marry me?"

I can't make my voice work. I'm hyperventilating. "You left your home for me?"

His dimples pop out. *Have mercy.*

"You want to marry me?"

He nods then stands to slide the ring on my finger. "That's how we do it down South."

I poke him in the chest with my finger. "I can't let you do that."

His face loses all expression. He scrunches up his brow, and pain stretches across his face.

"Gunnar, you are going to march yourself right back down to Smithville. I won't hear of it anymore."

"But—"

"I'm not raising a family here. This isn't home. Besides, Mrs. Cavanagh needs an apprentice." I plant a soft kiss on his lips. "I love you, Gunnar. Let's go home."

"Is that a yes?"

"Yes."

Relief washes over his face. I giggle. He kisses me with more passion than he's ever kissed me before. I don't care if we are in the middle of one of the biggest cities in the country. He's mine, and I want the world to know.

I pull back from him, holding out my engagement ring for all the strangers to see. "Hey, y'all, we're getting married."

A total stranger gives me a high five, and I tug Gunnar back down for another kiss. "If you know what's best for you, you'll get on the phone and tell them you're not interested in that job."

He pulls out his phone and makes a call. "Hey, this is Gunnar Wills. I just saw you about a position? Yeah, well, my plans have changed. My fiancée won't let me take the job."

I poke him in the side.

"Yes, sir. Southern women can be so bossy, but I wouldn't have it any other way."

Fittin' in, Granny!

He hangs up the phone. "Darlin', let's go home."

Home. I love the sound of that. Nothing has ever sounded sweeter.

Acknowledgements

To my awesome critique partners: Jymie Smith, Kelly Ann Hopkins, Casie Bazay, and Stacey Kuhnz. I couldn't have done this without all of you.

To the #amediting crew — Hugs.

To the entire Red Adept family, and in particular:

Lynn McNamee — Thanks for believing in this story and in me.

Erica Lucke Dean — You are the best mentor ever.

Alyssa Hall & Neila Forssberg, my awesome editors. I learned so much from you, and I hope I taught you a few Southern phrases along the journey.

Jessica Anderegg – The cover is so pretty.

To Daisy Mae, the best canine writing partner ever. We did it again!

To Mark — Thanks for being a small-town police officer in a former life. I'm so glad you keep putting up with me.

Maddie, I love you. Never give up on your dreams. Stay colorful.

About the Author

A fter several decades of writing medical research documents, Cindy Dorminy decided to switch gears and become an author. She wanted to write stories where the chances of happy endings are 100% and the side effects include satisfied sighs, permanent smiles, and a chuckle or two.

Cindy was born in Texas and raised in Georgia. She enjoys gardening, reading, and bodybuilding. She can often be overheard quoting lines from her favorite movies. But her favorite pastime is spending time with Mark, her bass-playing husband, and Maddie Rose, the coolest girl on the planet. She also loves her fur child, Daisy Mae. She currently resides in Nashville, TN, where live music can be heard everywhere, even at the grocery store.